The Kate Huntington Mystery Series:
MULTIPLE MOTIVES
ILL-TIMED ENTANGLEMENTS
FAMILY FALLACIES
CELEBRITY STATUS
COLLATERAL CASUALTIES
ZERO HERO
FATAL FORTY-EIGHT
(coming Fall, 2014)

The Kate On Vacation Series (novellas):
An Unsaintly Season in St. Augustine
Cruel Capers on the Caribbean
Ten-Gallon Tensions in Texas
(coming 2015)

ECHOES, A Story of Suspense
(a stand-alone ghost story/mystery)

ILL-TIMED ENTANGLEMENTS

A Kate Huntington Mystery

Kassandra Lamb

ILL-TIMED ENTANGLEMENTS
A Kate Huntington Mystery

Published in the United States of America by *misterio press*,
a Florida limited liability company
www.misteriopress.com

Copyright © 2012 by Kassandra Lamb

First Edition

All Rights Reserved. No part of this book may be used, transmitted, stored, or reproduced in any manner whatsoever without the author's written permission, except brief excerpts for reviews.

ILL-TIMED ENTANGLEMENTS is a work of fiction. Names, characters, events and most places (including The Villages of Lancaster retirement community) are ALL products of the author's imagination. Any resemblance to actual events or people, living or dead, is entirely coincidental. Real places may be used fictitiously.

Cover and interior design by Melinda VanLone,
Book Cover Corner

ISBN 13: 978-0-9913208-7-5 (misterio press LLC)

ISBN 10: 0991320875

This book is dedicated to the men entangled in my life:

*To my brother who has been there from the beginning,
and who advises me on guns and guy things;*

*To my husband who puts up with me, which is no small feat,
and who proofreads my manuscripts,
(also no small feat);*

*To my awesome and creative son
who had the good sense to marry my daughter-in-law
and who came up with the title, Multiple Motives,
for the 1st book;*

*And to the most precious little men of all,
my grandsons.*

PROLOGUE

Enough was enough! The woman was evil.

The memory rankled still. "What do *you* want?" she'd sneered. Then the heartless creature…you couldn't call her a *woman*, shriveled up old thing that she was…she'd turned and walked away.

She had it coming. She didn't deserve to live.

CHAPTER ONE

Betty Franklin's phone rang at eight o'clock in the morning. She'd been up since six-thirty, but nonetheless no civilized person, in her opinion, should be calling before nine.

Still in her slippers and bathrobe, she shuffled over to the phone on the wall of her kitchen. At eighty-five, she didn't move all that fast in the morning.

Heck, I don't move fast at any hour of the day anymore.

Betty picked up the receiver, and a cheerful voice said in her ear, "How's my favorite author this morning?"

"I'm fine, dear. How are you?"

"I'm absolutely wonderful! Just got off the phone with your publisher. They love your latest book!"

"That's good news, my dear."

"Wait, there's more. Are you sitting down?"

"Yes," Betty lied, as she shuffled to the stove to retrieve the tea kettle. She liked her new agent, but the young woman's exuberant personality could be a bit over the top at times.

"This book fulfills your current contract. *But* they're offering you another two-book contract. Aaannd…"

"That's wonderful, dear." She wasn't the least bit surprised. After all, she was a best-selling author. She started filling the kettle with water.

"Wait, I haven't told you the best part yet," her agent's voice bubbled through the phone. "The advance is eighty thousand dollars, forty per book!"

Betty almost dropped the kettle into the sink.

Maybe not so over the top this time. That was twice the size of her last advance.

She patted her chest in a vain effort to still her racing heart. "Well... that truly *is* great news, dear." She managed to keep her voice reasonably steady.

"Thought that would make your day. I'll send along the contract as soon as I get it."

Betty paused. For some reason, she could never keep this girl's name straight. Was it Sally or Sarah? "Thank you, dear," she finally said, but her agent had already disconnected.

She could hardly wait to tell her friends the news, but Betty didn't rush through her morning routine. Her face and figure retained vestiges of the beauty she had once been, and she didn't consider advanced age an excuse to let oneself go.

Finally she stepped out of her apartment door, impeccably dressed, her short, white hair combed and patted into place. There was a slight skip in her step as she headed for the recreation building where The Villages writers' group was about to convene its weekly meeting.

Betty considered pinching herself to make sure she wasn't dreaming. Some days, the entire last two decades of success felt like a dream. In her younger years, she'd tried to pursue her passion for writing, but the demands of a teaching career and a family had gotten in the way. In her sixties, as a retired widow, she'd needed to supplement her pension, so she'd started writing articles for *Senior Travels* magazine. Her editor there had encouraged her to try her hand at fiction.

And the rest, as they say, is history.

She grinned as she stepped through the conference room door.

A half hour later, Betty's mood was as low as it had been high earlier. The writers' group had applauded her announcement, and then someone had asked how she'd tied up all the loose ends at the end of the book. She'd started explaining how she'd woven one of the subplots into the main story at the end. Doris Blackwell had jumped up and accused her of plagiarism, claiming the subplot was suspiciously like an idea for a book she'd described to Betty months ago.

Other group members tried to calm Doris down while Betty just sat there, too flabbergasted to speak up in her own defense. The last words Doris threw over her shoulder as she left the room were, "I'm calling my lawyer. I'm going to sue you!"

Back in her apartment, Betty dialed her agent's number with a shaky hand. Once again the girl's name was rattling around in her brain, just beyond the reach of conscious awareness. Why was it she could remember the phone number by heart but couldn't come up with the damn name?

"Forgive me, Lord," Betty muttered under her breath as the phone rang in her ear. She never even thought in curse words, much less used them out loud. It was a sign of how upset she was.

"Hello, dear," she said to the receptionist who answered the phone. She didn't even *try* to remember her name. "This is Betty Franklin. I have a bit of an emergency. Is she in?"

Her agent picked up a moment later. "Sara Burnett."

"I'm afraid we have a problem, dear."

"What's up, Betty?"

She told the agent about Doris's accusations.

"Are you sure this woman isn't just blowing hot air?" Sara asked.

"I doubt it. Doris Blackwell is a very litigious person. She's involved in one or two lawsuits a year."

"How hard would it be to take that subplot out?"

"Very. It would require a major re-write. It's entwined with the main story in several places. And I'd have to totally rethink the ending..." Betty's voice trailed off. She did *not* want to re-write the book. Her mind had already moved on to the next one.

But Sara jumped to another possibility. "When did you develop that subplot? Before or after this woman talked with you?"

"I don't know for sure, but I think it was before. I'd have to look back through the earlier drafts in my computer. I don't think it was in the original outline."

"You save all the old drafts?"

"Yes. I'm always afraid I'll have second thoughts about something I've changed, and I'll want to go back to the earlier version."

"Okay, put them on a flash drive and hop on a plane. Your contract requires your publisher to back you up in the event of a plagiarism claim, if there's reason to believe the claim is unfounded. I'll get the publisher's lawyers on the phone and set a meeting up for late this afternoon or first thing tomorrow."

"Honey, I'm eighty-five. I don't just hop on planes anymore. Never did like to fly anyway. I get airsick."

A beat of silence. "So how'd you end up writing all those travel articles?"

Betty thought she detected a note of doubt in her agent's voice. Her stomach quivered. Did Sara think she'd plagiarized those articles?

"I flew when I had to, but I was a lot younger then, in my sixties. Mostly I got there by tour bus or cruise ship."

A longer silence. Betty hoped the girl was just checking her calendar.

Finally Sara said, "Okay, so when can you get here?"

"I'd have to get someone to drive me to Philadelphia or New Jersey to catch a train, and probably by the time I get there I'll be incoherent with fatigue." The very thought of the trip made her shoulders sag and her joints ache. "I could get there by day after tomorrow."

"Okay, I'll see if I can get something set up for Friday morning. And don't forget to bring those earlier drafts."

"I'll get them together right now. Soon as I call around for a ride for tomorrow morning. Uh, just one other question, dear."

"Shoot."

"What's a flash drive?"

~~~~~~~

Kate's stomach growled as she sat in a booth at Mac's Place, waiting for her lunch date. She blew a dark curl out of her blue eyes and licked her lips at the thought of the savory crab cake she was planning to order, now that she'd gotten her weight back down.

Recovering her figure after the baby was born had been the least of her many concerns regarding her late pregnancy. Fortunately, little Edie had gone full term and was a healthy, cheerful baby.

So why are you leaving her to go back to work?

Damn! Why did her mind insist on going over and over that guilt-ridden topic, like a tongue probing a sore tooth?

One third of her guilt was about leaving her baby daughter with a nanny three days a week. Two-thirds was because she was looking forward to it.

I'm no different from any other professional mom. I love my child. I love my job, she told herself for the umpteenth time.

But there was a difference. Kate didn't have to work, thanks to the foresight of her late husband and the sizeable life insurance policy he'd taken out several years before he was killed. Bottom line, she just wasn't cut out to be a stay-at-home mom. And she loved her work. Being a psychotherapist felt more like a calling than a career.

Besides, she was leaving Edie in good hands. Maria Hernandez, the cousin of her friend Rose, was wonderful with the baby. But her English was practically non-existent. Her presence in the household had done little to alleviate Kate's loneliness.

A blur of movement surged past her booth. The blur came to a halt and took two steps back. Rose Hernandez's short, sturdy body was swathed in an apron two sizes too big for her.

"Cute waitress costume," Kate said, "but it's a little early for Halloween."

Rose rolled her eyes. "Very funny. Waitress went home sick. I'm helping out until her replacement gets here." She quickly scanned the restaurant.

Kate looked around. All the patrons seemed focused on their food or their companions at the moment.

Rose dropped onto the bench across from her. "I've got news. Big news."

"You and Mac gettin' hitched?" Kate teased, not sure how she'd feel about it if the answer was yes.

Rose rolled her eyes again. A pink tinge crept up her cheeks. "Hardly."

Kate and Mac Reilly had grown up together–their parents had been best friends. She loved him like a brother, but she would be the first to admit he was an irascible curmudgeon. She was glad that Rose was taking things slow, giving herself time to assess if she could deal with him full-time, especially since two Mrs. Reillys before her could not.

"You remember Skip Canfield?" The young woman's chocolate brown eyes sparkled with excitement.

Kate just nodded, not at all sure where this was going. Of course she remembered Skip. He'd been her bodyguard for several weeks, when Eddie's murderer had also tried to kill her. Skip was six-five, built like Hulk Hogan, and had turned out to have as much brain as brawn.

"He's got his private investigator's license now," Rose said, "and I'm training with him to get mine, helping out with cases when I'm off duty." She leaned forward and lowered her voice. "He and I are talking about starting our own agency, but keep that to yourself for now. He doesn't want his boss to find out yet."

"So you're really gonna do it, quit the police force?"

"Yup." White teeth flashed, momentarily transforming Rose's reserved and rather plain features into a face any beauty queen would envy. "But not for a few months yet. I need the income for now."

"Phew." Kate beamed back at her. "For a minute there I thought you were gonna tell me you were dumping Mac for another man."

"Who? Skip? Naw, he's not my type."

A man two tables away was anxiously looking around. Kate tilted her head in his direction. "I think a customer needs you."

Rose looked over her shoulder, then jumped up. "Later."

"Congratulations," Kate called after her.

She spotted her lunch companion coming into the restaurant. At six-two and well over two hundred pounds–he wasn't saying how far over these days–he was hard to miss. He saw her and walked in her direction. She noted with concern that he looked tired and harried, and the salt was starting to gain on the pepper in his hair.

Rob Franklin settled his bulk into the booth. "Hmm, I never, ever would have thought to put the words *Rose* and *waitress* together in the same sentence."

Kate grinned. "Somebody went home sick so she's helping out."

"Sorry I'm late. Emergency call."

"Important client?"

"Important, yes. Client, no. It was my Aunt Betty. Do you remember her from the party? She's my great aunt really. She was married to my grandfather's youngest brother."

Kate chuckled softly, recalling her conversation with the octogenarian at the surprise anniversary party the Franklins' daughters had thrown for their parents the previous month. "Aunt Betty would be hard to forget. We had a delightful discussion of child-rearing practices, past and present. Apparently she had to research those of the eighteenth century for her latest novel."

"Well, that novel's the cause of the current emergency, I'm afraid."

A young waitress, whom Kate had never seen before, appeared at their table.

"And sorry again," Rob said, "but I can't stay to eat. I'm swamped." He turned to the waitress. "Crab cake sandwich with fries, to go please. And put her pickle slices," he tilted his head in Kate's direction, "on my sandwich."

"Crab cake sandwich," Kate said, "and you might as well make mine to go, too. And yes, you can put my pickles on his sandwich." In response to the confusion on the waitress's face, she added, "Just tell Mac the order's for Kate and Rob. He'll understand."

They were regular customers at Mac's Place. In addition to the owner's connection to Kate, he served the best crab cakes in Towson, no small feat in the state of Maryland.

"I should've realized sooner that I wouldn't have time for lunch," Rob said, once the waitress had left. "I thought I had things under control with this case. But Murphy's Law has been in full play today, and we go to court tomorrow."

"I understand. You didn't need to come over in person. You could've just called."

"Uh, I have a huge favor to ask." Rob dropped his gaze to the table, then looked up again. "I figured it would be easier to explain face to face. Aunt Betty needs to get to her publisher's office in New York by Friday morning. Her son's out of the country, and my court case will probably last into next week. It's a complicated custody battle, and the children will be at physical risk if things don't go our way."

Thus the tired, harried look, Kate thought. Rob was the most dedicated lawyer she knew, which was how they'd originally become friends. He'd always been a strong advocate for her therapy clients whenever they needed legal counsel, even if they couldn't pay him.

"I can't possibly get away," he said, "and Aunt Betty doesn't fly anymore. She was calling to get a ride to the train station. But I can't see her dragging a suitcase on and off trains by herself. Besides I think she needs someone to go with her. I'm afraid the publisher's lawyers are going to try to steam roll over her and do whatever they think is expedient."

"Okay, I can see this coming. The huge favor is you want me to go with her. Liz can't go?"

"She's swamped at work right now too. Big project deadline coming up next Tuesday. She's been working practically 24/7."

Rob hesitated, conflicting emotions doing battle on his broad face.

Anxiety fluttered in Kate's chest. He was a trial lawyer, well practiced at hiding his emotions. Whatever he let show externally was usually only a fraction of what he was feeling internally.

"I know it's a lot to ask, but it's a bad situation. Aunt Betty's been accused of plagiarizing part of her latest novel."

"Oh, no!" No wonder he felt torn. "Where does she live again? In Pennsylvania, right?"

"Yeah, in Lancaster."

Guilt twisted Kate's stomach. She only had a few weeks with the baby before returning to work, but Rob needed her help. She never would have gotten through the months since Eddie's death without his and Liz's support. They'd practically adopted her into their family.

Could she take Edie with her? That would work for the trip up and back, but she couldn't take an infant carrier into a business meeting with New York publishers. That would hardly establish the image of a powerful advocate that was needed here.

She could take Maria, too. She and the baby would have to be alone in a hotel room for a few hours though. No, they'd be better off at home, in a familiar environment. But Maria's English was so poor, if something happened she wouldn't be able to deal with it.

Rob was watching her face, tension in his own. "We're talking a couple days," he said, "to get up there and back. I was thinking about something on my way over here. How would you feel about Maria and the baby staying with us while you're gone? We can set them up in the spare bedroom downstairs. Samantha's at loose ends. She got laid off from her summer job. I thought I could hire her to help Maria out during the day. She took Spanish in school, and if they have any problems, Liz and I are only a phone call away."

Kate considered that plan. After several years of rebelliousness, Rob and Liz's youngest seemed to finally be maturing as she headed into her senior year of high school. But Samantha at loose ends was probably still a scary thing for her parents. The arrangement Rob was proposing killed two birds with one stone.

Still she struggled with maternal guilt. The baby was comfortable with Maria now, and Sam adored the child. Kate had to admit that her hesitation was mainly about her own resistance to being away from her daughter.

It's only two days, for Pete's sake. You're acting like you're going to be on the other side of the planet for weeks.

She'd hesitated too long. Rob backpedaled. "I'm sorry, I shouldn't have asked this of you. It's too much. I'll think of something else—"

"No, I'll do it," Kate quickly interrupted. "I was feeling kind of bored lately anyway. This will be a little change of pace for a couple days."

Rob had just finished giving her the details of the plagiarism accusation when Mac appeared next to their table. He was a wiry man, on the short side but with a ramrod straight spine, thanks to the decade he'd spent as a Green Beret. His jeans and faded Army T-shirt were partially covered with a grimy apron.

"Here's your crab cake, sweet pea," he said, using his childhood nickname for Kate as he handed her a paper bag. He dropped a second bag in front of Rob. "And for the gentleman, a pickle sandwich with crab cake garnish."

Kate snickered. Rob, the pickle addict, gave Mac a mock scowl.

Standing up, Rob fished some bills out of his wallet and dropped them on the table. He leaned down and kissed Kate on the forehead. "Thanks a million, sweetheart. It's a load off my mind knowing Aunt Betty's in good hands. If you run into any problems, call me."

He picked up his lunch and headed for the door. "See ya later, Mac."

Kate's catch-up-on-life chat with Mac was cut short by a loud crash coming from the kitchen. He raced off.

She gathered her things and headed out as well. As she drove home, she fought another round with maternal guilt. Samantha adored Edie, and vice versa, she reminded herself. Her little girl would be fine.

And it'll only be for two days.

~~~~~~~

Early the next morning, Kate's Prius zipped along I-83. Traffic going her way was light compared to the rolling back-up on the other side, as Pennsylvania commuters headed to their jobs in the Baltimore area. The outside temperature was already soaring due to a July heat wave.

As she drove, Kate imagined different scenarios with the publisher's lawyers. It was a technique she used with clients to rehearse anticipated confrontations. Imagine the worst case scenario and figure out how you'll deal with it. Then you'll go into the situation calm and confident. In this case, the tricky part was that she had to advocate for Betty without usurping her autonomy.

Ultimately any decisions were Betty's to make. But Rob was concerned that the lawyers would see his aunt as a sweet, old lady and try to push her into doing something she didn't want to do. Kate's job, in addition to chauffeuring, was to help Betty back them off, should the meeting head in an undesirable direction.

She grinned to herself. If Betty was anything like the other Franklin women she knew, the folks in New York were going to discover she wasn't all that easy to push around.

As she took the exit for US 30, Kate realized her mental rehearsals were moving toward obsessive ruminating. It was time to think about something else. Her adorable daughter, Edwina Huntington–named after her father–was always a good topic for inner contemplation.

Better not go there this morning, however, or she'd be turning around to head back home, abandoning Betty to her fate.

At the thought of Edie, Kate felt a slight tug in her breasts. She'd just finished weaning the baby to a bottle and formula the previous weekend. Guilt poked at her heart. Was she a bad mother? Going back to work when her child was so young, weaning her because she couldn't face the idea of pumping breast milk at the office. And now she was gallivanting off to Pennsylvania.

You're a great mom, love, her late husband's voice echoed in her head. *Our baby girl is fine.*

Kate smiled. Shortly after Eddie's death, she'd started having these internal conversations with him. At first she'd say something, then decide what he would probably say in return, scripting both sides of the conversation herself. But after a while, Eddie's soft baritone had started responding on its own. Every time she had herself convinced the conversations were just products of her imagination, Eddie would say something that took her totally by surprise.

These internal chats had helped her cope with her grief. She'd never told anyone, not even Rob or Liz, about them. She feared even they would think she was crazy. And she never intended to tell anyone either. These special moments with the love of her life were too precious to share.

Kate was now off the highway and entering Lancaster. She shifted mental gears again and searched for Abbeyville Road. She made that turn, and a half mile later spotted a sign, nestled in a clump of evergreen bushes—*The Villages of Lancaster, A 55+ Adult Community.*

Driving along the entrance lane, the word *tranquil* came to mind. The property was beautifully landscaped. Kate passed a white, one-story building on the left, identified as the administration building by a discreet wooden sign. Then on either side of the lane were several taller, look-alike buildings—red brick, with a large ground-to-roof section of glass in the middle of each slightly peaked front. According to Rob's directions, the three-story recreation center would be on the left around the next curve, and across from it would be the road leading to Betty's building.

When Kate turned onto that road, she found her way blocked by a police cruiser, parked crosswise, lights flashing. A young, uniformed officer got out and approached her car.

She lowered her window. "What's going on, Officer?"

He ignored her question. "Road's closed, ma'am."

"What's going on?" Kate asked again. It couldn't be a simple medical emergency. They wouldn't close off the whole road for that.

"I'm not at liberty to say, ma'am."

"Officer, I'm here to pick up one of the residents to take her to a very important meeting. And I've just driven for over two hours to get here." Kate tried to keep the whine out of her voice. She hated the thought of having to drive home, and then do this all again another day, because of something that undoubtedly had nothing to do with Betty.

"Who is it you're here to see, ma'am?" the officer asked.

"Elizabeth Franklin."

Something shifted in his face. He stood up straighter. "I'll move my car. Take the second left and ask for Detective Lindstrom."

Kate swallowed the lump that was suddenly clogging her throat. "Has something happened to Betty Franklin?"

The cop's face was unreadable. "Detective Lindstrom will explain."

CHAPTER TWO

With a growing sense of dread, Kate followed his instructions, passing a strip of woods on her right and another building and parking lot on her left. As she turned into the second entrance, she was immensely relieved to see Betty standing in front of her building, looking up at a tall, lanky man next to her. He was wearing a light blue, business suit.

Kate parked as close as the emergency vehicles clogging the lot allowed. Ducking under yellow crime scene tape and dodging the uniformed officer who tried to stop her, she hurried toward the elderly woman.

As she got nearer, her steps faltered. The man in the business suit was reciting the Miranda warning to Rob's aunt.

Kate raced across the last part of the hot asphalt and came to an abrupt halt next to Betty. "What's going on here?" she gasped, out of breath.

The man held up a hand to stop the officer who was about to grab her arm and drag her away. Then he turned his attention to Kate. She caught a hint of humor in his light blue eyes before they turned hard and unreadable. Reddish-blond hair was blowing across a forehead that sported a summer tan.

The breeze caught Kate's short curls and blew some into her face. She impatiently shoved them aside and was about to repeat her question when the man introduced himself.

"Detective Andrew Lindstrom. And you, I presume, are the young woman, friend of the family, whose name Mrs. Franklin couldn't remember."

"Yes, Kate Huntington, friend of her nephew."

"That would be the lawyer nephew, Robert Franklin."

"Yes. Now what's going on?" Kate repeated her question, trying not to sound as impatient and scared as she was. "Why were you reading Betty her rights?"

"I was informing Mrs. Franklin of her rights because she insisted I do so." His tone, along with an aborted eye roll, implied that he wished people would not watch so many crime shows on TV. "She also refused to answer any questions until you arrived."

Kate turned to Betty. "Did you call Rob?"

"He's in court. Can't be reached," the detective answered for her.

Kate felt a nervous flutter in her stomach. Apparently she was going to be Rob's stand-in as lawyer now as well. "What's this about? Why do you want to question Betty...Mrs. Franklin?"

Betty put a hand gently on Kate's arm. "Doris is dead, dear. She was murdered."

Kate's mouth fell open at the word *murdered*. "Who... who's Doris?" she stammered.

"Doris is, *was* the woman who said I stole her idea," Betty said.

Holy shit! Kate barely caught the words before they tumbled out of her mouth.

As much to buy time as anything else, she said, "We need to take this inside, out of the heat." Even at ten o'clock in the morning, the July sun was relentlessly beating down on them.

She noticed several of the elderly residents trying to inch past the police barricade around the building, no doubt hoping to eavesdrop on the detective's interrogation. Another good reason to move inside.

Detective Lindstrom was also looking in the direction of the residents creeping their way. He didn't move or say anything for a long moment.

The butterfly feeling in Kate's stomach shifted to full-fledged nausea as she watched his rugged face. She swallowed hard, praying he wasn't going to insist on taking Betty to the police station for questioning. Should she resist that idea, pointing out Betty's age and how stressful that would be? Or would it be better to be completely cooperative, for as long as possible?

He'd only been reading Betty her rights because she'd insisted. Maybe he didn't seriously suspect her.

"Can't go into this building," Lindstrom finally said. "It's a crime scene."

"There are conference rooms in the recreation center." Betty gestured toward the three-story building in the distance.

Kate's stomach untwisted a little. Betty didn't sound upset. The nausea was back the next second, when she contemplated how the policeman might interpret her matter-of-fact tone.

Both she and the detective eyed the labyrinth of wooden barricades, police cruisers, coroner's van and ambulance that stood between them and the recreation building, and the groups of elderly residents and curious staff gathered on the sidewalks of the roadway.

"Ladies." Detective Lindstrom extended a hand toward an unmarked police car parked a few yards away. As he opened the passenger door and solicitously helped Betty into the front seat, Kate shielded her eyes from the bright sun and squinted into the back.

The detective said, "No grill. I don't usually transport prisoners."

Kate opened the back door and climbed in. The backseat was an oven and the air conditioning had very little time to make inroads into the heat before they were in the recreation building's parking lot. When the car came to a stop, Kate pulled on the door handle. Nothing happened.

The detective, in the meantime, had circled the front of the car and was opening Betty's door. In a gentlemanly manner, he assisted the older woman out onto the sidewalk.

Kate banged on her window. The detective reached over and opened her door from the outside. "Sorry. The inside door handles are disabled," he said, a hint of humor in his eyes again.

"I thought you didn't transport prisoners." Kate heard the crabbiness in her voice and wished she'd thought before she spoke.

Lindstrom cocked his head slightly to one side. "Sometimes I do." He turned to escort Betty into the building with a light hand on her elbow. Reaching forward, he pulled open the building's door for her.

Betty beamed up at him. "Such nice manners, young man."

Kate, following behind them, rolled her eyes. *When a policeman who suspects you of murder is being nice, you can bet he has an ulterior motive.*

The detective caught the end of the eye roll as he reached back to keep the door open for her. He flashed a quick grin over the elderly woman's head.

Not sure what to make of this guy, Kate schooled her face into a neutral expression. "I'll be right in. Don't say anything, Betty, until I get there."

"Okay, dear."

Once the door closed behind them, Kate yanked her cell phone out of her purse and hit the speed dial for Rob's cell. It went straight to voicemail.

Of course. He's in court.

Heart pounding, she said in a frantic voice, "Don't know if anyone left you a message earlier or not. They may have just called the office. The woman who accused Betty of plagiarism has been killed, and I've got a real bad feeling the police think Betty did it. I'll try to keep a lid on the situation until I hear from you. Call me ASAP. Help!" The last word came out on a squeak.

Inside a young woman at a reception desk pointed Kate toward a small, glass-walled conference room. Betty and the detective were sitting at the oval table. She had her hands folded primly in front of her. He was drumming his fingers on the table.

Kate walked in and sat down next to Betty. She placed her

cell phone in front of her, willing it to ring soon.

"Perhaps now, Mrs. Franklin," the detective said, "you would be willing to answer my question as to her whereabouts between eight p.m. last night and eight a.m. this morning?"

"I'm not sure I should allow that," Kate said.

Lindstrom shot her an irritated look. "Has she been ruled incompetent? Do you have her power of attorney?"

Betty gasped. She looked as if she were about to take back her compliment regarding his manners.

"Of course not," Kate said.

"Then she's an adult and it's up to her to decide if she wants to answer me or not. Mrs. Franklin?"

"I'm afraid it's not a very interesting answer," Betty said. "I was in my apartment. Since I had to be up early this morning, I went to bed promptly at nine. The alarm was set for five-thirty, but I woke up before that, about five. Laid in bed for a few minutes and then got up. I showered and got dressed. Had to finish packing a few things. Then I walked over here for breakfast a little after seven. The cafeteria's in this building.

"My nephew said, uh…" Betty paused. Her eyes went to the ceiling, flitted back and forth, searching her memory. Then she let out a soft "Ah," as she looked at Kate with a small smile. "Robert said his friend, Kate, might get here as early as nine, so I left the cafeteria at eight-thirty to be back at my apartment and ready to go. But I couldn't get into the building. The security guards had the doors blocked. I guess someone had found poor Doris by then and you were on the way." She nodded toward the detective.

"Were you with anyone or did anyone see you during that time frame?" he asked.

"Not until breakfast. There's a few of us from the writers' club who usually eat together. Doris often does too, but we weren't too surprised when she didn't join us this morning, considering what…" Betty's voice trailed off, her expression sad.

The detective stared down at the table for a moment, tapping his index finger on the polished wood surface. "Did you wake up during the night? Hear or see anything?"

"Just to go to the little girls' room once."

"With all the tension yesterday at the writers' group, and a big day ahead of you today, I'll bet you didn't sleep too well." He sounded sympathetic.

Kate narrowed her eyes at him.

"Then you would lose that bet, young man." Betty's matter-of-fact tone said she wasn't buying the sympathetic routine. He'd blown his nice young man act with his sharp retort to Kate. "I take antihistamines for my allergies. They knock me out. I sleep like a rock."

Kate quietly blew out air and relaxed a little. Betty was no fool, and she was now on guard.

"But you did wake up once, to answer the call of nature. What time was that?"

"I have no idea, Detective. I didn't bother to put my glasses on nor turn on the light. I keep a nightlight on in the bathroom, so I can find my way. It felt like I'd been asleep for awhile so it was probably around one or two in the morning. But that's just a guess. I went right back to sleep, a few minutes after my head hit the pillow again."

"Okay." The detective paused to make a few notes in a small pad he had removed from the inside pocket of his suit jacket. "So why did you not want to tell me this until Mrs. Huntington arrived?"

"It's not that I didn't want to tell you, young man. But I knew my nephew would be angry with me if I answered your questions before she got here."

"That he would," Kate said..

Lindstrom inclined his head in a slight nod. "Tell me about the writers' club meeting."

"Not much to tell there either. Doris accused me of stealing her idea, which I didn't. But I was so taken by surprise, I couldn't even think of what to say to her. And before I could find my voice, she stomped out."

"I understand she threatened to sue you," the detective said.

Betty didn't say anything.

"Bet that would have created quite a mess in your life."

Betty shrugged. "Life gets a little messy sometimes, young man. You don't get to be my age without knowing that. I figured my nephew and Kate here, and my agent, they'd help me get it straightened out."

"It could mean your book didn't get published after all. That would have been more than just a little mess. Lots of bucks and your reputation on the line. Maybe no publisher would ever want to deal with you again."

"Actually, that's not quite accurate," Kate interjected. "Mrs. Franklin has four bestsellers on the market. It's unlikely that this situation would have kept her from getting published again. Indeed, many well-established authors get accused of plagiarism at some point, by someone who thinks they can get some money out of them. You know, 'pay me and I'll go away' kind of nuisance suits." Kate had no idea if that was true but it sounded plausible, and she wanted to deflect this line of questioning if possible.

Betty might have trouble remembering names but she took her cue well. "Yes, it was more of a nuisance than a mess, really."

The detective wasn't so easily deflected. "So would you have agreed to pay Mrs. Blackwell money, to make her go away?"

"Certainly not." Betty sat up straighter and gave the man a hard look. "I have proof that the subplot she claimed was her idea had been in the earlier drafts of my book. Written *before* she talked to me about her novel."

"Were there any witnesses to the discussion between you and Mrs. Blackwell about her book idea?"

"Well, no. She approached me after one of our meetings. Invited me to her apartment for a cup of tea. She wanted my help to get the book published, once it was done."

"So it would have been her word against yours as to when that discussion happened, and your word as to when the earlier drafts were written?"

Betty looked confused, as if it had never crossed her mind that anyone might question her word.

Kate jumped in. "Detective, these were all things that would have been discussed tomorrow with the publisher's lawyers. I'm quite sure all these legal ins and outs hadn't even occurred to Mrs. Franklin yet. And I think we need to stop at this point, until legal counsel is present."

As if on cue, Kate's cell phone played the opening notes of Brahms' lullaby. She looked at the caller ID window, and tried not to let her relief show as she answered it. "Hi, can you hold on a minute?... Detective, if you would excuse us, we need to consult with Mrs. Franklin's attorney now."

The detective stood up. "I'll check on the crime scene folks. Don't go anywhere." He left the glass-walled room.

Kate watched him as he stopped to talk to a uniformed officer in the hall. Lindstrom nodded toward the conference room, then walked away. The officer moved into position just outside the door.

Damn! He really does suspect her.

She tried not to stammer as she told Rob what was going on.

CHAPTER THREE

Betty followed Kate's end of the conversation with curiosity and only an occasional flicker of anxiety on her face.

When Kate had finished filling him in, Rob asked, "Has this detective indicated he's going to arrest her?"

"No, but I think it might be under consideration." She was choosing her words carefully, trying not to upset Betty.

"You think he's going to?" Rob said.

"Not sure."

"Is she holding up okay?"

"Yes, remarkably so."

"Hmm, they have motive and opportunity–"

"Shouldn't be enough," Kate said.

"But in some jurisdictions, it's considered enough for arrest while they dig for more concrete evidence."

Kate struggled to keep the dismay off of her face. "Are you licensed to practice in Pennsylvania?"

"No, but if she's arrested, I'll hire a local firm. And if it goes to court, I would probably second chair." Rob paused for a beat. "Look, I really need to be here for this damn case. Do you think you can hold the fort up there until tomorrow evening?"

"Yeah." Kate got up and tried to look nonchalant as she wandered over to the big window overlooking the parking lot.

Rob had apparently picked up on her hesitation. "Are you okay?" he asked, regret and concern in his voice.

"Yeah, I'm fine. I guess, uh…" She turned her back further away from Betty and whispered into the phone, "I'm just feeling a little inadequate here. I think I can deflect the detective for the rest of today, maybe. But I don't know about tomorrow."

"Do the best you can and I'll be on the road the minute I get out of court tomorrow. I'll leave my phone on vibrate in my pocket. If they arrest her, call me right away. If I don't answer, I'm in court and I'll get a recess as soon as I can and call you back. The police are going to want to search her apartment. Let them. They'll be able to get a warrant anyway, and refusing to allow a search would look suspicious."

"Okay." Responding to Betty's gestures, Kate added, "Here, your aunt wants to talk to you."

Betty took the phone but didn't get a chance to say more than "Hello." She listened, said, "okay," a couple times, then handed the phone back.

Rob had disconnected the call from his end. Kate pocketed the phone.

Betty pursed her lips. "I thought that boy had better manners than that. He wouldn't even let me talk."

Kate suppressed a smile. *That boy* was in his mid-forties. "He's in what I call court mode. You've probably never seen him that way. When he's in court, he has to be very direct, and sometimes downright aggressive. He's a bit brusque right after he gets out of court, until his normal personality reasserts itself."

"Well, he did say he had to get back to the courtroom, that they only had a few minutes' recess." Betty tapped her index finger against her upper lip in thought. "Hmm, maybe in my next book, I'll have the heroine get into some kind of legal trouble and have a courtroom scene, and then she falls in love with her lawyer."

Kate stared at her, then shook her head and grinned. "All things are grist for the mill, huh?"

Betty smiled back at her. "You betcha, my dear."

~~~

After going over the same questions a couple more times, Sandy Lindstrom noted on his pad that the answers were consistent, but not worded exactly the same each time. That often meant the person was telling the truth.

He eyed the old lady, a fiction writer.

Often, but not always.

"I need to search your apartment."

Neither woman objected. They drove back across the retirement community's campus in silence. He gestured for a uniform to follow them into the apartment.

Once inside, he pulled a small electronic device from his suit jacket's inside pocket and placed it on the breakfast bar that separated the apartment's kitchen from the living room and dining areas. "Mrs. Franklin, I need to take your fingerprints."

As he had the woman place her fingers in the device, Mrs. Huntington look on in fascination.

Lindstrom glanced over at her. "Clever little gadget, isn't it? Takes a digital image of the print. We only have two of them. Testing them out to see if it's worth getting more."

And this was the very kind of situation where such a device came in handy. He preferred not to expose his elderly suspect to the stress of taking her to the police station. If she had a coronary, the lawyer nephew would no doubt sue the department, and his superiors would eat him for lunch.

"I need to call my agent, Detective," Mrs. Franklin said. "Let her know we won't be coming up tomorrow. I'm assuming you don't want me to 'leave town.'" She made quote marks in the air.

He caught Mrs. Huntington's wince out of the corner of his eye but opted to ignore it. He nodded.

Mrs. Franklin disappeared into the small den off of the living room.

He told the uniform to start in the kitchen. To get away from Mrs. Huntington's relentless gaze, he took the bedroom. Donning gloves, he quickly searched the room. Then he picked up the hairbrush off the dresser and returned to the living room.

"I'd like to take a hair sample from this brush," he said to Mrs. Huntington, who hadn't moved from her position in the middle of the floor. She nodded, her face a blank mask. He removed several hairs, slipped them into an evidence bag, labeled it and then put it in his coat pocket.

Mrs. Franklin re-entered the room just as he said, "I also need to take the computer."

She went pale and turned to Mrs. Huntington.

The younger woman crossed her arms. "I'm not going to allow that, Detective. That computer contains Mrs. Franklin's books. It's the main tool of her trade."

"I can get a warrant for it," Lindstrom pointed out.

Her chin went up in the air. "You do that then."

Lindstrom suppressed a smile. He nodded back, keeping his own face blank.

He wasn't sure what he thought of Elizabeth Franklin yet, but he was beginning to like Kate Huntington. He admired her spunk.

~~~~

Once he was gone, Kate turned to Betty. "If you don't have your computer files backed up, do it now."

"I do. Everything's on disks."

"Get them then. We're going to put them in my car, because he *will* be back for the computer. I'd say by tomorrow at the latest."

"I'd already gathered them up for the meeting. I'll get them. Would you put the kettle on, dear? I need a cup of tea."

They stashed the box of disks in the back seat of her car, then settled down in the living room with their tea. Having scalded her tongue with the first sip, Kate blew gently on the hot liquid in the china cup, as Betty talked about the writers' club and how it would probably never be the same again.

Kate's mind wandered. The whole morning was starting to feel surreal. It felt like she'd taken a wrong turn and had landed in a British mystery novel, and Miss Marple was sitting across from her, sipping tea and calmly discussing suspects.

Kate's attention returned to Betty's words. She realized the older woman was now talking about the victim.

"Doris could be rather difficult at times, but she didn't deserve to be murdered."

Kate glanced up and saw unshed tears in the elderly woman's eyes. Jolted back to reality, her own throat tightened. This wasn't an Agatha Christie novel. A woman was dead and Rob's aunt was the prime suspect.

"Betty, tell me everything you can think of about Doris and the others in the writers' club."

Betty gave her a startled look. "Why, dear?"

"Because maybe something will pop out at us that would explain why someone would kill her."

"Shouldn't we leave that to the police detective? His manners aren't always what they should be, but he seems competent enough."

"No doubt he is, but you have the most obvious motive so he may not be inclined to dig too much deeper…" Kate trailed off, not quite sure how to end the sentence without unduly frightening the elderly woman.

But Betty was made of sterner stuff than she'd given her credit for. "So maybe we should be doing a little digging ourselves."

The doorbell rang. Both women tensed.

Not Lindstrom again, Kate prayed as she followed Betty to the door.

Her prayer was answered.

The woman who entered the apartment was Betty's polar opposite. In contrast to Betty's crisp linen slacks and pale green short-sleeved sweater, the woman she introduced as her friend, Frieda McIntosh, wore a bright red, shapeless house dress. Frieda was a couple inches taller than petite Betty and was almost as round as she was tall. Her steel gray hair was jammed into an untidy knot on the back of her head.

"Have a seat, my dear," Betty said. "Would you like some tea? I was about to have another cup."

"Tea would be great." Frieda plopped down on an armchair. "I guess it's too early for something stronger." She looked longingly at the wooden cabinet in the dining area.

Kate surmised that it contained Betty's liquor supply.

Betty headed for the kitchen. "Help yourself, dear."

Frieda hesitated, then shook her head. "Best I keep my wits about me, in case that handsome detective has more questions."

"So Detective Lindstrom's been to see you," Kate said.

"Yes. He left my apartment a few minutes ago, and I'll tell you, I did *not* like the direction some of his questions were leaning. It sounded like he thought Betty was the killer, so I told him Betty Franklin wouldn't hurt a fly." Frieda nodded her head sharply, as if her opinion should definitively settle the issue.

"Thank you, Frieda." Betty handed her friend a cup of tea, and then settled down on the settee between the two armchairs.

"So tell me everything. What did the detective say? Did he fingerprint you, read you your rights?" Frieda asked, excitement in her voice.

Betty glanced quickly in Kate's direction. Ignoring the questions, she said, "We were about to go over what we know about Doris and the other members of the writers' group."

Kate took her cue from Betty. "Mrs. McIntosh, do you know if Doris had any enemies?"

"I'm Frieda, honey. Mrs. McIntosh was my mother-in-law and I never did like the old battle-axe. But to answer your question, I'm not sure Doris had anything but enemies. She was a pain in the caboose, always going on about how this person or that person had done her wrong."

Frieda paused, took a swig of tea, then went on. "In my day we would've called her a C.T." She shot a glance at Betty. "A you-know-what teaser, or at least she would've been if she weren't a wrinkled up old prune, and most of the men around here weren't impotent."

At Kate's surprised expression, Frieda laughed. "I know I'm a bit over the top sometimes. I decided awhile ago that I didn't have enough time left on this planet to waste any of it mincing words, so I tell it like it is. Most folks, by the time they get to be my age, don't care much what others think anymore. I certainly don't."

Kate struggled to hide a smile. "In what way was Doris a

C.T.?"

"She used to flirt all the time with the men, even the married ones. She even flirted with Henry, and *nobody* can stand him. She told me one time that a couple of the men had actually asked her out." Frieda snorted. "No accountin' for taste! But she turned 'em down flat. She flirted with our maintenance man, Joe, too, and he's gotta be at least forty years younger than her. Bet she wouldn't have turned him down. He's a hunk."

As Frieda kept talking, Betty got up to fetch a pad of paper and pen from her den. She handed them to Kate, who started taking notes. Then Betty headed for the kitchen and pulled the ingredients for sandwiches out of her refrigerator.

"You'll stay for lunch, won't you, dear?" she asked when Frieda paused for breath.

An hour and a half later, Frieda had polished off two sandwiches, most of the plate of cookies Betty had produced, and three cups of tea. And they now had all the latest dirt on the members of the writers' group, along with the information that Detective Lindstrom had implied there'd been no forced entry into Doris's apartment.

While saying her farewells at the door, Frieda took Betty's hand. "Now you pay no never mind to what Doris said, honey. We all know you didn't steal her idea. I think she was just jealous 'cause you'd gotten published and she hadn't."

Betty gave her friend a hug. "Thank you for your support, dear."

Frieda went out the door, and Betty turned around. She burst out laughing when she saw Kate's face. "I'm afraid Frieda takes some getting used to."

"Well, I did say I wanted to know all about Doris and the writers' group members," Kate said, with a chagrined smile.

Betty's gray eyes twinkled. "Watch what you ask for, my dear."

CHAPTER FOUR

Friday morning dawned sunny, hot and humid. A typical summer day. As Kate stretched to relieve the stiffness from sleeping on the uncomfortable sofa bed in Betty's den, she realized it was probably going to be one of the least typical days of her life.

She found Betty frying eggs in the small kitchen. Kate headed for one of the stools at the breakfast bar.

"Good morning." Her hostess gave her a warm smile. "I figured we might want to eat in this morning, so we can plan our day. And I'm not quite sure I'm ready to deal with the others in the cafeteria yet." She placed a heaping plate of eggs and bacon on the breakfast bar.

Kate closed her eyes and breathed in the delicious blend of fragrances. She picked up her fork and dug in.

They'd barely finished eating when Detective Lindstrom was ringing the doorbell. He presented Kate with a search warrant for the computer. She made a show of reading it, although she only understood about one quarter of the legalese.

Handing it to Betty, she watched Lindstrom and a uniformed officer go into the den.

Good thing we got the disks out of here.

The uniform came out carrying Betty's hard drive. He left with it as Lindstrom sauntered over toward the sitting area. "I have some more questions, Mrs. Franklin."

Betty invited him to sit down and offered coffee. Lindstrom declined the offer as he settled into an armchair.

Once again, he went over the same ground as the day before.

Then he threw in a new question. "Mrs. Franklin, can you explain why your fingerprints and several of your hairs were found in Mrs. Blackwell's living room?"

Betty didn't miss a beat. "Of course. That was where we discussed her book idea."

"How long ago was that?" Lindstrom asked.

Betty stood up and walked over to the calendar hanging on her kitchen wall. She flipped back a few months. "It was around the middle of April, after one of our meetings. The 11th was just before Easter. We didn't meet then, so it had to have been April 18th."

Kate winced and swallowed hard. That was the day after the one-year anniversary of her husband's death. She shook her head to bring herself back to the here and now.

"But surely the apartment would have been cleaned since then," the detective was saying in a skeptical tone.

"Did you look at the place?" Betty said. "Doris was the world's worst housekeeper, and she was too cheap to use the cleaning service."

Kate jumped in with a question of her own. "Detective, what was the cause of death?"

Lindstrom hesitated. "Won't know for sure until the autopsy this afternoon, but it looked like she was hit with a fireplace poker. It was lying next to her."

"Oh, please," Betty scoffed. "Next you'll be telling us the butler did it."

"Mrs. Franklin, this is hardly a joking matter."

Betty raised her eyebrows at the detective's tone. "I didn't mean that as a joke. I just meant to say that someone getting clobbered with a poker is the second biggest cliché in murder mysteries. The first being the butler did it."

"Well, cliché or not, that was probably what happened. It looked like Mrs. Blackwell was arguing with someone. They lost their temper and grabbed the nearest convenient thing to hit her." He paused, looking at Betty. "It wouldn't be premeditated murder. Only second degree. Maybe could be plea-bargained down to manslaughter." He paused again, a sympathetic expression on his face.

The silence dragged out. Finally, Lindstrom asked, "Want to guess where Mrs. Blackwell was hit?"

Kate quickly said, "On the back of her head."

"I wasn't asking you, Mrs. Huntington." The detective shot her a perturbed look. "And how did you know that?"

"I guessed it from the rest of what you described. If you're assuming the attacker was acting on impulse during an argument, then she was probably hit when she turned her back on them. Were Mrs. Franklin's fingerprints on the poker?"

Lindstrom hesitated, then shook his head. "It had been wiped clean, which is the other reason we think it was the murder weapon."

Betty excused herself with her little girls' room euphemism.

Once she was out of the room, Kate said, "Surely, Detective, you don't really think that little old lady is a killer?"

The detective gave a half shrug. "It looks like *all* of my likely suspects are little old ladies, or little old men."

"So you are looking at other suspects?"

"I would, if I had any."

Kate disguised her exasperated sigh by pretending to blow an unruly curl out of her eyes. "I know there's no way I can convince you of this, but Betty Franklin wouldn't hurt a soul, and you're wasting your time focusing on her."

The detective let out a small chuckle. "You left out the part about how meanwhile a murderer is going free."

When Kate just glared at him, he softened his tone. "Look, I'm not in the habit of railroading old ladies into jail on bogus murder charges. I've got officers questioning every resident of this community and I will be looking at this case from all angles, and then I'll turn it over and look at it some more."

"Thank you," Kate said. "That's reassuring." After a quick internal debate, she decided to propose her idea. "It occurs to me, Detective, that some people might be more forthcoming with a female civilian than they would be with an intimidating police officer. I'm stuck here anyway until this evening, when Mrs. Franklin's nephew gets here. I'd be more than happy to help with the interviews."

The detective's reply was quick. "That's best left to the professionals, the trained observers."

"Which is what I am," Kate said. "I'm a psychotherapist. I'll bet I can tell when someone's lying or leaving something out better than some of your uniformed officers. Quite a few of them look like they still belong in high school."

The detective, whose weathered face and gray-sprinkled hair pegged him as forty-something, smiled. "They do seem to be getting younger every year."

He paused for a long moment. "As an agent, so to speak, of Mrs. Franklin's attorney, I can't stop you from asking questions. But stay out of the way of my people, and anything you find out, I want to hear about it immediately. And be careful." He rose and offered Kate his hand. "This isn't a game."

She shook his hand as Betty re-entered the room. "I know that all too well, Detective."

Kate decided not to elaborate that she'd had some previous experience with investigating murder, that of her own husband.

Detective Lindstrom took Betty's hand in both of his. "Try not to worry, Mrs. Franklin. As I was telling Mrs. Huntington, we are going to be looking at this case from every angle." He patted her hand, then made his exit.

Kate wasn't sure if he was truly trying to reassure Betty or he was trying to throw her off guard. Maybe whichever applied, depending on whether or not she was guilty.

~~~~~~~

By the time the doorbell announced Rob's arrival that evening, Kate and Betty had the beginnings of a plan. With the help of the community's directory, they'd compiled two lists–one of those residents who definitely knew Doris and had reason to dislike her, the other of those who only knew her in passing and might or might not have strong feelings toward her.

Unable to just sit and wait, Kate had decided to start interviewing the women on the second list by herself. The risk that she would be confronting a killer was slight, and she could at least eliminate those people from their rather long potential suspect list. She'd tracked down several of the ladies that afternoon. But none had told her anything helpful, other than to confirm that Doris was universally disliked.

Greetings were exchanged, and Betty asked Rob if he had stopped for dinner. He hadn't. She went into the kitchen to make soup and sandwiches.

Rob reassured Kate that Edie was being spoiled rotten by his daughter and wife. Then Kate told him about their conversation that morning with the police detective.

Rob took a sandwich from the plate Aunt Betty held out. "Don't let your guard down with this guy," he said to her. "He may truly be seeing you as one of many possible leads or he might be trying to trick you into saying something he can use against you."

"I know, dear." Betty patted his arm. She handed the sandwich plate to Kate, who was contemplating how easy it was to fall into the trap of assuming Betty was naive just because she looked so sweet and innocent. After all, the woman had been alive for eighty-five years.

"Lindstrom has assured me he's going to look at this case from all angles, as he put it, but..." Kate hesitated to say out loud that the detective might not pursue other leads with great vigor when he had a suspect with a good motive. She and Rob knew about that firsthand. The detective investigating Eddie's murder had jumped to the conclusion that they were lovers and had accused *them* of killing her husband.

"So Betty and I have come up with a plan." Kate outlined their ideas for investigating on their own and showed Rob the lists of names.

"We were thinking you and I could interview the people who disliked Doris this weekend. Since people are less likely to be totally honest with Betty, her job will be to organize our notes from the interviews."

"Sounds like it's worth a try." Rob shot her a guilty look. "But maybe you should—"

Kate put a restraining hand on his arm. "No, I'm not going home yet. Yes, I miss Edie, but it's not like she's going to be ready to leave for college by the time I get back. I want to stick around and help. The sooner we can clear Betty, the sooner everyone's lives can get back to normal."

She desperately longed to hold her child, but she'd taken note of the drooping shoulders and the fatigue in Rob's face. Edie was being well cared for. He needed her more right now.

~~~~~~

By Saturday evening, their enthusiasm for the plan was waning. The interviews were taking far longer than anticipated. Half the time, people were not home and they had to try again later. Kate was realizing that the stereotype of retirees sitting around doing nothing was a myth. Quite a few of the residents seemed to spend very little time in their apartments, as they went about their busy lives of leisure.

Those people who were home had greeted Kate and Rob with enthusiasm and had plied them with tea, coffee, and cookies, as they were asked about their life stories. Interviews that should have taken fifteen to twenty minutes had taken closer to an hour each.

After dinner, Betty took them into the den to show them her handiwork. She had listed the names of the members of the writers' club on one of two large pieces of white posterboard, with room under each name to add notations. The second she had titled *Other Suspects*, with the rest of the remaining names from the *Disliked Doris* list. All she lacked was a bulletin board to tack them to.

"You can take the teacher out of the classroom," Kate teased.

Betty smiled at her.

They compared notes from their interviews and Betty made

notations. Their main accomplishment of the day had been the elimination of several people from the suspect list.

By nine, Betty was yawning. She went into her bedroom to get ready for bed, but she would be sleeping on the small settee in the living room as she had done the night before. She had insisted her tall, big-framed nephew should take the queen-sized bed in her bedroom.

"I'm way too wired to sleep yet," Kate said. "Too much tea and coffee today. I'm not used to it anymore." She'd been avoiding caffeine for over a year, while she was pregnant and then nursing.

"I'm still a bit wound up myself," Rob said. "Why don't we take a walk. I've got a key, so we can slip back in later and not disturb Aunt Betty."

Kate and Rob walked down the short hallway to the atrium in the center of the building. At nine, the area was already deserted, although they could hear televisions playing and the low murmur of conversations in several of the apartments.

"Pretty much roll up the sidewalks at sunset around here, don't they?" Rob said, as they headed for the front doors of the building.

Kate glanced outside at the gray July dusk. "Yeah, it's not even completely dark yet."

As they pushed through the doors, Kate studied her friend's broad face. Rob was looking downright haggard.

They chose a direction at random and strolled along the sidewalk. Streetlights surrounding the parking lots were coming on, then some blinked off again, their sensors unable to make up their minds.

"Anything the matter, Rob?" Kate asked.

Rob gave a low chuckle. "Besides the obvious that my aunt is a murder suspect?"

"Yeah, besides that." Kate smiled up at him.

"This case is getting to me a bit. It's going okay so far, but a lot's at stake. My client's wife is an alcoholic. Originally, she was divorcing him so she could party without him nagging her about trivial things." He gave a slight shake of his head. "Like not leaving the kids home alone when she wants to go to the bar, and not driving drunk with them in the car. So he assumed she would agree to let him have custody, but she's balked at that. Now we're duking it out in front of a judge. If she gets custody, the kids will be at even more risk than before."

"How old are the kids?"

"Six and four."

Kate winced.

"Yeah," Rob said, "way too young to be the rope in a parental tug of war."

"Not that there's ever a good age for that." Kate noticed a bench beside the sidewalk. "Let's sit for a while."

They sat down. The temperature was dropping with nightfall but heat still radiated from the asphalt of the parking lots. A slight breath of cool breeze ruffled their hair. Rob stretched his long legs out in front of him and let out a sigh.

"So is your client going for full custody?" Kate asked.

"Yeah, and supervised visitation for the mother, which he's not going to get. Now she's claiming she's sober, going to AA. But she's promised him before she would clean up her act, and it's only lasted a few days."

"With the courts still leaning toward the idea that young children need to be with their mother, he may not get custody at all."

"That's what I'm afraid is going to happen. I can present the best possible case, give a performance to rival Perry Mason, and this still may not turn out good."

"You're dating yourself with that reference, my friend," Kate said.

He gave her a lopsided grin, then his face sobered again. "I should be back in Maryland right now, working on my arguments and combing through case law to find more precedents for giving dads custody. But I couldn't let Aunt Betty down."

Kate took one of his big hands and held it in hers, unable to think of a thing to say to bolster his mood. Realistically his client wasn't likely to get even most of what he was asking for.

After a long pause, Rob squeezed her hand. His voice came out of the darkness now gathering around them. "You don't need to cheer me up, Kate. As usual, just talking out a case with you is helping."

Rob knew her so well he'd developed a sometimes disconcerting ability to read her mind. As she could his at times. In addition to consulting on mutual cases, they'd socialized outside the office for years. Long before Eddie's death, the Huntingtons had considered Rob and Liz their closest friends. Then the three of them had endured those horrible weeks following his murder.

Shared adversity had been powerful glue, leaving them even closer.

~~~~

The last of the lights around the adjacent parking lot finally decided it was truly dark and snapped on. Rob willed his muscles to relax. Liz had been bugging him to lower his stress level, and he'd promised to cut back his workload.

He'd been moderately successful at keeping that promise, until this week. First this divorce case had exploded into a nasty custody battle, and now this mess with Aunt Betty.

Kate stirred next to him on the bench, then let out a soft sigh.

"So how have you been, my friend?" Rob said.

She sighed again. "Looking forward to returning to work, and then feeling guilty because I'm actually glad my maternity leave is almost over. I'm just not cut out to be a stay-at-home mom."

"You should talk to Liz, sweetheart. She's had the been-there, done-that experience with that. She loved being a mom, but all day, every day pretty much drove her up a wall when the girls were little."

"Don't get me wrong," Kate said. "It's great when I'm actually interacting with Edie. But there's way too much time when she's sleeping. Of course there are always chores to do, laundry and such…" Her voice trailed off.

"But laundry's boring," Rob said. "Not exactly in the same

league as helping people get sane."

"Yeah, I'm bored to tears most days."

He glanced sideways at her, then twisted around to examine her face more closely. The nearest streetlight reflected off the actual tears pooling in her eyes.

"And lonely," she added in a whisper.

He wrapped an arm around her shoulders and pulled her up against his side. "You still miss him a lot." A statement, not a question.

"Every minute that I'm not thinking about something else." She leaned her head on his shoulder.

"I miss him, too," Rob said, his voice husky. His connection to Kate had always been stronger, but over the years he'd become good friends with her husband as well. Ed Huntington had been the kindest and most easygoing man he'd ever known.

He cleared his throat. "Sometimes I still catch myself, when I hear a good joke, thinking I gotta remember to tell Ed that one." His eyes burned. He was grateful for the dim light, so she couldn't see his face.

Kate sniffled.

He reached into his pocket for his handkerchief and handed it to her. While she was wiping her eyes, he furtively swiped at his own with the back of his hand.

There were very few things he kept from this woman with whom he was closer than anyone else on the planet, with the exception of his wife. But he had tried to hide from her his own grief for her husband. She already had so much to deal with–losing Ed and then having to face childbirth and parenthood on her own. And he'd had Liz to help him cope with the loss of his friend.

"Guess we'd better be getting back and get some sleep, so we can go pester old people again tomorrow." Rob stood up and pulled Kate to her feet. As they walked back toward Betty's building, he put his hand on her shoulder.

"Here I was trying to cheer you up," she said. "And once again you end up comforting me."

"Actually I feel better than I did earlier. Maybe having to come up here isn't all bad. It's given me some distance. Made me realize that I'm not responsible for the mess my client's life has become. All I can do is try to help him as best I can."

They entered the building. The lights in the atrium had been dimmed and there were now only a few murmurs of conversation coming from behind closed doors.

Kate dropped her voice to a whisper. "It's such a tough balance to maintain, in both our jobs. To care, but not be sucked into the misery ourselves."

Rob put his key in the lock of Betty's door, but before opening it, he turned to Kate. "I always know, sweetheart, that when the undertow starts sucking my feet out from under me, you'll help me get my balance back."

He opened the door and ushered her into the quiet apartment, the dim light over the stove in the kitchen the only illumination. "Thanks, Kate," he whispered, then kissed her on the forehead.

"Goodnight, dear," she said softly, and headed for the sofa bed in the den.

CHAPTER FIVE

Sunday morning brought more frustration. After knocking on mostly unanswered doors–apparently many of the residents had gone to church–Kate and Rob headed back to Betty's apartment to regroup.

"We need more hands on deck here," Rob said. "I'm going to call Skip Canfield and hire him. Hopefully he can get up here by tomorrow."

Kate nodded enthusiastic approval of that idea. "Hey, I just had a thought. We hid Betty's back-up computer disks in my car, in case Lindstrom decided to confiscate them. Do you think Liz would have time to go through them, to see when that supposedly plagiarized subplot first appeared?"

"How would we prove when those earlier drafts were written?"

Kate hid a smile. Rob was a technophobe. His understanding of computers was rather fuzzy. The technophobe's wife, ironically, was a computer whiz. "Files are electronically date-stamped. Liz'll know how to access the date when each draft was last modified."

Rob thought for a moment, then nodded. "Wouldn't totally eliminate the motive, but it would take the teeth out of it. I'll take the disks with me and see what Liz can do with them."

Over lunch they told Betty about Kate's idea. "I'll write out the gist of the subplot," she said, "and as much as I can remember about Doris's idea. The premise was similar, but the way she'd planned to develop it was different." Betty sighed heavily. "Unfortunately, I can't prove that."

Kate felt bad for the woman. "Try not to let this get to you, Betty. Remember you're innocent until proven guilty."

After lunch, they headed out of the building to locate the next person on their interview list.

Rob cleared his throat. "I didn't want to say this in front of Aunt Betty, but unfortunately in the real world, innocent until proven guilty doesn't always apply. The police and prosecutors often get jaded. They start to assume that if the person looks guilty, they probably are. Then their agenda becomes to find the evidence to convict the person, or to scare them into a plea bargain."

"Do you really think Lindstrom could build a case against Betty?" Kate said.

Rob held up his big fist. His index finger went up as he started ticking off points. "He's got a half dozen witnesses who heard the victim make her accusation and threaten to sue, and the defendant reacted with shock. The prosecutor would pound that point, that Betty was so upset, she was speechless." He extended the next finger. "The very next morning the victim is found dead." Another finger went up. "The scene says it was a crime of passion. An impulsive striking out during an argument."

His little finger joined its buddies. "The defendant's fingerprints and hair are found at the scene. And a defense attorney would sound pretty lame trying to make a case that the victim hadn't cleaned her living room in three months."

Rob wiggled his thumb. "The defendant has no alibi. Lindstrom's got opportunity, means and motive. Actually a less dedicated detective might have already arrested her. The fact that her nephew is an attorney may be all that's stopping him."

Kate was having trouble digesting what he was saying. She stopped walking and turned to face him. "Hell, Rob, this is the United States in 2006, not medieval Europe. How does Betty *maybe* wanted to kill Doris, and possibly could've killed her, become she *did* kill her? Don't they have to prove she did it?"

"In theory, but in practice the prosecutor looks at the case and asks 'Can I convince a jury this person is guilty?'"

They started walking again, along the stretch of road between Betty's section of The Villages and the buildings clustered around the recreation building.

"There was a case up here in Pennsylvania, a few years ago," Rob said after a pause. "A man was found dead in his car, the side of his head bashed in. A woman was seen getting into the car and her fingerprints were found in it. She was arrested for second degree murder.

"Her story was that a stranger stopped his car and asked for directions, throwing open the passenger door to talk to her. When she leaned over to answer his question, he dragged her into the car and took off. She said he took her to the spot where the car was later found, and tried to rape her. She fought him, he hit his head against the side window and she assumed he was just knocked out. She took off and went home, shaken and ashamed of her stupidity."

"So she didn't report it," Kate guessed.

Rob nodded. "Prosecutor claimed she and the guy were lovers, and they'd had an argument. She'd hit him and left him for dead. There was no evidence that she even knew the man, but the prosecutor was persuasive and her fresh-out-of-law-school public defender was an idiot. A female police officer had come forward and reported she'd been approached by the same guy when she was off duty, in exactly the way the woman claimed. She'd flashed her badge at the guy and he took off."

Rob shook his head, a disgusted look on his face. "The prosecutor ignored that piece of information and her lawyer, for some obscure reason, didn't use it. After the prosecutor had mopped the courtroom floor with his green opponent, a better lawyer was hired by a local rape victim advocacy group. He filed an appeal and had the cop testify. The appeals court's hands were tied, though. It was not new evidence. Her defense attorney had known about it at the time of the first trial."

"Wait a minute, I read about that case somewhere," Kate said. "The woman was eventually pardoned by the governor of

Pennsylvania."

"Yes, *nine years* after she was convicted. Her daughter was fourteen. The girl's foster parents had thought it would be too upsetting to bring her to prison to visit her mother, so the woman hadn't seen the child since she was five."

Kate felt the blood drain out of her face as she imagined being separated from Edie for nine years, not being able to watch her grow up. Her steps faltered.

Rob grabbed her arm to steady her.

"Holy...crap," she said, although that wasn't the word she was thinking. She shook her head to dispel the image of a teen-aged Edie standing in front of her, a stranger. "Okay, I get it. The legal system's not to be trusted to actually care whether or not someone's guilty."

"Now you know why I've been so worried." Rob turned to face her. "I know it's a lot to ask, but would you be willing to stay up here for another day or two? I'd feel a whole lot better if you were here to run interference with the police. My court case will hopefully be finished by Tuesday or Wednesday. At the very least, Liz'll be available by then."

"Wait a minute," Kate said. "Where the hell is Betty's son?"

Rob grimaced. "On a cruise in the Mediterranean."

Kate shook her head. "By the time he gets here, this will probably already be resolved."

Annoyance flashed in Rob's eyes. "He's not coming."

"What?"

"I'm afraid my cousin takes after his father. My great uncle was one of the most self-centered men I've ever known. When I finally caught up with Jake by ship-to-shore phone, he listened politely, then said, 'Keep me informed.'"

They started walking again. "Before I could point out that it was his filial duty to come help his mother, he'd hung up. I'm amazed Aunt Betty was able to stand living with the two of them."

"Women of her generation didn't question their lot in life," Kate said. "They just made do."

They fell silent as they entered one of the apartment buildings. She was trying to decide what to do. Her guilt and longing for her baby were escalating by the hour, but the thought of Betty incarcerated, even for a day or two, outweighed her maternal angst. Edie was safe and cared for, no matter how much Kate hated being away from her. The physical and emotional risks to Betty if she was arrested were much greater concerns. She needed someone here who could quickly move to arrange for a local lawyer and bail.

"Okay, I'll stay," Kate said.

"Thank you." Rob breathed out a sigh of relief, and she knew she'd made the right decision.

"I've got Fran checking out the reputations of criminal lawyers up here," he said. "I'll have her call you with some names, just in case."

Kate nodded.

There'd been no sign of Detective Lindstrom all weekend, although they'd seen various police officers also interviewing residents. Maybe he'd already come up with other leads, and tomorrow morning he'd be stopping by to tell them that Betty had been cleared.

Then she could go home to her child and her blissfully boring life. And to think she had wanted a little excitement.

"Watch what you ask for, indeed," she muttered under her breath, as Rob rang the doorbell of their next interviewee.

Monday morning, Kate went to talk to the retirement community's director, Alice Carroll. At the small building that housed the management and sales offices, she was kept waiting only a few minutes before being ushered into the director's office.

"Thank you for seeing me on such short notice, Mrs. Carroll," Kate said, as she shook the middle-aged woman's hand and took the offered seat. The director, tall and thin, was meticulously dressed, but her plain face was bare of make-up. Her mousy brown hair was cut in an outdated page boy.

Kate explained why she was there, representing Betty Franklin. "I'm sure you want to clear up this matter quickly as much as we do. I was hoping you could give me some insights into the members of the writers' club."

"Well, Mrs. Huntington," the director huffed. "I really am not at liberty to discuss my residents."

"I understand, Mrs. Carroll. I'm a psychotherapist so I am certainly aware of confidentiality restrictions on medical records and such. But anything you do feel comfortable sharing, such as your impressions of their personalities, would be very helpful."

Despite her protests, once Kate got the woman talking, she was a fount of information. Kate scribbled notes as quickly and unobtrusively as possible, while nodding and making tell-me-more noises.

When Mrs. Carroll wound down a bit, Kate prompted, "What about the Morrises? I notice they were the only couple who were both in the writers' group."

"Oh, they're a sad case. You know Mrs. Morris is no longer with us." Kate shook her head slightly, even though she did know the woman was dead. She wanted to keep the director talking.

"Yes, the poor dear. She died a year after they moved here," Mrs. Carroll said. "I feel sorry for Mr. Morris, although he is a bit of a difficult man. Quite frankly I don't know how Mrs. Morris put up with him all those years."

~~~~~~~

The rest of Kate's morning was quite frustrating. At three of the apartments she'd tried, no one answered the doorbell. The two women she did catch up with confirmed that they hadn't really known Doris well, but they'd only admitted that after they'd plied her with refreshments and tried to pump her for information about the murder investigation.

At eleven-fifty, Kate was sitting in the atrium in the center of Betty's apartment building. She'd just called the Franklins' house for an Edie fix. After reassuring her that the baby was doing fine, Samantha had held the phone to the little girl's ear so Kate could tell her how much Mommy loved and missed her.

Trying to distract herself from her homesickness, Kate was re-writing her scribbles from her interview with Mrs. Carroll, so Betty would be able to make sense of them. Her notes covered the small wrought iron table, nestled amongst lush plants that were thriving in the filtered light from skylights two stories above her head.

She was almost finished her task when someone tapped her on the shoulder. She jumped a little, then looked up into Skip Canfield's smiling face.

Kate smiled back, glad reinforcements had arrived and also, she realized, glad to see him. "Hi." She gestured toward one of the other chairs at the little table.

As he pulled out the chair, she noted that changing roles from bodyguard to private investigator didn't mean he was letting himself go. His tall body still looked quite buff. The hem of his crisply-ironed shirt hung loose over his jeans to cover the pistol, which Kate knew, from their past association, rested in a waistband holster at the small of his back.

He sat down across from her.

She blushed a little when she realized she'd been staring a bit too long at his broad shoulders and muscular chest. Bringing her gaze up to his face, she noticed that his tan shirt matched the gold flecks in his hazel eyes.

Those gold flecks danced, and a slow, easy smile spread across his face. "How have you been, Kate?"

She felt her cheeks grow hotter. She ducked her head and fiddled with the pages of notes in front of her. "I've been good, thanks. Uh, let me tell you what we've done so far."

Kate started filling him in, but she was distracted by Frieda and another woman, who were sitting on a bench across the atrium from them. Frieda waggled her fingers at Kate by way of a greeting but didn't interrupt her conversation.

The other woman was apparently partially deaf. She kept saying in a loud voice, "What did you say, Frieda? Speak up."

It was also apparent that Frieda was trying not to speak up any more than was necessary, no doubt because she was gossiping.

Kate tried to ignore them so she could finish her report to Skip, but the words *Betty's book* and *poker* jolted her attention back to Frieda and her bench mate. They were talking about the murder.

Skip had noticed her divided attention. He followed her line of vision to the cause of her distraction.

There was a rustling movement in the plants behind the women's bench.

Skip and Kate exchanged a quick glance, then she went back to discreetly observing the ladies.

Skip leaned toward her. His straight brown hair–slightly longer than most men wore their hair–fell across the side of his face. The casual observer would assume he was looking at her, but he was watching the women out of the corner of his eye.

Kate only caught the occasional word, mostly names, some of which she recognized from the list of the writers' club members.

The plants moved again. There were no drafts that Kate could detect in the atrium, but maybe there was an air-conditioning vent near the plants.

The women got up and parted company. The plants rustled.

Frieda headed toward a door that was adorned with a wreath of dried flowers. Before entering her apartment, she turned and gave Kate an exaggerated wink.

They watched the plants for another minute. The foliage remained still.

She looked at Skip. He shrugged.

Her stomach growled loudly.

He grinned at her. "Still have a hearty appetite, I see."

"Yes, and I don't have pregnancy as an excuse anymore. Let's get some lunch in the cafeteria while I finish filling you in."

"Mrs. Franklin isn't joining us?"

"No, she's eating her meals in her apartment for now. Says she's not ready to deal with the funny looks and comments behind her back."

Once they had selected their food in the cafeteria, they settled at a table some distance from those occupied by other diners. It only took a few minutes for Kate to finish her summary of what had been accomplished so far.

They ate their sandwiches in companionable silence. Kate was reminded of another time when they had sat eating sandwiches, while Skip had explained his incongruous nickname to her. To make conversation, she said, "You told me before how you came by your nickname as a kid. But I'm curious. Why did you keep it as an adult?"

"I did talk to my dad about changing it," Skip said, "when I was sixteen. I was tired of being picked on at school because of it. By that time my grandfather, Reginald William, Sr., had died. I didn't want to go by Bill. That was my father's name. And the last thing a teenager wants to be is more like his parents."

He took a bite of his sandwich and quickly chewed and swallowed. "My dad suggested I go by Reggie, now that Gramps was gone. Well, that lasted less than a day. The bullies at school who'd made fun of *Skip* went into hysterics when I informed them that my real name was *Reggie*. They ganged up on me and almost beat me to a pulp before a teacher finally intervened."

His face had grown serious. "I decided from that day forward, I would be Skip. I wasn't letting a bunch of bullies define who I was. I also started working out, and then I had a growth spurt. By the end of that school year, I was bigger and stronger than the leader of the bullies. Suddenly they weren't so eager to pick on me."

Kate gave him a small smile. "And heaven help anybody who's snickered at your name since then, huh?"

"Any guy, that is." The easygoing grin was back. "With the ladies, I just charm them with the idea of me as a cute little baby named Skippy."

Kate chuckled, and realized she was feeling more relaxed than she had in days. She smiled back at him. "I can understand the whole identity issue thing. My husband was a junior. It's certainly tougher to sort out who you are as a teen when you're carrying around someone else's name. As a kid, he was called Eddie to differentiate him from Ed, Sr. Once he was an adult, his mother and I were the only ones who could get away with calling him that. It got pretty confusing at family…" She trailed off, wishing she hadn't brought up the subject of Eddie.

Ducking her head to hide the unshed tears stinging her eyes, she managed to finish the thought. "At get-togethers, whenever someone referred to Ed you were never quite sure who they meant." She hoped her voice sounded reasonably normal.

Unfortunately her attempts to cover up her feelings were too successful.

Skip leaned forward. "Uh, Kate, I was wondering if you would consider maybe having dinner with me some time?"

One of the tears escaped and trickled down her cheek.

"Damn! I'm sorry. I guess it's too soon, huh?" Skip handed her his handkerchief and scooted his chair a bit closer so he could pat her arm.

Kate nodded as she dabbed at her eyes, momentarily distracted by the random thought that men of her generation rarely carried cloth handkerchiefs. It was a dying tradition.

When she could trust her voice, she said, "I'm sorry, Skip. But thank you for asking. A girl always likes to know she's still attractive." She gave him a small smile, as she returned the damp handkerchief.

Skip flashed her his easygoing grin again.

She couldn't help noting that his personality was very much like Eddie's.

Cut that out.

It really was way too soon, and she wasn't at all sure that any man could ever live up to her husband's memory.

They became aware of the silence in the room and looked around. It was not because they were alone, but rather the other diners had stopped eating and were enjoying the show. "Oh, great," Kate whispered. "It looks like we've become the latest installment in *Days of Our Lives*."

Skip laughed nonchalantly. He stood up. In a louder than normal voice, he said, "If you're done, darlin', shall we go?"

Wondering what he was up to, Kate rose to her feet. He took her hand and tucked it into the crook of his arm. She stifled a snicker as he escorted her from the dining room.

Once in the hall, Kate tugged her hand free and lightly smacked his arm. "You're terrible," she said, laughing.

"Aw, come on. We made their day." He smiled down at her, his hair flopping onto his forehead.

"I gotta warn you." His expression turned serious as he brushed the hair back with long slender fingers. "I'm a patient man. I will be asking again."

Kate wasn't sure what to say so she opted for a small smile.

~~~~~~~

Back at Betty's building, they headed for Henry Morris's apartment. Rob and Kate had tried to interview him over the weekend, but they'd gotten no answer when they'd knocked on his door.

The walkway surrounding the second level of the open atrium area would have afforded a lovely view of the foliage and small fountain below, if it weren't for more lush plants in large clay pots, sitting on a small shelf at the top of the walkway's railing.

Kate figured the community's management meant well. They were trying to make the buildings attractive. But there was a little too much greenery, in her opinion. She was starting to feel like she was in a jungle.

Skip rang Mr. Morris's doorbell. After several moments with no response, he rapped on the door.

A gruff "Go away!" came from inside.

"Sorry to bother you, sir," Kate called through the door. "We just need to ask you a few questions."

The door cracked open slightly. Kate had a quick impression of a lean, wiry man, average height, his weathered face scowling at her.

"You the police?"

"No but—"

"Already talked to the police."

"Yes, but—"

The door slammed in her face.

"Go away!" came from the other side of it.

Now Kate knew what Mrs. Carroll had meant about Mr. Morris's personality. Apparently "a bit difficult" was the local euphemism for totally obnoxious.

Skip and Kate succeeded in interviewing two of the married couples on their list, to explore the flirtation/jealousy issue. The others had not been home. Then they split up, Skip going in search of the maintenance man, while Kate attempted to track down more of the women on the list of those who might or might not have known Doris well enough to dislike her.

As Kate walked past the door with the dried-flower wreath, it opened and Frieda stuck her head out. "Hey, Kate, can I talk to you for a minute?"

"Sure." Kate followed the older woman into her apartment.

Once they were settled in her living room, Frieda said, "I heard a rumor that the murder weapon was a poker. Have you heard anything about that?"

Kate wasn't sure how to answer her. She didn't want to fuel the rumor mill but she also didn't want to lose Frieda's trust. "The detective mentioned something along those lines," she finally said.

Frieda nodded. Then her expression turned sly. "So who's that strapping young man I saw you with earlier?"

"He's, uh, another friend of the family. Rob asked him to come up and help us clear Betty's name."

"Looked to me like he's sweet on you." Frieda grinned at her, a sly look in her eye. "The way he was leaning forward, gazing into your eyes."

Kate resisted the urge to laugh. "No, he's just a friend." She wasn't about to tell Frieda that Skip had been attempting to disguise his surveillance of her and her bench mate.

"Uh huh, you go right on believing that, honey, but I say he's sweet on you." Frieda glanced at Kate's left hand. Her eyebrow shot up at the sight of her wedding band and diamond ring.

"I'm a widow," Kate said. "A relatively recent widow actually, so I'm not ready to date yet."

Frieda's expression shifted to remorseful. "I'm so sorry, honey. I didn't mean to stir up something painful."

"That's okay. It's not a completely healed wound, but it's not a fresh one either."

Frieda pushed her bulk forward in her chair. "The main reason I wanted to talk to you… I hope Betty doesn't find out about this. Some folks are acting as if it's a given that she killed Doris."

Shocked, Kate sat up straighter. "How could anybody who knows Betty assume that?"

"These weren't people who know her all that well."

"Who was it?"

"I'd rather not say," Frieda replied.

Hell of a time for a gossip to get coy.

Out loud, she said, "Frieda, this could be important. One of those people could be the killer."

"Well, one of the times was when a group of people were talking. They were standing in front of me in line for dinner the other night. Can't remember if it was Friday or Saturday. Their conversation kind of evolved from the police suspect Betty to maybe she really did it, and then to she must have done it. I don't even know most of their names. They're from a couple buildings over, but I do remember the Forsythes were there."

Kate jotted down the name on her notepad.

"The other time was when I was talking to Carla Baxter. She lives in the building next door. I was talking to her about… something else, and then she started saying that Betty must be guilty. Her comment was 'Where there's smoke, there's fire.'"

Kate noted that name as well. "Thanks, Frieda. I'll make sure Carla Baxter gets added to our list to interview. I think the Forsythes were already on there." She stood up.

"I feel so bad for Betty." Frieda lumbered to her feet to escort her guest to the door. "I can't believe people are jumping to the conclusion that she's a killer."

"Unfortunately, it's human nature to make that kind of leap. All too often what could be becomes what is."

Especially when people are gossiping and spreading rumors, she thought, but resisted saying it out loud.

At the door, Frieda patted the younger woman's arm. "I hope that young fella's still hangin' around when you're ready to date, honey, 'cause he's one gorgeous hunk of manhood."

Kate smiled at her. "I did notice that."

~~~~~~~~

That afternoon, Kate was able to eliminate several more people who didn't seem to know Doris well. Other than that, she had little to show for her efforts when she met Skip at five and they headed back to Betty's building.

"Did you find the maintenance man?" she asked.

Skip shook his head. "Saw a youngish guy, in work clothes, going into one of the buildings, but when I got there I couldn't find him... Oh, by the way, Rose is off duty tomorrow. She's coming up to give us a hand."

"Good. Otherwise, at the rate this is going," Kate dropped her voice to a whisper as they entered Betty's building and started across the atrium, "most of our suspects will have died of old age before we get a chance to interview them."

Skip was still chuckling when he glanced up.

Kate started to follow his line of vision. In the next instant, she was lying under him on the cold slate floor. She'd opened her mouth to ask what the hell he thought he was doing, when a tremendous crash echoed through the atrium. Flying dirt and bits of something harder pummeled her skin, wherever Skip's body wasn't covering it.

He rolled off of her and onto his feet in one motion, his gun in his hand.

Gasps rippled through the group of residents heading toward

the door. Some ran. Others stood frozen and wide-eyed.

Skip slowly spun in a circle, eyes up, scanning the railings of the upper levels. He stopped abruptly, stared for a moment. Then he extended his hand to Kate to help her up. His eyes weren't on her, however.

She followed his line of vision to a gaping hole in the line of pots along the railing one level above their heads.

Skip smoothly slipped his gun back into his waistband, but kept his hand resting on the butt. "You okay?" he asked Kate, still not looking at her as he scanned the upper levels again.

"Yeah," she said, although she suspected she'd have a few bruises in the morning from being squashed between his big body and the hard floor. She wasn't about to complain, though. His tackle had saved her from being smashed on the head by a potted plant. She wasn't sure if it would have killed her, but it would have definitely given her one hell of a concussion.

"Stay here," Skip ordered. She ignored his words and followed him as he sprinted toward the fire stairs door. He stopped and turned back to her. "It would be helpful if you stayed down here and watched for anyone suspicious while I'm in the stairwell."

Okay, *that* seemed like a good reason to stay here. She modeled his scanning behavior, although she wasn't real sure what she was looking for.

She realized how difficult Detective Lindstrom's job was. Assuming Doris had been killed by another resident, how could you tell who was suspicious? They all just looked like what they were, senior citizens–some of them now scowling at the intrusion by these strangers, some curiously staring at her or at the shards of terra cotta clay and dirt on the floor.

The only people in the building who looked out of place were *her and Skip*.

Lindstrom. She should call him. She took her cell phone from her purse and looked up his number, which she'd added to her contacts list on Friday. She punched send and did another scan of the atrium. It was quickly emptying of residents as they went in search of their supper.

A flash of stealthy movement on the second level. Kate frantically waved her hand to get Skip's attention, then pointed to the railing on the opposite side from where he was examining the gap in the pots.

But by the time he raced around the walkway, no one was there.

CHAPTER SIX

An hour later, Detective Lindstrom was examining the debris scattered across the atrium's slate floor, while Mrs. Carroll stood nearby, asserting in a too-loud voice that the pot must have been bumped by someone walking past it. The director glared in Kate's direction, as if she were the cause of the problem.

Lindstrom made no comment to the director's assertions. He turned to Kate and Skip.

For the time being, they had decided that Skip would be introduced as a friend of the family. Cops rarely appreciated private investigators sticking their noses into official police investigations.

After they gave the detective their account of what had happened, Skip quietly pointed out that there was a four-inch side along each edge of the shelf holding the plants. It was no doubt there to prevent the plants from being accidentally knocked off. Someone had to have lifted the heavy pot up over that side.

The potted plant had been dropped on them intentionally.

Lindstrom turned to Kate. "Mrs. Huntington, I suggest that you go home. It isn't safe for you to continue poking around in this."

Kate didn't respond. She wasn't quite sure how she felt about the situation at this point. She was certainly rattled, and a part of her was definitely frightened, not only for herself, but at the thought of leaving Edie an orphan.

But another part was really pissed. Bad enough that this killer was trying to frame a little old lady, now he or she was trying to frighten them away from investigating and clearing Betty's name. Kate was adverse to the idea of running back to Maryland like a scared puppy. And she had Skip to protect her. They would just have to be more vigilant.

She nodded at the detective to let him know she'd heard him. If he chose to take that as acquiescence, well, she couldn't help it if he misunderstood her.

When she and Skip were finally allowed to go their way, it was after six. They went down the short hall off of the atrium to Betty's apartment.

Betty answered the door and exclaimed, "Thank God, Kate. I was beginning to worry."

The fragrance of crab soup simmering on the stove had Kate's mouth watering, but first she introduced Skip and they filled Betty in on the pot incident.

The elderly woman covered her mouth with her hand and turned pale. "You can't keep asking questions then. I'll not have you getting hurt on my account."

Kate felt Skip's gaze on her. She turned to him.

There was a half smile on his face, but his eyes were serious. He said to Betty, "Give it up. She isn't going to stop. She's one of the most stubborn women I know."

Kate glared at him. "I like to think of it as determination."

"Hey, I didn't mean that as an insult." Skip raised his hands in mock surrender. "Personally, I *like* stubborn women."

Only partially mollified, Kate said, "Well, I *don't* like the idea of letting some... bozo chase me away." The word she was thinking of was much stronger than *bozo*, but she didn't want to offend Betty.

Skip was shaking his head at her, and grinning at the same time.

"I want to go knock on some doors on the upper levels," he said, his face sobering, "before folks start settling down for the night. See if anybody saw anything. Can you save some of that wonderful-smelling soup for me?"

"Of course, young man."

Suspecting Betty had called him "young man" because she'd already forgotten his name, Kate said, "Be careful, *Skip*."

He tilted his head at her, an odd expression on his face, then gave them both a small salute before heading for the door.

Over Maryland crab soup and homemade biscuits, Kate filled Betty in on their interviews that day, handing over the notes she'd taken. "We caught up with two of the married couples today. Mr. Murphy didn't even realize Doris had been coming on to him. And his wife seemed amused by the whole thing."

Mrs. Murphy had chuckled at her husband's startled expression and had told them, "I don't worry about him straying. Marilyn Monroe could be batting her eyelashes at him and he'd think she had something in her eye."

"The other couple, the Petersons," Kate said. "He looked kind of embarrassed and then tried to downplay the flirting. The wife did seem a bit pi... uh, annoyed about it all. But I think maybe the undercurrents between them were about past transgressions. I didn't get the impression that he'd actually responded positively to Doris's attention."

She hesitated. "We also overheard Frieda and another woman talking earlier today. They seemed to be talking about Doris and your book, and something about the poker." She wasn't sure how important this was but she figured they should note everything. You never knew what pieces of information, seemingly innocuous by themselves, might connect with each other.

Betty shook her head. "I love Frieda dearly, but she's an incurable gossip."

"Did you talk to Rob or Liz today?" Kate asked, as she scraped the last few strands of crabmeat from the bottom of her bowl.

"Yes, Robert called around five. I think he was still in that court mode you talked about. He was rather brusque." Betty pursed her lips. "Said he was working on his closing argument for his case. He's hopeful it will be finished by tomorrow, or Wednesday at the latest."

Kate nodded, trying to decipher the odd expression on the elderly woman's face. "What's the matter, Betty?"

"This just doesn't sit well with me. It's just not right."

"Of course it's not. Someone's killed a woman and is letting you take the blame."

"No, that's not what I meant, dear, although that's certainly not right either." Betty shook her head slightly. "It doesn't sit well with me that you and Robert, and now this young man, are having your lives disrupted like this, because of me. And now someone's tried to harm you."

At that moment, Betty looked every minute of her eighty-five years. Worry and guilt were etched on her face. Gently covering the older woman's thin fingers with her own, Kate softly said, "Betty, we all *want* to help. You're family."

Betty turned her hand over and wrapped her fingers around Kate's to give them a gentle squeeze. "Thank you, dear, but I'm worried you'll get hurt, because of me."

"Betty, Skip's a licensed investigator and he's also a trained bodyguard. We'll be on the alert now. It'll be okay."

The older woman's lips formed a thin, tight line. "That nephew of mine implied that Skip was a friend, returning a favor. But he's paying him, isn't he?"

Kate was reminded of a time when she was ten and her mother demanded to know if her brother Jack had broken the crystal vase lying in shattered fragments on the floor. Bridget O'Donnell had worn that same no-nonsense scowl on her face, a look that said Kate had better choose honesty over filial loyalty.

"I don't suppose you'd believe me if I told you that he's family, too." Kate gave Betty a lopsided grin.

"Trust me, young lady, I would remember if I had ever seen *him* at a family party before." Betty relented and let her stern expression melt, returning Kate's grin. "He tends to give tall, dark and handsome a whole new meaning."

"To answer your question, yes, Rob is paying Skip, but I know he considers it money well spent. He wants to clear your name."

"Well, I'll just have to insist that I'm paying that bill," Betty said emphatically.

"You might not want to go there right now." Kate caught herself before she blurted out that Rob was already stressed out and might react poorly. She didn't want to add to Betty's guilt and worry.

"When this is all resolved might be a better time to have that argument," she said instead. "I'll tell you what's worked for me when we go out to lunch together. You let him argue long enough to appease his male ego, then you offer to split it with him."

Betty nodded, flashing Kate a conspiratorial grin. She pushed herself to a stand and headed for the den with Kate's notes. "Excuse me, dear, while I make a few notations on the lists," she said over her shoulder.

Betty had just finished writing *might be jealous* under Mrs. Peterson's name and *gossiping about book/poker* under Frieda's when a knock on the apartment door announced Skip's return.

He shook his head at Kate's questioning look, then sat down at the breakfast bar while Betty ladled up soup for him.

"Everybody was either already downstairs on their way to the cafeteria, or in the cafeteria," he said, between spoonfuls. "Except for a couple of folks who decided to eat in their apartments. One of them came out when he heard the pot hit the floor." Skip paused to devour a biscuit in two bites. "Fella said he didn't see anybody on the upper level, but he wasn't really looking there. He was looking down into the atrium. Once he saw no one was hurt, he went back to his supper."

Betty yawned, and the contagion spread. Kate's mouth stretched so wide, her jaw made a cracking noise.

"My bedtime," Betty said.

After traipsing all over the retirement community for several days, Kate was ready for an early night as well.

Skip looked dubiously at the silk-covered settee in the living room. Before Betty could offer to take the settee and give him her bed, he said, "I saw a Travel Lodge on my way into town.

Doubt they're booked up on a Monday night. I'll see you ladies in the morning. Thanks for the supper, ma'am."

Kate walked him to the door. Once there, he stopped and whispered, "Make sure you put the security chain on. And don't allow Mrs. Franklin to let anybody in, even one of her closest friends... On second thought, maybe I should stay here tonight."

"We'll be fine," Kate reassured him. "This guy'll wait to see if he's managed to scare us off before trying something else, I would think."

"Probably." Skip thought for a moment. "And a direct attack against you, that didn't look like an accident, would clear her and intensify the investigation, neither of which would be his desired result. You still have my cell number?"

Kate smiled up at him. "Yes, and it's still on speed dial."

He returned her smile, then left.

~~~~~~~

Kate didn't sleep well. Almost being clobbered by a potted plant had rattled her more than she'd realized. With every little night-time noise outside her window, adrenaline shot through her system.

When she did doze off, she started dreaming about being on trial for murdering her neighbor up the street, a grumpy little man who let his dogs poop on everybody else's lawn. The prosecutor was telling her that if she didn't take a plea bargain she wouldn't see Edie again until she was grown.

Kate jolted awake. She breathed a sigh of relief when she realized it had been a dream, then punched her pillow and tried to find a more comfortable position on the thin mattress.

At one o'clock in the morning, she was just drifting off again when she could have sworn she heard the apartment door open and close. She lay perfectly still, listening intently. She knew she would never get to sleep until she investigated. Putting on her bathrobe, she slipped quietly out into the main room of the apartment. Going to the door, she saw that it was locked, the safety chain in place.

Back in bed, she endured a couple more hours of dozing on and off before she finally fell into a sound sleep.

And of course, she overslept. The smell of coffee brewing finally penetrated her sleeping brain. She stumbled out to the breakfast bar in her bathrobe.

Skip was already there. He snickered at her disheveled appearance. "Good morning, sleepyhead." His tone was annoyingly cheery.

Kate stuck her tongue out at him.

"Ah, so we discover she is not a morning pers–" He was cut off by a blood-curdling scream.

Skip unlocked the apartment door and threw it open. He raced down the short hall to the atrium.

Kate was on his heels, no longer the least bit groggy.

As they turned the corner, a young Hispanic woman in a maid's uniform was running frantically toward them, yelling in Spanish. The only word Kate could make out was *"policia."*

Doors were popping open throughout the building.

Skip intercepted the woman. He held her by the forearms and shook her gently. "Stop! Tell me what's the matter."

She was babbling in what sounded like English, but stress was thickening her accent. Her words were indecipherable.

Kate stepped up and wrapped an arm around her shaking shoulders. "Calm down. Take a deep breath." She demonstrated with an exaggerated inhale of her own.

Skip let go of the young woman. "*Señorita, por favor. ¿Cual es el problema?*"

She made a valiant effort to breathe deeply. It came out on a shudder. "*La Señora...*" She pointed to a door standing open several apartments away. "*¡Está muerta!*"

Kate's eyes followed the direction of the young woman's finger, to the small wreath of dried flowers on the apartment door. Her hand flew to her mouth.

"Frieda! Frieda McIntosh?" she cried.

"*Si. Señora* McIntosh. She eez dead!" The young woman

mimicked stabbing herself in the chest.

Kate's knees buckled.

Skip grabbed her arm to keep both her and the young maid from falling. "Are you okay?" he whispered, concern in his voice.

Kate shook her head. She tried to follow her own advice, but the vice around her chest was making it hard to take a deep breath. When she found her voice, she said, "No, but thanks for asking."

"I need to..." Skip tilted his head toward Frieda's door.

Kate nodded that she'd be okay, and he headed toward the apartment to investigate. He was careful not to touch the door as he slipped inside.

She led the still trembling maid to a bench in the atrium.

In stumbling English, the young woman explained that she always cleaned the *Señora*'s apartment first thing on Tuesdays. Apparently Frieda was an early riser and the maid had expected her to have already left for breakfast in the cafeteria.

"*¡Dios mio!* I was in de living room cleaning for long time, and she..." The young woman crossed herself. "She eez lying dead in de bedroom."

Betty, pale and shaking, was standing in the middle of a group of residents who had gathered at the corner of the atrium. Skip came out of Frieda's apartment, again slipping sideways past the door without touching it.

Kate patted the maid's arm again before getting up and going over to him.

He shook his head slightly, then whispered, "She's in bed. Knife sticking out of her chest."

"Dear God!" Kate swallowed a lump in her throat. "My cell phone's in my purse on Betty's coffee table. Lindstrom's under contacts. I probably oughta put him on speed dial at this rate."

As Skip headed off to retrieve her cell phone, Kate hurried to Betty's side. The woman looked like she had aged a decade in the last ten minutes. Tears streaked her wrinkled cheeks and her hand shook as she reached toward Kate. "Is it really Frieda?" she asked in a wavering whisper. "Is she... Are you sure?"

Kate gathered the woman up in her arms. "I'm afraid so," she said quietly. Betty started sobbing as Kate gently turned her around and helped her back toward her apartment.

Rose arrived to witness Kate, still in her bathrobe, leading an elderly woman down a short hallway, away from a crowd of people milling around the atrium. Her teasing remark about her friend's attire died on her lips when she saw Kate's pale face and realized the old woman was crying.

Kate tilted her head toward Skip, who was talking into a cell phone. She and the old woman kept moving.

Rose quickly gathered the gist of the situation from Skip's end of the conversation. She pulled out her own cell phone.

Kate got Betty settled in the living room with a box of tissues and put the teakettle on to heat. She rummaged in cabinets until she found a box of tea bags. She put two in a couple mugs, along with a healthy dose of sugar.

When she offered one of the mugs of tea to Betty, the woman took it with a shaking hand. "Thank you, dear."

For the next hour, Betty fluctuated between tearful reminiscences and bleak silences, during which she stared into space. Sitting next to her on the settee, Kate held her hand and listened.

Betty finally patted her hand. "I think I need to lie down for a little while, dear. Thank you for listening to an old woman's rambling."

"You weren't rambling, Betty," Kate reassured her. She helped the woman to her feet and watched as she slowly moved to her bedroom doorway. Holding onto the doorjamb with one hand, Betty took an audible deep breath and straightened her spine.

Kate waited until the bedroom door had closed before letting out her own breath. That triggered a yawn.

She figured with all the police running around they wouldn't be able to do much investigating for a while. Might as well take a nap herself.

She glanced at the apartment door. Reassured that the security chain was in place, she trudged into the den and collapsed onto the sofa bed without bothering to remove her robe. She was asleep in seconds.

It never occurred to her that the killer would make another move so soon, with police officers swarming all over the building.

CHAPTER SEVEN

Kate jolted out of a sound sleep. Disoriented, she tried to figure out what had woken her. Had she heard a scream, or had she just been reliving the morning's events in a dream?

She looked at the clock on the wall of the den. Almost eleven. She'd slept two hours.

"Kate!" Betty's voice, high-pitched and frantic. "Somebody's breaking in!"

Kate bolted out of bed and ran into the living room.

Betty was standing in the middle of the room, staring at the door. It was partway open, caught at the end of the security chain.

Kate raced to the door and tried to shove it closed, only to be met with a resisting force on the other side. "Police!" she yelled.

"That you, sweet pea?"

Relief washed through her. Mac Reilly was the only person on the planet who called her sweet pea. Kate fumbled with the chain. She yanked Mac into the apartment, then slammed and locked the door.

She turned around, breathing hard, and saw horror on Betty's face. The elderly woman stood—one hand clasping the front of her blouse, the other covering her mouth—staring at Mac as if he were an axe murderer.

"It's okay! He's a friend." Kate turned to Mac. "I didn't know you were coming up."

"Rose called. Told me 'bout the other old lady. Figured you could use reinforcements."

"But why...?" She was totally confused. Mac wouldn't

break in.

"Heard screamin'. Saw the door partway open," Mac said in his usual cryptic manner.

Betty finally found her voice. "I...I heard a noise as I came out of the bedroom. Then the door popped open and caught on the chain. That's when I screamed."

"You must have scared him off, Betty. Did you see anybody running away?" Kate asked Mac.

"Just a flash of movement. Behind the foliage. What's with the jungle out there? Thought I was back in–" Mac stopped abruptly.

Kate glanced up from rummaging in her purse for her cell phone. It wasn't like him to almost slip like that. When he was in Special Forces, he'd disappeared for months at a time. Even his parents hadn't known where he was. Kate had always assumed he was involved in covert operations.

Was he more rattled by the risk to her than he seemed on the surface? As a kid, he had played the role of protective big brother, even more so than her real brothers had.

The doorbell rang. Mac took it upon himself to check through the peephole. Then he opened the door. Skip and Rose came in.

"Police are done with us for now," Rose said.

Mac awkwardly gave her a peck on the cheek, which brought a pink tinge to her skin. Then he brusquely started filling her and Skip in on the attempted break-in.

Kate went back to rummaging in her purse. She was about to dump it out on the coffee table when Skip handed over her cell phone.

"Sorry, I forgot to give it back to you. And maybe Lindstrom on speed dial isn't such a bad idea."

Kate started to chuckle, then realized he was serious. She located the number and hit the send button. It went straight to the detective's voicemail. She left a message.

Heading for the den to throw some clothes on, she said, "Nobody touch that outside door knob until the police get here."

But when Lindstrom arrived, that precaution turned out to have been unnecessary. He didn't seem to take the attempted break-in all that seriously.

He examined the doorframe and found no scratch marks. "Probably just somebody confused about where their apartment was." Left unsaid was that old people get confused easily. "All these doors look the same."

Betty gave him an annoyed look. "Except for the big fat apartment numbers in the middle of them."

Lindstrom shrugged. "If you're feeling vulnerable, ma'am, you could move to a motel for a while. Just let us know where you are."

Betty's expression shifted from annoyed to downright angry, and stubborn. "I'm not letting this bozo chase me out of my home!"

"Again, ma'am, I don't think this was an attempt to do you harm—"

Kate held up her hand in a stop gesture. "Then how do you explain that the lock was picked, Detective?"

"Mrs. Franklin probably just forgot to lock it."

Betty glared at the man. "I remembered to put the safety chain on but forgot to turn the lock on the knob? I am not senile, Detective."

"It's something anybody could forget," Lindstrom said, with another shrug.

Kate tried to interject that she was the one who'd locked the door earlier, but Betty snapped back, "Not, young man, when two people have been murdered in the same building, within the last forty-eight hours!"

"Speaking of which, ma'am, I need to ask you some questions about Mrs. McIntosh. How well did you know her?"

Tears sprang to Betty's eyes and her angry expression melted into sorrow. She sank into the nearest chair. Visibly struggling not to break down, she motioned Lindstrom toward the settee. "Frieda was a good friend," she finally said in a soft voice.

Kate sat down in the other armchair. The others stepped back, standing roughly in a line and looking like a military guard at parade rest.

As the detective asked several questions about Betty's relationship with the deceased, he was having trouble staying upright on the slippery silk upholstery of the settee. It was a piece of furniture designed for nineteenth-century ladies' tea parties, not for twenty-first century tall, lanky policemen. He had to keep his feet planted firmly in front of him. But he would occasionally forget and relax his legs. Then he'd start to slither toward the edge of the antique's short seat.

Kate struggled to keep a straight face. She glanced over at the others. Only equally tall Skip seemed to have noticed the detective's plight. He winked at her and pinched his lips together in an effort to avoid laughing out loud.

Lindstrom asked, "Did Mrs. McIntosh have any enemies that you know of?"

Betty paused to wipe her eyes. "Frieda could be provocative. She did not mince words. Some people found her candor… disturbing."

"Could you be more specific, ma'am? Who found her disturbing?"

"Let me get paper and pencil." Betty pushed herself up out of the chair and headed for the den. "I'll make you a list."

Once she was out of earshot, Kate quietly said, "She's trying not to speak ill of her dead friend, but Frieda McIntosh was more than just forthright, she was also a gossip. Also, Frieda told us that Doris was a flirt, that she even flirted with married men. Maybe there's a jealous wife involved."

Lindstrom digested that for a moment. He rose from his seat, as Betty came back into the room. "It never occurred to me to have my people ask about romantic motives with this crowd. I'll have to add that question to their list—"

Betty bristled. "We're old, not dead, Detective!" Then she looked chagrined at her poor choice of words. She handed him a sheet of paper. "These are the folks who most tended to find Frieda abrasive."

"I'll walk you out, Detective." Kate stood and followed him to the door. She slipped outside and pulled the door partway closed behind her, without touching the outer knob.

"So does this eliminate Betty Franklin as a suspect?" she asked in a low voice. "She had no reason to harm her friend." She decided not to push the idea just yet that the attempted break-in put Betty more in the category of potential victim than suspect.

"Not completely. All three of these ladies were in the writers' group. We'll be looking into what other connections there might be between them." In response to Kate's frown, he added, "I told you before, I look at my cases from *all* angles."

"You can't seriously still suspect her. And what about the attack on myself and Mr. Canfield? Betty would have no reason to go after us. We're trying to help her."

"It's conceivable the pot got knocked off accidently."

Kate put her hands on her hips. She caught herself before she said Rob's name. Not a good idea to turn Lindstrom against him. Instead, she said, "I've been told that all too many police officers these days don't care about getting the true culprit. They just try to make a case against the most likely suspect."

Lindstrom sighed. "Mrs. Huntington, I assure you that I am not one of those officers. But my captain… he's a by-the-book kind of guy. This second murder does confuse the issue, as do the attacks against all of you. But I know what Captain Davis will say. Maybe that's what the murderer wants, to throw us off."

"That sweet little old lady killed a good friend of hers just to throw you off her trail? Oh come on, Detective!"

"She didn't seem all that sweet today. Kept biting my head off."

"Maybe that's because you were spouting one ageist stereotype after another," Kate snapped at him.

To her surprise, his expression turned sheepish. "Yeah, I need to stop making assumptions about this crowd, just because they're old."

Kate's anger evaporated. "It's easy to do. I keep catching myself falling into the stereotype trap, too. But elderly people find it insulting when you lump them all together."

"It's not just insulting. It's dangerous. I could miss something vital." Lindstrom's voice was sharp with self-criticism. Then, with a small grin, he said, "But I have a feeling you and Mrs. Franklin are going to keep reminding me to keep an open mind."

"Just doing our civic duty, sir." Kate gave him a mock salute.

Lindstrom's face grew serious. He scrubbed his hand over it, then ran fingers through his sandy hair. "Look, it's early on in the investigation and some much better suspects may very well be discovered soon. But for lack of anybody better right now, Mrs. Franklin's at the top of the suspect list in the Blackwell murder. She has the most compelling motive by far and physical evidence places her at the scene–"

"At some point in the past," Kate interrupted. "Not necessarily the night Doris was killed."

Lindstrom nodded slightly. "She's got no alibi, so from the captain's perspective, we have motive, means and opportunity." He echoed Rob's words from Sunday.

Kate studied his face for a few seconds. "But your gut's saying she didn't do it, isn't it?"

Lindstrom didn't answer as he looked down at her. After a moment, he said, "I think it would be a good idea to convince Mrs. Franklin to go to a motel for now, to be on the safe side."

"Then why aren't you taking this attempted break-in more seriously? And by the way, I was the one who locked the door earlier. You should at least take fingerprints off the doorknob."

Lindstrom pointed to the door. "Do you realize how many prints will be on there? It would take hours to take everyone's fingerprints, just in this building, in order to compare them. And then what would we have proved? That someone grabbed her doorknob at some point in the past."

The detective scrubbed his face with his hand again. "My

resources are stretched a bit thin at the moment. Had another major case land on my desk this morning, as well as this new murder. I think it's more important to have my people chasing down real leads rather than fooling with fingerprinting a doorknob."

"But you do believe that someone tried to break in to get to me or Betty?"

His cop face back in place, he looked at her for another long moment. "I'm keeping my mind open to all possibilities."

Lindstrom turned and strode away down the hall. He admired Mrs. Huntington's loyalty to her friends, but perhaps she was a bit naive.

He had talked to his cousin, who was an author, and had found out that it was likely the woman's publisher would have dropped her if the plagiarism accusation had any validity.

Mrs. Franklin might not have a motive in this last murder, but she definitely had a very strong reason to kill Doris Blackwell.

And it was quite plausible that Betty Franklin had opened her door herself, just before she started screaming that someone was breaking in.

CHAPTER EIGHT

Back inside the apartment, Kate filled the others in on her conversation with the detective.

Skip turned to Rose and handed her his keys. "Fingerprint kit's in the back compartment of my truck. This is a good opportunity to teach you how to lift prints."

"But how do we compare them to the residents' fingerprints?" Kate said.

Skip shook his head. "We won't be able to. Actually we'll be lucky if we get anything clear. But if we do, we can at least run them through the system to see if the owners of the prints have police records."

After Rose's print-lifting lesson resulted in nothing but smears, everyone grabbed a sandwich from the plate Betty had placed on the breakfast bar. Then they gathered in the living room area to regroup. Betty brought her posterboard lists out and propped them up on the settee. Mac and Skip grabbed chairs from the small dining alcove. Rose just sank to the floor, legs crossed in front of her.

Betty was putting two asterisks next to some of the names on the lists, when Kate's cell phone rang. She checked caller ID.

"It's Rob," she told the others as she answered the call.

"Hey," he said. "Court's adjourned for lunch. What's going on up there?"

As succinctly as possible, Kate filled him in on the second murder and the rest of their harrowing morning.

When she got to the attempted break-in at Betty's apartment, he said, "Shit! Can you convince her to move out temporarily?"

Kate glanced at Betty. "Already been suggested," she said into the phone. "Skip's going to camp out on the living room rug tonight. We'll be okay."

"Hopefully this case will be over today or tomorrow. I'll be on the road the minute after the judge's gavel comes down. Thanks again, sweetheart." His voice was rough with emotion. "You all be careful up there."

"We will be. Good luck with the case." She wanted to say more, to somehow reassure him, but the others were watching her. She said goodbye and disconnected.

Betty pointed to the names that she had put asterisks next to. "These are the folks that Frieda really rubbed the wrong way, but lots of other people found her a bit irritating. I love…" She stopped and closed her eyes. After a moment, she blinked twice, then continued, "I loved Frieda dearly, but she did tend to carry telling it like it is to the extreme."

"Were any of the men who found her particularly irritating among the guys Doris flirted with?" Kate asked.

Betty pointed to three names: James Berkeley, Fred Murphy and Henry Morris. "But Henry finds everybody irritating and his wife's been gone for months now."

"He's in the writers' group, and we haven't been successful at getting him to talk to us yet," Skip pointed out.

"I don't know why he stayed in the group after Sally died," Betty said. "She was the writer. He just dabbled some. Says he's writing his memoirs, but he almost never has anything ready to share with us, and when he does, it's pretty awful. I always thought he came with Sally just to know what she was doing. The man seemed to be a bit on the jealous side."

As Kate started making two lists of interviewees, Skip said, "Back to the drawing board. We need to re-interview everybody who knew both women. If we can find a common motive, then we'd be cooking."

"Yeah, we should try to find out if Frieda gossiped about

them," Kate said, as she handed the first list to Mac who was sitting next to her. "Skip and I'll check out the flirtation/jealousy angle with the rest of the married couples, and see how they react to Frieda's death. And we'll try again to get Morris to talk to us."

Skip nodded his agreement. "But we better wait until after Lindstrom's people have talked to these folks. He'll have our heads if we get in the way of his investigation."

"Good point," Kate said as she watched Mac stand up, then lean down to offer Rose a hand.

Rose grabbed his forearm in a gesture reminiscent of soldiers or athletes helping each other up. As Mac hauled her to her feet, Kate hid a grin. These two sometimes acted more like military comrades-in-arms than a romantic couple.

But apparently his respect for Rose as a comrade-in-arms had overcome Mac's sexist tendencies–tendencies that, along with his gruff personality, had led to two divorces. Maybe, just maybe, her childhood friend had finally found true love. Kate hoped so.

As the other two headed out the door, she turned to Skip. "Do you think it's safe to leave Betty here by herself?"

Before he could answer, Betty firmly announced that she would be fine. "I'll stay out here in the living room and keep an eye on the door. The chain held before so it should again. Somebody tries to get in, I'll scream bloody murder."

She looked chagrined again. "I never realized before how much we sprinkle our sentences with words like *dead* and *murder*, not realizing…" Her voice trailed off as tears pooled in her eyes.

Kate patted her shoulder. She caught herself as she was about to ask if Betty was okay. Of course she wasn't okay. She'd just lost a good friend.

Instead she said, "You have my cell phone number. Call if you need us, for any reason."

～～～

Skip and Kate headed out of the building in search of the first couple on their list. From beside him, she heaved a sigh.

Skip glanced over, trying to read her mood. "Are you okay?"

"Actually I'm not sure I *know* how I am. Everything's happened so fast, I haven't really had a chance to process all of it. I'd only met Frieda a couple of times, but I really liked her. She was quite a character."

He was tempted to take her hand to comfort her, but decided against it. He wasn't sure how she'd interpret the gesture.

Kate was quiet for a moment as they walked along the sidewalk in the hot sun. Then she said, "She told me something yesterday that I didn't share with Betty. Frieda didn't want her to know that some people had already jumped to the conclusion that she did kill Doris. The most emphatic of them was a woman named Carla Baxter. I gave Betty a vague reason for adding her name to our suspect list."

She fell silent again, her face serious, sadness in her eyes. "I can't help but think that Frieda's gossiping is what got her killed. She told the wrong thing to the wrong person. I should have warned her yesterday to be careful who she talked to…" Kate's voice trailed off. She blinked hard, then looked off into the distance.

Skip put his hand on her shoulder as he stopped walking. He turned her toward him. "I feel funny saying this to a therapist, but isn't that a pretty typical grief reaction? To think you could have done something to keep the person from dying."

Kate looked up at him. He could see the struggle on her face not to break down. She nodded mutely, then turned and started walking again. He fell into step with her.

"Thank you," she said softly after a moment.

"You're welcome." This time he did take her hand and gave it a squeeze, then quickly let it go again.

~~~~~~

By two-thirty, they had finally tracked down both members of the Forsythe couple. He had been getting a haircut in the barber shop on the second level of the recreation building.

Mr. Forsythe was a robust-looking gentleman with a thatch of thick white hair and broken veins on his large nose. Kate wondered if he was an alcoholic.

He'd laughed when they'd asked him about Doris's flirting. "That old hag... Oops, sorry, guess I shouldn't speak ill of the dead, but really, she was kinda pathetic. Always sidling up to me and making comments that I guess were supposed to be clever innuendoes."

"So you weren't even a little bit interested?" Skip had asked.

Forsythe laughed again. "Go see for yourself why I wouldn't be. You said you wanted to talk to my wife. She's in the gym downstairs, doing her daily workout."

They'd understood what he meant when they'd located Mrs. Forsythe on a treadmill in the gym. Slightly taller than average, she had excellent posture, elegantly styled ash blonde hair, and her latex shorts and light blue tank top revealed a figure that many women much younger would envy. Betty had said she was in her late sixties, but she looked more like mid-fifties. And a well preserved mid-fifties at that.

They'd had to wait for the timer on her treadmill to ding before they could get her attention. She had given Skip an appreciative once-over as she used a towel to pat the sweat off her carefully made-up face and a neck that showed only a hint of the crepey texture common to older women's skin.

Mrs. Forsythe had also expressed a mixture of amusement and pity regarding Doris's flirting with her husband. "If the woman hadn't been such an irritating person in general, I would have felt sorry for her."

When asked about Frieda, Mrs. Forsythe had shuddered dramatically. "I heard she was killed. I was telling Bob over lunch that maybe we should go visit our daughter for a while. But to answer your question. I didn't really know Frieda McIntosh. I mean I knew who she was, but I tried to steer clear of her."

Leaning closer to Skip, she whispered, "She was a bit of a gossip. I didn't want to end up one of her so-called friends that she talked about behind their backs." She batted eyelashes, heavy with mascara, at him.

"Frieda told me that she overheard a conversation," Kate said, "Friday or Saturday night, while standing in line for dinner in the cafeteria. A group of folks from your building were talking about Doris's murder and someone said, or implied at least, that they thought Betty had actually killed her. Do you happen to recall who made that comment?" She watched the woman's body language closely while Mrs. Forsythe gave that some thought.

Finally she shrugged. "I remember the conversation but not who actually said that."

Which was more than they'd gotten out of Mr. Forsythe. He hadn't even remembered the conversation.

And they'd had even less success with the Berkeleys. The husband had refused to open the door further than the security chain would allow. Through the narrow crack he'd appeared to be a short, frail man, probably in his mid to late eighties. "The Missus ain't home. She said I can't talk to nobody unless she's here." When Kate asked if his wife was expected back soon, the man had shrugged, then closed the door.

Kate planned to ask Rose and Mac to talk to the couple. If the wife was as frail as the husband, they might find Skip's size too intimidating.

As Skip held the door to Betty's building open for her, Kate said, "I've been thinking that we should get a stronger lock for Betty's apartment."

"I had the same thought, but I don't know how much good it would do. Someone determined to get in usually succeeds. I'm actually hoping he'll try to break in tonight. I'll be waiting for him this time."

"Don't be sexist now. The killer could be a woman," Kate admonished in a teasing tone, as they started around the atrium. "I wouldn't put it past Mrs. Forsythe, if she had a motive."

Skip smiled down at her. "She's a piece of work, isn't she?"

Kate looked across the atrium and spotted a man, laden with groceries, entering the elevator. She thought she recognized the weathered face and wiry build. Taking off for the elevator, she left a startled Skip behind.

The man saw her coming and quickly lowered the box he was carrying in one hand to the floor. He jabbed at the close-door button. The doors obeyed before Kate could get close enough to insert a hand between them.

Turning, she collided with Skip, then ducked around him. "I think that was Morris," she said breathlessly. She raced back across the atrium toward the door for the fire stairs.

Skip passed her and took the stairs three steps at a time. By the time Kate made it to the second level, he was halfway down the walkway.

However, even Skip's long legs couldn't outdistance the other man, whose apartment was only two doors down from the elevator. Kate saw two thin, weathered hands reach out to snatch the last of the groceries out of the hallway.

Then the door slammed shut just before Skip got there.

Kate caught up to him and leaned over, hands on her knees, gasping for air. "Damn. Probably no point in knocking," she huffed out. She narrowed her eyes at Skip. He wasn't even breathing hard.

"Kinda feel like a hound dog chasin' a car," he drawled, a hint of Southern roots creeping into his voice. "What was I s'posed to do with him if I'd caught him?" He was grinning down at her.

She gave him a mock scowl and sucked in more oxygen. "I was hoping to get to his door before he did. Block his way and maybe sweet talk him into letting us in and talking to us."

"Don't think he's in the mood for sweet talk right now," Skip observed, still grinning at her.

Kate ignored him and took out her cell phone to call Mac. Morris might relate to him, curmudgeon to curmudgeon. It was worth a try.

"What's up, sweet pea?"

"Skip and I just tried to catch up with Morris but he got away from us. How about you and Rose come knock on his door. See if he'll talk to you."

She and Skip went down the stairs to the first floor. As they reached the public restrooms near the elevator, Skip tilted his head in the direction of the men's room door. "Need to make a stop."

Kate gestured toward one of the benches. "I'll wait over there. My feet are killing me."

Skip looked up at the second level railing. "Watch out for pots falling out of the sky."

She looked up, then back at the bench. "Hm, maybe I'll go over there instead." She pointed to the small table and chairs, that were not directly under the railing overhead.

Skip nodded.

Kate headed for the table. She had no sooner settled into one of the chairs when she caught movement out of the corner of her eye. Turning, she saw the back of a khaki shirt, a work boot and khaki-covered leg disappearing through a door.

Was that Joe, the elusive maintenance man?

Kate quickly moved over to the door, then hesitated. A small sign on it read *Employees Only*. She opened it partway and stuck her head in to look around. Most of the room was taken up by a large piece of machinery that emitted a constant rumbling noise. She guessed it must be the furnace or air conditioner, or maybe the air handler for both. There were about four feet between it and the walls on all sides. To Kate's right was a narrow workbench running along the adjoining wall.

Again she hesitated.

All I'm going to do is walk to that corner and look around. How can that hurt anything?

She moved toward the workbench. Rounding the corner, she was disappointed to see nothing but a few jars and paint cans sitting on it. No Joe.

She jumped when someone tapped her on the shoulder and growled, "What the hell do you think you're doing?"

The man's angry tone turned to syrup when she spun around. "Well, hello there." Standing too close to her, he flashed a charming smile.

She took a step backward.

Kate got a fairly good look at him, before he moved in too close again. Frieda had been right. He was a good-looking man–a few inches taller than herself, lean and muscular, with that bad-boy James Dean look.

And from the way he was leering at her, he apparently was well aware of his attractiveness.

A shiver of anxiety ran down Kate's spine. Trying to keep her voice calm, she said, "Sorry to disturb you. You must be Joe."

"That I am. And what's *your* name, pretty lady?"

"I'm Betty Franklin's friend." She felt resistant to giving him her name so she left it at that. Trying to be subtle as she shifted back away from him a bit, she continued, "I'm, uh, trying to clear her. You may have heard she's a suspect in Mrs. Blackwell's death."

Having succeeded in putting a semi-reasonable amount of space between them, Kate relaxed slightly. "I figured that since you're in and out of this building regularly, you probably see and hear a lot. Maybe you could give me some insights, you know, into the personalities of the residents here?"

"Yeah, I'm in and out a lot." He cocked an eyebrow at her suggestively, then stepped in too close again.

Kate pretended not to notice the lewd double entendre as she edged away once more.

"But I don't pay much attention to the oldsters," he said. "Just do my work, so's I can get through the day and then go *party* at night."

"I think someone mentioned that you did sometimes talk to Mrs. Blackwell. I hear she was a bit of a flirt." She was fighting the temptation to cut and run.

"Yeah, she musta thought she was matty hairy or somethin'." Joe chuckled derisively.

It took a second for Kate to realize he meant Mata Hari. She was afraid to ask him outright if he'd ever had sex with Doris.

This guy might interpret such a query as interest on her own part, and he did not need any encouragement.

"So you didn't have any other contact with her, other than talking to her?"

"Nah, I like older women." He wiggled his eyebrows suggestively, then gave a mock shudder. "But not *that* old."

"Okay. Well, thanks for your time, Joe."

He didn't take the hint and move aside so she could pass. Instead, he closed the small gap between them again and leaned toward her. "Well, now, since I've answered your questions, how 'bout we spend a little time on some other subjects. You like to party, pretty lady?"

She tried to step back. Her heel hit the wall.

Joe had backed her into a corner.

CHAPTER NINE

Skip stood outside the ladies' room door, his arms crossed over his chest. Two elderly women came out together, chatting to each other.

"Excuse me, ladies. Was there anyone else in there?"

"No," one of them answered. Her companion was silently looking him over, an appreciative glint in her eye.

He didn't usually care for being somebody's eye candy, but he decided to make an exception for the octogenarian set. He smiled.

The woman fanned her fingers in front of her face, pretending she was about to swoon.

"Thank you, ladies."

"Our pleasure," the flirtatious one said. She winked at him over her shoulder as they walked away.

Grinning, he took several steps toward the table where Kate was supposed to be and did a scan of the atrium. Where the hell was she?

Shrugging, he turned to go back to Betty's place. There in front of him was a door marked *Employees Only*. His hand reached out and nudged the door open a few inches.

His brain caught up with his instincts. *Joe could be in here. And Kate as well.*

They may have gone into the room to talk.

In front of him was a wall of sheet metal. He pushed the door further open and stepped into the doorway. The wall was the side of a massive air handler. It was chugging away in its efforts to cool the three-story building.

Raising his voice a little to be heard over its rumbling, he called out, "Anybody in here?"

"Yes!" Kate's voice, a shrill yelp.

Skip's hand flew to his gun, but he kept it holstered for now. Two strides brought him to a wooden workbench. Turning the corner, he took in the scene.

Kate's scared, pale face behind a man who had spun around, fists halfway up, face twisted in anger. When the guy got a good look at his adversary, his demeanor changed abruptly.

His expression bland, he stepped aside. He kept his gaze on Skip as he said, "Glad to be of help, ma'am. You have any more questions, you know where to find me."

Kate eyed the guy nervously as she turned sideways and edged past him.

Unwilling to turn his back on the creep, Skip backed around the corner, pulling her along with him. Then he quickly maneuvered her around him and out the door.

He wrapped his hand around her upper arm and hustled her across the atrium.

Pressure built in his chest. *Why the hell had she gone in there? What was she thinking?*

He ground his teeth. As they neared the hallway leading to Betty's apartment, he tightened his grip and veered sharply toward the outer door of the building instead.

"Hey, what are you doing? Where are we going?"

Looking straight ahead, his jaw tight, Skip ignored her questions as he dragged her out the door into the summer heat. He took a half-dozen long strides away from the building.

Kate was forced to jog to keep up with him. When he stopped, she shook her arm loose and stepped back.

"What the *hell* do you think you're doing?" she spat at him.

"What the hell do I think *I'm* doing!" he yelled.

A group of elderly residents turned to stare.

He lowered his voice to a growl. "Have you lost your mind? Going into that room with that...that scumbag."

Kate just stood there, hands belligerently on her hips. They glared at each other, neither saying anything.

Her face shifted. The anger drained away. She lowered her hands to her side, then rubbed her arm where he'd grabbed her. "Okay, I shouldn't have gone in there. But I was just looking for the guy and he crept up behind me. I... I didn't know what was in there when I opened the door. It didn't occur to me how easily he could get me cornered in there or I never would've gone in."

"Shit, Kate, I thought you were smarter than that!"

Her hands were back on her hips. "Now wait a damn minute, Skip Canfield. I already admitted it was a stupid move. Anyone can have a lapse in judgment. And don't you *ever* lay hands on me again!"

Skip's anger deflated like a popped balloon. "Aw, Kate, I'm sorry. I shouldn't have grabbed you like that. But you can't even imagine how scared I was when I came around that corner and saw that weasel about to..."

"Ha! *You* were scared. Not half as scared as I was." She tried to laugh but it came out on a sob. And suddenly she was shaking and crying.

Aw, shit!

He closed the gap between them and gathered her into his arms. Holding her, he whispered, "Sh, sh, sh, you're okay," into her hair.

Her tears subsiding, she put both hands on his chest and gently pushed. He resisted letting her go for half a beat, then reached into his back pocket for his handkerchief.

Not looking at him, she dried her cheeks and eyes. "It was pretty stupid. I just didn't think. I saw him go in there and thought how we'd been trying to catch up with him, and I grabbed at the chance to question him."

She started trembling again.

Skip put an arm around her shoulders and steered her toward a bench, next to a small pond between the buildings.

As they sat down, she asked, "What made you think to come

looking for me in that room?"

"I don't know. At first I thought you might have gone into the ladies' room. When I saw the employees-only sign on that door, something, some instinct I guess, told me I should check in there."

"Well, thank God you've got good instincts."

They sat for a few moments, until the silence grew awkward.

Kate looked down at the crumpled, soggy cloth in her hand. "You know, you're a member of a dying breed—men who carry cloth handkerchiefs. My husband carried one, and so does Rob. But I don't know anybody else who does. It's a tradition I hate to see fade away." She looked up, gave him a small smile. "'Cause I seem to use the handkerchiefs of the men in my life more than they do."

Skip's heart gave a lurch in his chest.

She considers me a man in her life. Hot damn!

He smiled back at her. Eyeing the gooey blob of cloth, he said, "Uh, I think I'll let you keep that one. I've got a spare in my bag back at the motel."

She glanced down. "I'll get it back to you. I figure eventually I'll be able to go home and do mundane things like laundry."

When she looked up at him again, dark lashes still damp around sky blue eyes, his heart did a funny little flip. He felt light-headed.

She looked away. Staring across the small pond in front of them, she chewed on her lower lip for a moment. "A man giving someone his handkerchief, it's very...I guess *supportive* is the right word. It's a supportive gesture." She turned back toward him. Her voice dropped almost to a whisper. "I saw Eddie slip his to Rob one time, when Liz was in surgery..."

Skip was staring into her eyes, her words no longer registering. His heart raced. Before, he'd just been interested in this woman. But now... something had shifted. His mind resisted naming it. But somewhere in the last ten minutes or so, since he'd walked into that room and saw her in jeopardy.... Yeah, something had shifted alright.

Damn, Skippy, you're in trouble now.

He put a finger under her chin. Her eyes went wide as he leaned down to kiss her.

But she didn't pull back.

He kept the kiss chaste and tender. After a moment she closed her eyes. He closed his own and lost himself in the soft warmth of her lips. That warmth spread through him, igniting fires that had lain dormant for a while. His fist clenched the back of the bench, resisting the desire to grab her and crush her against him.

Eventually she broke free. "Skip…" she gasped.

"I know. Too soon," he said softly, his lips still hovering close to hers.

Then he made himself sit back. He tried to grin but it felt kinda lopsided. "Consider that a preview of, uh, future possibilities."

He knew if he kept looking at her he'd kiss her again, so he turned on the bench and looked straight ahead. Sitting side by side, their arms were just barely touching. He couldn't resist leaning slightly toward her, his arm pressing more firmly against her shoulder.

To his amazement, she leaned back.

He sat perfectly still, savoring the warmth flowing from that shoulder.

"It really is too soon, Skip."

"I know." For a second, he leaned a little harder against her. Then he moved away. "But I can still be your friend, can't I?"

She stood up abruptly. "Of course." She took several steps away from the bench.

He pushed himself to a stand.

She pivoted back around. "And I value that friendship, Skip. I really do." Then she turned and marched off toward Betty's building.

He trailed after her, trying to suppress his grin, but it spread across his face despite his best efforts.

Hot damn! I think she likes me.

Kate glanced back.

Crap, he's grinning.

Why the hell had she leaned against him like that. It had totally sent the wrong message.

She'd needed the contact comfort, she told herself, after her scary encounter with Joe. In fact, she admitted, she'd really wanted Skip to put his arms around her again. It had been so long since she'd been held by a man. For a brief second, she'd even considered faking more tears.

Instead she'd indulged in leaning against his muscular arm a bit longer.

This was crazy. Rob gave her hugs, as did her female friends. It wasn't like she didn't get plenty of support.

She pulled open the door to Betty's building and shivered a little when the air-conditioned air hit her hot skin.

So why had it felt so different being held by a man?

She glanced back again. Skip had entered the building a few steps behind her.

She could feel his strong arms around her again. She told herself she was just recalling the memory in order to analyze why that felt different from a woman's hug.

Because men are more solid, she answered her own question. Women were warm and soft, but men... they were warm and *solid.* Both comforting, but in different ways.

He gave her a nod, only a small smile on his lips now. But the gold flecks were dancing in his eyes.

The man was solid alright, in more ways than one.

Stop that!

Out loud she whispered, "It's too damn soon."

~~~~~~~

The plan had been to check in with Betty, then head out again to track down the Berkeleys. But as Kate and Skip were getting ready to leave the apartment, the doorbell rang.

It was Detective Lindstrom, and he did not look happy.

Betty invited the detective to sit down in the living room.

Kate followed them toward the settee and armchairs. Movement in the corner of her eye had her glancing toward the breakfast bar.

Skip had settled onto one of the stools, his back turned toward the sitting area. He picked up a newspaper lying on the counter and pretended to be absorbed in it.

A surge of gratitude and respect for this man–and something else she opted not to analyze–swelled inside her chest.

"Mrs. Franklin," Detective Lindstrom said, "I've talked to several members of the writers' group, and some of them mentioned something I found interesting. It seems you're not above using a cliché in your own mysteries. There's a scene in your latest book where someone hits somebody else with a poker, is there not?"

Betty looked puzzled. "I write historical romances, not murder mysteries, Detective." Then her face cleared. "Oh, you mean the flashback the heroine has to her childhood. When she saw her father murder her mother and then he tells everyone the woman slipped and hit her head on the hearth stones. That's there to explain why she's so mistrustful of men."

"Yes, that must be the scene that was mentioned to me. It seems Mrs. McIntosh had commented to a couple members of the group about the similarity between that scene and Mrs. Blackwell's death."

Lindstrom was watching Betty intently, but again she just looked confused.

Kate had a bad feeling about where this was going. "I suppose, Detective," she said in a mild voice, "that bashing people with a poker in the heat of an argument has become a cliché in novels, because it's often a weapon that's close at hand, if one has a fireplace, that is."

Betty, however, hadn't seemed to catch the drift of the detective's thoughts. "I don't know why Doris even had that set of fireplace tools. Our fireplaces all have those modern ventless gas fires."

Kate gritted her teeth, but telling Betty to stop talking would just make the hole she was digging that much more obvious.

"If she hadn't been such a horrible housekeeper, I would've said she had them there for show." The elderly woman shrugged. "Maybe they had sentimental value."

Detective Lindstrom allowed a moment of silence to pass.

Damn, Kate thought. The man had planted an idea in her head, and her analytical mind kept poking at it. What would be the psychological motivation for an author to act out a crime from his or her own work?

She forced her attention back to the discussion. Lindstrom had changed tacks. "The medical examiner's preliminary report says Mrs. McIntosh died between nine p.m. and four a.m. Where were you during that time, Mrs. Franklin?"

"Sound asleep in my bed, of course."

The detective turned to Kate. "You stayed here last night, Mrs. Huntington?"

"Yes, on the sofa bed in the den."

"And did you sleep soundly through the night?"

"Actually no, I was kind of restless. Just dozed off and on most of the night."

"Did you get up at any time?"

"Yes, once." Kate looked toward the door and hoped he wouldn't ask if she had heard anything strange. "I was a little spooked by the pot incident. I got up and checked the door to make sure it was locked."

"And was it?" Lindstrom asked.

"Yes." Too late she realized she wasn't making eye contact with the man.

The detective stared at her for a long moment of silence. "Anything else bothering you about last night, Mrs. Huntington?"

"No, I just kept hearing the night critters chirping and rustling outside my window." Kate made a concerted effort to give him a natural smile and look him in the eye. "And you know how it is when you're not sleeping in your own bed. Sometimes it's hard to get comfortable." She knew her claim that she had slept lightly did not give Betty an airtight alibi.

She was a bit startled when the detective flashed a brief smile back at her. "I do know how that is." Then he turned to Betty. "Do you have a key to Mrs. McIntosh's apartment?"

"Why, yes, we each had a key to the other's place."

Lindstrom nodded.

Kate read that to mean that again there had been no sign of forced entry. Either the killer had a key to both women's apartments or he or she knew how to pick locks.

"Did you know, Mrs. Franklin," Lindstrom said, "that your friend Frieda was gossiping with others about the similarities between your subplot and Doris Blackwell's idea? Apparently Mrs. Blackwell had also described it to her."

Betty was silent for moment. Then she said, "Frieda's a good friend in other ways, but she can't resist–" She stopped, sucked in her breath. Tears pooled in her eyes. "She *couldn't* resist gossiping, even about her friends."

The detective was watching Betty intently. Kate's heart ached for her. She wanted to intervene, but wasn't sure that she should.

Lindstrom leaned forward in his chair–he had wisely avoided the settee this time.

In a surprisingly gentle voice, he said, "One person reported that Mrs. McIntosh implied fairly blatantly that she thought you might have killed Doris Blackwell."

Betty looked at him and blinked. Tears broke loose and trickled down her wrinkled cheeks, but her voice was steady. "I find that hard to believe, Detective. Frieda was an incorrigible gossip but she never would have said anything like that."

Kate jumped in. "The person who told you that wouldn't happen to be Carla Baxter by any chance?"

Lindstrom's eyebrows went up as he turned toward her. "How'd you know that?"

"Frieda told me that they'd been talking and *Baxter* said point blank that she thought Betty was guilty."

"Are you saying Ms. Baxter is lying?" Lindstrom asked.

"Maybe. Or she's just not remembering the exchange accurately. It's hard sometimes, when people think back on a conversation, to remember who said what."

"And you're an expert on memory now, Mrs. Huntington?" Lindstrom said, annoyance creeping into his voice.

"Yes, as a matter of fact," Kate replied, not bothering to keep her rising anger out of her own. "As I mentioned before, I'm a psychotherapist. I specialize in trauma recovery. One cannot do that work without gleaning a fair amount of knowledge about what to believe, and what not to believe, in people's memories. Especially in the conveniently distorted recollections of child abusers, or boyfriends who've committed date rape, or husbands who've beaten the crap out of their wives...."

She paused for a beat, leaving the unsaid *or potential suspects in a murder case* hanging in the air.

"If you would bring Mrs. Franklin's computer back, I could find the references for you. Quite a few studies have been done on the fallibility of human memory."

Movement at the breakfast bar. Kate glanced up. His back still toward them, Skip was doing a small fist pump in the air.

She had trouble maintaining her defiant glare at the detective.

Lindstrom didn't answer her. He turned back to Betty. "Mrs. Franklin, did your friend's gossiping, which was strengthening the case against you for murder, did that anger you enough to want to kill her?"

Betty winced.

Kate jumped in again. "She didn't even know Frieda was gossiping about those things until you told her, just now."

Lindstrom narrowed his eyes at her. After a pause, he said, with exaggerated patience, "We don't *know* if that was the first time Mrs. Franklin heard about the gossiping. Some well-meaning mutual acquaintance could have told her."

"She's hardly left this apartment since this whole mess began, and when she has gone out, one of us has been with her."

"She could have gone out when you weren't here, or someone

could have dropped by, and there is always the telephone. Now would you *please* be quiet while I finish my interview."

Betty pursed her lips. "Would you two stop talking about me as if I weren't here."

The detective looked at her. "Mrs. Franklin, did your friend's gossiping make you angry enough that you put a knife in her heart while she lay helpless in her bed?"

Betty gasped and reared back in her seat. Her hand flew to her own chest. "Of course not."

Kate jumped up. "Good Lord, Detective, are you trying to give her a heart attack?"

Lindstrom pushed himself to a stand and turned toward her. For the briefest moment, there was regret in his eyes. Then he said to Betty, "Mrs. Franklin, I'm going to have to ask that you not leave the jurisdiction."

"I have no intentions of doing so, young man."

~~~

As the man walked past his stool, Skip spoke quietly, so the women wouldn't hear him. "Detective, can I talk to you outside?"

Following Lindstrom to the door, he called over his shoulder, "Be right back."

Out in the hall, he opened the newspaper he'd tucked under his arm and pointed to the front page. "Is this your case, sir?"

Lindstrom nodded.

"I might have a possible suspect for you, but I'd prefer you not say anything about what I tell you in front of the others. It would embarrass Mrs. Huntington." Skip told the detective about Kate's encounter with the maintenance man.

Lindstrom's face was set in a grim expression by the time he finished.

"Thanks," the detective said and walked away.

Skip folded the headline–*Rapist Terrorizes Lancaster Women*–back inside the paper before re-entering the apartment.

CHAPTER TEN

Although the interview with Lindstrom had been rough on Betty, Kate was grateful for one thing that came out of it. It seemed to have relieved the tension between Skip and herself.

"Remind me never to piss you off," he'd teased as they'd headed for the Berkleys' apartment.

She gave him a small smile. "Lindstrom seems to be more convinced than ever that Betty's guilty."

"He strikes me as a good cop," Skip said. "He may not want to believe she's guilty, but who else does he have? In Doris Blackwell's case at least, Betty's the only one, so far, who has a motive strong enough to merit murder."

"So far," Kate said. "So let's go find somebody with a better motive."

"If wishes were horses," Kate muttered under her breath at five o'clock. Again, they had encountered mostly unanswered doors, the rustling behind the Berkleys' indicating their lack of response was quite intentional.

They'd decided to call it a day and returned to Betty's apartment. Skip rang the doorbell.

Nothing happened.

Oh, come on," Kate thought irritably. She knocked on the door and called out, "Betty, it's me, Kate." She put her ear to the door. Was that a shuffling noise?

Another moment passed. She reached into her pocket. "Betty gave me her spare key on Friday, for this very reason. She said she doesn't always hear the bell if she's napping." She inserted the key in the lock.

"I thought she promised to stay vigilant," Skip said. "Napping doesn't sound vigilant to—"

His words hadn't quite covered the sound of footsteps running through the apartment. Kate shoved the door open. It caught on the chain.

Through the narrow opening, she could see a shoe, with a foot in it, lying on the kitchen floor. Her heart stuttered in her chest. She screamed Betty's name.

Skip shoved her aside and put his shoulder to the door. The chain gave way, the bracket ripping loose from the wood.

He took off through the apartment as Kate rushed to Betty's side. Shee crouched down, frantically feeling Betty's neck for a pulse, and collapsed onto her butt in relief when she found one.

A shrieking whistle from the kitchen. Kate jumped and yelped.

A moment later, she was punching 911 into the kitchen wall phone with one hand while turning off the tea kettle on the stove with the other. Movement out of the corner of her eye.

She jumped again and whirled around, then shook her head in confusion.

Skip was standing just inside the still-open front door. He nodded grimly toward Betty crumpled on the floor.

"She's alive," Kate said. Into the phone, she told the emergency dispatcher to send an ambulance, and the police.

After she'd hung up, Skip said, "He came in through her bedroom window. I went out that way to see if I could catch the guy. Ran around the side of the building, but no sign of him."

He crouched down next to Betty's still form and gently ran his fingers over her scalp. "Don't feel any bumps or cuts. Ah, what have we here?" He leaned over something lying on the floor nearby and sniffed it.

"Whew!" He sat back on his heels. "Smells like chloroform to me."

Kate dug her phone out of her purse and scrolled through her contacts. She found Lindstrom's number, then muttered, "This time I *am* putting him on speed dial." She got his voicemail and left a message.

Betty moaned and stirred. Kate moved quickly around the breakfast bar to help her.

"Don't disturb the rag," Skip said.

She dodged around the piece of fabric. Her foot kicked something that rolled away from her with a soft tinkling sound.

She helped Betty sit up. A fragment of white paper fluttered from the elderly woman's hand onto the floor.

"Are you okay?"

"I think so." Betty rubbed her forehead with a slightly trembling hand. She tried to stand up.

Kate helped her to her feet, then carefully backed them out of the kitchen area. She steered Betty over to the settee. "The paramedics should be here soon to check you over."

Kate patted Betty's arm, but then curiosity got the better of her.

She walked back around the breakfast bar and leaned over Skip, who was stooped down examining the objects on the floor. "What is it?" she asked, squinting at what looked like a clear tube.

"Glass vial of some sort. Do you see any puddles of liquid anywhere?"

Kate looked around. "No." Then she noticed the small rug in front of the sink, near where she had been when she'd kicked the vial. Gingerly she stepped around Skip's bulk, trying to steer clear of the rag and scrap of paper on the floor. She leaned over and touched the rug. The edge was wet. She lifted one finger to her nose and sniffed cautiously. "Rug's damp, but it doesn't have any odor, so not chloroform."

"Get a couple of chairs from the dining room. Let's put them over these things to mark and protect them."

"Good idea."

She had put one chair over the damp spot on the rug and was going back for a second one when a rap of knuckles on the open door announced the arrival of the paramedics. Kate pointed to the living room. "Patient's over there."

She led them to Betty. They quickly and efficiently started taking the elderly woman's vital signs and asking her questions. Kate stepped back out of the way.

"Come look at this, Kate," Skip called over. He was squatting again, examining the scrap of paper.

She knelt down beside him. "What is it?"

"Looks like the corner of a note to me. Something's written on it."

Kate was trying to get her face closer to it without touching it, when they heard the crunch of breaking glass. "Oh, no!" She sat back on her heels.

"What?" said the paramedic who was standing between the breakfast bar and the sink. "The lady wanted some water." Inches from his feet, where the glass vial had been, there were now only tiny slivers of glass, sparkling in the overhead light.

"Never mind, man," Skip said. "You didn't know it was there. But you just stepped on some evidence."

"Shit!" The paramedic said, then gave Kate an apologetic look. "Sorry, ma'am."

It was a day late and a dollar short, but she went to get another chair to put over the broken glass.

When she returned, Skip was holding the scrap of paper pinched between the fingernails of his index finger and thumb. "Find me a plastic baggie, would you?" he asked. "And something to mark where my right toe is. That's where it was. But I figure it's not that crucial where it was, since it fell out of her hand. More important to make sure it doesn't get damaged."

"Good point." Kate rummaged through cabinets to find Betty's storage supplies. She located a pencil in a drawer. Handing a freezer bag to Skip, she crouched down and made a small x next to his toe.

Skip brought the baggie, that now contained the tiny piece of paper, up close to his face. "Looks like something's typed on it.

Can you make it out?" He handed it to her.

"Hmm, capital S, then o and maybe an r just before the torn edge, and I think a capital I under the S."

"Let's bag the chloroform rag as well," Skip said. "I've got a hunch about what happened here, and that rag is crucial to proving my theory."

Kate leaned over and carefully drew a line around the edge of the rag. Then she dug out another plastic bag and handed it to him.

He pinched a corner of the cloth to lift it off the floor, then dropped it into the bag. "Better slightly compromised evidence than damaged evidence."

"Hope Lindstrom sees it that way."

"You hope Lindstrom sees what that way?" the detective said from the open doorway.

CHAPTER ELEVEN

When Rob saw his great aunt's door standing wide open, he broke into a run, quickly outdistancing his petite wife. He skidded through the door. Kate, Skip and a tall, thin sandy-haired man in a suit were in the kitchen area, all talking at once. Aunt Betty was sitting on her couch, holding her head, with two paramedics hovering over her.

Rob raced over and crouched down in front of her. "Are you okay? What happened?"

"I'm fine." Aunt Betty rubbed her temples. "Just a headache. And I'm not real sure what happened."

Rob straightened up and closed the distance to the breakfast bar in two strides. He felt more than saw Liz come in the door behind him. "What happened?" he demanded.

Everyone stopped talking and turned toward him.

Kate looked over his shoulder at Liz and anger blossomed on her face.

Rob held up his hand. "Edie's fine. Shelley got home from Europe yesterday."

Kate's expression shifted to mild anxiety, but apparently the news that his eldest daughter was also now spoiling her baby had mollified her.

"Tell me what happened," Rob said.

Kate and Skip started talking at once again. The tall stranger held up his arms and they went silent.

One of the paramedics took advantage of the pause and stepped up to Rob, clipboard in hand. "The lady says you're her nephew. She doesn't want to go to the hospital. Are you her medical surrogate?"

Rob nodded. "Is she really okay?"

"Seems to be," the paramedic said. When Rob glared at him, he shrugged apologetically. "I'm not a doctor so I'm not allowed to make pronouncements about someone's medical condition, but I see no reason for you to insist she go to the hospital."

"In other words, she's okay."

The paramedic smiled and shrugged again. "We need a signature saying the patient is voluntarily refusing transport." He handed Rob the clipboard.

He starting skimming the form on it

"Betty's not incompetent," Kate said. "She can sign for herself."

The paramedic blinked at her. Then his cheeks turned pink. "Yes, ma'am." He held out his hand to take the clipboard back.

Rob resisted the urge to shake his head, at both the paramedic and himself. *How easy it is to assume old people can't do for themselves.*

As he handed the clipboard over, he decided to save the young man some face. "I'm her lawyer too. I looked it over, Aunt Betty," he called across the room. "It's okay to sign it."

His aunt nodded as the young man headed back in her direction.

Rob turned back to the others. "So is anybody gonna tell–"

At the same moment, the stranger stuck out his hand. "So you're the lawyer nephew. Detective Andrew Lindstrom."

Rob shook his hand.

Lindstrom said, "Why don't we all sit down?"

Good idea, Rob thought, and started to sink into the nearest chair. *Why are dining room chairs scattered all over the place?*

"Not there!" Kate and Skip yelled in unison.

Rob grabbed for the breakfast bar in an attempt to stop the momentum of his butt headed for the seat of the chair. Half hanging from the edge of the granite top, he said, "Why the hell not?"

"Because there's evidence under it," Kate said.

"What evidence?" Lindstrom's voice was sharp.

Kate and Skip both started to explain. Rob got the gist of it. Apparently Kate had accidentally kicked a glass something that was on the floor, and then the paramedic had stepped on it.

He put his cheek down on the cool surface of the counter, sighed and then mimicked banging his head against the countertop.

Liz's voice boomed across the noise. "Will somebody please tell the man what happened before he has a heart attack."

Mac and Rose came through the still open door, and stopped abruptly at the sight of the crowded room. "What the hell?" Mac said.

Rob groaned, pushed himself upright and walked around the end of the breakfast bar and into the living room. He flopped into an armchair. "You sure you're okay?" he asked his aunt.

"Yes, dear. I'm fine."

"Good. What's in your liquor cabinet? I need a drink."

Half an hour later, they were all sitting around the living room, again with several chairs dragged over from the dining area. This time, Mac was the one sitting cross-legged on the floor, between Rose's and Skip's chairs.

Liz had made coffee. "Decaf," she'd said pointedly.

The paramedics were gone and two crime scene techs were taking pictures in the kitchen area and gathering up the compromised evidence. Another was in the bedroom, dusting the window frame around the jimmied lock for prints.

Rob swirled the ice cubes around in the remainder of his bourbon. He was considering having another one. Since he didn't drink very often, he decided he'd better not.

They'd finally gotten the story out of his aunt and Kate. Aunt Betty had been in the kitchen making tea. The water running had apparently covered the sound of the intruder breaking in. She'd put the kettle on the stove and turned the burner on, when an arm came around from behind her and yanked her head backward. She struggled as best she could, but a smelly rag was held over her face. The next thing she knew she was waking up with Kate crouched beside her.

Kate had taken over from there, describing how she and Skip had found her and why they'd decided to bag some of the evidence to keep it safe.

"You may have to testify in court, if and when the time comes, to establish the chain of evidence," Lindstrom was now saying to Skip. He nodded.

"Humph, a defense attorney will have a field day with that," Rob said.

Lindstrom shrugged. "When we catch the culprit, we'll be charging him with bigger crimes than breaking and entering and assault. But we gotta find the guy first."

"Or woman," Kate said.

"Nope," Skip said. "I think this had to be a man."

"Why?" Kate turned to Betty. "Did you see anything that would indicate it was a man or a woman?"

Betty closed her eyes and thought for a moment. "The arm was bare, no jacket or shirt sleeve. I don't remember it being particularly hairy. The hand with the rag had a glove on it, dark brown, like a work or gardening glove." As she opened her eyes, she shuddered slightly. "Other than that, I couldn't tell you. It all happened so fast."

His wife was sitting next to his aunt on the settee. Liz reached over and gave Aunt Betty's hand a squeeze.

Rob's eyes flicked back to Lindstrom, who was jotting things in his little pad.

"I don't think a woman could've outrun me," Skip said.

Liz shook her head. "I'm not sure that an elderly man could run all that much faster than an elderly woman."

"Good point, Mrs. Franklin," Lindstrom said.

"Aunt Betty's Mrs. Franklin. Call me Liz. Too confusing otherwise."

Lindstrom nodded, as Kate was saying, "Besides, Skip, whoever it was only had to get around the corner of the building before you got to the window. Once they were on the sidewalk they could just innocently stroll along. Did you see anybody out front?"

"Two women walking by. They weren't together. Mrs. Forsythe and another one I didn't recognize. And I concede the point." Skip smiled at her. "Mrs. Forsythe would definitely be strong enough and fast enough to pull this off."

"They didn't see anyone running away?" Rob asked.

"I didn't take the time to ask them," Skip said. "I wanted to get back inside and make sure Kate and Betty were okay. It occurred to me that there could be two people working together, and one could've still been in the apartment."

"What's this about Mrs. Forsythe?" Lindstrom asked. "I don't recall there being anything significant in the report from the officer who interviewed them."

"Wait," Rob said. "Who is she again?"

"Wife of one of the men Doris flirted with," Kate said. "When Skip and I talked to them, she and her husband both dismissed the flirtation, but she's very fit for her age. She was working out in the gym when we caught up with her."

Skip pulled his list of interviewees out of his pocket and consulted it. "They're two buildings over, near the recreation center, apartment 210."

"Any other impressions of them?" Lindstrom asked.

"He probably likes alcohol a little too much for his own good," Kate said, with a shrug.

"How'd you figure that out?" Skip flashed her a smile.

Kate tapped her nose. "There's a skin disease that causes that kind of large nose with broken veins, but it's aggravated by alcohol abuse."

Rob slouched in his chair, swirling the ice cubes in his glass and contemplating that second bourbon again.

"Detective, I'm assuming the same thing has occurred to

you," Skip said. "I'm thinking that scrap of paper was the corner of a bogus suicide note, in which Mrs. Franklin was supposedly admitting that she was the killer. The intruder was probably planning to knock her out with the chloroform, then inject her with whatever was in the vial. If he, or *she*," he smiled at Kate, "could make it look like Betty had taken her own life out of remorse, you would have your case tied up in a nice pretty bow and the killer'd be in the clear."

"What about the broken lock on the window?" Kate asked.

"The frame's scuffed up but the lock's not broken," Lindstrom said.

"Killer probably used a slim jim," Skip said.

"What's that?" Kate asked.

"A slim metal strip that you push up between the two parts of the window to work the lock open."

Kate gave him a warm smile. Skip smiled back at her.

Rob glanced back and forth between them. What was it with these two and their mutual admiration club?

"If we hadn't interrupted him," Skip said, "the killer probably would've locked the window and slipped out the door. Scuff marks on the window frame might not have even been noticed if we hadn't known that someone got in that way."

Lindstrom pushed up out of his chair. "I think I'll be paying the Forsythes a visit this evening."

"We're done, Detective," one of the techs said.

"Good. Let me know what the lab comes up with as soon as you can."

Rob rose and extended his hand.

As the detective shook it, he said quietly, "I suggested before that she go to a motel. Maybe you can convince her."

"I'll try," Rob said.

~~~

Lindstrom paused outside the apartment door. He'd acted like he believed Mrs. Franklin had been attacked, but he really wasn't sure what to think. The department's computer geek had sent over her report that afternoon. The contested subplot idea first appeared in Mrs. Franklin's earlier drafts of her book four days after she had met with Mrs. Blackwell. The victim's plagiarism accusation seemed to be legitimate.

Lindstrom was hoping the lab results would help him figure out what had really happened here today. Had the killer tried to set up a fake suicide to frame Mrs. Franklin? Or had this best-selling writer of fiction come up with a creative ruse to throw suspicion off of herself? Easy enough to scrape up the window frame, then leave the window hanging open while she set up the rest of it.

Canfield had said they'd heard the intruder running away through the apartment, but people sometimes thought they'd heard or seen something because it was what they *expected* to hear or see in those circumstances.

～～～

Once the detective and his technicians were out the door, Kate sensed more than saw Skip lean forward in his chair next to her. She startled when light glinted off the mother-of-pearl handle of his gun.

"Sorry," he said quickly, then flashed her a quick grin. "I'm not planning on shooting anybody. One of the downsides of waistband holsters. It's been digging into my back for the last half hour." He started to slip the pistol into his pocket.

From his spot on the floor beside him, Mac said, "Nice lookin' piece."

Skip held the gun on the flat of his palm so Mac could get a better look.

"May I?" Mac asked.

"Sure." Skip handed the gun to the other man butt first.

"Any coffee left?" Rose asked.

"I'll get it." Skip stood up. "Wouldn't mind another cup myself." He stepped around behind the chairs.

Kate felt his warm hand on her shoulder.

"You want any?" he asked.

She twisted around to smile up at him and shook her head.

He gave her shoulder a light squeeze, then took Rose's cup from her. "Anybody else?" The others shook their heads and he headed into the kitchen.

Kate realized that Rob was staring at Skip. Then he got up and went over to the liquor cabinet. He poured himself another bourbon.

Is that his second or his third?

Mac held Skip's pistol up, carefully keeping the barrel pointed away from the occupants of the room. "Nice. Double action?"

"Yeah. It was my grandfather's." Skip poured the coffee and came back into the living room. He handed Rose her cup.

Mac had laid the pistol on Skip's chair.

Kate leaned over without touching it. She pointed to the mother-of-pearl handle. "It's pretty, for a gun."

Mac groaned. Rose rolled her eyes.

Skip chuckled as he scooped it up and sat down. "Guns aren't usually described as pretty."

Kate gave them all a mock glare. "Okay, it's handsome then."

She glanced across the room. Rob was studying them through narrowed eyes, and he was rapidly polishing off his drink.

What's wrong with him? Did he lose his court case?

With all the chaos, there'd been no chance to find out how that had gone. And she couldn't ask him now, in front of the others.

She turned toward Liz. "Did you have any luck with the back-up disks?"

Liz grimaced. "I'm sorry, Aunt Betty, I'm afraid the subplot does start to show up in the drafts in mid-April, around the time you met with Doris."

Oh, no!

Betty's expression moved from surprise to dismay. "Are you sure, Elizabeth?"

Liz nodded.

Betty dropped her face into her hands. "I'm a plagiarist."

Kate felt awful for her. "Did you mention the subplot idea at the club meetings before you included it in the story?"

Betty raised a tear-stained face to look at her. "Maybe. I don't remember. We talk about so many things."

"It's possible that Doris got the idea from you. Or maybe you did come up with the subplot after your talk with her, but thought it was your own idea. That happens more than you think. It's even got a fancy psychobabble name. It's called source amnesia. As in you remember the information but not the source it came from."

Betty shook her head. Her voice trembling, she said, "I can't write anymore if I'm getting too old to remember what are my ideas and what I've heard from other people."

"No, no, it has nothing to do with age." Kate moved across the room and knelt down in front of her, taking both of Betty's hands in her own. "College students unintentionally plagiarize ideas all the time. They read something while doing research for a paper, then forget where they read it and put it in the paper as their own idea."

Liz patted Betty's arm. "It's an honest human mistake."

"It definitely doesn't mean you're too old to write," Kate said. "And you'd better finish that next book. I want to find out if the heroine gets the lawyer to fall in love with her or not."

Betty gave her a weak smile. "Thank you." She took the tissues Liz offered and wiped her eyes.

As Kate struggled up off her knees, Rob said, "I think we all need to go to a motel for tonight. It's not safe here, especially now that the security chain's broken."

"If I can find a hardware store," Mac said. "Get some supplies. I can fix it tomorrow."

"I saw a Home Depot on Route 30," Kate said. "But shouldn't you two be heading home? You're on duty tomorrow, aren't you, Rose?"

"Called my sergeant this afternoon. Told him I needed to take a few days' leave. Personal business."

"You shouldn't be using up your leave for this," Betty protested.

"Counts toward my training hours, for my PI license. Right,

Skip?"

He nodded.

"Got things covered at the restaurant," Mac said. "We're in this for the duration."

Kate hid a smile. Even without the Rose factor, she figured Mac found chasing murderers more interesting than running a restaurant. When it came to careers, her childhood friend had a short attention span. Kate suspected his next one might be private investigating.

Liz had turned to her. "We were assuming *you* would want to go home tonight, now that we're here."

Kate silently debated with herself. She wanted nothing more than to go home, kiss her sleeping baby, then wake up tomorrow morning to a day of childcare and laundry. But maternal guilt was doing battle with other emotions.

She was worried about Betty. And despite Skip's efforts to reassure her, she still felt guilty about Frieda. She did not want to see the woman's murderer go free.

She was also increasingly concerned about Rob. Besides looking physically exhausted, something was definitely troubling him. She couldn't in good conscience just walk away from this. And if she went home now, she'd be worrying constantly about what was going on up here. Better to be here and help out.

Finally she said, "I'll stick around and help for another day or two, if you think Shelley won't mind holding down the fort back home."

"I don't think she'll mind," Liz said. "She doesn't have any plans for the next few days, other than resting up from her trip."

Skip stood up. "There's a Travel Lodge near here. Has an Indian restaurant attached to it, so we can get room service for dinner."

"I'm paying for the rooms," Betty said.

Rob opened his mouth, but his aunt cut him off. "You all are here for my benefit, and I cannot tell you how grateful I am. Besides, nephew, my books have made enough money, I couldn't possibly spend it all if I live to be a hundred."

Liz offered to help Betty pack some clothes and they went into her bedroom. Skip walked over to retrieve his duffel bag from the corner of the living room.

Kate started toward the den to gather her things. Out of the corner of her eye, she caught Rob frowning at Skip's back.

He seems upset with Skip. But again, now was not the time to ask what was going on.

As they were heading out the door, Liz held her hand out and wiggled her fingers. "Gimme the keys, Big Guy. I'm driving."

CHAPTER TWELVE

Kate had trouble getting to sleep that night. Lying in one of the double beds in the room she was sharing with Betty, she stared at the ceiling. She missed her child horribly. Her whole upper body ached from longing to hold the little girl in her arms. She imagined Maria bathing Edie and envy shot through her. The thing she loved most about being a mother was cuddling with her freshly bathed, sleepy baby.

But as soon as she started contemplating going home, leaving the Franklins to deal with this mess without her, the image of Rob's drawn face came into her mind's eye. Her stomach felt queasy from worry. She hadn't seen him this tired and stressed out in a long time, not since those horrible weeks when they had been trying to track down Eddie's killer.

Sighing, Kate thought, *I miss our baby girl, Eddie.*

I miss you, love!

I miss you too, darling.

She rolled over, punched her pillow, and decided to try the age-old tactic of counting sheep. After thirty or so, she did, indeed, begin to feel drowsy. As she drifted off, it only half registered that the sheep were starting to have Skip's big, easygoing grin on their faces.

She woke up early the next morning and couldn't get back to sleep. Pulling on the previous day's clothing, she slipped out of the bedroom.

Skip was stretched out diagonally on the too-small sofa bed in the suite's living room. Kate tiptoed across the room, trying not to disturb him. She quietly rummaged through drawers, searching for notepaper.

"What are you looking for?" Skip whispered.

Kate jumped.

"Sorry, didn't mean to startle you."

Kate glanced at the door to the Franklins' adjoining room, then walked closer to the bed so they could keep their voices down. She stopped at the sight of broad, bare shoulders above the sheet and tousled brown hair falling across the well-formed planes of his face.

He blinked and brought a hand out from under the sheet. As he rubbed the sleep from his eyes, Kate swallowed hard, staring at the muscular arm attached to that hand.

She flashed again to the sensation of his arms around her. Clearing her throat, she said, "Uh, I was going to write you a note. I'm slipping out to Denny's for some breakfast. I, um, could use some alone time."

Mainly to figure out how I feel about you.

She was suddenly self-conscious in her rumpled clothing.

Skip propped himself up on his elbows, worry on his face. The sheet slid down to his waist, exposing sculpted pecs sprinkled with dark hair.

Kate sucked in her breath, then prayed he hadn't heard her. But the slow grin spreading across his face told her he had. She felt heat in her cheeks.

"Don't worry. I kept my pants on, in case I had to jump up to fend off the bad guys in the middle of the night."

"I'll be back… in a little while," she stammered and she moved toward the door.

His grin faded. "Kate, wait." He swung his legs out of bed and stood up, then gestured for her to come closer as he grabbed his shirt from the back of a chair.

She stopped a few feet away, her gaze on the floor. The heat in her face was now spreading elsewhere. She was relieved when he put his shirt on.

"Kate, listen. That other case of Lindstrom's, it's a serial rapist. There have been three attacks so far, in the last two months. First two didn't report it until the third one hit the paper."

Kate grimaced. Thus the worry in his face and voice. She thought for a moment. "When do the attacks happen?"

"At night, so far, but there's no guarantee he'll stick to that MO."

"I know, but he probably would only go after a woman during the day if she were in an isolated spot and not paying attention. I'll be sure to be paying attention now."

"The key word is *probably*. You can never tell for sure what these guys are going to do. Now that he's getting media attention, he may go underground, but he also might escalate to something more daring, to thumb his nose at the police and keep the attention coming." He stepped closer and took her hand.

She hoped her reaction to the zing she felt didn't show on her face. "I appreciate your concern, and the warning. I'll be on guard now, and make sure I'm always near other people."

He wrapped both of his hands around hers, as if to keep her there. Naked fear flashed across his face, then was gone so fast she wondered if she'd imagined it.

Kate tugged her hand. He let it go reluctantly.

She knew he'd once been on the Maryland State police force. "I'm sure when you were a state trooper, you received training to help you understand how rapists think and behave. Maybe went to a workshop about it?"

"Two or three over the years."

"Skip, this is my field. I've taught some of those workshops, plus ones for women on rape prevention. I know how to handle myself to minimize the risk."

Tension still on his face, he nodded. Silently, he walked her to the door. "Just be careful," he said as she stepped past him. "Remember there's also a killer out there, who's probably not very happy that we're trying to find him."

He kept watch as she walked to her car. When she was pulling out of the parking lot, she glanced back. He was still standing in the doorway, barefoot, his half-buttoned shirt flapping in the breeze, sleep-tousled hair sticking out in all directions.

The small tug around her heart both pleased and scared the crap out of her.

～～～

Kate sat in the Denny's a few blocks from the motel, eyes closed, waiting for the waitress to bring her coffee.

Edie would be waking up about now. Trying to block out the breakfast smells of the restaurant, Kate imagined nuzzling her little one's neck and breathing in the scent of clean baby skin. Her mouth turned up at the corners as she realized she was even beginning to miss changing diapers.

She heard rustling and felt a familiar presence. Opening one eye, Kate saw Rob slide into the booth across from her.

So much for alone time.

"Good morning," she said out loud. "Skip ratted me out, didn't he?"

"Morning," Rob said, without answering her question.

There was definitely something bothering him. "What's the matter? Did your case go badly?"

"No, I won. Or at least got the ruling I expected."

As Kate's expression invited him to elaborate, he said, "What we got was the best any judge was likely to give him, joint legal custody, sole physical custody, wife got liberal visitation."

"At least he got custody," Kate said, breathing out a small sigh. "Are you worried about the kids when they're with her?"

Rob shrugged. "She says she's in recovery now, volunteered to get a breathalyzer installed on her car. The kind that won't let you start the car if you register above a certain alcohol level."

"Which can be circumvented."

"Yeah, but I'm not unhappy with how the case went. I did my job and got him the best deal he was likely to get."

"Then what's bothering you? Other than the obvious, that someone is trying to frame your aunt for murder."

He didn't answer her as he consulted the menu. The waitress arrived with her coffee and took their orders. The woman grabbed a cup from an empty table and poured coffee for Rob as well.

After the waitress left, Rob said, "What's with you and Skip?"

Hunh?

She stared at him for a beat, trying to process the abrupt change of subject. "What do you mean?"

"The smiles and the shoulder squeezing. What's going on with you two?" His tone was borderline accusatory.

Wha... Where the hell is this coming from?

Out loud, she said, "We're friends."

"Since when? At the point that I hired him..." Rob made a dramatic show of consulting the date and time on his watch, "... roughly eighty-four hours ago, he was just an acquaintance."

He was starting to piss her off. "I'd say, roughly sixty hours ago."

He frowned at her without responding.

"Rob, what is your problem? This is the man *you* hired last year to protect me."

He busied himself doctoring his coffee with cream and sugar. "Look, I just don't want you to get hurt."

Softening her tone, she said, "Rob, what part of 'we're friends' don't you understand?" She was still irritated, but also touched by his concern.

"What do you know about this guy anyway?"

"What did you know about him when you hired him to guard me back then?" Kate countered.

"That's different. I contacted an agency to hire some bodyguards. Not quite the same thing as becoming 'friends' with someone." He made quotation marks in the air.

Kate sat back in her seat and stared at him.

You hypocrite!

He hated it when they encountered the attitude in others that a man and a woman could not be *just* friends. And here he was assuming, based on one shoulder squeeze, that she and Skip were more than friends.

Deciding she would cut him some slack, considering his stress level at the moment, Kate tried to keep her tone calm. "Skip and I have been working very closely together for the past few days. And somewhere along the way, we became friends. He's a nice guy."

"Okay, but other than some insights into his personality, what do you really know about him?"

The waitress chose that moment to bring their food.

"What do we know about anybody when we become friends?" she said, once the waitress had moved on. "Something resonates between you, and a budding friendship is born. Sometimes it grows as you get to know each other better, and sometimes it doesn't."

After a moment, Rob looked down at his untouched food. "I just don't want you to get hurt," he said again.

She reached over and patted his hand. "I appreciate your concern, but I'm a big girl. I get to choose my friends, and I can handle it if things don't work out."

"If things don't work out? That sounds like more than friends to me."

"Rob!" Kate stopped herself and took a deep breath. "Okay, Skip did ask me out. I told him it was too soon for me to date, and we have agreed to be friends." Despite her best efforts, anger was creeping into her voice. "So yes, we are just friends, and that's all we are going to be for the foreseeable future."

Rob pressed his lips together in a thin line. He picked up his fork and started eating.

As Kate took a bite of her food, she couldn't help thinking that he had a point. She didn't know much about Skip's life, past or present. Any guy who looked that good had to be used to seducing women on a regular basis. She couldn't help but wonder why he was interested in her, a woman of average attractiveness with all kinds of baggage, including unresolved grief and a seven-month-old child.

After a few minutes, Rob said, "I need your opinion on something."

She nodded, grateful for the change of subject.

"I'm debating whether or not I should insist on taking Aunt Betty back to Maryland with us, until this killer is caught." He took a sip of coffee. "I've got two concerns. One is legal. Has Lindstrom said anything to her about not leaving the area?"

"Yes, he did say that at one point, and I thought it a little odd. Where did he think she was going to run off to?"

"Usually if a suspect packs up and leaves the jurisdiction, it's seen as a sign of guilt. But if I approach Lindstrom first and tell him I'm taking her to my house to keep her safe, that should take care of that issue."

"Does that mean you want to scrap the idea of trying to find out who the killer is ourselves?"

"Yes and no," Rob said. "I'd still have Skip and Rose look into it, but the rest of us could get back to our own lives. It wasn't easy clearing my schedule for the rest of this week, especially since other things had gotten backed up while I was working the custody case."

Kate was surprised that her second emotion, after joy at the thought of going home to Edie, was a twinge of regret that she would no longer be in Skip's company on a regular basis. Actually it was more than a twinge.

"My other concern," Rob said, "what I wanted your opinion on, is Aunt Betty's mental state. She seems to be holding up so far, but would it be better to get her away from all this? Or would being uprooted from her home and her friends indefinitely be more stressful for her?"

She thought for a minute, determinedly shoving aside her own longing for her baby to assess it from Betty's standpoint. "It's a tough call," she finally said. "Being a murder suspect and not feeling safe has certainly got to be pretty stressful. As to the uprooted issue, she's already experiencing that by having to stay in a motel, but it probably feels temporary to her. I don't know how moving in with you and Liz, for an indefinite length of time, might affect her…" Kate trailed off as she realized what they were doing. "Hey, we're sitting here acting like it's our decision to make. It's up to her to decide what she wants to do."

"Well, yeah, I would ask her. But I wanted your opinion first, so I'd know whether I should push it or not."

"Wait, on second thought, you can't ask her. She's already feeling guilty because we're here, putting our lives on hold, to help her. She'll say yes to going with you, whether that's what she wants to do or not." Kate suddenly had a mental image of the elderly woman sitting forlornly in the Franklins' family room, staring at the walls. Betty was in good health, but at her age mindset had a lot to do with physical well-being. Feeling uprooted and depressed could send her into a downward spiral.

After she'd shared those thoughts with him, Rob asked, "So what do you advise?"

"Let's give it another day or two and see how things go."

Rob sighed. "Hopefully this mess won't drag on any longer than that."

Kate found the discouragement in his voice worrisome. He was a take-charge, make-things-happen kind of guy. But in this situation, all they could do was keep talking to people and hope they unearthed some nugget that would turn into a fresh lead in the case.

She reached over and patted his hand again. "Something's gotta break loose soon," she said with more confidence than she felt.

~~~

They ordered carry-out breakfasts for the others. When they returned to the motel, everyone was up, including Mac and Rose, who had a room several doors down from the suite.

Those who hadn't eaten yet squeezed in around the table in the suite's living room. Kate sat down on the sofa.

Rob eased his bulk into the armchair next to it. He looked around the room. "This place is costing a bundle."

"I don't mind the expense," Betty said, "but I do dislike the idea of being driven out of my home."

Rob and Kate exchanged a look.

Liz patted Betty's arm. "We understand, but it isn't safe for you to be there, not after what happened yesterday."

"I've got an idea," Rose said. "Might speed things up. How about we lure the killer into trying again? I'm close to Betty's size. I could dress in her clothes and a wig. Rob escorts me home, then makes a big deal about leaving. We sneak Mac into the apartment and we wait for the perp to show up."

Mac paused, a forkful of scrambled eggs suspended in midair. "Maybe sneak Skip or Rob in as well. So we've got somebody in each room. No matter what door or window he comes through, we're covered."

"Is this guy, or gal, likely to try again?" Liz asked.

"Maybe," Skip said. "He grabbed the note back so it wouldn't be obvious that it was a staged suicide. He may not realize he left the rag and vial there, might think he dropped them somewhere outside in his haste to get away." Skip cut off a wedge of pancake and stabbed it with his plastic fork. "Or he might write a new note that accounts for the earlier botched attempt."

"Like I tried to stage an attempt on my life the first time," Betty said, "but now remorse has overcome me and I really am committing suicide."

Skip nodded as he chewed.

Kate had a horrible thought. "It's also possible that setting up your death as a remorseful suicide was just a side benefit for the killer." She looked around at the others. "Betty might be next on his list, for some other reason."

Betty showed no reaction to this possibility, but Rob's face paled. He leaned forward in his chair. "You're trap idea's worth a try, Rose. What else needs to be done? Have all the interviews been completed?"

Skip shook his head. "We've narrowed the list down a good bit, but there are a few people we still haven't caught up with.

And I'm thinking we should talk to the folks in Betty's building again. Ask them if they saw anybody outside her door yesterday afternoon, or running away outside the building. And Kate and I definitely need to take another crack at Mrs. Forsythe."

"Lindstrom was going to do that last night."

Kate wondered if the others had noticed the edge to Rob's voice.

"True," she said, "but she might be more forthcoming with us than with a police officer. Skip can mention he saw her out front right after Betty's assailant got away. See what her reaction is."

Rob frowned. "Maybe we should mix up the interviewing pairs. See if that shakes things up any."

Liz gave him a quizzical look.

Keeping her voice calm, Kate said, "Skip and I have already talked to her. She's more likely to be comfortable with us."

"Once we get the trap set back at Betty's place," Mac said, "I can slip out and talk to the folks in her building."

Kate moved on quickly, to forestall further attempts to change the interviewing teams. "You two caught up with Carla Baxter yesterday afternoon, right? What did she have to say about her conversation with Frieda?"

Rose nodded, setting her coffee cup down on the table. "At first she claimed that Frieda did say Betty might be guilty, but when I pushed a bit, she backpedaled. I think what really happened was that Baxter said it, Frieda stood up for her friend and then Baxter insisted where there's smoke, there's fire. And assumed she'd convinced Frieda because she'd gotten the last word."

"She reminded me of a sergeant I once had," Mac said. "Believed if he was the last one talkin', he'd won the argument."

Liz snorted.

"Where there's smoke, there's fire," Kate said. "Those were the words Frieda quoted her as saying."

"There was something about her that felt off," Rose said. "She was giving off strange vibes." She looked at Mac.

"I didn't sense nothin' weird."

Rose thought for a moment. "Well, I don't know what it was, but I was picking up on something."

"It's a good idea to trust one's instincts," Kate said, "until you have further information at least. More often than not there's something to them. Usually something we've sensed on a subliminal level that didn't quite register consciously."

Skip stabbed a chunk of pancake and swirled it in a puddle of syrup. "Sounds like Ms. Baxter deserves another interview. She may be pushing the idea that Betty's guilty because she's the real killer."

"Talked to old man Morris too," Mac said.

Kate was impressed. "How'd you get him to let you in?"

"Told him we weren't goin' away. Just kept knockin' and ringin' the bell. Old fart finally surrendered. Once we got him talkin', couldn't get him to shut up."

"He's lonely. Misses his wife," Rose said.

"Then why'd he keep bitchin' 'bout her. Called her an old bat. Kept complainin' 'bout how she cluttered up the place. Little tables and knickknacks everywhere. Looked like one of them froo-froo gift shops."

The corners of Rose's mouth twitched as she hid a smile. "It was pretty crowded in there," she conceded.

"His wife's been dead for months," Kate said. "If he really hated the clutter, he would've long since cleaned it out. I agree with Rose. He's still grieving for her. What did he say about Doris flirting with him?"

"Dismissed it," Mac said. "Called her a crabby bitch."

Betty frowned at him.

"Sorry, but that's what he said."

Rose finished off her eggs, then tossed her fork on the table. "Morris said he wouldn't give Doris the time a day. Claimed he hardly knew the other lady, outside of seeing her at the writers' club."

"Do you think he was telling the truth?" Kate asked.

Rose shook her head slightly. "Hard to tell with crotchety old men." She tilted her head slightly in Mac's direction and cocked an eyebrow. Rose had very expressive eyebrows.

Kate stifled a snicker.

"Know someone's lying when the emotions are off," Rose said. "With them, always the same emotion. Grouchy."

Mac grumbled under his breath and leaned forward to shovel more eggs into his mouth.

Kate struggled to keep a straight face. "What's your best guess?"

Rose thought for a moment, then shook her head again. "Really can't say. He did seem a little off. But could be just because he was trying to hide his feelings about his wife."

Kate nodded. "Damn! Oops, sorry, Betty. I meant to ask Lindstrom about... where the second weapon may have come from."

"Uh, I made a point of doing a visual scan of Frieda's kitchen," Skip said, "when I was in her apartment. There was an empty slot in the knife block on her counter." When Betty paled, he quickly added, "It looked like she was killed in her sleep. She never knew what happened."

"So it was another case of using whatever weapon was convenient," Kate said.

"Hmm." Liz tapped her fork against her lips. "I wonder how easy it is to get one's hands on chloroform?"

"That's a very good question, my love," Rob said. "Does anyone know?" Everyone shook their heads. He nodded at his wife. "That could be your assignment for this morning, Lizzie. This place probably has wireless. Did you bring your laptop?"

Liz nodded. "I was planning on staying here to keep Aunt Betty company anyway."

Betty sat up straighter in her chair. "I don't need a babysitter, Elizabeth."

Skip shook his head. "You actually shouldn't be alone, Betty. There've been some assaults in town recently. So far the guy's only attacked women at night, but as Kate and I were discussing earlier, any woman who is alone and vulnerable is a potential target."

Rob shot Kate a worried look. "Maybe it's not safe for Liz and Aunt Betty to be here by themselves then."

"We should be okay," Liz said. "We'll keep the doors locked up tight."

"I think they'll be safe, Rob," Kate reassured him. "Rarely does a rapist go after more than one woman at a time. Many of them are actually not all that brave. They want the deck stacked in their favor, to be sure they'll be able to overpower the woman."

Liz pointed her fork toward the lists of names. "Who interviewed the maintenance man?"

Kate and Skip exchanged a look. She gave him a slight shake of her head. "I talked to him. He's kinda creepy. Seems to think he's God's gift to women. He claimed to not have any interest in Doris though. Said she was too old."

"Do you think he was telling the truth?" Liz asked.

"Not sure, but I think so. His general attitude was that he could do a lot better than someone that much older than himself. I think he's capable of rape, but he didn't come across as a murderer. Just an oversexed jack… uh, creep."

She glanced over at Rob. He was watching her through slightly narrowed eyes.

He's too damn good at reading me. He knows I'm hiding something.

But she wasn't about to tell him what had happened with Joe. In his current mind-set, who knows what his reaction would be.

Skip stood up. "Thanks for the food, Rob. Denny's sure beats the heck out of a room service breakfast. You ready to go, Kate?"

"You're welcome," Rob mumbled.

Kate rose and headed for the door. She could feel Rob's gaze on her back.

CHAPTER THIRTEEN

Rose changed into the clothes Betty had worn the day before when she'd left the retirement center. She was curvier than the elderly woman so the slacks and knit top were a bit snugger in places. Checking herself out in the mirror over the desk in the suite's living room, she decided it would do.

Not so tight that I look like a slut.

Liz was checking online for wig stores in the area. "We're in luck. There's one in an outlet mall not far from here."

Their luck didn't hold. The store had no gray or white wigs. After looking through the entire shop, Liz and Rose asked a salesperson.

"We have a few," he said, "but we don't usually put them out until closer to Halloween. Not much demand for gray or white the rest of the year."

He rummaged in the stock room and came out with three wigs. One of them came close to matching Betty's hairstyle, although it was a little curlier.

Liz held it up and turned it around. "If we wet this some and smooth it down, will it stay that way?"

"Oh, yes. This wig is made from real hair. You can style it the way you would your own. A large hot roller would probably do the trick."

Rose, who always wore her straight black hair in a tight bun, whispered to Liz, "What's a hot roller?"

"Never mind. I can fix it," Liz whispered back. Rose looked at Liz's carefully arranged strawberry blonde hair and nodded.

Rose's eyes went wide when she saw the price tag. She thought she heard Liz gasp a little beside her.

But then Liz said, "Try it on."

Rose pulled off the band holding her bun in place and let her hair cascade down her back. She pulled the wig on.

Liz nodded. "It's worth it," she said in a low voice. "If you keep her head down and round your shoulders a little, from a distance you can definitely pass for Aunt Betty."

Back at the motel, Liz set to work on de-curling the wig, while Rose and the others hammered out the details of their plan.

Mac would go first. He would hang out in the atrium and look for an opportunity to slip into Betty's apartment when no one was around.

Rose, in disguise, would enter the building with Rob. They would be hoping now that people *would* notice as they walked to the apartment. A few minutes later, Rob would leave, loudly calling back into the apartment that he would stop up next weekend to check on his aunt. Then he would slip around behind the building, and Mac would let him in through the window in the den.

Rose nodded. It was a good plan, even though a few parts of it depended on luck, and the cooperation of the killer.

~~~~~~~

Kate and Skip decided to try the gym first. Sure enough Mrs. Forsythe was there. Once again, they waited for her to finish her time on the treadmill, then they stepped forward.

"Well, hello there." Mrs. Forsythe ran her eyes up and down Skip's body.

Oh, yes, Kate thought. It was definitely better to have buff Skip interviewing this fitness nut rather than Rob, for whom the battle with middle-aged spread was at best a stand-off at this point.

"Hi, Mrs. Forsythe." Skip's lips were smiling, but the smile came nowhere near his eyes. "Sorry to bother you again, ma'am, but we really need your help with something."

"No bother, and please call me Ellen." She fluttered her eyelashes at him.

Skip widened his smile but the rest of his expression still didn't match it.

He doesn't like being ogled by a woman anymore than women like that from men. Kate wished she could do something to rescue him, but the interview must go on.

"Well, Ellen," Skip said, "I saw you walking in front of Mrs. Franklin's building yesterday afternoon. And the thing is, someone had just broken into her apartment, and I was chasing the intruder around the corner of the building. I was wondering if you saw anybody running away, or otherwise looking suspicious, as you were walking by?"

Ellen Forsythe didn't look surprised by the news of the break-in, but that didn't necessarily mean anything. No doubt that information was already making its way through the community's grapevine, or Lindstrom may have told the Forsythes about it last night.

"Hmm." Ellen looked up at the ceiling, her eyes darting back and forth a couple times.

Kate suspected the woman was only pretending to contemplate Skip's question, while she made up a lie. But was that because she was the intruder Skip had been chasing? Or was she stalling before answering in order to seem cooperative and get into Skip's good graces?

"I seem to recall there was someone who looked suspicious. He came around the building rather quickly, and then abruptly slowed his pace." She rubbed her chin.

Not exactly an Oscar-quality performance.

Out loud, Kate asked, "Can you describe him for us?"

"Oh, that would be hard to do. All these old men look the same to me. I really only pay attention to the *younger* men." She smiled at Skip, then added, "The ones closer to *my* age."

"The man you saw, what was he wearing?" Skip asked.

"Hmm, let me think. Short-sleeved shirt. Blue, I think. Dark pants, kind of baggy, but then most of the geezers around here seem to be wearing their pants two sizes too big."

Kate was liking this woman less and less as the interview progressed. Condescending bitch thought she was attractive to Skip, who was three decades her junior, but she felt free to sneer at men who were only a decade or two older than herself.

"Height, build?" Skip asked, a smile still plastered on his face. Kate could tell it was fake but Mrs. Forsythe didn't seem to notice.

"Hmm, about average height, not heavy, more on the thin side. I didn't really get that good a look at him. He turned and walked in the opposite direction from me. He had white hair, of course." She smiled demurely at Skip.

Great. She just described at least half the men in this place.

Kate was trying to keep her expression neutral. "Mrs. Forsythe, if we could go back for a moment to the subject of Mrs. Blackwell and her flirting. You seemed to be amused by it, but do you know of any of the wives who might have taken it more seriously?"

"Well, I guess some of these old biddies might be worried, but *my* husband..." The woman actually ran her hands down her lean hips. "He *knows* what he has, and he wouldn't dare risk losing it now." Kate caught a glint of anger in her eyes.

Skip asked the woman a few more questions. Kate was impressed by how he managed to make even inquiries about where she had been at certain times sound nonthreatening.

"Thank you for your time, ma'am, uh, Ellen," Skip finally said.

Mrs. Forsythe smiled and fluttered her eyelashes again. "Come around any time. I'm always happy to talk to a handsome man."

Skip kept his voice low as they crossed the recreation building's lobby. "So what'd you think of that performance?"

"I think it's likely she was lying through her teeth," Kate said quietly. "But the question is, was she the person you were chasing or is she just making stuff up in order to seem helpful, because..."

"Because she wants me," Skip finished her sentence, grinning down at her. His hair flopped down onto his forehead.

Without thinking, Kate reached up to smooth it back. Her hand halfway to its target, she caught herself and pretended to be covering a yawn instead. "Didn't sleep well last night."

Skip's grin grew wider as he held the door for her.

The hot, humid air hit them like a wet blanket. Nonetheless, Kate was glad to be out of the aggressively air-conditioned building. They started down the sidewalk.

"Did you ask Joe about Frieda yesterday?" Skip asked.

"No, I didn't get to that before he started backing me into the corner."

"I think I'll have another go at him then."

"Do you mind if I pass on that particular interview?" Kate tried to hide the slight shudder that ran through her body. She glanced up at the side of Skip's face. His tight jaw suggested she had not been successful.

"Not at all. He might be more open about his interactions with the female residents if he's talking to another man." His words were casual enough but there was tension under the surface in his voice.

She gave him another sideways glance. His eye was twitching. "What's the matter?"

"Nothing. Sun's too bright." He looked up at the sky and squinted.

You're a lousy liar, Skip Canfield.

She hoped he wasn't planning on hitting Joe. Rob's words came back to her–*How well do you know this guy anyway?*

"Well, I like being out in the sun," she said, just to make conversation. "The heat feels good after being in that meat locker back there." She pointed down the road leading to Betty's building. "I'll wait for you on the bench where we sat yesterday."

"Okay," Skip said, glancing up at the sky. "Should be safe from falling pots there."

Kate snickered. "Yeah, unless I've pissed God off lately."

~~~

Skip saw a large shed in the distance, under some trees. Good a place as any to start looking for the maintenance man. He had a plan to get Joe talking, one guy to another, about his sexual exploits. The bastard might even let something slip about preying on the young women around town.

The thought of having to act like a sleaze himself in order to gain the creep's trust made his eye twitch again.

His mind flashed to that scene in the machine room and Kate's face, wide-eyed and pale. Joe had better not mention her, or he might just have to beat the crap out of the bastard.

Skip willed his clenched fists to relax.

~~~~~~

Finally, Kate thought as she strolled down the road, *a little alone time to get my thoughts straight.*

This was a peaceful stretch, one side of the road occupied by a large parking lot that served the building adjacent to Betty's and the other side bordered by a strip of woods. Kate could hear the gurgle of a stream somewhere in the trees.

She dug her cell phone out of her pocket to check on Edie. Shelley answered and told her everything was under control. Then Maria brought the baby to the phone so she could babble in her mother's ear. Reassured but homesick, Kate disconnected.

She looked up when she heard the rumble of a truck engine. A moving van was turning out of the parking lot of the building next to Betty's. She lifted her foot to step up onto the sidewalk.

The truck driver blew his horn. Startled, Kate caught her toe on the edge of the curb.

She stumbled forward for several steps and went down on her knees in the grass beside a large tree.

As the moving van rumbled past, another engine roared, just feet away. Instinctively, Kate scrambled behind the tree, then peered around it.

A large, dark-colored sedan was racing away from her. She caught a glimpse of the driver's silhouette, wearing some kind of cap, before the car turned the corner beyond Betty's building.

Real bright, Kate, walking in the road when there's a perfectly good sidewalk available.

She shoved herself to her feet and leaned over to brush grass and dirt off her knees. At least she was wearing dark slacks today so the stains wouldn't show.

A black tire mark on the sidewalk caught her eye. She couldn't tell if it was old or freshly made by the car that had almost hit her. Apparently around here, with elderly drivers whose eyesight and reflexes weren't what they once were, one had better keep their wits about them even on the sidewalk.

She looked around for her cell phone. Belatedly, it dawned on her the driver could have been intentionally aiming for her. Lack of sleep was definitely making her brain fuzzy. Maybe that was why the truck driver blew his horn, because he saw the car bearing down on her.

But would the killer try to run her down with the truck driver there to witness it? Unlikely.

Kate found her phone in a clump of weeds beside the tree. It seemed undamaged. As she wiped it off and returned it to her pocket, she decided not to tell Skip about her embarrassing lapse in alertness.

Looking carefully both ways, she crossed the road and walked over to the bench. One end of it was in a little patch of shade from a small dogwood tree. She sat down there and tried to gather her scattered thoughts.

The image of Rob's frowning face from that morning popped into her mind's eye. What was going on with him? She'd always thought he liked Skip. So why the negative attitude now? She could understand, and appreciate, that Rob didn't want to see her get hurt. But there was more to it than that.

She reviewed his comments at breakfast. Finally her sleep-deprived mind produced a theory.

Rob's jealous.

She sat back against the bench. "Phew," she gasped out loud.

Rob jealous? That can't be.

They had been platonic friends for years, and she knew beyond a shadow of a doubt that he was devoted to Liz. He was her closest friend, but she couldn't begin to think about him in terms of romance. It would be like dating her brother.

Then a second revelation hit her. Maybe it wasn't romantic jealousy. It might be a territorial thing, the kind of jealousy that fathers feel when their teenage daughters start dating. Maybe with a little bit of misguided loyalty to Ed thrown in. How dare this man try to take his friend's place.

That made more sense. Rob was very protective of the people he cared about. And he and Liz had made her part of their family after Eddie died. Knowing Rob as she did, that meant he was feeling responsible for her, like he did for Liz and his daughters. And now here was this other man stepping into his territory, and Rob wasn't sure about his intentions.

Was Rob aware of all this? Probably not. He was mentally healthy enough to rein in the feelings if he were consciously aware of them.

Ho, boy, just when you think relationships can't get any more complicated.

How was she going to address this? She valued Rob's friendship above all else in her life, with the exception of her daughter. But she wasn't going to back away from other relationships because they might upset him. There was no way she would let anyone, not even Rob, have that kind of neurotic hold over her life.

"Okay, wait a minute here," she said out loud. Rob was not neurotic. If she talked to him about it, he would back off.

Kate started rehearsing in her head what she might say to him. *Look, Rob, You're my closest friend... Hmm, no... Rob, I love you for being so concerned about me, and it's too soon for me to consider... a new romantic interest.* She shook her head.

"I'm still grieving for Eddie," she said out loud. "But someday, I probably will become romantically interested in another man. Very possibly Skip..." A surge of warmth ran through her body.

Cut that out!

"I appreciate that you're trying to protect me from hurt, but you need to stop acting like my father. Skip's a sweet, wonderful man–"

"Did I just hear what I thought I heard?"

CHAPTER FOURTEEN

Kate froze, then jumped up from the bench and whirled around.

Skip watched the red tide creep up her neck and into her cheeks, giving them a nice rosy glow. Several emotions chased each other across her face, too fast for him to identify them.

Finally she said, "Come sit with me for a moment." She sat back down and patted the empty space beside her.

He walked around the end of the bench and joined her.

"I'm worried about Rob's stress level." A slight breeze blew dark curls into her face. She shoved them back. "First he had a tough court case, then came directly up here to deal with all of this. But I think there's something else going on as well. Did you happen to notice that he didn't really seem like himself last night and this morning?"

Skip hadn't noticed any such thing, but he nodded obediently. Never say no when a woman asks if you've noticed something, his father had taught him, unless the question is, "Have you noticed that I've gained weight lately?"

"I think he's jealous, in a strange kind of way," Kate said. "Don't get me wrong. There isn't any romantic interest there. Rob and I have been good friends for years, and it's strictly platonic. But it's just that he kind of took over the role of protector when Eddie died…"

"And he's not sure of my intentions," Skip finished for her.

"Well, yeah, that's part of it…" She hesitated.

He guessed what was coming next. "In a way, I'm stepping

onto his turf."

Again, an array of emotions waged a battle on her face–relief at first, but anxiety ended up dominating. "You can't tell him we had this conversation."

"Of course not." The breeze flipped another curl forward. He reached over and tucked it behind her ear.

Her cheeks flushed again.

He withdrew his fingers reluctantly. "Don't worry. I know how much Rob means to you. I'd never do anything that might damage your friendship with him."

A sigh whooshed out of her and she collapsed against him. Then she abruptly pulled back.

He put his arm around her shoulders, gave them a quick squeeze and let go. "Before you say it, I'll say it for you. 'It's too soon, Skip.'" His voice rose in a shrill falsetto.

Kate laughed, then her expression turned serious. "Someday, Skip, I can't begin to tell you when, it will no longer be too soon."

~~~~~~~

Sandy Lindstrom spotted his quarry coming into the building. He waved to her and Canfield from across the atrium, gesturing for them to wait up. He was becoming increasingly curious about this woman, who wore a wedding ring and answered to *Mrs.* Huntington, and yet none of the men in this group of amateur investigators seemed to be her husband. Where was he?

"Mrs. Huntington, Mr. Canfield," he said when he caught up to them. "I was hoping to run into you. Uh, could I speak to you for a moment, Mrs. Huntington?"

"Sure." She turned to Canfield. "I'll catch up with you."

Lindstrom held out a hand toward the small wrought iron table and chairs. She led the way and they sat down across from each other.

Business first. "I thought you were taking Mrs. Franklin to a motel?"

Mrs. Huntington eyed the foliage around them for a second. "We did last night, but she wanted to come home this morning."

She leaned forward. In a whisper she added, "She's actually still at the motel. Mr. Franklin and our friends are setting a trap in her apartment to see if the killer will make a move against her again."

"They shouldn't be doing that," Lindstrom whispered back. "It's too dangerous."

"Don't worry. Rose Hernandez is a Baltimore County police officer, and Mac Reilly is an ex-Green Beret. They can handle themselves."

Lindstrom frowned and scrubbed a hand over his face. It rasped against his stubbled cheeks. He was wishing he'd found the time to shave when she leaned even closer to him.

"Look, Detective," she hissed under her breath. "We need to do everything we can to resolve this. Betty isn't safe in her own home, and we can't go back to our lives until she is."

She sat back a little. "I can understand why you don't want us messing in police business." Her tone was more conciliatory. "But the others have jobs they need to get back to and I have a small daughter at home."

As good an opening as he was likely to get. "Is she with your husband?"

"No, her nanny. I'm a widow."

Lindstrom hid his relief behind an appropriately sorrowful expression. "My condolences, Mrs. Huntington."

"Thank you, and please call me Kate." She smiled at him.

He smiled back. "Folks call me Sandy, Kate."

He leaned forward. "I wanted to warn you to watch out for the maintenance man here, Joseph Fielding." Honoring his promise to Canfield and not wanting to embarrass her, he pretended he wasn't aware of her previous encounter with Fielding. But he did want her to know just how dangerous the man might be.

She winced a little, then her face closed. She'd said she was a therapist. He guessed they needed to know how to hide their feelings too, like cops do.

"Why's that?" she said.

"He's got a record. Mostly little stuff–petty theft, drunk and disorderlies, but there were a couple of domestic violence calls from an ex-girlfriend. He's spent quite a bit of time in the local jail."

"Do you suspect him of the murders? Was robbery the motive?"

"I don't know yet if anything was taken from the victims' apartments. As Mrs. Franklin pointed out, Mrs. Blackwell wasn't a very neat woman, so it's hard to tell if her things had been disturbed. And she doesn't have any close relatives who can tell us what should be there. Mrs. McIntosh's daughter is taking an inventory of her mother's place today. She's going to let me know if she finds anything missing."

"Would you let me know what she says?" Kate asked.

He gave her a small nod, although whether or not he told her would depend on what the McIntosh daughter did or didn't find. "What I do suspect Fielding of are the sexual assaults that have occurred in town over the last couple months. His alibis are shaky. I'm trying to break them."

The creep claimed he'd been drinking with his buddies and his low-life friends had backed him up. Lindstrom actually found it suspicious that he was alibied for all three crimes. Most people stay home and watch TV at least some of the time.

"Were there any signs of sexual assault with Doris or Frieda?" Kate asked.

He shook his head. "I talked to the Forsythes last night," he said, mostly to keep the conversation going. He liked talking to her, and looking at her. She was an attractive woman. "They told me the same thing they'd told you about Mrs. Blackwell."

"Skip and I talked to her again this morning. She said she saw someone coming around the corner of Betty's building yesterday, an elderly man. Her description of him was very generic though. Supposedly he turned and walked away before she got a good look at his face."

"Supposedly?"

"I think she could have been lying. I also got the impression that Mr. Forsythe might have strayed at some point in the past."

He got out his pad and made a few notes. Mrs. Forsythe had claimed she hadn't seen anyone when he'd talked to her last night.

He pretended to still be writing, as he glanced up at Kate from under his eyebrows. Did he dare do what he was contemplating. He swallowed and took the plunge.

"Kate, I was wondering… uh, I was hoping you might have dinner with me, or a coffee or something, sometime? Once this case is resolved, of course."

She stared at him, her mouth slightly open.

What is this? Kate thought. *Am I suddenly wearing a sign that says, "I'm lonely. Ask me out!"*

No man had hit on her in the last sixteen months, and now two invitations in a row. Maybe she was starting to put out availability vibes. Maybe she was closer to it no longer being *too soon* than she'd thought. She tucked that idea away for later contemplation.

She realized she'd paused too long. Sandy was waiting expectantly, his expression becoming more anxious by the second. No wonder he'd been somewhat freer with information than a police officer would normally be. He was trying to get her to like him.

"I'm sorry, Sandy. I've only been a widow for a little over a year. It's too soon for me to consider dating. But thank you for asking. I'm flattered."

The man's face fell, but he quickly covered up his disappointment. "Again, I'm very sorry for your loss, Kate. Would you think it callous of me if I asked permission to call you at some point in the future?"

Kate debated for a second. She had a strong feeling that when she was ready to date, she would be going out with the man who was already first in line, Skip Canfield. But she didn't want to disappoint this poor guy again. She nodded, and gave him a small smile.

There was an awkward lull. Kate decided this might be a good time to feel him out about taking Betty back to Maryland.

"Uh, Sandy, Mr. Franklin and I are becoming concerned about his aunt's stress level. And as I said before, we've all got lives we need to get back to. Surely it couldn't be construed that she's fleeing out of guilt if her nephew takes her back to stay with him in Maryland, until your investigation is completed."

Kate was pleased with her carefully chosen words. While waiting for his agreement to this plan, she tried to decide how exuberantly she should thank him. She didn't want to seem to be encouraging his romantic interest.

He shocked her when he shook his head. "I'm afraid I can't allow that."

"But you can't make her stay here? Not when there's been an attempt on her life," she blurted out.

So much for carefully chosen words.

"If I arrest her, I can. Don't force my hand."

She blanched. "Sandy, please don't do that. It could kill her."

The detective raised his gaze to the skylights for a minute. Kate watched as his Adam's apple bobbed in his lean neck.

The thought flashed through her mind that he was actually more her physical type–lean and lanky like Eddie–than Skip was. And yet she wasn't the least bit attracted to him. She wondered if she would have been, if Skip hadn't come along first.

Now cut that out!

He brought his eyes back to her face. "Kate, have I mentioned that my captain is a by-the-book kinda guy?" When she didn't respond, he continued, "In *his* book, we have motive, means, and opportunity. In the Blackwell case, at least."

"Her motive's not a very strong one, and anyone could've picked up that poker. As for opportunity, most of the folks in this community live alone and go to bed early. If you ask any of them about their alibi, you're going to get the same answer Betty gave you, 'home alone in bed.' And she's got even less motive to kill Frieda."

He looked at her for a long moment. "I talked to Mrs. Franklin's agent. Her publisher had just offered her a lucrative new contract, but that offer would have been withdrawn if Doris Blackwell had sued. I'd say that $80,000 is a pretty strong motive in that case."

Kate decided to change tactics. "Sandy, you must have pretty good instincts or you wouldn't have earned that gold badge. You've talked to Betty Franklin, watched her face, her body language. You know she's not a killer, and she's definitely not capable of killing a close friend."

"Yes, they seem to have been friends, but I only have her word for it that they were close friends. It's also possible someone else killed Frieda McIntosh. She had made some enemies with her gossiping. Maybe her murderer is figuring Mrs. Franklin will take the blame, which would explain the attempt to fake her suicide, so we would think both cases were resolved."

"Aren't cops supposed to trust their instincts. Can you look me in the eye, Sandy, and tell me you actually think Betty Franklin is capable of murder?"

The detective sighed and looked her in the eye. "Kate, you've been watching too much TV. Yes, cops use their instincts, but most of police work is doggedly following leads, searching for evidence. I can't ignore that evidence just because my gut says someone's probably not a killer."

He paused. "And Captain Davis is not the least bit interested in what my gut says. He's sitting back in his office, reading my reports, that are saying I've got no other real leads, and then he's looking at his open and closed cases stats."

"But Sandy…"

"Don't push me, Kate." He stood up. Then his cop face fell away for a moment as he looked down at her. "I wish I could give you a different answer." He walked away.

~~~~~~~

Knuckles rapped on the apartment door. Then Kate's voice calling out, "Betty, it's Kate."

Rose, in her new wig and Aunt Betty's clothing, got up to let her in.

Kate walked into the living room, then paused in mid-step.

She looked at him, then at Canfield, then back at him.

Rob shifted in his chair and made sure his court face was in place.

"Any coffee available?" she asked, her voice too cheerful.

"Finished the pot a little bit ago," Rob said. "But there's iced tea in the fridge."

"Even better. Anybody else want some?"

Canfield smiled at her. "I'll take a glass."

Rob frowned at the man.

Kate narrowed her eyes at him. She turned toward the kitchen cabinet and got out two glasses. "Did you tell them about our interview with *Ellen* and yours with Joe?" she called back over her shoulder.

"Who the hell is Ellen?" Mac said.

Kate came back with two glasses of tea. "Mrs. Forsythe. She asked Skip, but *not* me, to call her Ellen." Kate wiggled her eyebrows and snickered.

Rose chuckled.

Mac was sitting next to Canfield. He slapped the big man on the shoulder. "Made a conquest, huh, buddy?"

His cheeks turning pink, Canfield muttered, "Not intentionally."

Kate handed him one of the glasses and sat down on the settee.

"I told them about the interview with *Mrs. Forsythe*," Canfield said. "But I was waiting for you to report on the one with Joe."

"Lindstrom told me that Joe has a police record," Kate said. "He suspects him of being the rapist whose been in the news lately."

Canfield nodded. "Wouldn't surprise me to find out he's a rapist. His attitude toward women would make the Neanderthal man look liberated. Couldn't get him to admit to anything regarding Doris but in general he seems to have a take it wherever you can get it attitude."

"Emphasis on *take*," Kate said.

"At first he pretended he didn't really know who Frieda was. But later on, he made a lewd comment about her." Canfield curled his lip. "Uh, let's just say that neither weight nor age are major turn-offs for him."

"So the man's a sexist creep, a thief, and maybe a rapist," Rose said. "But not necessarily a killer."

"Not unless he got caught in the act of searching for valuables in Doris's apartment," Kate said, "and then whacked her over the head. I think he's quite capable of using whatever degree of violence is necessary to get what he wants or to avoid getting arrested."

She glanced Rob's way. He realized he'd been silent too long, just watching them. He leaned forward, schooling his face into a more attentive look.

"Yeah, I can see that," Canfield was saying, "but would he kill Frieda in her sleep in order to rob her?"

"Lindstrom said Doris and Frieda were not sexually assaulted." Kate looked around. "It's a good thing Betty's not here, or we wouldn't be able to talk about this openly."

Rob faked a smile in her direction. "Yeah, she's pretty old-fashioned."

"One guy could be doin' both," Mac said. "Gettin' his sexual jollies with the younger gals. Stealin' from the old ones."

Canfield shook his head. "A rapist rapes any woman he can overpower. Age and appearance aren't all that important, just whether or not she's vulnerable. He wouldn't break into an old woman's apartment, steal from her and kill her, and refrain from raping her. Not when he already had control over her." He looked at Kate for confirmation.

She nodded, but then held up a hand. "Wait, there's another possibility. Rapists have almost always been sexually abused as children, and often physically abused as well. If this guy had been sexually abused by his father or his mother's boyfriend, and the mother failed to protect him, he could be a rapist *and* also harbor a hatred for older women. He might then start symbolically killing his mother by murdering older women, but without any desire to have sex with them."

"Because they're his mother, in his mind," Rose said.

Kate nodded. "Normally, as Skip pointed out, the tendency would be for him to rape them too, but with psychopathic killers, the word *normal* doesn't always apply."

Now Rob was paying attention for real as the horror of what she was saying sunk in. "You think this could be a serial killer?"

She nodded again.

They all were silent for a minute, digesting that disturbing idea.

"I'm afraid I have some other bad news," Kate said. "Lindstrom pretty much admitted that his captain is pressuring him to arrest Betty for Doris's murder, even though he doesn't have enough to charge her for Frieda's."

Rob sucked in his breath. "Shit!"

"I was trying to get him to let us take her back to Maryland. He as much as said he'd arrest her if we did that. His exact words were 'Don't force my hand.'"

Fear for his aunt twisted in Rob's gut. "Shit!" he said again.

"Yeah," Kate said. "That was my reaction, although I didn't say it to him."

They all sat in silence again for a moment.

Finally Rose said, "So the sooner we solve his case for him, the better."

"Back to our suspect list," Kate said. "I think Joe should be near the top, and Mrs. Forsythe's being in front of the building yesterday and then lying to us today puts her up there as well, in my book."

"Mr. Forsythe is a possibility, too," Canfield said. "If he's strayed before, maybe he did respond to Doris's flirting, they had an affair, and then she threatened to tell his wife."

"Ah, so you picked up on that 'he wouldn't risk losing me *now*' comment." Kate smiled at him approvingly.

"And the flash of anger when she said it." Canfield smiled back at her.

Rob cleared his throat. Kate glanced at him, anger in her eyes.

Guilt squeezed his chest. Those eyes were the washed-out gray they became when she was stressed or tired.

And she's both, thanks to me. I got her into this.

Guilt morphed into worry. Being stressed out made her even more vulnerable to Canfield.

Kate turned toward Mac and Rose, her back now toward him. He suspected the maneuver was intentional.

"Any of the residents see anything suspicious outside Betty's apartment yesterday?" she asked.

Mac shook his head. "Nobody saw nothin' strange."

"But it occurred to me," Rose said, "that these folks are so used to seeing each other wandering around the building. If it was another resident they saw, they wouldn't have given it another thought."

Kate nodded. "Even someone who doesn't live in this building, someone they see regularly, maybe in the cafeteria. It wouldn't even register."

"Nor would Joe," Rob said. "Since he no doubt goes into people's apartments sometimes to do maintenance."

"He probably has a master key," Rose said.

Kate shuddered. Canfield shot a concerned look in her direction.

They're keeping something from me. Rob was surprised by how much that realization made his chest hurt.

"Havin' a key would explain why no scratch marks on the door, first time the bastard tried to get in," Mac was saying.

Rob's cell phone rang. It was Liz calling from the motel.

"Got some info, hon."

"Hold on." He put the phone on speaker and set it in the middle of the coffee table so the others could hear.

"Chloroform's not that easy to come by," Liz's disembodied voice boomed. "Can't just walk into a store and buy it. Only schools, hospitals and labs that have a good reason for needing it can order it from chemical companies. It's illegal, in most states, for an individual to possess it."

"So who, among our suspects," Kate said, "would have access to it?"

"I tried to hack into the retirement community's records–"

"You've got to stop doing that, Liz," Rob interrupted. "One of these days, you're going to get caught, not to mention I could get disbarred if it came out that I knew you were a hacker."

"I only do it for worthy causes, hon. It's not like I'm planting computer viruses or hacking into bank records to steal money."

Rob frowned at the phone but let it go.

"So what did you find?" Kate asked.

"Not a thing, unfortunately. The only references in their computer records to residents is in their accounting program, showing when they've paid their rent and fees. Any personal info must be kept in paper files only. I'm thinking that if we could find out what jobs our suspects retired from, we'd know who might have been able to get their hands on chloroform."

"Mrs. Carroll, the community director, might know that information," Kate said. "However, I'm not her favorite person at the moment. You could probably get her to talk to you, Liz."

"I'll call her."

"Might get more out of her in person," Kate said. "How about I come over to keep Betty company. She and I can fill in some things on her lists while you go talk to Mrs. Carroll."

"Sounds like a plan," Liz said. "I'll call and make an appointment with her. Maybe act like we're thinking about moving here when we retire. That ought to soften her up some. See ya in a bit, Kate."

In the back of his mind, Rob was still digesting the information he had gotten from his admin assistant a little while ago. He'd had Fran do a background check on Skip Canfield, and he hadn't liked some of the details from his work history that she'd uncovered. So he'd made some calls. Until he heard back from a couple people, he wanted to get the man away from Kate.

He figured there was no point in trying to send her home to her child. Her knew the signs. She was already invested in helping

Betty, and she was the stubbornest woman he knew.

He stared at the now mute phone on the coffee table. Make that the second most stubborn woman. His wife, the Robin Hood of hackers, was first.

This was probably the best opening he was likely to get.

Rob tried to keep his voice nonchalant as he leaned over to retrieve his phone. "Well, Skip, it doesn't look like there's anything for you to do at the moment. You might as well go back to Maryland for this evening. I'll let you know if we need you back up here later. Hopefully, we'll trap ourselves a killer tonight."

Silence. The others were all staring at him. Rose's right eyebrow was cocked at a forty-five degree angle. She and Mac exchanged a quick glance.

Canfield's face was a neutral mask. He turned to Kate. "Are you staying?"

Her mouth was hanging partway open. She continued to stare at Rob for a moment. Then she said, "Yes, I want to see this through."

Which is what I knew you would say, Rob thought.

"Then I'm sticking around." Canfield's voice was neutral, to match his face. "On my own time, Rob. No charge."

"That won't be necessary, Canfield."

Kate gave Rob a sharp look.

Canfield cocked an eyebrow and pressed his lips together. "Nothing better to do right now. I'll take Kate back to the motel and grab a nap. Since I was on guard duty last night, I only dozed." He got up and carried his empty glass into the kitchen. He put it in the sink and walked back around the breakfast bar.

Rob stood up and took a step toward Canfield. Too late, he realized his fists were clenched.

Kate stepped between them.

Canfield's face was no longer neutral–a muscle throbbed in his jaw–but his voice remained calm. "You ready to go, Kate?"

She shot Rob a worried look, then nodded.

Mac and Rose glanced back and forth between him and

Canfield, inscrutable expressions on their faces.

You're making an ass of yourself, Franklin.

"Y'all be careful tonight. Call if you need reinforcements." Canfield opened the door. After Kate preceded him out of the apartment, he said in a louder voice, "Thanks for the iced tea, Mrs. Franklin. We'll see you tomorrow."

Rob watched the door swing shut behind them. His cell phone rang.

CHAPTER FIFTEEN

Once they were in Skip's SUV, Kate let out a long pent-up breath.

"My sentiments exactly," Skip said, staring straight ahead at the road. He worked his jaw, trying to get it to relax.

"If it weren't for the fact that he called you Canfield, I could try to convince myself he just wants to save some money."

"No way," Skip said. "He's not thinking straight. He's gonna leave three women he loves on their own at the motel tonight? With a rapist and a killer in town."

She laid her head back against the headrest of her seat. "Why does life have to be so complicated sometimes?"

"You gonna have that conversation with him, darlin'? The one you were rehearsing out by the bench."

She gave him a sharp sideways glance.

Oops!

"Sorry. *Darlin'* just slipped out."

After a beat, she said, "It looks like I'm going to have to talk to him."

Skip decided a change of subject was in order. He cast about for something safe to talk about. "How's the baby doing?" He knew she was calling to check on Edie every chance she got.

"She's doing fine. It's her mother who's not dealing well with separation. I don't know why I'm feeling so guilty. Between Shelley and Sam, Edie's no doubt being spoiled rotten."

"I've always gotten the impression that guilt comes with the territory for moms." Skip flashed a grin at her.

She smiled back. "Yeah, probably some guilt gene on the X chromosome that turns on once we give birth."

～～～

Back at the motel, Kate suggested Skip would be more comfortable napping on one of the beds in the suite's bedroom, while she and Betty discussed what they had learned that morning about their suspects. Kate called room service to have them send over some lunch.

She'd finished filling Betty in when there was a light tap on the door. After checking through the peephole, Kate opened the door to take the plate of sandwiches from the young waitress. She was surprised to see Rob getting out of his car across the parking lot.

She waited as he approached.

"Kate, we need to talk." He tilted his head toward the outside door of his room. His face had the hard look she'd only seen in the courtroom, when the opposition was trying to screw his client.

Her stomach clenched. "Okay. Be over in a minute."

Kate closed and locked the door, then deposited the plate on the dresser. "I'll be next door," she said to Betty who was making notes on her posterboard lists of suspects.

Dreading the conversation to come, she stepped through the door between the rooms.

Rob closed it behind her. He gestured toward the small table by the window. They sat across from each other.

"Kate, how well do you know Skip Canfield?" Rob's voice was calm. Too calm.

Anger flared. She reined it in. "I'm getting to know him. Why do you keep asking me that?"

Rob ignored the question. Still in that infuriatingly calm voice, he said, "Did he tell you he has a temper?"

"No, although..." She flashed back to the scene after her encounter with Joe. "I know he can get a bit intense at times."

As can you, like right now!

"Did he tell you he quit the state troopers after he blew up at his superior officer?"

Kate's narrowed her eyes at him. Pressure was building in her chest. "No, he didn't, and how is it that *you* know that?"

He held up his hands, as if to ward off her anger. "Look, I know you're going to be pissed, but please hear me out. I had Fran run a background check on Canfield."

For a second, disbelief overrode anger. She stared at him. "You did *what*?"

"Let me finish, please. I also called a buddy of mine who's a retired state trooper. He just got back to me."

It felt like her chest was going to explode. Her hands balled into fists under the table.

Rob talked faster. "He made some calls and found out about the blow up. Canfield quit after *eleven years* on the force, without notice. Then he drifted from job to job for three years. Those aren't the actions of a stable or responsible man."

Kate was beyond pissed. A small part of her mind was trying to process what he was saying about Skip. But most of her mental energy was focused on resisting the urge to tell this man, whom she'd loved as a friend for over a decade, exactly what he could do with his damned background check. How dare he go behind her back and check up on one of her friends!

Through clenched teeth, she said, "Apparently I didn't make myself totally clear at breakfast. I thought I'd conveyed the message that you needed to back off."

"I'd already told Fran to order the check. If nothing negative had come back, I would have dropped it. But..."

She didn't say anything

In a softer voice, he said, "You're vulnerable right now, so soon after Ed's death."

"Rob, I'm not a child. I'm thirty-nine years old and I have an advanced degree in psychology. I *know* I'm vulnerable, which is why I told Skip I'm not ready to date yet."

"I just didn't want you getting attached to this guy," he said. "And then finding out later that he wasn't on the up and up."

"And what about quitting a job after an argument with his

boss makes the man not on the up and up?"

"He didn't tell you about it, did he?"

"The subject of past employment has not yet come up in conversation. I can't believe–" Kate stopped herself, realizing she was too angry to continue this discussion. They were dangerously close to the edge of a precipice. If either of them said the wrong thing…

She shoved her chair back and stood up.

Rob rose. He reached out a hand.

"Don't!" She took a step back.

He froze.

"I can't believe you did this." She walked toward the door between the rooms.

"Kate, please! I just didn't want you to get hurt."

She turned back and looked at him. His big frame was sagging, his face pale, his eyes pleading.

This is what hurts, what you've done. She managed not to say the words out loud.

Pain squeezed her heart. Her eyes stung.

He started toward her.

She held up her hand. "You need to leave me alone now, before I say something I'll regret later." She went through the door, closing it carefully behind her.

~~~~~~

Kate jolted awake. She knew she'd been dreaming and it hadn't been good, but she couldn't remember the details.

Trying not to wake Betty, she felt around for her watch on the bedside table. She couldn't read it in the dark. She got up and went into the bathroom, closing the door before fumbling for the light switch.

One-fourteen. She put the watch on, then stared into the mirror over the sink. Her eyes were washed-out gray, rimmed in red.

She was feeling claustrophobic. With Betty in the same room, she couldn't turn on the light to read, or watch TV to distract herself from her thoughts. She couldn't go out into the living room.

Skip would wake up and want to know what was going on. And she couldn't get in her car and go to Denny's because there was a rapist running around Lancaster.

She walked across the floor of the small bathroom and back again, and cracked her shin on the toilet. "Shit!" she said softly. She couldn't even pace.

Sitting down on the side of the bathtub, she propped her elbows on her knees and rested her chin in her hands. The porcelain edge was cold through the thin fabric of her nightgown.

What the hell was she doing here, sleeping in a strange bed miles away from her child, trying to catch a killer who had so far eluded the entire Lancaster police force? In the morning, she should just pack up and go home.

Most of her didn't even want to wait for morning.

But a smaller, more rational part knew if she did that, with things the way they were right now, the rift between her and Rob could become irreparable. Her eyes stung, but she refused to let herself cry.

Damn the man! What had he been thinking, invading Skip's privacy like that?

Her tired mind wandered to what Rob had found out. Skip had ended an eleven-year career by blowing up at his boss and quitting without notice? That did not fit with what she knew about the man. He was one of the most laid-back people she'd ever met.

No, she didn't know much about his past, but she'd thought she had a good sense of his personality. After all, the man had camped out on her sofa for weeks after Eddie's murder, and he'd helped them trap the killer. On several occasions during that awful time, Skip's calm, easygoing manner had helped to steady her.

There had to be some logical explanation for the information Rob had discovered. She'd worked enough domestic violence cases to know that someone could hide an explosive nature under a layer of charm.

She shook her head. No, Skip Canfield was not a superficial charmer, nor was he an impulsive man. It wasn't possible she'd misread him like that.

He'd been furious after her encounter with Joe. She rubbed her arm where he'd grabbed it. But that short-lived outburst had stemmed from fear for her.

Arrgghh!

Kate grabbed a hunk of curls in each hand. "Damn you, Rob Franklin," she whispered out loud, "for planting this seed."

Okay, what am I going to do about Rob?

She knew she couldn't leave, at least not right away. Even though she had Edie as a good excuse, one the others would buy without question, Rob would know the real reason. And he would be hurt, terribly hurt, that she would withdraw from him like that without trying to work things out.

As angry as she was with him right now, she couldn't intentionally hurt him. But her brain was too tired to figure out how to deal with this. He'd crossed a line he shouldn't have crossed, and she wasn't sure how they would find their way back to where they had been.

Suddenly she was so exhausted she was afraid she'd slide right off the side of the tub onto the floor. Better go back to bed and see if she could get some sleep. Tomorrow was going to be stressful enough without being sleep-deprived.

She decided she would do her best to pretend everything was okay, until she could figure out what else to do.

~~~~~~~

Earlier, when they'd been planning how to set their trap, Rob had worried he might not be able to stay alert. After his confrontation with Kate, that was no longer a problem. Wide awake and fully clothed, he lay on Aunt Betty's bed, staring into the darkness.

Shortly after two in the morning, he thought he heard a noise. He got up quietly and tiptoed into the living room. There was very little ambient light in the apartment. Rob moved carefully across the room, then reached down to the settee to wake Rose.

And felt nothing but air. He patted around on the settee. It was empty. "Rose, where are you?" he whispered.

"Damn thing's too slithery," came the whispered reply from the floor.

"I thought I heard something, outside the door." They both were quiet, until they heard it again, a soft scratching sound.

Rob was still looking down into the darkness on the floor, assuming that was where Rose was. He felt warm breath on his neck and jumped. "Get Mac," Rose whispered right next to his ear.

He felt his way along the living room wall to the den doorway, then found the end of the sofa bed in the dark and shook Mac's foot. Mac was out of bed in an instant, poking a gun barrel into Rob's gut. "It's me, you idiot," Rob hissed.

"Who you callin' an eejit," Mac growled softly. "You're the one almost got shot."

"Someone's trying to get in," Rob whispered.

They crept back into the outer room, just as the front door swung silently open and a dark figure slipped inside.

Rose flipped the light switch by the door. Gun in her hands, she barked, "Police! Don't move!"

But the black-clad, ski-masked figure surprised them by whirling around. Neither Rose nor Mac could shoot without risking hitting the other. The figure plunged back out the door. Rose took off after it.

Rob ran for the door.

"Oof." He and Mac had collided in the doorway.

Mac turned sideways and slid past him. He took off.

Rob raced after him. Rose was turning the corner into the center area of the building.

The foliage rustled on the opposite side of the dimly lit atrium. The three of them bolted toward the spot, but nothing was there. Mac gestured that they should split up and go around the outside of the plants. He started in one direction, with Rob and Rose going the other way, all of them squinting into the dark foliage to detect anyone hiding there.

They had gone halfway around when Rob heard the soft swish of the building's outer door opening. He whirled in time to see a dark silhouette disappearing out into the night.

Again they gave chase. There was no moon and the outside lighting, clustered in front of the building and in the nearby parking lot, left large pockets of pitch black.

"Go back inside," Mac hissed at Rob. He gestured to Rose and they moved in different directions around the building.

Rob stood there for a moment, feeling like an idiot.

We should've had Skip here and me at the motel.

The total lunacy of his earlier effort hit him. What if Skip had complied? Then there would have been no one to guard the women. He would've had to go to the motel and leave Mac and Rose here by themselves.

They'd have been better off without me.

Shoulders sagging, he walked back to his aunt's apartment.

Ten minutes later, Rose and Mac jogged up the hall. Rob was standing in the open doorway of the apartment.

"No sign of the bastard," Mac growled softly.

"I screwed that up," Rob said.

"Not your fault," Mac said. "Most people do what ya tell them when you're holdin' a gun on them."

"But not always murderers," Rose said. "Sometimes suicide by cop is preferable to life without parole."

"No point in waking the others," Rob said, "just to report failure."

Failure caused by my screw-up.

CHAPTER SIXTEEN

As Kate came out of the bathroom the next morning, towel-drying her curly mop, she could hear Liz's voice through the bedroom door. Betty was still asleep, which had her worried. The older woman was usually an early riser.

Quickly pulling on her clothes, Kate tiptoed to the door and slipped out into the living room of the suite.

Skip whispered a summary of nocturnal events that he had gleaned from Liz's side of the conversation.

Liz continued to commiserate with Rob over the phone. Finally she said, "I'm thinking we should all come over there, even Betty. She and I have some information to share and we can all confer to decide where to go from here... I know, but we'll just make sure someone is always with her."

She dropped her voice and echoed Kate's concerns. "Another day cooped up in this room with nothing to do, I'm not sure that's really good for her... Okay, we'll grab some breakfast and be there in a little while."

Over their room service breakfast, Liz gave the others the physical description, such as it was, of the previous night's intruder. "Most useful information is that the killer is average height and build and fairly physically fit, to be agile and fast enough to get away from them."

"We already knew they had to be strong enough to lift that pot off the ledge," Skip said.

Liz looked at him in confusion.

"Dear Lord," Kate exclaimed. "We didn't tell you about that?"

Betty scowled at her from across the table.

"Sorry, Betty." Kate turned back to Liz. "Somebody tried to drop a potted plant on our heads, out in the atrium...When was that anyway?" she asked Skip.

"Tuesday. No wait, it was Monday, late afternoon."

Alarm on her face, Liz asked, "Were you hurt?"

"No, other than a few bruises the next day from Hulk Hogan here diving on top of me."

"Hey, I resent that. I'm much cuter than Hulk Hogan."

"True," Kate said. "He doesn't have your boyish grin."

Liz was looking from one to the other of them. The corners of her mouth quirked up.

Crap, are we that transparent?

"So how strong would one have to be to knock those pots off?" Liz asked.

"Somebody just brushing against them wouldn't do it," Kate said. "Which is what Mrs. Carroll kept insisting happened."

"There's a little side on the shelf," Skip said. "Someone would have to lift the pot up over that."

"Or maybe pull the pot a little bit toward them." Betty pantomimed the action. "And then get it rocking so they could tip it over the edge."

"That might work, too," Skip said, forking in his last bite of scrambled eggs.

He turned to Kate. "Want to show me where that Home Depot is? I think it's time for a stronger lock."

Liz nodded her agreement with that idea. "We'll head on over."

"I'll walk you to your car," Skip said.

~~~~

After a swing out to US 30 to buy a deadbolt lock and the tools to install it, Skip and Kate were headed back across Columbia Avenue, the main drag through the western side of Lancaster.

Kate suddenly leaned forward, straining against her seatbelt. "Oh, I was hoping to see some Amish while I was up here. All these years I've lived only two hours away, and I've never been to Amish country before."

Skip followed her line of vision. Half a block ahead was a black buggy, a neon orange triangle attached to its back. The cars behind were easing around it, as breaks in the traffic coming the other way allowed.

As Skip carefully maneuvered his Explorer around the buggy, he admired the shiny coat and lively step of the horse pulling it.

Kate waved at the Amish family, a couple with a small boy, no older than four. The bearded father kept his eyes stoically ahead, but the modestly dressed mother gave Kate a shy smile. The young woman's hair was tucked up under a small white bonnet.

The boy, wearing a miniature version of his father's straw hat, blue shirt and suspendered black trousers, was much less reserved. He waved back, a big grin on his face.

At the sight of the boy's cheerful face, Skip experienced a sharp stab of something he had never felt before. Easing back into his lane in front of the trotting horse, he realized it was envy. He wanted what that man had. A family.

In his thirty-eight years, he had dated many women, loved some of them and even lived with one. But, much to his mother's dismay, he'd never felt the urge to marry or have a family. And he'd never felt like he was missing out on anything, until now.

He glanced at Kate, who was still looking over her shoulder at the receding buggy and its occupants. He'd never met little Edie but he recalled the picture her proud mother had shown him. The baby was a tiny version of Kate–dark curly hair, blue eyes and a big grin.

A warm sensation spread through his chest, followed by a sinking feeling in his gut.

Aw, shit, Skippy. You've got it bad, man!

~~~~

At Betty's apartment, Skip began installing the deadbolt just below the newly repaired security chain. While the others gathered in the living room, Kate stood by the breakfast bar, handing

Skip tools as needed. She was watching Rob out of the corner of her eye. His emotions were hidden behind the neutral mask he wore in court.

Liz pointed to the lists propped up on the settee. "Between Betty's knowledge of them, what I could get out of Mrs. Carroll, and some computer searches, we've identified the former occupations of most of these folks. We thought we were really onto something with Mr. Forsythe. He was a high school chemistry teacher. But your description of the intruder tends to eliminate him."

"He's the only one of our suspects it eliminates," Kate said. "Except maybe one or two of the ladies in the writers' group, and Mr. Berkeley. He looked quite frail."

"Even if neither Berkeley or Forsythe could be the intruder," Rose said, "they could be in it with their wives for some reason."

Liz leaned over the list of the writers' group members. "We tried to find out the occupations of spouses as well. Jill Winthrop, widow and homemaker, deceased husband was retired military, a colonel. And get this, in charge of a VA hospital for the last five years of his career. Henry Morris, widower, maintenance worker for the Lancaster school system, wife was a nurse's aide at the hospital."

Kate handed Skip a screwdriver. "They must have been careful savers to be able to afford this place."

"True." Liz pointed to the next name on the list. "Julie Thompson, divorcee, retired elementary school principal. Don't know what her ex did for a living."

Skip tightened another screw. "So Mrs. Winthrop or Morris could conceivably have chloroform lying around, that their deceased spouses may have brought home."

"But that's not very likely," Rob said.

"True," Kate and Skip said in unison. He looked over his shoulder at her and flashed a grin.

Kate glanced at Rob. He was looking their way, his court mask still in place. But his big body seemed deflated. He made eye contact with her, and his face sagged.

Her chest ached. Then worry shot through her.

Is he having some kind of breakdown?

Betty had written *might have access to chloroform* next to a star at the bottom of the list. Now she took out a marker and put a star with a question mark next to Winthrop's and Morris's names. There was already a star beside Mr. Forsythe's.

Liz continued, "Janet Maccabe, widow and homemaker, husband worked for the railroad; Fred Murphy, forensic technician for the local police department, wife was a nurse."

"Either one of them could get their hands on chloroform," Rob said.

Mrs. Murphy already had a star. Betty put one by Mr. Murphy's name. There were also two asterisks next to it, indicating he was one of the married men Doris had flirted with and he'd particularly disliked Frieda.

"Nothing popped when we interviewed them," Kate said. "Did you sense anything suspicious about them, Skip?"

Skip shook his head without turning around. He tightened the last of the screws in the deadbolt. "Seemed like nice boring people. But they're both average height and build, and looked reasonably fit."

"Boring's a good description of them," Betty said. "Frieda was the only one they didn't get along with. Fred's got a rather dry wit and Frieda never got his jokes. She'd take offense and tell him off."

As Kate and Skip found seats in the living room, Liz said, "Peggy Foster is divorced. She was a school teacher, no idea what her ex did for a living."

"I interviewed Foster," Kate said. "She's petite. She couldn't have been the intruder last night." Betty nodded in agreement.

"That's it for the writers' group," Liz said. "The Petersons. He was a manager at the Armstrong plant here in Lancaster. She worked in the pharmacy at the hospital." There was already a star next to her name. "The Berkeleys owned their own hardware store."

"Would they be able to get chloroform?" Rob asked.

"Maybe," Liz said. A star with a question mark went up next to the Berkeleys. "Carla Baxter never married. She was a mathematics professor at Drexel in Philly. Last but not least, we have the Forsythes, chemistry teacher and aerobics instructor."

"Why am I not surprised," Kate muttered under her breath.

She'd been chasing an elusive thought around in the back of her head. Finally she was able to grab it. "Betty, what were the members of the writers' group working on? Did any of them have stories in progress, or ones they'd written before, that had a plot at all similar to what's been happening here?"

Betty thought for a moment. "Only two members write mysteries. Well, actually Janet writes political thrillers. Jill Winthrop's been working on a volume of short stories…" She paused for a couple seconds. "I seem to recall one of them is about an artists' commune. A jealous member is killing off the other artists."

"Anybody in the group who tends to be jealous of the others?" Kate asked.

"Doris," was Betty's immediate reply.

"How about Winthrop herself?" Rose asked.

"Jill's a hard person to read," Betty said. "She's very private. It was like pulling teeth sometimes to get her to talk about what she was writing. Which after all is the whole point of the group, to hash out our ideas with other writers."

"Could we have a life-imitating-art scenario here, perhaps?" Rob said.

The doorbell rang before the others could respond. He got up to answer it.

Mrs. Carroll stepped into the apartment and stood by the breakfast bar. She was clenching and unclenching her hands, her expression an odd mix of anxiety and anger. "I'm afraid you will all have to leave."

"Excuse me," Rob said into the stunned silence.

"The rules clearly state that no one who is not related to a resident by blood or marriage can stay in a resident's apartment for more than one week. This has been going on for a week now, so you all need to leave."

"Mrs. Carroll," Rob said, in a matter-of-fact tone, "first of all, my wife and I *are* related to my aunt, and secondly, this isn't exactly a routine visit."

"Well, I can't allow you to go on asking questions, bothering the residents, and keeping everything stirred up." Her voice rose, an hysterical edge to it. "I've had four residents move out, and several more have given me notice that they're leaving. When I called people on the waiting list to take their places, all but one turned me down."

"Mrs. Carroll," Kate said, in as gentle a tone as she could muster. "We're not the problem. People are being murdered. We're trying to help the police figure out who the murderer is."

"But you're not helping." The woman was almost in tears. "You're just making it worse. Keeping everybody upset." She wrung her hands.

Betty stood up. "How dare you come in here and tell my guests they have to leave. This is my home!"

"I'm sorry, Mrs. Franklin, but I'm supposed to keep everything calm around here. I can't have all this trouble." The woman took a deep breath and straightened her back. "I must insist that your guests leave."

Fire flashed in Betty's eyes but before she could respond, Rob said, "Mrs. Carroll, you have no legal standing to do that. Residents have the right to have guests and we have the blessing of the lead detective on the case."

"Well, we'll see about that. I'm going to call our lawyers." The director turned and left in a huff.

As Rob closed the door and flipped the new deadbolt, Kate asked, "Can she make us leave?"

Rob turned back toward them, his expression grim. "I don't know. It's a bit of a gray area. Hopefully we'll catch a break before she catches up with her lawyers."

But a big break in the case was not in the cards that morning. They had to settle for several little ones.

Most of the doors they knocked on went unanswered, despite the rustling noises they frequently heard behind them. As the rumor mill spread and exaggerated the details of the murders, residents were becoming more wary about opening their doors to strangers.

Kate and Skip had been able to eliminate Janet Maccabe. She had moved slowly around her apartment, complaining about her arthritis. It was highly unlikely she could have been the intruder who had gotten away from Skip, and then Rose and Mac as well.

Her reaction when they'd asked about chloroform had been mild curiosity. "Do they still make that?"

Jill Winthrop was another story. She lived on the third level of Betty's building. She'd become rather nervous as the interview progressed, fingering the string of pearls at her throat. She was tall and slender, a prim-looking woman wearing an old-fashioned shirtwaist dress, with short, curly gray hair bracketing her wrinkled face. She'd adamantly denied that her husband had ever brought home any chloroform or other supplies from the VA hospital.

When Kate brought up the subject of her writing, the woman became resistant. "I don't discuss my work."

"Other than with the writers' group," Kate said.

"Not even there, if I could help it. It's too easy for one's ideas to be plagiarized, as we have now seen happen."

Kate resisted the temptation to defend Betty. She was convinced the plagiarism had been accidental. But now was not the time to try to explain source amnesia to this woman.

Instead she said, "Betty told us one of your stories was about an artists' commune—"

Mrs. Winthrop stood up. "You'll have to excuse me. I have a doctor's appointment in twenty minutes. I must get ready."

As they headed down the fire stairs to meet the others for

lunch in Betty's apartment, Skip said, "I believe Mrs. Winthrop merits closer scrutiny."

Kate agreed.

~~~~~~~

Mac and Rose walked along the secluded stretch between the recreation center and Betty's building, discussing the results of the only two interviews they had successfully conducted that morning.

After looking around to make sure no one was in sight, Mac took Rose's hand. She flashed him one of her beautiful smiles. After all these months, he still went all soft inside at the sight of them. He grinned back at her.

Mac glanced down at the sidewalk and noticed a black tire mark.

Some old geezer's one reckless driver.

He turned to Rose and opened his mouth. Before words could form on his lips, an engine roared.

Rose looked over her shoulder. In the next instant she was shoving him off the sidewalk and diving after him. Together they rolled several times across the grass.

The engine gunned. Tires squealed.

Mac leapt to his feet. The car was already over fifty feet away and moving fast into the sun. He squinted, but could only make out the first two letters of the license plate.

"You okay?" he asked Rose, still watching the departing vehicle.

"Yeah," she said from beside him. "You get the plate?"

Mac shook his head. "Just D-P. Older car, I think."

Rose nodded. "Engine sounded like it could've been a V-8."

"Think that was intentional?"

Rose thought for a moment. "Maybe."

"Funny thing is…" Mac pointed down to the two tire marks on the sidewalk, the original and a fresh one. "I was about to say that somebody 'round here's a careless driver."

CHAPTER SEVENTEEN

The group again gathered in the living room. Rose and Mac were the last to arrive. Returning to his armchair after letting them in, Rob glanced over at Kate, who was, of course, sitting next to Canfield on two of the dining room chairs.

Her expression was neutral, too neutral.

Liz was helping Aunt Betty in the kitchen. As she worked, she filled them in on her computer research that morning. "I found out that Carla Baxter's undergraduate degree was in chemistry. She started out pursuing that field in her graduate work but then switched to math. So she might know how to get chloroform."

She brought the plate of sandwiches over and put it down on the coffee table. "I checked into Alice Carroll's background as well. I thought her little tizzy fit this morning a bit of an over-reaction, so I did some digging. She was a nurse until ten years ago, when she came here as an administrator. Worked in an assisted living and hospice facility. They had several suspicious deaths. Folks who were terminal but who died sooner than was expected. Local police were starting to suspect they were mercy killings by one of the staff, but could never prove anything. Shortly after that, Carroll resigned."

"So are you thinking she had something to do with the murders here?" Rob asked.

Liz shrugged as she passed out glasses of iced tea. "I don't know about that. But it does give her a strong reason to want us to stop investigating. She probably feared we would dig this up."

"And ironically," Kate said, "she brought that on by drawing attention to herself. She seemed rather hung up on keeping the peace. Is it possible she got wind of Doris's threat to sue Betty and went to talk her out of it and…"

"Things got out of hand," Skip said. "She certainly seems like the type who could come unglued easily."

Rob caught himself as he was about to scowl at the man. Now he was finishing Kate's sentences.

Turning to his aunt, he asked, "How well do you know Mrs. Carroll?"

Aunt Betty shook her head. "Not very, but I do know the woman's a wimp. I can see her going to talk to Doris, and maybe hitting her if Doris provoked her. And Doris was good at provoking people. But I doubt Alice Carroll has it in her to stab somebody."

"And why would she kill Frieda?" Kate said. "If she's trying to smooth things over, keep things calm, murdering people is not exactly the best way to accomplish that goal."

"Maybe Frieda found out something that would link her to Doris's death," Rose said.

Skip grabbed another half sandwich off the plate on the table. "Or... Gossips are good at weaseling out information. They make great informants for the police. Maybe Frieda found out about the suspicions regarding Carroll as a mercy killer."

Kate's eyes widened. "That would be a good motive."

"And if she was killing the people there," Skip said, "it wouldn't be that hard for her to justify killing old people here, to protect herself and her job."

Kate nodded. "Once someone's rationalized taking a life, it gets easier to rationalize again."

Liz waved a hand in the air, part of her sandwich in it. "But could she have been the intruder last night?"

Rose looked skeptical. "She's about the right build and height. And she's what, maybe fifty. I guess with enough adrenaline pumping she could've gotten away from us."

Aunt Betty shook her head. "I have trouble imagining Alice Carroll breaking in and attacking me."

"People can do things that are fairly out of character," Skip said, "when they feel threatened, and desperate enough."

Kate nodded vigorously, her mouth full of food. She quickly swallowed. "And if the attempt against you had been successful, Betty, your suicide–"

"Complete with remorseful note," Skip threw in.

Kate nodded again. "The case would've been closed, and things would've quieted down."

Rob suppressed another frown. "She should go on our suspect list."

"But how do we go about investigating her?" Kate said. "I doubt she'll give any of us the time of day now."

Liz grinned at Skip. "Mr. Handsome here might be able to charm her into talking to him."

Skip shrugged. "I can try."

"We caught up with Mrs. Berkley," Mac reported. "Somethin's off about her. Wouldn't let us in. Came out in the hall. Said the place was a mess. Claimed she didn't have much to do with Doris or Frieda."

"What's she look like?" Kate asked. "Could she have been the intruder last night?"

Rose nodded. "About your height. Built a bit sturdier. Looked to be in her sixties, maybe."

"They're a May-December couple," Aunt Betty commented. "Mr. Berkeley's in his eighties."

"She's a tough-lookin' broad," Mac said.

Kate crumpled up her napkin. "But we've got no motive for her except that Doris flirted with her husband."

"We also talked to Mrs. Thompson," Rose said. "Don't think she's fast enough to be our perp, but we got her talking about some of the others. She said Mrs. Berkeley tends to be very protective of her husband."

"That jives with something Janet Maccabe told us," Kate said. "She called Mrs. Berkeley controlling. Said she hardly ever lets her husband even talk to anybody, male or female."

Mrs. Winthrop wouldn't tell us much of anything," Skip said, "but she acted nervous."

Rob leaned forward. "Okay, she stays on our list for now. I think Kate and I should interview Carla Baxter again. See if, with her chemistry background, she knows how to get her hands on chloroform. Rose picked up on something strange about her. Maybe Kate can figure out what it is."

Afraid to make eye contact with Kate, he prayed she didn't misunderstand his motives. He wasn't trying to keep her from Skip this time, but somehow he had to get things back on an even keel with her.

From across the circle, she said, "That's a good idea, Rob."

He glanced up. Her expression was still neutral.

~~~

They walked along the hot sidewalk between the two buildings. Kate was trying to think of something to say to break the awkward silence. Rob held the door to Baxter's building open for her.

"I hope Baxter's home," she said as she stepped past him. Lame, but the only thing she could come up with.

The math professor was home. When she answered the door, Kate explained who they were. Baxter escorted them into her living room area.

Kate was having serious *deja vu* since all the apartments were laid out basically the same as Betty's, but in Baxter's the decorating could best be described as Early Shabby.

"Would you like some coffee?"

"Yes, thank you." Kate gave the older woman her warmest smile.

She watched Baxter as she moved around her kitchen making the coffee. She was a tall, big-boned woman. The baggy knit shirt and loose jeans she wore made her look even bigger. Her face was free of make-up and her straight gray hair was cut in a short and not very becoming style. The word *frumpy* came to mind.

Baxter brought over a tray of mismatched mugs and sat it

down on a pile of dusty professional journals on an end table. She passed the mugs around and offered cream and sugar.

Kate took a sip of coffee. It was quite good. "Dr. Baxter–"

The woman raised her eyebrows. "I don't usually use my professional title here at the Villages." Her lips pressed together into an unhappy line. "How did you know I have a doctorate?"

"Please forgive us for being nosy," Kate said. "But under the circumstances, we felt the need to research people's backgrounds."

Baxter blanched, then struggled to hide her dismay. "How can I help with your inquiries?" she said in a formal tone.

Kate and Rob asked her several questions about her impressions of the other suspects on their list. Regardless of who asked the question, Baxter addressed her answer to Kate. The woman's expression had relaxed a little, but she still sat stiffly in her chair.

Kate leaned forward slightly. "In our research, it was discovered that…" She intentionally paused for a beat and saw what she'd expected. Baxter tensed. "You'd originally majored in chemistry as an undergraduate."

Undisguised relief on her face, Dr. Baxter laughed a fake little laugh. "Oh, yes, I did start out in chemistry. But I soon discovered I was much more fascinated by the statistics involved in the research, than in the research itself. I shifted gears in my graduate studies and have never regretted it." The woman's ease increased with each word. "I had a very successful and satisfying academic career."

Kate gave her another warm smile. "Well, Dr. Baxter, the detective isn't allowing us to give out any details, but chloroform was used in some of these crimes. What can you tell us about that chemical?"

The professor leaned forward and launched into a description of the chemical make-up, uses and hazards of chloroform, including its official name, trichloromethane. She aimed her remarks at Kate, virtually ignoring Rob's presence.

When she ran down, Kate asked, "How difficult is it to get chloroform?"

"Oh, an individual can't, at least not legally. The black market is another matter. But universities and other institutions that have a legitimate reason for needing it can purchase it. There are forms to fill out, of course."

"You mentioned a black market," Rob spoke up. "How might one go about getting chloroform other than through legal channels?"

Dr. Baxter turned toward him. "I wouldn't know." Her voice was chilly.

"Of course, you wouldn't," Kate said, in a conciliatory tone. "But anything you could tell us about how someone might have access to chloroform, that would be very helpful."

Baxter looked at Kate and shook her head. "I wish I could help you there, but it's been decades since I was a chemistry student. I know a black market for such chemicals exists, but that's really all I can tell you about it. I'm sorry."

"Well, thank you for all this information. It's very helpful," Kate said, even though they already knew most of it from Liz's research.

Keeping her voice gentle, she changed the subject. "Frieda McIntosh told me, the day before she died, that she had talked to you about the possibility that Betty Franklin had killed Mrs. Blackwell. Do you recall that conversation?"

The woman bristled, sitting up straighter in her chair. "The police asked me about that already, and so did those other two friends of yours."

Kate said nothing.

Under her constant but sympathetic gaze, Baxter deflated a bit. "Frankly, I'm not sure anymore who said what first."

"Did you tell Detective Lindstrom that?" Rob said, also in a gentle voice.

"Yes, the second time he came around," Baxter answered him, then turned back toward Kate. "I feel bad about... I'm afraid my memory's starting to slip some."

Kate gave her another sympathetic look, genuine this time.

"Actually remembering who said what in a conversation is sometimes difficult at any age, and it's human nature to trust our memories more than we should. Thank you for admitting to Detective Lindstrom that you might have mis-remembered."

She rose from her chair. "And thank you for your time, Dr. Baxter. You've been very helpful."

Baxter stood up. "You're certainly welcome. I'm glad to have been of help," she said warmly to Kate, then added as an obvious afterthought, "Uh, nice to meet you, Mr. Franklin."

They were quiet until they were out of the building and away from eavesdropping ears. Then Rob said, "Okay, that was strange. What the hell was going on there? Oh, and by the way, you're a damn good interviewer. All these years I've known you, I don't think I've ever seen you in action like that."

"Thank you," Kate said, grateful mainly that he was finally loosening up and acting more natural with her. "As to what was going on there, she doesn't like men. That much was obvious. And she definitely puts out different vibes toward women than she does toward men."

"Vibes, smibes. She mostly ignored me."

"I really hate to speculate about this, but it occurs to me that Dr. Baxter may be a lesbian."

Rob stopped walking. "Really? Was that why she was watching you so closely, to see if you were interested in her."

Kate shook her head as they started walking again. "No, I don't think so. I think she was worried about what we might have found out about her. Could be she's still in the closet and she's afraid of being outed."

"Even though it wouldn't matter all that much these days."

"I don't know about that with this older crowd. Those around her age would probably have mixed reactions–many accepting, others not so much so, but still willing to let her be. But not all the folks in their seventies and eighties would be that tolerant."

She shoved damp curls off of her forehead. "We tend to think of the residents here as one homogenous group, but there are actually two generations represented. The folks in their eighties are old enough to be the parents of the ones in their sixties."

Rob rubbed his chin. "Okay, that's a somewhat mind-boggling thought, but you're right. Twenty years constitutes a generation."

"Anyway, she has a secret," Kate said. "I'm just speculating that it might be about her sexual orientation. The question is whether or not she'd be afraid enough of having her secret revealed to commit murder? Doris and/or Frieda could have somehow found out whatever it is… "Wait a minute."

Kate stopped walking. She stared into space, reaching for a memory. "Monday, when I talked to Frieda, she said something… At first, she didn't want to tell me who was assuming Betty was the killer. I thought at the time it was strange for a gossip to suddenly get coy. And when I convinced her to tell me who it was, she said that she and Carla Baxter were, quote, 'talking about something else' when the issue of Betty's guilt came up."

"Something that Baxter then asked Frieda to keep to herself," Rob said.

"But I doubt Frieda would have been able to resist gossiping about it, and Baxter probably knew that. So we're back to, is it a secret worthy of murder to keep it quiet?"

"I strongly suspect Baxter could get her hands on chloroform if she wanted to," Rob said. "Her disclaimers about the black market aside, she knew a little too much about it. Hard to believe she was reaching back several decades to her undergraduate studies for that knowledge."

"Could she have been the intruder the other night?"

Rob thought for a moment. "She's about the right height but my impression was of a slimmer person. Of course, we only got a quick look at him or her, before they took off."

"And you said the intruder was wearing a black jacket and ski mask. Baxter might look thinner in that than she did in the baggy clothes she's wearing today."

~~~

Baxter's was the last successful interview of the afternoon.

No one else answered their door.

The others had similar luck. Gathered in Aunt Betty's living room at the end of the day, they commiserated with each other's frustration. Rob filled them in on the interview with Carla Baxter.

He watched as Aunt Betty wrote *Has a secret Frieda probably knew about* next to Baxter's name on her chart of suspects.

Canfield reported going to the administration building but Mrs. Carroll was not in her office. "I tried to get Morris to come out of his lair," he said, "so I could ask him about chloroform, but he refused to come to the door."

"Sure he was home?" Mac said.

"Yeah, I could hear movement inside the apartment."

"I found out something interesting," Liz said, "when I was researching the Berkeleys. They moved to this town and opened their hardware store twenty years ago. They don't seem to have existed before then."

Eyebrows shot up around the room.

"Don't know what that means," she continued, "but I'm going to do some more poking around tomorrow. Aunt Betty, is there any way to get pictures of these people?"

"Oh yes, dear. The community has a pictorial directory. They update it every couple years. To help people learn the names and faces of new residents, I think, as well as giving us contact information for each other."

"That's a nice touch. This really is a good place to retire," Liz said.

"It is." Aunt Betty's face fell. "Or at least it used to be."

"It will be again," Rob tried to reassure her.

The doorbell rang and he got up to answer it. What he looked through the peephole, he sucked in his breath.

A grim-faced Lindstrom was smacking a folded official-looking paper against his palm, with a uniformed officer hovering behind him. Would the man be so callous as to arrest his aunt this late in the day, when it would be difficult to schedule a bail hearing before the next day?

The thought of his aunt spending the night in jail made the blood drain from Rob's face. For a brief moment, he considered not opening the door.

Lindstrom rapped sharply against the wood. Rob jumped. Reluctantly he unlocked and opened the door.

The man didn't even bother to say hello. He handed over the paper.

Rob glanced down and tried to hide his relief. "It's a search warrant," he told the others, as Lindstrom directed the officer toward the den.

The detective headed for Betty's bedroom. Rob followed the uniformed officer, hoping a lawyer standing over him would discourage him from making a mess as he searched.

A few minutes later, Rob heard Lindstrom's voice. "How did you happen to come by this, Mrs. Franklin?"

He raced back into the living room. The detective was holding up a clear evidence bag containing a piece of silver and turquoise jewelry.

"Oh my, I forgot I had that," Aunt Betty said before Rob could stop her. "Frieda lent it to me months ago. I had an interview with someone from the local TV station and she was helping me decide what to wear."

Tears filled his aunt's eyes and her voice dropped to a whisper. "She insisted I wear her necklace because it matched the suit we picked out."

Lindstrom was giving her a skeptical look when the uniform returned to the room. The detective gestured with his head, and the officer moved into the kitchen. He quietly began going through drawers and cabinets.

Lindstrom turned back to Aunt Betty and opened his mouth.

Kate jumped in. "Was that the same suit you wore for Liz and Rob's anniversary party?"

"Yes, dear."

Kate and Liz exchanged a look. Liz stood and headed for the bedroom. "Be right back." In less than a minute, she came out again, holding up a suit on a hanger. The tweed fabric was navy, burgundy and turquoise.

Lindstrom didn't look happy.

Kate gave him a sympathetic look that Rob suspected was quite intentional. "Was there anything else missing from Frieda McIntosh's apartment, Detective?" she said.

After a moment of hesitation, he said, "Her daughter thinks there are three pieces of jewelry missing, all fairly valuable."

"So the killer could have stolen the other two," Rob said. "Or Frieda might have lent them to other friends. I take it you did not see the other pieces in my aunt's jewelry box?"

Lindstrom frowned at him.

"Was one of them a pearl necklace, by any chance?" Kate asked.

Lindstrom's head jerked around toward her. "Yes. How did you know?"

Kate reported on the interview with Jill Winthrop, including the fact that she was nervously fingering a pearl necklace the whole time.

Lindstrom made notes in his pad without commenting.

The others filled him in on the rest of what they had found out that day.

The uniformed officer, working around where they were sitting, had managed to discreetly search the rest of the living and dining areas. He shook his head slightly when Lindstrom looked his way.

"Thank you," was all the detective said to them. He and the officer headed for the door.

Once it was closed behind them, Rob let out his breath. "Okay, folks, let's head back to the motel for dinner and a good night's sleep."

"Rose and me'll stay here," Mac said. "In case the perp tries to break in again."

"Thanks, Mac. We'll take a fresh look at things in the morning."

But by morning they would be dealing with a whole new scenario.

CHAPTER EIGHTEEN

As Kate headed for his Explorer, Skip noticed Rob was staring at her back. He was careful not to make eye contact with the other man.

They were on Columbia Avenue, when Kate said, "I wish they had a different kind of restaurant at the motel. I'm not overly fond of Indian food."

She'd given him the perfect opportunity. Spotting the sign he'd noticed that morning, Skip swung his truck into the parking lot of Florentino's restaurant.

"Skip, I'm not having dinner with you."

"Why not? You just said you'd like something other than Indian food."

"Because it's too soon for me to date, that's why not."

He gave her his most innocent look. "Who said anything about a date? This is handy and we're both hungry, so might as well eat together, as friends. You go out to lunch with Rob all the time."

Kate stared at him for a moment. "True, but us not showing up…" Her voice trailed off.

Skip could guess at her thoughts. She didn't want to aggravate the situation with Rob.

To hell with Rob Franklin. He wanted to spend some time with this woman, away from the others and not focused on the investigation for a change.

"Give them a call. Tell them we saw this place and decided to stop. Ask if they want us to bring them anything." When she didn't move or say anything, he added, "Kate, you're the one who's making this a big deal. I just want to have a decent meal, with a friend, and away from all the scowling. Be nice to relax for a while."

Kate finally gave him a small nod. She took out her cell phone. Her finger hovered over it for a moment, then she punched in a number.

Skip heard Liz's booming voice answer on the other end.

Kate told her that they weren't in the mood for Indian food so they'd stopped at another restaurant. "You want us to bring you some carry-out?"

Liz's muffled voice, rumbled from the phone. Then he caught a few clear words. "…bring…two steaks, medium, with…" The rest was indecipherable.

Kate pulled the phone away from her face and stared at it for a second, then put it back to her ear. "Okay, who are you and what have you done with my friend?"

Skip snickered, remembering that Liz was a bit of a health nut.

Booming laughter, then Liz said something he couldn't make out.

Kate disconnected.

"What was that last part?"

She hesitated, then turned to him. "She said she figured if we fed Rob some red meat, maybe he'd be less likely to take a chunk out of you."

"Liz doesn't miss much, does she?"

"No, she doesn't," Kate said. "Come on, let's eat. I'm starved."

~~~~

After they gave the waitress their food order, Skip selected a bottle of wine with enough ease to tell her that he knew his way around a wine list.

"I thought this was a *non*-date," Kate mock scolded when the waitress had left.

"What, after the day we've had–make that the week we've had–you're objecting to a little liquid tranquilizer?"

"Hard to believe it's been a week since I fell down the rabbit hole into this strange and scary place."

"At least nobody's tried to drop any pots on us lately," Skip said.

Kate pulled a bread stick from the basket the waitress had left on the table. "Lucky for us you happened to look up when you did."

"Not luck really. It was what you said the other day. I had this sudden feeling that I should look up. I've learned to pay attention to those feelings, but I never realized before that they actually have some basis in something our senses have picked up on. I wonder what it was. Maybe the sound of the pot scraping against the railing."

"Or a shift in the light, a shadow cast by the pot," Kate said.

The waitress arrived with the wine. She showed Skip the bottle. He glanced at the label and nodded.

"You told Lindstrom you were nervous about it later, but you didn't seem all that scared at the time," he said to Kate.

As the waitress worked on pulling the cork, Kate answered the implied question. "I did have a little bit of a delayed reaction later. But when it was happening, by the time I realized what was going on, the risk had already passed."

Skip took a small sip of the proffered half glass of wine, then nodded again. The waitress poured Kate a glass, then topped off Skip's, leaving the bottle in an ice bucket on the end of the table.

Kate noted it was a white wine to complement the shrimp fettuccini she had ordered, rather than a red, which would have gone better with Skip's steak. She took a sip. It was a crisp, light Chardonnay. "Nice choice."

"Thanks," Skip said. "You don't scare that easily, do you, Kate?"

She took another sip of wine as she contemplated his question. Her muscles began to relax. "Oh, I think I scare about as easily as most people, but I try not to let fear be the deciding factor. I don't want it to control my actions. I guess a big guy like you doesn't have to be scared of much."

Skip shrugged. "I probably don't scare as easily as most guys, which is one part my size and one part my personality."

"You have a fearless personality?"

"Heck, no. Only fools are completely fearless."

"And psychopaths," Kate pointed out.

"Yeah, and I like to think I'm neither of those. But I'm pretty unflappable. My dad was the same way."

"Serves you well in your work, I'll bet, to be able to keep your head in a crisis." Kate's brain was madly scrambling for a good segue into a discussion of other personality traits.

"Most definitely," he said.

The waitress arrived with a tray. She slipped a salad in front of each of them, then left again.

Kate picked up her fork. "So you don't get scared easily. How about angry?"

Okay, that was a little lame.

"The other day was the first time I've ever seen you lose your temper," she added.

Skip gave a low chuckle. "Oh, I get mad every few years, just to keep in practice."

"Every few years?" She was trying to keep her tone light. "When was the last time?"

He took a bite of salad without answering her. His expression sobered as he chewed and swallowed. "Four years, ten months and thirteen days ago."

"Wow! You keep that close track of every time you lose your temper?"

"Not every time. Just that time. It was the day my father died."

The ache in her heart took Kate's breath away for a second.

"Oh, Skip, I'm so sorry." She covered his hand, lying on the table, with her own. "I didn't mean to stir up something painful."

"It's okay." He turned his hand over and wrapped long fingers around hers.

Heat and energy jolted through her. She tried to jerk her hand back.

He held on. "Someday I'll tell you about it," he said in a low voice, "but not tonight, if you don't mind."

The sensation in her hand mellowed to a slow wave of warmth flowing between their palms. "No, I don't mind." She squeezed his hand, then tugged.

He let hers go.

Neither of them commented on what had just happened. Kate dropped her gaze to her plate, trying to sort out her jangled emotions.

Relief was one of them. The timing fit. He had to be referring to the blow-up with his boss when he'd quit the state troopers. She didn't need to hear the details. She knew the sanest of human beings could go a little crazy when a beloved parent dies.

But what the hell was that other thing, that energy that had passed between them? It wasn't just the zing of sexual attraction. And the empathy she'd felt, it was more intense than any she'd ever experienced before. Which was saying something, since the ability to empathize was an essential tool of her trade.

I already care about this man, she admitted to herself.

But she was also afraid of him. No, not of him. Of the potential for a connection with him. *That* was downright terrifying. One could lose oneself in a connection that strong.

Another reason why it's too soon.

Rob had been right about one thing. Grief and loneliness made her too vulnerable right now.

Skip had his head slightly down, pretending he was concentrating on his salad. But she could tell he was watching her through the veil of brown hair that had flopped down in front of his eyes. He looked up and scraped the hair back with long fingers. "Are you okay?"

"Yeah, I was just…thinking about some things," she said softly.

"Anything you can share?"

She shook her head, then gave him a small smile. "Someday. Not tonight."

He moved his hand toward hers, then aborted the action when the waitress arrived with their entrees.

Kate placed the order for two steak dinners to go.

Skip topped off their wine glasses, then cut off a bite of his steak.

She ate some of her shrimp fettuccine. It was delicious.

She was looking at her plate, twirling more noodles onto her fork, when he said, "I think I need to talk to Rob."

Her head jerked up. "No!"

He held up his hands, palms out. "Please hear me out. I would bring it up real casually. Say that I know what good friends you are and I want to reassure him that I'd never do anything to hurt you."

She shook her head vehemently but he kept talking. "It's a guy thing, Kate. I bring it up. We talk it out man to man, slap each other on the back, then it's all good."

He put down his fork and leaned toward her. "I know how important Rob is to you. I don't want to have our, uh, friendship come between you two."

Too late, Kate thought, but she couldn't tell him that Rob had already put a strain on the friendship by checking him out.

"He's not going to bring it up," Skip said. "He's just going to keep scowling at me. As the intruder in his territory, it's up to me to hold up the white flag and start the peace talks."

Kate stabbed a fat shrimp off her plate and stuffed it in her mouth, to buy herself time to think. She swallowed and took a sip of wine.

"What you're saying makes sense, Skip, but I have my reasons for asking that you not talk to him. At least, not yet. I'm going to have a talk with him myself, something along the lines of 'I love you for caring so much but stop acting like you're my father.'"

His gaze on his plate, he cut a bite of steak into two smaller pieces. "What if that doesn't work?"

He looked up. She saw the anxiety in his eyes as he tried to appear nonchalant.

Dropping his gaze again, he further mangled his steak. He

forked some into his mouth and chewed.

She reached for his hand. "Rob's a reasonable man. He'll come around. It'll be okay."

He stopped chewing. Leaning forward, he tugged her toward him.

The food in his mouth saved her. While he quickly chewed and swallowed, she pulled back and extracted her hand from his.

"And if he doesn't come around?"

She wasn't sure how to answer him. Finally she said, "My life is my own."

He nodded slightly and went back to his steak.

They ate in silence for a few minutes.

Deciding it was time to turn to lighter subjects, Kate asked Skip if he had always lived in Maryland. He told her he was from Texas. He'd come to Maryland to study criminal justice at Towson University and had stayed when he'd landed a job with the state police.

"Aha, I thought I caught a hint of Texas in your voice now and again," she said.

"Yes, ma'am," he drawled. "I'm Texan born an' bred." Then in his normal voice, he said, "But I've been in Maryland long enough now, I talk funny like you Northerners."

"Is that where you learned Spanish? In Texas."

"Yup, had a couple Chicano buddies in high school. I wouldn't say I'm fluent but I can get by."

There was something else she was curious about, more than curious. But it would be outrageously bold of her to ask. Then again, his answer could be a deal breaker.

Despite the lip service society gave to the idea that looks shouldn't matter, she knew people tended to be attracted to romantic partners who were at their own level of physical attractiveness. She could still remember her social psychology professor talking about the research on the subject, and then saying how this was good news for everyone, that even if you were butt ugly, there was still someone out there for you. The class had laughed.

Oh, what the hell.

If this man wanted a relationship with her, he might as well get used to the way she was. He'd either handle it, or not. She smiled a little as she recalled Mac's pub-owner father saying, *Straight up, no ice, no soda, that's our Katie.*

Skip had been watching her again, through his veil of hair.

She took a sip of wine to bolster her nerve. "I have another question for you."

"Shoot."

"I think of myself as reasonably attractive but I'm far from beautiful. And I would describe you as just shy of an Adonis. So how come you're attracted to me?"

Skip dropped his fork and sat back in his chair. "Phew! You don't mess around on non-dates, do you? I'm a little afraid to find out what you might say on a real date."

He skimmed the hair out of his eyes, then gave her a long appraising look. "You're right. I would not call you beautiful, at least not in the classic sense of the word. But you're a very attractive woman. Nice features, good skin–"

"Good heavens, he's going to be prying my mouth open in a minute to look at my teeth."

"Hey, when a woman fishes for a compliment, she should not get snitty about how it is delivered."

"Is snitty a word?"

"It is now," he said. "Are you going to let me finish?"

"Of course. You were saying how attractive I am." She gave him an exaggerated flutter of her eyelashes.

Skip chuckled, but then his voice turned serious. "To me you are. Pretty much the most attractive woman I know."

"Oh, come on. With that physique and handsome face." Kate blushed a little when she realized what she was saying. "You mean to tell me you don't have beautiful women flocking to your doorstep all the time."

Annoyance flashed in his eyes. "Do you think I'm that shallow?"

Oops! I've offended him.

She shook her head. "No, that's not what—"

He held up his hand and leaned forward. His expression softened. "Okay, let me clarify two things. First, inside this Adonis beats the heart of a scrawny sixteen-year-old who got the crap beaten out of him because of his goofy name. Second, I am attracted to women, not Barbie dolls. When I find a woman attractive, it is because of the whole package."

He stopped to appraise her again for a moment, his lips curling up on the ends. "The adorable face, the nice figure, the *sound teeth*."

She smiled.

"The intelligent mind and the… hmm, I think in your case the word would be *refreshing*, the refreshing personality."

"Ding, ding, ding! Right answer, Mr. Canfield! And your prize is several more non-dates with your friend, Kate Huntington."

Skip burst out laughing. "Kate, you are…"

"Refreshing?" she suggested.

"This time I was thinking incorrigible." He grinned at her.

They ate for a few minutes in companionable silence.

Skip topped off her wine glass but left his half full. "I was serious, Kate, about the scrawny sixteen-year-old trapped inside. I don't know if it's true for people in general, but for me that image of myself, that I developed as a teenager, is still there. I've looked like this for two decades now." He pointed to his muscular chest. "But I still do a double-take sometimes when I see myself in a mirror. It's like I momentarily forget that I'm not still five-eight and a hundred and thirty pounds."

"That makes sense." Kate realized that although he joked about it, his adolescence had left some emotional scar tissue. "Our teens are when we're forming our sense of identity, and body image is a huge part of that for kids. I was incredibly self-conscious about my hair. Straight hair was in vogue, and no matter what I did, my curls were out of control. My mother wouldn't let me get it straightened. She said God had given me a beautiful head of curls and straightening them would be a sin."

Skip reached across the table and briefly fingered one of her dark curls. "She was right," he said softly.

Sweet Jesus! This man's touch could even make her hair follicles tingle.

Kate dropped her eyes to her plate. She reached for her wine glass and took a healthy gulp. To change the subject, she said, "So sixteen plus two decades. You're thirty-six?"

"Thirty-eight. Missed being a baby-boomer by just a few years."

Kate breathed a soft sigh of relief. He was only a year younger than she was.

The waitress delivered the to-go meals and the check.

After a short tussle over who would pay, Skip won the argument. "Kate, this may be a non-date, but *I'm* paying. It was my idea to stop here to eat."

As they walked across the parking lot to his truck, Kate suddenly stopped. Skip turned toward her.

She smiled up at him. "Skip, this was the best first non-date I've ever had."

CHAPTER NINETEEN

Conversation over their room-service breakfast the next morning was stilted. Only Betty seemed oblivious to the undercurrents, or maybe she was pretending not to notice.

The previous evening when they'd returned to the motel, Kate had knocked on Liz and Rob's outside door. Liz had answered. Kate had handed over the bag with their dinners and then ducked into the suite, thinking she'd avoided Rob.

But he was sitting on the sofa in the suite's living room. He'd stood, given them a stiff nod, and went through the door to his room.

They were halfway through breakfast when Rob's cell phone rang. He answered it, listened for a moment, then swore under his breath. "We'll be there soon." He disconnected.

Fear clogged Kate's throat. "What's wrong? Are Mac and Rose okay?"

"They're fine, but there's been another murder."

Her stomach clenched. "Oh, no!" She dropped her fork on the table.

"A man this time. No official release of the name yet, but Mac overheard a couple people say Jeff–"

"Jeff?" Betty cried out. "Jeff Morgan?"

Kate, sitting next to her, leaned over and put an arm around the elderly woman's shoulders. Betty started sobbing into her hands.

Liz moved around the table to kneel on the other side of her chair. "Is he… was he a friend?"

Face still buried in her hands, Betty shook her head. "Not

close friends, no." She raised her head and looked at Liz. "Why would anyone want to harm Jeff? He's one of the kindest people I've ever known." Her face crumpled again. "Why is somebody doing this?"

Kate tightened her arm around Betty's shoulders, sensing the woman's reaction was to more than this man's death. Somebody was turning her safe, well-ordered world into chaos.

Liz patted Betty's arm. "Can I get you anything? What can we do to help?"

"Take me home!"

"Okay," Rob said in a soft voice. "We'll come back here to sleep tonight, but for now, we'll take you home."

At Betty's building, they were blocked from entry by uniformed officers and yellow crime scene tape. When arguing, begging and cajoling didn't work, Kate said, "Could you please tell Detective Lindstrom that Kate Huntington would like to see him? Right away. It's very important."

Rob took his aunt back to sit in their air-conditioned car.

After a few minutes, Sandy Lindstrom came out of the building. Kate rushed toward him.

He scrubbed a hand over his unshaven face. "Somehow good morning doesn't seem like the right thing to say. What can I do for you, Kate?" He was wearing the same suit as the previous day. She wondered how long it had been since he'd been home.

"I'm sorry to pull you away from your investigation, Sandy." She kept her voice low. "But we need to get Mrs. Franklin into her apartment. She's very upset, and has been getting more depressed as this whole thing has dragged out. I'm really getting concerned about her health."

Sandy took her arm and led her out of earshot of the uniforms and some curious residents standing nearby.

Kate caught the look on Skip's face out of the corner of her eye. He was scowling at the detective.

Sheez! Men! But she couldn't deal with that now.

Sandy said, "There's been another death–"

"I know. Mac called and told us."

"Well, this one did a header off the second level onto the atrium's slate floor."

Kate grimaced.

"Yeah." He ran a hand through his hair. "It's pretty gruesome in there. Right now I've got the uniforms keeping everybody in their apartments, and nobody else is supposed to come into the building."

"Isn't there some way we could get her in without her seeing..." Kate's voice trailed off.

"Hmm, there's an emergency exit at the end of the hall by her apartment. No handle on the outside, but I'll go in and open it from the inside. Bring her around to the side of the building."

Kate grabbed his hand and shook it. "Thanks, Sandy. You're a... good man." She'd been about to say a *sweetheart* but decided that would be too encouraging.

Kate raced over to Rob's car. He and Liz escorted Betty to the emergency door while the others trailed behind, Skip carrying the posterboard lists.

~~~~

Rob sank gratefully into one of the armchairs. Damn, he was tired.

Aunt Betty was on the settee with a cup of tea. She seemed more composed now that she was back in her own space.

The others were scattered around the living room, some of them again in the straight-backed chairs from the dining area.

The doorbell rang. Rob groaned.

"I'll get it," Canfield said.

Rob let him.

Canfield bent his knees and lowered his eye to the peephole. "It's Lindstrom."

Rob stifled another groan.

Canfield let the detective in and gestured toward the chair he had just vacated. Then he walked around and stood behind Kate, resting one hand on the back of her chair in a possessive gesture.

Kate didn't seem to notice.

Rob stifled the urge to frown at the younger man. He turned his attention to the detective who was asking Aunt Betty about her association with the newest victim.

By the time she had finished describing a quiet, gentle man, her body was slumping and tears filled her eyes. "Excuse me. I think I'll lie down for a while." Her voice had a tremor in it.

The men stood as she rose and shuffled from the room.

Fear for her health squeezed Rob's heart. He wasn't ready to lose her. He blinked the grit out of his own eyes.

"Is it possible this was a suicide?" Kate asked.

"Possible." Lindstrom settled back onto his chair. "But it would be one heck of a coincidence. Several plants were knocked off the ledge. He could have done that himself if he just dived over, but it would make more sense to lift them down and then climb onto the shelf."

"And there's no guarantee a one-story drop would kill you." Canfield said. "Wouldn't be most people's first choice as a method of committing suicide."

Rob leaned forward in his chair. "May I point out, Detective, my aunt has a solid alibi this time. One of us has been with her day and night, and we've been taking her back to the motel to sleep at night. Not to mention, she has no motive to harm Mr. Morgan."

Lindstrom nodded slightly. But his next words took Rob by surprise.

"Honestly, Mr. Franklin, I'd love to be able to say that this latest crime has cleared your aunt of suspicion. But that would only be true if indeed all the murders are related. There's the possibility that someone else had a reason to kill Jeffrey Morgan and decided now would be a good time to do it, so his death would be blamed on whoever killed the women." The detective scratched his stubbled jaw. "Or the purpose of this murder may have been to throw us off. He doesn't fit the pattern. Different gender, not in the writers' club."

Rob shook his head at the thought of someone taking a life

just to confuse the police. "So with nothing tying this victim to the others, you're basically back to square one." He wasn't able to completely keep the frustration out of his voice.

The detective didn't reply. He looked around the room. "I thank you all for your input but I really don't think you should keep trying to investigate this yourselves. It's gotten way too dangerous for amateurs."

"Lindstrom, this is ridiculous!" Rob snapped at him. "You won't let us take Aunt—"

"Detective," Canfield interrupted, "I'm a licensed PI and I was a Maryland state trooper for eleven years. These two have military and police background as well." He nodded toward Mac and Rose. "We're trained investigators, not amateurs. And Mr. Franklin and Mrs. Huntington are both in professions that require keen observational and analytical skills. Not to mention Mrs. Franklin is a whiz at computer research. Frankly, I think we're a damned formidable team."

Lindstrom looked surprised. "Elizabeth Franklin is a whiz on the computer?"

Liz raised her hand and wiggled her fingers. "This Elizabeth Franklin."

Despite the gravity of the moment, Rob wanted to grin at his wife. Instead he studied Lindstrom's face.

The detective frowned but said nothing. Seconds ticked by. The man looked around the room, his gaze settling on Kate's determined face.

"What are you going to do if we continue investigating, Sandy?" she said. "Arrest us? Rob has an excellent point. If you're not going to let us take his aunt to Maryland, where she would be safe, how can you insist we just sit around and wait?"

Rob remained silent. She'd presented the case as well as he could. He knew cops were notoriously territorial, but his sense of this detective was that he was a reasonable man. And Kate seemed to have some influence with him.

Lindstrom's cell phone rang. He yanked it out of his pocket

and answered it. After a couple cryptic yeahs, he stood up and strode over to the door. "Just be careful," he threw back over his shoulder as he left.

Rob blew out air, then got up to lock the door.

"I don't know about square one," Canfield said. "But we do need to question our prime suspects regarding their association with Jeffrey Morgan."

"I think we need to speed things up here," Rose said. "Before somebody else gets killed. Could be the perp's starting to enjoy his work. How about we split up? Skip, Mac and I, the *trained investigators* in the room." She flashed a grin in Skip's direction. "We each take some of the names of those who need to be questioned."

"And Kate and I will pair up," Rob said.

Mac chuckled. "Pooling your keen observational and analytical skills."

Rob faked a smile. He suspected Canfield's earlier interruption had been intentional. He turned to the man. Pumping as much sincerity as he could into his voice, he said, "Thanks for stopping me from pushing Lindstrom too hard."

Canfield nodded. "No problem."

"Do you think it's safe to leave Liz and Betty here by themselves?" Kate asked.

"With the new lock," Liz said, "I think I can handle guard duty during the day."

Rob leaned forward in his chair. In case his aunt wasn't actually asleep in the next room, he kept his voice low. "I'm worried we may never find the killer now that residents are moving out. I'm going to approach Lindstrom again about letting us take Aunt Betty back to Maryland."

"What if he still refuses?" Liz asked.

"Don't leave the area is really a request," Canfield said, "even though it may be said as an order. The police don't have the authority to enforce it, unless you've been arrested and are out on bail."

"That's my concern," Rob said. "I don't want to get Aunt Betty arrested, which is what I think would happen if we just packed her up and left. And I'm not one hundred percent sure the police don't have the authority here to order suspects to stay put. It tends to be a bit more of a law-and-order type state than Maryland. I've got my staff researching the Pennsylvania statutes for me."

"In the meantime," Canfield said, his voice grim, "we keep looking for the killer. If we get lucky today, you won't have to uproot Betty from her home."

Rob felt a glimmer of gratitude toward the man. He wasn't real sure what to do with that feeling.

Unfortunately they weren't able to begin their new round of interviews until the police and crime scene investigators were finally finished in the atrium, and allowed the building to return to relative normalcy.

Rob's chest tightened as he and Kate walked past the Wet Floor caution signs in the atrium. He grimaced.

Kate averted her eyes.

In Baxter's building, Rob rang her doorbell. After a minute, he rang it again, hiding his impatience behind his court face in case she was checking him out through the peephole.

Kate leaned toward the door. "Thought I heard something. I'll bet she's in there, but doesn't want to talk to us again."

Rob nodded and hit the bell a third time, more to express his irritation than out of any expectation of a response.

As they walked out of the building, Rob spotted a moving van pulled up in front of Aunt Betty's building next door. Beside it, an agitated Mrs. Carroll was talking to an elderly man, who was blatantly ignoring her.

When she saw Rob and Kate she broke off her efforts and raced in their direction. "You have to leave. I won't have you continuing to bother my residents." Her voice was slightly slurred.

Rob thought he smelled alcohol on her breath.

"Mrs. Carroll, there was another murder this morning," Kate

said, exasperation in her voice. "People are moving out because they're afraid they'll be next. It has nothing to do with us."

"But you're making things worse by reminding people." Her voice rose on an hysterical note. "If you don't leave, I'll find a way to make you." She stomped away.

Kate shot Rob a look and shook her head. Then she pivoted back toward Aunt Betty's building.

She jumped and let out a little shriek.

Rob whirled around.

CHAPTER TWENTY

A slender man was standing right behind them.

"Who are you?" Kate blurted out.

He took off his Phillies cap to reveal an egg-shaped, totally bald head, which was a slightly lighter shade of red than his ruddy face. "Sorry, I didn't mean to startle you. I'm Paul Johnson. Live over there." He gestured with his hat toward the building they'd just exited.

"I heard you folks were looking into the murders. I'd like to help if I can. Jeff Morgan was a friend of mine." He returned his baseball cap to his head. "Would you like to go inside? Get out of the heat."

Rob nodded. Kate patted her chest as she followed the two men, willing her racing heart to slow down.

Johnson ushered them into his apartment. It was beautifully decorated with rich mahogany furniture and wing-backed chairs. The artwork on the walls looked like originals.

Their host noticed Kate admiring the furnishings. "My partner was an antiques dealer. He passed away three years ago."

Paul Johnson apparently *was* out of the closet.

After a few minutes of chit-chat about antiques, Kate let Rob take the lead while she observed. As the interview progressed, she had a growing sense of unease. Something about this man was nagging at her.

Again, Jeff was described as a kind, gentle man. Whenever Rob paused for breath, Johnson asked questions about the progress of the investigation, which Rob expertly dodged.

When Rob seemed to be running out of questions, Kate asked, "Mr. Johnson, is there much of a gay community here at The Villages?"

Johnson hesitated before saying, "No. My partner and I were the only openly gay people here."

"Was Jeff gay?" Kate asked.

Johnson let out a small chuckle as he shook his head. "No, what brought us together was loneliness, not shared sexual orientation. Jeff was a widower. He reached out to me when Tim died. He was the only one who did, really. Nobody was rude or anything, and most folks offered their condolences when they saw me. But Jeff made a point of befriending me."

"Do you know if anyone else in the community is gay?" Kate asked.

"If they are, they're still in the closet. Why do you ask?"

Kate shrugged. "No particular reason. Just exploring all angles."

"Is there some reason to think the murderer is gay?" Johnson asked.

No, but one of the suspects might be, and might be worried about being outed."

"Who is that?"

Kate wasn't about to answer that question. "I'd rather not say."

Johnson smiled. "I'm hardly going to hold being gay against someone, Mrs. Huntington."

"Still, it's only speculation on our part, so I'm not comfortable naming names."

Rob thanked the man for his time, and they made their exit. Once outside on the sidewalk, he asked, "So what'd you think of that?"

"I think," Kate said, "that for someone who claimed to be his friend, Mr. Johnson did not know Jeff Morgan very well."

Rob nodded. "That was my take. But the guy sure was nosey about the investigation."

They reached Betty's building, and Rob held the door open for her. Walking through the atrium, Kate was thinking this might be a good time to have that talk with him.

She was bracing herself to suggest they sit down, when Rob said, "Kate, I owe you an–"

Both of their good intentions were thwarted by Detective Lindstrom heading their way.

Rob waved him over. "If you have a minute, Detective, there's something I'd like to discuss with you."

The three of them sat down at the wrought iron table. "We have a rather untenable situation here," Rob said. "The residents are starting to move out and the killer could have been among them–"

Lindstrom interrupted. "We're keeping track of who's left, and where they've moved to."

"Yes, but you've told my aunt that she *can't* leave, and it isn't safe for her to be here by herself. This could drag on for quite a while. We all have jobs and other commitments we need to get back to."

"And it's possible," Kate said, "that the killer has moved out and lied to you about where they were going."

"Which means," Rob said, "that this case may never be solved. Maryland and Pennsylvania have a reciprocity agreement–"

"Mr. Franklin," Lindstrom interrupted again, "I understand your concerns but I can't let your aunt leave the state."

Rob opened his mouth.

Kate put a restraining hand on his arm. "Sandy, we're not just concerned about Betty being attacked again, but also about her stress level. And you don't really have any concrete evidence against her."

Lindstrom gave her a hard look as she lifted her hand from Rob's arm to swipe an errant curl out of her face.

"Depends on your definition of concrete. There are a few too many coincidences here, starting with the fact that Mrs. Franklin had a major dispute with Doris Blackwell the day before she was murdered."

Kate was startled by his sharp tone. This man had denied being the kind of cop who'd arrest someone just to close a case. Now she wasn't so sure she believed him.

"But Betty had no motive to harm Frieda," she said, "much less Jeff Morgan."

"And she has a solid alibi for when Morgan was killed," Rob said.

"What are the sleeping arrangements at the motel?" Lindstrom asked, his voice still brusque.

"We have a suite with a second adjoining bedroom," Kate said. "Rob and Liz are in that room. Betty and I are sharing the suite's bedroom, and Skip Canfield is sleeping in the living room, between us and the door. There's no way Betty could have left the other night without waking us up. Not to mention the fact that she doesn't drive anymore."

"We *do* have cabs in Lancaster."

"There's no way she could have gotten out of the suite," Kate said again, trying to keep her voice calm. "Not without waking Skip up. I know for a fact that he's a very light sleeper."

Too late she realized that was probably the wrong thing to say. Two sets of eyes glared at her.

"And how *exactly* do you know that, Kate?" Lindstrom asked.

Kate sighed. "Sandy, my husband didn't die of natural causes. He was murdered." The detective's face registered shock. "For several weeks after his murder, the killer was stalking Rob and me. Skip was hired by Rob as my bodyguard." She remembered that she'd introduced Skip to the detective as a family friend. "Uh, that's how we all first met him. I personally witnessed him come up out of a sound sleep with his gun in hand, when he heard my father *whispering* across the room."

She turned to Rob. "He was in the recliner in your family room. Ask Liz. She was there."

Rob gave her an apologetic look. She acknowledged it with a small smile.

Lindstrom looked from one to the other. His voice was clipped as he said, "I'll still need to talk to Canfield myself. Have him call me."

Rob's cell phone rang. He pulled it out and glanced at the caller ID. "Excuse me, Detective." He answered the call.

A second later, he jumped up. "I'll be right back." He took several strides away from the table.

Kate watched him talking into the phone, his face and body tense. Anxiety gnawed at her stomach.

"Kate." Sandy Lindstrom's sharp voice pulled her back. "Exactly what is your relationship with Franklin?"

She bristled but managed to catch herself before blurting out that her relationships were none of his business. Choosing her words carefully, she said, "Rob and Liz were *my husband's* and my closest friends, and are still my closest friends. I would not have survived losing him without their support."

Lindstrom's angry face collapsed into chagrin. "I'm sorry, Kate. I was out of line."

She decided to press her advantage, while Rob was out of earshot. "Sandy, you can't possibly believe that Betty Franklin could wrestle with a man and pitch him over that railing. And what about the person who broke into her apartment the other night, while she was back at the motel with us?"

Lindstrom shook his head, his expression still apologetic. "I told you, Kate, I have to explore every angle. I truly wish I could let Mrs. Franklin go with you, but you can't imagine the pressure I'm getting from above. The press is turning ugly on us. The mayor is calling the–"

Rob was suddenly at Kate's side, grasping her upper arm and practically yanking her out of her seat. "We've gotta go. We'll have Canfield call you, Detective."

He race-walked her across the atrium.

"What's the matter?" Kate whispered.

"Don't know. Liz said she couldn't talk about it on a cell phone. She reassured me they were safe, but she sounded very rattled."

They picked up their pace. They both knew that Liz did not rattle easily.

CHAPTER TWENTY-ONE

Rob was surprised when his aunt answered the door. "Nephew," she whispered, as he and Kate stepped into the apartment, "I don't know what's gotten into your wife. She's acting like a nervous Nellie."

Liz was standing in the middle of the living room. She wasn't quite wringing her hands, but she looked like she wanted to.

Rob walked over and wrapped a steadying arm around his petite wife's shoulders. "What's going on, hon?"

"Come look." She led them into the den where her laptop was sitting on Aunt Betty's desk. She pointed to the computer screen.

There was a picture of a woman, probably in her late thirties but she looked like she'd had a rough life. Under it were the words, *Wanted for armed robbery, assault with a deadly weapon, and suspected treasonist activities.* In bold letters at the bottom was *Federal Bureau of Investigation* and a toll-free number.

"I have to admit you were right, hon. I think my computer adventures have come back around to bite me." Liz's words were flippant but her voice was shaky. "I scanned the photos of our mysterious hardware store owners into a new search engine Google just came out with, that has a face-recognition feature."

She pointed to the photo. "This was in the list of results for Mrs. Berkeley. It's possible she didn't exist before coming to Lancaster because she's really Rayanne Caldwell, a member of a paramilitary organization that robbed a bank and set off a bomb in the town hall of Danville, Indiana, twenty-one years ago."

Kate gasped.

Aunt Betty tartly said, "Somehow that doesn't totally surprise me."

"We'd better call the FBI," Liz said. "They may have a cookie on the wanted poster that leads them back to any computer that hits on it."

Rob had every intention of doing so anyway. He took out his cell phone. After giving his reason for calling, he was asked for his location, then told to sit tight. Agents would arrive within the hour.

"I'm going to go head off the others," Kate said. "You don't need a room full of people whose presence you have to explain to the FBI."

Rob nodded, but Liz was still staring anxiously at the computer screen.

Kate looked at him and tilted her head slightly in his wife's direction.

He got the hint. "I'm not all that worried about the feds. Liz didn't do anything wrong, in *this case* at least." He couldn't resist getting in a small dig in about her sometimes questionable computer activities.

Then he relented and gathered her into his arms. "Honey, you were just checking out people who might be involved in what's been going on here. And you happened to stumble on a federal fugitive. Heck, they may give you a medal."

"I have a question, Elizabeth," Aunt Betty said, as Kate headed for the door. "What do cookies have to do with computers?"

Good question, Rob thought, but he wasn't real sure he wanted to know the answer.

~~~~~~~~

Skip stood outside Henry Morris's door. He glanced up and saw Kate coming toward him. Before she could say anything, he whispered, "I've been trying Mac's tactic. Isn't working this time. He's been ignoring me for almost an hour."

Kate whispered back, "There's been a development. We need to stay away from Betty's apartment for a while." She half turned, gesturing for him to follow her. "Mac and Rose are meeting us in the cafeteria."

"Where's Rob?" Skip asked as they started toward the stairs.

"In Betty's apartment."

"Why can't we go there?"

"They're waiting for the FBI."

"The FBI?"

It's complicated. I'd rather not have to explain it twice."

As they headed down the stairs and out into the heat, Kate filled him in on the conversation with Lindstrom. She handed him her phone, after hitting the detective's speed dial number.

Skip confirmed that Betty would not have been able to get past him in the motel suite the previous night. Then he said into the phone, "I saw you had another incident in your other case."

"Yeah, fifteen-year-old girl." Lindstrom's voice was grim.

Skip stifled a curse. The morning paper had given no details about the victim.

"He got careless this time, though," Lindstrom said. "Left some physical evidence behind, a smear of semen and some hair. Hey, thanks for the tip about Fielding. It might just pay off. Brought him in first thing this morning, before he had a chance to line up a bogus alibi with his buddies."

"Have your victims ID'd him?" Skip asked.

"Bastard wore a ski mask, so I don't have enough to hold him. Yet. The lab's working on the hair samples. If it looks like it's Fielding's, he's off the streets, and if the DNA matches, then we've nailed him good."

Skip grinned at the thought. He disconnected and handed the phone back to Kate.

"What'd he say?" she asked.

"About Betty's alibi, not much. Mostly grunted. But he thinks he might be able to nail Fielding for the rapes. And here's an interesting tidbit. The rapist wears a ski mask."

"Ah, like our intruder."

"Yeah, but ski masks are a pretty common way for perps to hide their identity. May not mean the two crimes are related."

"Lindstrom's change in attitude worries me," Kate said. "He seems to be caving to the pressure from above and is now trying to build a case against her."

Skip nodded grimly. "Worries me too. Unfortunately, cops get cynical after a while, and they definitely develop an aversion to coincidences."

In the cafeteria, they found Mac and Rose waiting for them at a table as far away from the few diners as they could get. The only person nearby was a young woman who was clearing away dirty dishes and setting up the tables for dinner.

In a low voice, Kate said, " Liz found out something rather startling about the Berkleys."

When she finished giving them the details, Skip sat back in his chair and let out a soft whistle.

"Maybe the Berkleys are our killers then," Rose said. "Doris and Frieda might have found out their secret."

"But why kill Jeff?" Kate asked.

Rose shrugged. "Maybe he found out, too. Or maybe Lindstrom's right and he was killed by someone else."

"Phew! I'll never assume the elderly lead bland, boring lives again." Skip looked around to make sure the cafeteria employee was out of earshot. "In addition to our best-selling author, a bitchy tease and an outspoken gossip, we have a closeted lesbian academician and now a fugitive from the FBI."

"You forgot your hot-to-trot ex-aerobics teacher," Mac said, his blue eyes twinkling. "Did Mrs. Forsythe do it in the atrium?" he continued in a credible imitation of a British accent.

They all snickered a little guiltily.

"It is starting to sound like a weird version of the game of Clue, isn't it?" Kate said. "And I'm starting to lose track of the players. Wish we had Betty's lists… Or better still maybe we need to make a new chart that shows how these people's lives intersect with each other." She stood up. "I'll be right back."

Skip followed her line of vision to the young woman setting up the tables. She was putting a tablecloth on each one, then tearing off a square of white paper from a large roll to place on top of it, before setting salt and pepper shakers and a small vase with a single flower in the center of the table.

Kate approached the woman and came back with a large square of paper. She laid it out on their table and pulled a pen from her pants pocket.

Skip leaned over and watched her write the victims' names across the top of the paper, and then the suspects in a column down the middle.

"Have I got them all?"

"You forgot Alice Carroll," Rose said.

Kate added her name. Across the bottom, she wrote *access to chloroform* in one corner, *avg. height/build* in the other, and *not weak or slow* in the middle.

"Okay, let's connect the dots." With input from the others, Kate went down the suspect list, drawing lines from their names to any of the victims with who they had a connection.

"I talked to Mrs. Winthrop again this morning," Rose said. "She claimed Frieda lent her the pearls. Lindstrom's confiscated them, by the way. Winthrop still refused to talk about her stories. Said she didn't know Jeff all that well."

Kate drew a line between Jill Winthrop's and Frieda's names. "That reminds me. Rob and I ran into a man who said he was a friend of Jeff's. But he didn't seem to know him as well as he claimed."

Skip frowned. "Was this guy the right height and build to be our intruder?"

Kate gave him a startled look, then nodded. "He's on the thin side, but that wouldn't be very obvious if he was wearing a jacket."

Rose looked at Skip. "He's inserting himself into the investigation."

He smiled approvingly at his protégé. "He could have a motive for doing in Jeff Morgan. Hell, he could've killed the women for all we know. We need to check him out."

Kate added *Paul Johnson* to the suspect list, then drew a line to Jeff.

Skip leaned over the chart. That was the only connection to Jeff so far. Everyone they'd talked to that morning had said they didn't know him well and had no idea who his friends or enemies might be.

"Now then," Kate muttered under her breath as she looked down at the bottom of the paper. A stray curl fell across her cheek.

Without thinking, Skip hooked a finger around the curl and tucked it behind her ear. She kept her eyes on the paper as a blush crept up her neck and into her cheeks.

Rose's eyebrow went up. She and Mac exchanged a look.

Skip avoided eye contact with them, praying Kate wouldn't be mad at him.

She was studiously drawing lines from *access to chloroform* to suspects' names, some solid, some dotted with question marks next to them. She tapped the pen point on *not weak or slow*.

"Hmm, Mr. Berkeley's fairly frail, but you said the wife's not." She drew a line. "Is Henry Morris strong enough to wrestle with another man and pitch him over a railing?"

"Yeah," Rose said. "He's not all that old. In his late sixties. Kinda wiry, like Mac."

Kate added that line and sat back in her chair. "What do you think, folks?"

They all stared at the chart for a full minute.

Skip placed the tip of his index finger on one of the names. "I think that the boring Murphys are the only ones connected to everyone and everything, although a couple of the lines are still dotted."

"Okay, next step." Kate picked up her notepad that she'd consulted a few times while making the chart. She flipped to a fresh page. "Summaries of each suspect. What we know, and what questions still need to be answered about them."

They'd completed summaries for Joe Fielding and the Forsythes when her cell phone rang.

She checked caller ID. "Rob," she told them, then answered the call. "What's going on?...Okay, be there in a few minutes." She disconnected. "The feds are gone."

Putting her phone back in her pocket, she started folding up her chart. "Let's go, Gang. Back to the Bat Cave."

"Dana, dana, dana, dana, Batman," Skip sang softly, pretending to swish an imaginary cape around himself as he stood up.

Mac and Rose fell back a bit from the other two as they walked along the sidewalk. "He musta been smokin' happy tobaccy," Mac said softly, a chuckle in his voice.

"Nah," Rose whispered back, flashing him a smile. "He's just in *looove.*"

CHAPTER TWENTY-TWO

Rob was grinning when he opened the apartment door for them. Everyone trooped in and arranged themselves around the living room. Rose dropped to the floor.

Mac nudged the last two empty chairs closer together, then sat down cross-legged next to Rose on the floor.

Kate felt the heat rising in her cheeks again. She sat in one of the chairs, discreetly scooting it over a couple inches before Skip sat down in the other.

Liz was looking smug. Betty's eyes flashed with excitement.

Kate wondered how long ago the FBI had been established. She had a funny feeling the early years of the agency would be featured in one of Betty's future novels.

"Feds were very grateful for my lovely wife's assistance," Rob said. "They are discreetly staking out the Berkeleys' apartment as we speak, waiting for the appropriate warrants."

"Well, we've been putting our time to good use while you all were dealing with the feds." Kate unfolded the chart and held it up for them to see. "Betty, do you have any more of that posterboard, and maybe some tape?"

"I certainly do," Betty said, and got up to fetch both from the den. Kate moved the magazines and coasters off the coffee table and placed them on the floor underneath it.

When Betty returned with the supplies, Kate laid the posterboard out on the table, then taped the chart to it.

Betty watched her appraisingly. "Young lady," she said in her best schoolmarm voice, "I believe your project should receive a

B plus."

Kate faked a Valley girl accent. "Aw, gee, Mrs. Franklin," she whined. "Like, I thought fer shure you were gonna, like, gimme an *A* on it." She snapped imaginary chewing gum.

Betty grinned at her. "All it needs," she paused dramatically, then pulled a fistful of colored markers out from behind her back, "are these. May I color code it for you, my dear?"

"That would help tremendously. The lines are kinda blurring together."

Betty began to turn the chart into a work of art.

Kate's stomach growled, reminding her that they hadn't actually eaten lunch while they were in the cafeteria.

"Elizabeth, would you mind making some sandwiches?" Betty asked without looking up from her work.

"Glad to, Aunt Betty." Liz headed for the kitchen.

Meanwhile Kate continued writing summaries for each suspect. She tore the first page off of her notepad and looked around for a place to put it.

Skip plucked it out of her fingers.

She leaned over the chart again to study the lines to the Berkleys. She'd finished summarizing the information on them and was leaning over to decide who to list next, when Skip burst out laughing.

"Kate, do you realize you've listed these people in the order in which you dislike them?"

Kate glanced over at the sheet in his hand. "Not true. I put Mr. Forsythe before *El-leeen*." She dragged out the woman's name.

They made eye contact. She giggled.

"Kate, have you finished whatever the hell you're doing over there?" Rob said from the armchair across the room.

"Robert, watch your language."

"Sorry, Aunt Betty."

Skip shot Kate a look that eloquently said, *You haven't talked to him yet, have you?*

Kate shook her head slightly.

Rob was watching them through narrowed eyes.

"Be done in a minute." Kate bent again to her task.

She paused to grab a sandwich from the plate that was circulating the room. She took a bite, then rolled her eyes. "Liz, how do you manage to make even sandwiches into a gourmet treat?" Having never mastered the skill of making palatable food herself, she was in awe of those who could.

Liz thanked her for the compliment.

Kate finished the suspect summaries and asked Betty for a pair of scissors. After swallowing her last bite of sandwich, she started cutting the summaries apart, so that one suspect was on each slip of paper.

"Joe's more likely to agree to another interview if the interviewer is female, but the guy's a real creepo." Kate turned to Rose and Mac. "You guys willing to take a crack at him?"

Mac nodded and Kate handed Joe's slip to them.

"The Forsythes–"

"Tried to talk to her this morning," Mac said. "The bit.... ouch!" Rose had elbowed him in the side. "The *lady* wouldn't give me the time of day."

"Well, *Skippy* here has developed a certain rapport with *Ellen*."

Skip lightly punched her shoulder. "I'm bigger'n you, remember?" he drawled.

She snickered. "I'd better go with him, though, as his protection."

"I'll go with him," Rob said.

Yeah, not gonna happen, buddy.

Out loud, she said, "Actually, I was suggesting I go with him so he can concentrate on charming her while I observe. It's a combination that's worked well with her before."

Rob frowned but let it go.

"I want to do some more research on the other two couples," Liz said. "Hopefully they won't turn out to be wanted by the FBI."

"Okay, we'll put off talking to them for now–"

"Kate, I don't think we should wait to talk to the Murphys." Skip pointed to the chart on the coffee table. "They're the ones with the most solid lines. We can go back to them again later if Liz digs up something new."

"Okay. You want them, Rob?" Kate asked. He held out his hand and she passed their summaries over to him.

"I'll take Morris," Skip said. "I'm bound and determined to get that man to talk to me."

Rob glanced down at the chart. "Why's Paul Johnson on the suspect list?"

"*Who's* Paul Johnson?" Liz asked.

"He approached Rob and me and said he was Jeff's friend," Kate said. "Skip's suspicious that he could be the killer, or at least Jeff's killer, and he's inserted himself into the investigation to find out what's going on."

"He did ask a lot of questions." Rob turned to his aunt. "Do you know whether this Johnson guy was really a friend of Jeff's?"

Betty shook her head. "I don't know. I've never seen them together."

Liz grimaced. "He's gonna be hard to research. That's such a common name."

"I'll call on him to offer my condolences," Betty said. "I think I can draw him out."

Rob frowned. "That's too danger—"

"I think that's a great idea," Kate intentionally interrupted. Betty was rallying, and the best antidote for depression was action. "But it's not safe for you to go by yourself."

"Mac or Skip could go," Rose said, "as her bodyguard. Stand by the door."

"Hmm." Betty tapped her index finger against her upper lip. "I think Mac. Skip would be far too distracting for the poor man." She winked at Skip.

They all stared at Betty for a beat.

Kate heard someone stifle a snicker. She hid a smile of her own. Betty was definitely rallying.

Skip squirmed a little in his chair. "I've got Mrs. Carroll. That just leaves Carla Baxter."

"I'll try her again," Rob said.

Kate passed the appropriate slip of paper to him.

Rose stood and offered a hand up to Mac. Then she headed for the door.

Kate followed her out, with Skip trailing behind.

~~~

Out on the sidewalk, Kate turned in the direction of the Forsythes' building. "This late in the day," she said over her shoulder, "Ellen's probably not at the gym."

"I thought you were going to talk to him, Kate." Skip tried to keep the anger out of his voice, but he was getting tired of being frowned at. "How are you supposed to do that if you're not with him?"

Kate came to a halt and Skip was a long stride past her before he realized she'd stopped walking. He turned back and stepped in close to her.

She looked up into his face. Her hand moved up and brushed the hair off his forehead.

The light touch sent shock waves through his body. He closed his eyes and groaned.

He felt her start to pull away and captured her hand in his, holding it against his chest. She left it there for a moment. His heart pounded wildly under it.

Then she gently pulled free. "Tired of my company, *Skippy*?" She smiled up at him.

He managed to return her smile with a lopsided grin. "I'm bigger'n you, remember."

His good sense did battle with the desire to crush her against him and kiss her. The former finally won and he forced himself to take a step backward.

They turned and walked side by side in silence. As they neared the Forsythes' building, good sense lost the second skirmish.

Skip grabbed Kate's hand and dragged her around the corner,

away from prying eyes. He did manage, barely, to resist the urge to kiss her. Holding her hand in both of his, he started to blurt out, "Kate, I–"

The fingers of her other hand were on his mouth, stopping the flow of words. "No, Skip. Don't take us to a place we can't back up from."

She stepped back. His lips tingled where her fingertips had been.

"Let's get through this," she said. "We need to catch this killer... so life can go back to normal. And then we'll see."

For the first time since his father died, Skip wanted to cry. He blinked, felt wetness on his cheeks from his eyelashes.

He also took a step back. Sucking in air, he let it out in a long shuddering exhale. "I was just going to say that I really want to kiss you."

He was lying. What had been about to come out of his mouth was "Kate, I love you." And, damn it, she was right. It was way too soon for that. Despite the difference in the length of their legs, she would run away so fast he'd never be able to catch her.

"Skip, that's a very tempting proposition. But I'm pretty darn sure if we did that, there would be no turning back."

"And that would be a bad thing why?"

Her smile was soft, indulgent. "It wouldn't be if... It won't be *when* the time is right."

She looked around, then tugged on his arm. "Let's sit down for a minute."

There was a shade tree with a bench under it about ten feet away. They walked to the bench. Kate sat down at one end of it.

Skip tried to leave some room between them, but he was a big man. There were only a couple inches of the bench seat showing.

They both knew it wasn't enough.

"Look, Skip, I'm not trying to tease you–"

"More like torture," he said mournfully.

"I know, and to be truthful, it is for me too. But if and when we... get together, I want it to work. I think there's a lot more potential here than just a nice little romance that will fizzle out after a while." She paused, looking off across the grass.

Skip smiled, encouraged by her words.

She turned back to him. "I'm not making any promises, but I have every intention of going out with you at some point in the future."

"And once we get there, can I kiss you?" He tried to keep his voice light and teasing.

She grinned. "When we get to that point, Skip Canfield, I will be *extremely disappointed* if you don't kiss me." Her face sobered. "But I'm afraid if we gave in now… to the desire… to kiss… I'm afraid once we…" Her voice trailed off on a croak as a blush crept up her cheeks.

He decided to let her off the hook. "We should probably stop talking about it."

"Skip, I know this isn't fair, to ask you to wait. But if we go there too soon… I'd be very disappointed if things didn't work out."

"How can a man argue with that?"

She gave him a small smile. "Oh, I knew plenty in high school and college who'd be arguing right now."

"That's because getting what they wanted then was more important to them than the long-term benefits."

His body was aching to hold her, but his brain acknowledged that he wouldn't be able to stop there. If he held her, he'd want to kiss her, and if he kissed her, he'd want….

He stood abruptly and took a long stride away from the bench, then turned back toward her. "I want it to work, too, Kate. But honestly, I'm not going to be able to keep my hands off you if… Look, I have an idea. Suddenly I'm reminded of those damn dance lessons my mother decided I needed when I was twelve. Guess she thought it would help me get over my awkward phase, as she called it." He gave an exaggerated eye roll.

"The teacher was a real throwback to the past, a total prude. She would run around with a ruler, sticking it between the boys and girls to make sure we weren't dancing too close to each other." He mimicked holding a girl at arm's length. Then he pursed his lips in a prim expression and pretended to hold the end of an imaginary ruler against his chest. "If we hadn't all been so totally self-conscious, we probably would have laughed at her. Most of us were still in the other-gender-has-cooties stage."

Kate had been smiling at his antics for the last few seconds. Now she laughed out loud. "I think I know what you're leading up to. What does the rule need to be, three feet?"

"Naw, my arms are almost that long, and if I lean over a bit." He leaned toward her to demonstrate. "No, I think it needs to be more like four feet."

Kate nodded her head, but this time her smile didn't reach her eyes. "Uh, Skip, I know it's supposed to be ladies first, but could you do me a favor and walk away now. Before I jump up off this bench and do something I've just spent the last ten minutes convincing you we shouldn't do yet."

Skip grinned at her, downright giddy with relief. She truly did want him, maybe even as much as he wanted her. The timing wasn't right, that's all.

He could wait. He was a patient man.

"Happy to oblige. Well, not exactly happy, but I'll do it." He gave her end of the bench an exaggerated wide berth as he walked back toward the front of the building.

She followed at a healthy distance behind him. He grabbed the door handle and stepped back, holding the door open for her. She stopped in her tracks and cocked her head at him.

"Okay, okay." He let go of the door handle and took two backward strides. Clasping his hands behind his back, he looked up at the sky and whistled tunelessly under his breath, while she opened the door and entered the building.

~~~

Ellen's low cut, red silk top and snug black pants seemed a bit dressy for lounging at home. She informed them in a whisper that her husband was taking a nap and tiptoed over to pull the bedroom door closed.

She invited them to sit down. Kate sat in one of the beige armchairs bracketing the ends of the black, plush velvet sofa in the living room.

Skip moved toward the other chair, but Mrs. Forsythe stepped in front of it. "Big man like you," she purred, "would probably be more comfortable on the sofa." She waited until he sat down. Then ignoring the chair herself, she perched on the arm of the opposite end of the sofa.

Kate had no doubt the woman would find an excuse to sit down next to him soon.

"Sorry to keep bothering you, Mrs. Forsythe," she said. "But we needed to touch base with you again about a couple things. First of all, we were wondering if you could tell us anything about Mr. Morgan. Such as who his friends were and if he had any enemies?"

"Oh, I didn't really know the man that well. He was on the quiet side."

"Did you ever notice who he hung out with, ma'am?" Skip asked. "Did he sit with anyone in particular at meals, for example?"

"Hmm, let me think. No, he usually sat alone."

"Did you ever talk to him?" Kate asked.

"Not all that much. I said hi a few times but he got kind of awkward, you know, like he wasn't real comfortable talking to a woman."

Curious, Kate thought. None of the other women had reported that Jeff was uncomfortable or awkward with them, just that he was quiet by nature.

"So you never noticed him hanging around with anyone in particular? Someone that might have been a good friend of his." Skip smiled at Mrs. Forsythe. "We're having a little trouble getting a handle on this guy."

She stared at the ceiling in thought, then casually swung her feet around and put them up on the sofa. She was now sitting sideways on its arm. Returning his smile, she rested her elbows on her knees and put her chin in her hand, providing him with an excellent view of her cleavage.

Her feet were bare. Her bright red toenails were just inches from Skip's thigh.

"I'm trying to remember who I've seen him with the most. Probably Henry Morris. They seemed to have been buddies. Although how Jeff could put up with that old sourpuss, I'll never know."

She wiggled her toes and edged them slightly closer to Skip's thigh. He tensed.

Kate gritted her teeth, then carefully schooled her face into a neutral mask.

"Uh, so Mr. Morris was his friend," Skip said. "Did he have any enemies that you know of?"

Mrs. Forsythe shook her head. "I can't imagine anyone disliking him. As I said, I didn't know him well, but he always struck me as a very sweet man."

"That's how everyone's been describing him, ma'am."

"I thought I told you to call me Ellen," Mrs. Forsythe scolded him. Her right big toe was now bumping against his thigh.

Suddenly *Ellen* snapped her fingers. "You know, I just thought of something. I'll bet he was gay." She used her mock surprise as the excuse to slide down from the arm onto the seat of the sofa. "That would explain a lot, wouldn't it? But I'm surprised I didn't pick up on that sooner. My gaydar's usually better than that."

Skip looked confused. "Ma'am...uh, Ellen?"

Ellen gave a fake little laugh. "Oh, Mrs. Huntington, I'll bet you know what I'm talking about, don't you?" She turned back toward Skip and patted his thigh. "Women can usually tell when a man is gay, because they don't put off any vibes that they're attracted to you."

Ellen was now watching her with a sly smile. She patted Skip's thigh again.

Ho, boy. This woman is a true piece of work.

Kate managed to maintain a pleasant expression despite her

next, truly nasty thought. *'Ho' is the right word, alright!*

"Mrs. For...I mean, Ellen." Skip turned his torso slightly toward the woman, while shifting his weight to put more space between their thighs. "This is really helpful to us."

"Yes, very helpful, ma'am." Kate gave the bitch her warmest smile. "But I'm wondering if we could ask you about something else. Someone mentioned, I can't remember who at the moment, that Mr. Forsythe was a retired science teacher." She was trying to distract the woman as Skip eased further away from her.

"Yes, but what's that got to do with any of this."

"Well, of course we'd like to talk to him about it, but since he's napping, maybe you can help us in the meantime. Detective Lindstrom let slip that there was a certain chemical involved in some of these crimes. He wouldn't give us any details, but we–"

Skip jumped up and started pacing around the room. "Damn, what was the name of that stuff? I can't remember and it's driving me crazy." He paced across in front of the sofa, taut muscles rippling beneath snug jeans. "Chlorodine, no that's not it…"

He turned and faced Ellen Forsythe. Kate caught a glimpse of mother of pearl and gunmetal sticking out of his waistband holster as he reached up and grabbed some of his hair, tugging on it, elbows high in the air.

"Chlorine… no that's not it either."

It dawned on her that Skip was intentionally flashing a view of his abs at the woman.

"Damn… Help me out here, Kate."

She paused a second to suppress the laughter bubbling in her throat, then dutifully supplied the word. "Chloroform."

"Yeah, that's it!" He lowered his arms and flashed a grin at her over his shoulder, then turned the grin back toward the woman on the sofa. "Doncha just hate it, Ellen, when you can't think of a word." He walked over to the other armchair and sat down. "It's danglin' there on the tip of your brain." His voice had slowed to a drawl. He leaned slightly toward Mrs. Forsythe. "And ya just can't seem to wrap yer tongue around it."

Kate stifled a snicker as *Ellen* licked her lips. The woman was leaning so far forward, Kate thought she might slip right off the sofa.

"So Ellen," Skip said, "since you've lived all these years with a scientist, maybe you've heard him talk about chloroform. We're tryin' to find out more about what it's used for, how someone'd get it, stuff like that. 'Cause you never know what little piece of information might turn out to be the *key* that unlocks the *door* in an investigation like this."

Kate was carefully watching the woman's face and body language. Other than licking her lips again, there was no reaction to any of the well-placed words in Skip's little speech. No flash of fear in the eyes, no going suddenly still, no lifting her head in surprise or alarm.

The room had fallen silent. Finally Mrs. Forsythe realized she was the one who was supposed to be talking. "No, I don't recall my husband ever mentioning chloroform. All I know is that it used to be used in hospitals sometimes, to put people under for operations, you know, before modern anesthesia was developed." She gave a little laugh. "Like in those old movies when they'd put the mask over the patient's face and say, 'Now, breath deeply and you won't feel a thing.'"

Having recovered herself a bit, she smiled and fluttered her eyelashes at Skip. "I guess that's not a whole lot of help, is it?"

"Well, actually it just might be, Ellen." Skip beamed at her. "Maybe that's how it was used here. Could be the killer put some chloroform on a piece a cloth and used it to knock his victims out, so then he could do whatever he wanted to them, without a struggle."

Again, no reaction to this scenario. But the woman's expression was becoming more calculating by the second.

Okay, Skippy, time to get you out of here.

Kate glanced at her watch and jumped to her feet. "Skip, we've got to be getting back. Thank you for your time, ma'am."

Skip ignored her for a beat and continued to beam at Ellen

Forsythe.

"Skip!" Kate said, faking a sharp tone.

"Oh yeah. Sorry, Kate." He jumped up. Before Ellen was halfway to standing, they were both at the door. "No need to get up, ma'am. We'll let ourselves out. Thanks for all your help."

They bolted out of the apartment and race-walked to the building exit. Once outside, they jogged around the corner of the building. By unspoken agreement they headed for the bench.

Skip got there first and flopped down on it, holding his sides and laughing. "Oh, man, nobody's going to believe us when we tell them about this interview."

Kate grinned at him. Abiding by the new four-foot rule, she collapsed onto the grass. "I think we'll leave out most of the details. That was a stellar performance, Skip. The belly dance maneuver was downright inspired." She started giggling. "The poor woman was awestruck."

"Thanks. I liked that little jealous snit of yours at the end. It's a good thing I didn't come alone. She would have eaten me alive. But did it occur to you to wonder where her old man really was?"

"Indeed, it did," Kate said. "After the first few minutes, we forgot to keep our voices down. Unless he's stone deaf or sleeps like a log, we had to have woken him. I kept expecting him to pop out of the bedroom and challenge you to a duel."

"Why would she lie about him being there if he wasn't?" Skip said. "Or if he was there, why wouldn't he come out if we woke him up?"

"I don't know. That was the only strange thing about the whole interview. She didn't react at all to any of the buzz words you threw out there. She's not a very good actress, so I'd bet my last dollar that she wasn't our intruder. And Mr. *Ellen* is too big."

"You said he might be a heavy drinker. Kind of early in the day for it, but maybe he was passed out drunk."

"Could be. That would explain why she didn't seem worried about coming on to you." Then Kate snapped her fingers and mimicked Ellen Forsythe's higher pitched voice. "You know, I just thought of something. *Maybe* the man in her bedroom wasn't her husband."

Skip grinned at her Ellen impersonation. "What did you make of her gaydar comment? I was a bit surprised to hear a woman in her sixties using that term."

"All part of her trying to seem young and hip. Paul Johnson said Jeff wasn't gay and I'm inclined to trust his assessment over hers. I think it's more likely that *Ellen* scared the crap out of poor Jeff, so he acted awkward around her."

"And of course she would need some explanation for why her considerable charms didn't entice him, so she concludes he's gay." Skip stood up.

From her seat on the ground, Kate grabbed the arm of the bench to pull herself to her feet. He reached down to offer her a hand.

She pulled back, shaking her head. "Nunh-uh. No touchy, remember."

"Well, darnation! I almost had the innocent maiden in my clutches," Skip said, imitating the evil villain's voice from old cartoons. He laughed diabolically.

"Darnation? Is that a word?" Kate stood, brushing the grass off her clothes.

"I'm not sure. There's another socially acceptable expletive the cartoon villains used to use but I can't think of it right now." Then he started jumping around, clutching at his hair. "Oh, doncha just hate it when you can't think of a word. And it's right there on the tip of your brain... Help me out here, Kate."

Kate laughed. "Oh, stop it or I'll go tell Ellen that you're all hers."

Skip snickered.

They started back toward Betty's building, keeping a healthy distance between them.

After a moment, his face sobered. "Actually, I was starting to get a pretty good sense of what women must feel like when some obnoxious guy is coming on to them. And you know what dawned on me, in the back of my mind, while most of my brain cells were madly looking for an escape route." He kicked a pebble from the sidewalk. "I realized she was no physical threat at all. I could pick her up and throw her across the room. What kept me feeling trapped were social conventions. You're trying to keep things polite, not be blatantly rejecting or obnoxious. Meanwhile the… aggressor, for lack of a better word, is getting more and more blatant."

"Yeah, you're playing by the rules but the other person isn't," Kate said. "With women, they can end up being maneuvered into a spot where the guy can physically overpower them, before they realize they have to stop being so nice."

Skip stopped walking and turned toward her, his eyes anxious and sad.

"No, that's never happened to me, thank God!" she answered the unasked question. "My encounter with Joe was the closest I've ever come, but I've heard variations of that story too often to count, from my rape-survivor clients. That's why I felt so stupid for letting Joe back me, literally, into that corner. I should've known better."

"But that's mostly hindsight now. You can't blame yourself for not realizing ahead of time he would be that way."

Kate stared at him for a beat from across the width of the sidewalk. Those were almost the same words she used with clients. "Have I told you, Mr. Canfield, that one of the many things I like about you is how astute you are?"

"No, you haven't mentioned that before. What are the other 'many things' you like?"

"Oh, no. I think I'll save them for another time. Don't want to give you too many compliments in one day."

Skip grinned at her from across the sidewalk. "*So much* to look forward to."

CHAPTER TWENTY-THREE

Sitting on Paul Johnson's sofa, Betty was working on her second cup of tea.

Mac was standing just inside the apartment door, arms crossed and staring into space. Betty had introduced him merely as her bodyguard, then had scoffed, "My nephew insists he go everywhere with me. That boy is such a worry wart."

She'd told Johnson she was calling to express her sympathy over the loss of his friend and then had commented on the lovely antique china cabinet in his dining area. In no time, she'd had him reminiscing about his life with his late partner, telling her tales of their travels, of the junk shops and second-hand furniture stores they had frequented on the weekends, looking for finds.

"What did you do for a living, Mr. Johnson, before you retired?" Betty asked, when there was a lull in the conversation.

"I was an engineer," was Johnson's brief and not very helpful answer.

When she brought the conversation back around to Jeff Morgan, the man's comments remained vague.

"I feel so bad that I didn't take the time to get to know Jeff better." Betty shook her head sadly. "He was such a nice man. What kinds of activities did he enjoy?"

Paul Johnson hesitated. "He loved books."

"Oh, really. Who was his favorite author?"

Again the hesitation, and a flash of something else. "Faulkner I guess was his favorite, although his tastes were very eclectic."

Betty thought it was interesting that this man could go on

and on about his late partner, but he seemed to have no desire to reminisce about times spent with the supposedly dear friend he had just lost.

She decided to be more direct. "Do you know if Jeff had any enemies?"

Again there was a flash of some emotion on his face, gone before she could identify it.

"I can't imagine how anyone could dislike the man," he said. "I should be offering you my condolences as well. I understand that you and Mrs. McIntosh were good friends. Do the police have any leads in her death?"

"Not that I know of," Betty said. "I think they're trying to figure out what motive someone might have for killing these particular people. Do you have any thoughts about that?"

Paul Johnson made a show of thinking about the question. After scratching his bald head and then squeezing the bridge of his thin nose, he said, "I can't think of anything they had in common, other than living in the same building. Who are the prime suspects? Perhaps I can shed some light on their personalities."

Betty played dumb. "Oh, I don't really know. My nephew's been discussing all that with that nice detective. It's all so upsetting." She fanned herself with her napkin. "Well, I guess I'd better let you get on with your day. Do you mind if I use the little girls' room before I go?"

"Of course not." Johnson directed her to the powder room next to his den.

Betty stood inside the tiny room, her ear to the crack between the door and its frame. Sure enough, she could hear Johnson talking to Mac.

"This is obviously very distressing for Mrs. Franklin. Do you know if they're getting close to finding the murderer?"

"Don't know, sir," Mac said.

Johnson's voice again. "Please tell Mr. Franklin that I'm happy to help with the investigation in any way I can."

"I will, sir."

Kate knocked on Betty's apartment door.

After a moment, Rob opened it. "Where's Canfield?" he asked as she walked in past him.

She shot a sideways glare at him. "*Skip* went to try Morris again, and then to talk to Alice Carroll." She was about to say more but caught herself. Better not start such an important conversation with anger. Not when their friendship hung in the balance.

That thought stopped her in mid-stride. Fear of losing Rob shot through her, but an instant later she realized that if he wouldn't accept Skip in her life, she didn't know what she would do. She already cared for the man too much to let him go.

Was Rob not as mentally healthy as she'd always thought he was? Or had she run up against a psychological blind spot in him? Most people had at least one or two, she'd found, no matter how good their overall mental health may be.

All this flashed through her mind in a matter of seconds, as she looked up at Rob, willing the stinging in her eyes not to turn to tears. "Did you catch up with Baxter or the Murphys?" She tried to sound nonchalant.

"Haven't had a chance to try." He took a step closer and peered intently at her face.

Apparently she hadn't pulled off the nonchalant.

His eyes were worried, then they narrowed in anger. "Did something happen with Canfield?"

"No, of course not." She took a step back. For a second, she was a little afraid of him.

He was still staring at her, trying to read her face.

Kate turned and walked toward the sitting area. "What happened? To keep you from seeing them?"

"FBI agents came back."

Relief washed through her. That's why he was acting so strangely. "Why do I have the feeling that they…"

"Weren't as friendly this time? They weren't." He gestured toward the chairs and settee.

"Where are Liz and Betty?' Kate flopped down on the settee and kicked her shoes off.

"Aunt Betty's lying down. She just got back from seeing Johnson. Liz is in the den."

Just as well she hadn't tried to have their little talk then. It wasn't a conversation she wanted interrupted by someone else popping into the room.

Maneuvering around to put her feet up, she stretched out as far as the short couch would allow. She sighed as some of the tension drained out of her tired muscles.

"Yeah, it's been a rough day," Rob said, agreeing with her nonverbal commentary on the roller coaster ride of the last nine hours. He sat down in the adjacent armchair.

Kate breathed out another quiet sigh. He was back to finishing her sentences and reading her mind. Maybe they'd be okay after all.

"So why'd the FBI come back?" she asked.

"The Berkeleys have vanished."

"What?" Kate jolted upright and almost slithered off the settee. She quickly put a foot on the floor to catch herself.

"They were gone when the feds went in," Rob said. "Apartment wasn't completely cleared out but they'd obviously packed up most of their clothes and valuables. The feds assumed that Liz or I had alerted them."

"Holy crap!"

"It's fine now. We finally convinced them we had nothing to do with their fugitives taking a powder. I pointed out that the Berkeleys probably got nervous because of all the police officers wandering around asking questions. Oh, another interesting tidbit. One of the agents let it slip that Mr. Berkeley is not Mrs. Berkeley's husband, but rather her father."

Kate stared at him.

"Yeah, keeps getting curiouser and curiouser. Seems the whole family was involved in the paramilitary organization. Survivalists, out in the woods, doing drills, et cetera. Leader started ranting about how the government had been corrupted by all the damn liberals. So they planned an Oklahoma City-type attack on the Indiana state legislature."

He ran fingers through his hair and glanced at Betty's liquor cabinet.

Kate managed to suppress a frown. She'd never known him to drink alcohol except on special occasions, and then not much. Butterflies of worry fluttered in her chest.

"To finance that endeavor," he said, "they decided to rob a bank first. Some of them got away with the money but three of the men got caught. Then the group tried to break them out of the jail in the basement of the town hall. They tossed a homemade bomb at the front door to blow it off the hinges. But the bomb did more damage than intended.

"Mrs. Berkeley, or should I say Miss Caldwell, and her father were the only ones who got away. And apparently rethought the whole idea of treason. They came to Lancaster, developed whole new identities, and bought a hardware store with their ill-gotten gains. Fifteen years later they sold the store and retired. They'd apparently figured that pretending to be husband and wife would help throw the feds off the trail. The FBI would be looking for a father and daughter, not a couple."

Incredulous, Kate asked, "The FBI agents told you all that?"

"No, but they let slip enough to give my darling wife a hint of where to research from there. Most of the info came from old newspaper articles. Some's just educated guessing."

Kate glanced toward the open doorway to the den. "So Liz didn't learn her lesson from all this," she said quietly.

Rob also dropped his voice. "Oh, she said she's turning over a new leaf. Just legal searches from now on. No more hacking."

"And you believe her?" Kate whispered.

"Hell no. Next time she thinks it's a worthy cause, she'll be at it again." But Rob smiled as he said it. He shook his head. "I gave up a long time ago on trying to stop her when she feels strongly about something."

Kate smiled too. She was pretty sure her four-ten, ninety-eight pound friend had been a stevedore in a former life, or maybe a cigar-smoking precinct captain in the early 1900s.

"Did Betty get anything useful out of Johnson?" she asked.

"Not really, but she agrees with our assessment that he didn't know Jeff as well as he claims." Rob pushed himself up out of his chair. "Well, I guess I'd better get on with my assignments."

"You want me to go with you?"

"That's okay," he said. "Why don't you relax a bit."

The dog-tired part of her won the internal debate against the part pushing her to go with him and look for a chance to talk things out.

Kate got up to lock the deadbolt after him, then stretched out on the settee again with a sigh. She'd have to find that opportunity soon. One more day away from her child would probably be her limit.

She closed her eyes to fantasize about bathing Edie and snuggling with her at bedtime.

~~~~~~

Once again, Skip had not been able to get Morris to come out of his lair. He hoped he'd have better luck with Mrs. Carroll.

In the administration building, he found a sales person enthusiastically explaining the virtues of The Villages to a white-haired couple.

Either these folks live under a rock or they're from out of town.

Skip hoped for the poor salesman's sake that the couple didn't pick up on the note of desperation in his voice.

When there was a lull, Skip asked if Mrs. Carroll was in. "Third door on the right down that hall." The man had a touch of panic in his eyes.

The door was slightly ajar. After getting no response to his soft knock, Skip nudged it open a bit further.

His curiosity about the salesman's look was satisfied when the reek of alcohol hit him in the face.

Slipping into the room and closing the door behind him, he

assessed the situation. Mrs. Carroll was sitting behind her desk, face down on her crossed arms. Not sure if she was dead or just dead drunk, Skip quickly scanned the room for potential hiding places. Unless an intruder was crammed under the desk, along with Mrs. Carroll's knees, there was no one else in the room.

The woman raised her head and looked at him through bleary eyes. "Who're you?" she slurred.

He tried to hide his shock at her appearance. Her dress was rumpled, her eyes red and swollen, and her face blotchy. "Skip Canfield, ma'am. May I sit down?"

She waved vaguely at the chair in front of the desk. "Wha's ya wan'? Yer too yug ta live 'ere."

It took Skip a moment to translate her words. "True, but it sure is a swell place to retire. I'm gonna be keepin' it in mind when the time comes." Skip let a bit of Texas creep into his voice. For some reason, it often charmed the ladies.

Mrs. Carroll looked at him skeptically, then emitted a very unladylike belch. "Wanna drink?" She pushed back a bit from her desk and almost fell off her chair. "Where's m' glass?" She looked around in confusion.

A splash of wetness on the far wall and broken glass on the floor testified to the fate of the missing glass.

"Nev'r min'." The woman pulled a fifth of Scotch, half empty, out of her lower desk drawer. She took a healthy swig right from the bottle, then held it out toward Skip.

He took it, put his thumb over the top and pretended to take a drink, then lowered it to the floor beside his chair. "It's a darn shame that y'all have been havin' such a string of bad luck 'round here lately." He hoped she didn't notice that he hadn't returned the bottle to her.

"S'not my fault. Can't blame me dis time!" The blotches on her face grew redder with anger.

Skip shook his head in sympathy, figuring he could be bolder than he would normally be. "I heard about your previous troubles, ma'am, at your old job."

"I din't do it. Somebody else..." she belched again, "was puttin' 'em out a der misery, but police thought was me."

"Then you landed this here nice job, an' now that's goin' to hell in a handbasket." Skip shook his head again.

"S'not my fault. I tried ta calm ev'ybody down."

"It's a darn shame Doris Blackwell wouldn't listen to ya. Musta been purty frustratin'."

"Damn bitch... s'always makin' trouble. Wish I coulda kicked 'er out, but she'da sued us... sued da Vill'ges."

Skip kept his voice gentle, sympathetic. "I can certainly understand, ma'am, why you hit her."

Mrs. Carroll just stared at him. Then she looked around for her bottle.

"I think you finished it off, ma'am." He could not, in good conscience, let her drink anymore.

The woman gathered herself together. "Whoev'r hit 'er, yug man, did th'world a flavor." She lurched forward and passed out across her desk.

Skip stood and leaned over her. He felt for a pulse on her neck. It and her breathing were irregular, and her skin was cold and pale.

He took out his handkerchief, which he carried for reasons other than just drying ladies' tears. Lifting the telephone receiver with it, he used his knuckle to punch 911. He requested an ambulance be sent to The Villages' management office, for a possible case of alcohol poisoning. When the operator asked for his name, he hung up.

Skip was feeling a bit paranoid. Too many people were dying for no apparent reason. What if there was something other than Scotch in that bottle? He didn't want to go from an investigator of these murders to a suspect.

Now he was wishing he hadn't touched the damn bottle. For a second, he contemplated wiping it clean. But if the Scotch had been tainted, he would be destroying evidence. Both his conscience and his police training wouldn't let him do it.

He checked Mrs. Carroll's pulse again. About the same.

Pocketing his handkerchief, he walked out of her office, leaving the door open. The salesman and the couple were gone.

Skip could now hear an approaching siren. Making sure the outer door of the building was unlocked so the paramedics could get in, he headed back toward Betty's building.

The salesman would remember him. Would he get in more trouble for leaving, should Mrs. Carroll turn out to be the killer's latest victim? He almost turned around and went back.

A few minutes later, he was glad he hadn't.

CHAPTER TWENTY-FOUR

Rob hadn't thought he could get any more frustrated, but now he was. Neither Carla Baxter nor the Murphys had answered their doors. They could be out somewhere, or huddled behind those doors, or they might have moved out like so many of the other residents. The Villages was starting to look like a ghost town.

As he was walking back to Aunt Betty's building, his cell phone rang. He checked caller ID. It was his admin assistant. "Hi, Fran," he said into the phone.

"Sorry it's taken us so long to get your info, Boss. It's been kind of crazy around here lately."

"I'm the one who should be apologizing for abandoning you and Beth to the craziness."

"No problem, Boss. You need to be doing what you're doing. As to whether you can take your aunt out of there and bring her home with you, the answer seems to be yes. In Pennsylvania, the order to not leave the jurisdiction has no legal standing unless it's given by a judge. It took Beth so long to determine that because she was looking for a statute that doesn't exist."

"Thanks, Fran." Rob stopped walking. A vague plan was forming in his mind. He hated to ask his paralegal to work late on a Friday evening, and on a *pro bono* case at that, but this situation had become intolerable. "Hey, ask Beth to look through Pennsylvania case law to see if there's anything relevant to this mess."

"What are you looking for?"

"I'm not sure. I guess relatively recent cases, as in the last couple decades, where there were acquittals because all the state had was possible motive, the means was a weapon of convenience, and opportunity involved evidence that the accused had been at the scene at some point in the past, but not necessarily at the time of the crime."

"You got something up your sleeve, Boss?"

"Maybe. I might go to the Lancaster chief of police and threaten to sue his, uh, you-know-what off, if my aunt isn't allowed to leave the area, since his police department can't guarantee her safety in her own home."

Fran chuckled. "Boss, I've got teenaged sons. Trust me, I've heard the word *ass* before."

Rob chuckled in return. "Knee-jerk reaction at this point. Aunt Betty's been snapping 'Robert, watch your language' at me every time I let even a *damn* or a *hell* slip out."

Rob thanked Fran, asking her to pass along his gratitude to Beth as well, then disconnected.

He felt better. This idea just might work. Staring across the road, eyes out of focus, he contemplated his game plan.

Something slammed into his side, knocking the breath out of him. As he flew sideways, the tires of a car careened up onto the sidewalk. They came within inches of his feet.

Whoever had tackled him was up off of him again in a flash. He heard a roaring engine, screeching tires and cursing.

Skip Canfield leaned down, offering him a hand up.

"What the hell just happened?" Rob asked, as the other man pulled him to his feet.

"I came around the corner, saw that car coming right for you. Driver had a cap on, pulled down to hide his face. Or her face. Could've been a woman. Only caught the first letter and one of the digits of the license plate."

Rob brushed himself off. "Could've been a resident whose driving isn't what it used to be."

Skip gave him a skeptical look. "Then why'd he take off instead of stopping to make sure you weren't hurt? Nope, looked intentional to me."

"You see anything else?"

"Big dark car. Looked like an older model. Olds or a Buick, maybe."

"The guy, or gal, could be out of it enough they didn't even realize they'd almost hit me," Rob said, not willing to accept that someone had tried to kill him.

Skip shrugged again. "It happened fast, but that wasn't my impression. Car was aiming right for you. Then the driver floored it."

Rob was still convinced Canfield was overreacting to an elderly driver's miscalculation. He leaned over to examine a grass stain on the knee of his khaki slacks. Without thinking it through, he said, "Let's not tell the ladies about this. It'll just worry them."

By the time he straightened up, Canfield's face was a neutral mask, but annoyance flashed in his eyes.

"I'm not sure that's a good idea. They need to know, so they'll be more alert."

Rob looked at him for a beat, trying to decide if he should make that a direct order. He realized he'd lost that right when he'd tried to fire the man.

"Thanks for your quick response." He offered his hand.

They shook.

Rob knew Canfield was right, but he couldn't bring himself to admit it directly. "*I'll* tell Kate and Liz, but not in front of Aunt Betty."

Canfield didn't say anything.

~~~~~~

Kate jolted awake on the narrow settee.

"Sorry." Liz dropped into the armchair next to her. "I didn't realize you were asleep."

Kate sat up, rubbing her gritty eyes. The gesture reminded her of Edie. When she was tired, she would rub her eyes with her chubby little fists. Her arms ached with longing to hold the child.

Liz lowered her head to look at her over the tops of the reading glasses perched on her nose. "You should go home. This has turned out to be way more than you signed on for."

"I may do that, soon. I can't just yet." Kate stopped, not sure how much to say to Liz. She didn't want to put her in the middle. "Some things are up in the air, that need to get resolved first."

"He said you were royally pissed about the background check. If he'd told me he was going to do that ahead of time, I would've stopped him. Kate, he wasn't thinking. He has Fran and Beth run checks all the time for whatever's in the public records on witnesses, including his own. And even his own clients sometimes. He can't afford to get into court and have some skeleton fall out of somebody's closet that he didn't know about."

Kate digested that for a moment. "Later, when we go back to the motel, can you and Betty ride with Skip so Rob and I can talk?"

Liz nodded.

"Has he said anything else, about me and Skip?"

Liz shook her head. "We haven't exactly had a lot of down time for in-depth conversations. And Rob may be an enlightened man, but he's still a man. I've learned the hard way, when something's bothering him, not to push him to talk before he's ready."

"Do you have any insights into why he's reacting this way?"

"Actually yes." Liz reached over and gave Kate's hand a squeeze. "Sweetheart, if you had told Rob over one of your lunches that you thought you'd met someone you were interested in dating, he would've been thrilled for you. And if you'd then told him the guy was Skip, a man he knew and had good reason to like and trust, he would've been even happier."

"But instead this has all evolved while he's under a lot of stress," Kate said.

"Well, yeah, that's part of it. But I think the bigger problem is that he's watching the process unfold. You're not just telling him about it over lunch. He's actually *seeing* you develop the easy, non-verbal communication with Skip that you had with Ed." Liz cleared her throat. "I felt a twinge of grief myself earlier, when you and Skip were joking around so naturally…" Her voice grew husky. "I thought, 'That's the way she was with Ed.' And I almost started crying."

Kate swallowed the lump in her own throat. "Thank you for telling me that, Liz. It helps. I didn't realize how hard it would be for him, and you, to see me… I keep telling Skip it's too soon for me. I'm thinking it's too soon for all of us."

"Don't let our reactions stop you." Liz's voice took on a bit of an edge. "When *you're* ready, you go for it. We'll adjust."

Kate smiled at her.

Rob's key in the lock announced his return. He stomped into the apartment.

Kate felt herself flush a little. He'd almost caught them talking about him.

But he was apparently too frustrated to notice. "Neither Baxter nor the Murphys answered their door, *again*."

The others came in behind him.

"No luck with Morris either," Skip said. "I'll try again tomorrow morning. But I did have a conversation, if you could call it that, with Mrs. Carroll."

As they all found seats, Skip told them about his meeting with the drunk director. "She was showing signs of alcohol poisoning so I called for an ambulance. She was out cold when I left her." He shot Rob an odd look.

Kate lifted a questioning eyebrow at Skip. He gave her an almost imperceptible shake of his head. She wasn't sure what that meant.

Rob caught the exchange and scowled at Skip.

Kate resisted the temptation to throw something at both of them.

She was giving a sanitized account of their meeting with Mrs. Forsythe when Betty came out of the bedroom to join them. "I think we can take the Forsythes off the prime suspects list," Kate concluded with a grimace.

Skip grinned at her from across the circle. "You really hate to have to admit that, doncha?"

She hesitated, then returned the smile, turning her head so she couldn't see Rob's reaction.

After a beat, Rob said, "Aunt Betty, do you think Ellen Forsythe is right? Was Morris friends with Jeff?"

"I never heard anything about them being good friends. But they could've been and I wouldn't necessarily have known it. Henry almost never eats in the cafeteria. He's quite antisocial."

"So I've noticed," Skip muttered.

"We couldn't find Joe," Rose was saying, when the doorbell rang.

~~~

Rob looked through the peephole. At least Lindstrom wasn't holding any papers in his hand this time.

As he unlocked and opened the door, the others were debating what they should do for dinner, get room service again from the Indian restaurant or go to the cafeteria first before going back to the motel.

Lindstrom stepped into the apartment. "If you go to the cafeteria, you'd better keep a sharp eye on your food and drink. I got a preliminary report from the M.E. Turns out Jeffrey Morgan may have been dead before he went over that railing."

They all stared at him.

"No signs that he tried to catch himself. Even a suicide will instinctively put his arms out. Should be some soft tissue damage and broken bones in his wrists or arms."

The ladies gasped. Rob winced.

The detective gave them an apologetic look. "Medical examiner thinks he was poisoned. We'll know more when the tox reports come back. So since there've been attempts made against several of you, I wouldn't advise eating or drinking anything that someone else around here could've doctored. I know folks have been plying my officers with refreshments." Lindstrom reached for the doorknob. "Figured they were doing the same thing with you and I'd better warn you."

Rob was confused. What other attempts was the man talking about? He hadn't told him yet about the car possibly trying to hit him. "Attempts against several of us? What attempts besides the ones against Aunt Betty?"

"The attack on Kate and Mr. Canfield," Lindstrom said.

Rose and Mac stared at Kate, apparently as surprised by this information as he was.

Rob clenched his teeth against a surge of anger. She *had* been keeping something from him.

He closed the door behind Lindstrom, then pivoted to glare at Kate. "What the hell was he talking about? *What* attack against you two?"

CHAPTER TWENTY-FIVE

With a sinking heart, Kate realized Liz wasn't the only one she'd forgotten to tell about the falling pot incident. Her stomach clenched.

She stood and took a step toward Rob. "Skip and I were walking through the atrium on Monday, when a potted plant almost hit us. One of those around the railings of the upper levels."

He stared at her for a beat, then closed the distance between them. His face red, he loomed over her. "Somebody tried to *kill* you, and you didn't even bother to tell me!"

"Calm down, Rob, please. We didn't keep it from you intentionally. It's just with everything else that's happened, it slipped our minds." Too late, she realized the *we* and *our* were probably poor word choices.

She looked up at him. Behind the anger in his eyes was hurt. "Oh no, Rob, no!" She grabbed his big hand in hers. "I wasn't keeping secrets from you. I honestly forgot to tell you. I didn't even realize until just now that I *hadn't* told you."

He tried to pull his hand away.

Kate hung on. She felt tears pooling. "I'm sorry. I didn't mean to hurt you. I'd never keep something like that from you intentionally."

He stared down at her, his own eyes shiny. Suddenly he wrapped his arms around her and buried his face in her hair. "Shit, Kate, you could've been killed." His voice was muffled, choked.

For once, Betty didn't censure her nephew's language.

Kate slipped her arms around his waist. "But I wasn't." She

laid her cheek against his chest. A couple tears broke loose.

She opted not to tell him that Skip had saved her.

They clung to each other for several seconds.

When Rob let her go, he reached into his pocket for his handkerchief and gave it to her. He swiped his arm across his own damp cheeks.

Skip stepped forward, fishing his handkerchief out of his pocket. He extended his hand to grab Rob's. "Sorry, man. We should've told you. Things have just been happening so fast."

When Skip stepped away from him, Rob stared down at the other man's handkerchief in his hand. Then he turned away to swipe at his eyes with it.

Kate's heart swelled at the gesture. She watched Skip's profile, waiting for him to look her way so she could give him a grateful smile.

Belatedly, she noticed the tension in his jaw.

He turned to face her. "Why exactly are you now *Kate* but I'm still Mr. Canfield?"

His voice was deceptively calm, but Kate hadn't missed the touch of steel under the surface.

She closed her eyes for a second and prayed for patience. She wasn't sure how much more of this she could take in one day. Turning away from all of them, she went over to her customary chair.

Liz took her cue from that and gestured to the others to take their seats.

Kate was about to flash her a grateful smile, when Liz threw her to the wolves. "Yeah, I've been wondering why the good detective has been so open with us about the investigation."

Kate resisted the urge to put her head in her hands. If she wasn't so tired, she'd scream. She sighed instead. "He wants to go out with me."

She could hear Skip grinding his teeth beside her.

"I told him it was too soon, but I didn't want to be too rejecting, so I agreed that he could call me in a few months. I guess he's trying to stay on my good side."

Skip turned toward her, a scowl on his face.

Kate barely caught herself as she was about to take the Lord's name in vain in front of Betty. "For Pete's sake," she said to Skip, "I'm *not* interested in him. I hate to use the guy, but it is nice to have a cooperative relationship with the police for a change."

Skip's tense face only relaxed a little.

Arrgghh! Men! Life-long celibacy was starting to have considerable appeal.

Liz must have decided a change of subject was in order. She said, "I researched chloroform some more today. Mostly colleges and universities use it, for research. But one of its uses is as a solvent, so some industries and institutions in the past used it for that purpose, to clean built-up gunk off of machine parts, for example."

"So it's possible Joe might have access to some," Kate said, grateful to have the focus off of her love life.

"Well, probably not from that source. Hasn't been used that way for years, because it was discovered to be a carcinogen. But I did some digging on Joe. He has a police record not only in Pennsylvania but in several other states as well. Mostly petty theft, barroom brawls and such. He's been enrolled, off and on for the last couple years, at the Lancaster campus of Harrisburg Community College. And get this, *most* of the classes he's taken have been science classes."

"So he knows where the labs are and where they keep the controlled chemicals," Rose said. "He could've stolen some chloroform."

Skip leaned forward in his chair. "And Mr. Morris might conceivably have some, since he was a maintenance man for several decades."

Kate snuck a peek at his jaw. Not quite as tense as it had been.

"I'm afraid I didn't get anything new out of Mr. Johnson," Betty was saying. "I'm inclined to agree with Kate and Robert, though. He didn't know Jeff that well. And it definitely felt like he was trying to pump us for information about the investigation... I kept getting the feeling that he was angry, but was trying to hide it. I couldn't tell if he was mad at Jeff Morgan, or just irritated about the questions I was asking."

"Or that we weren't satisfyin' his curiosity," Mac said.

Kate nodded. "So he may have had something against Jeff."

"Or he just wants to be in on the action," Liz said. "I'm not having much luck researching him. I got several hundred hits for that name, and none of them, so far, seem to be him."

Betty excused herself and headed into the bedroom to get fresh clothes for the next day.

"I need to narrow down which Paul Johnson this guy is," Liz said. "I'll bet The Villages' financial records have his social security number listed." She got up and headed for the den and her computer.

Rob stood. "What'd I tell ya, Kate. She's totally unrepentant." Shaking his head, he followed his wife to attempt to rein in her felonious tendencies.

Skip leaned into the center of the circle. In a low voice, he said, "Rob didn't want to say anything in front of his aunt, but somebody tried to run him down with a car a few minutes ago."

Kate's heart jittered in her chest. Her hand flew to her mouth.

"He's fine," Skip quickly added, "but we all need to be extra alert. The killer's still trying to–"

"Big, dark car?" Rose said. "Older model?"

"Yeah."

"Tried to run us down yesterday," Mac growled.

"And the same kind of car almost hit me the day before." Kate stopped talking when Betty re-entered the room.

Liz came out of the den, followed by a slightly limping Rob. Kate anxiously looked him over. His clothes were rumpled and she spotted a couple grass stains, but other than the limp he seemed unharmed.

Rob noticed her perusal. He looked at Skip, a frown on his face.

Okay, this is really getting old.

Out loud she said, "Rob, can I ride with you back to the motel. Skip'll take Liz and Betty with him. I need to talk to you about something."

He looked at her for a beat. "Okay."

As they walked to Rob's car, Kate's stomach growled loudly.

He gave her a small smile. "Let's stop somewhere for a bite. Denny's okay?"

On the way over, he told her about the research his staff was doing. "Hopefully they'll come up with something I can use to pressure the police chief into letting us take Aunt Betty home with us."

Kate fervently prayed that they would, because she'd decided she was definitely going home by tomorrow evening. She wasn't willing to be separated from her child any longer. And now, rather than helping Rob cope, her presence was causing him more stress, because of the tension between him and Skip.

Once they'd ordered their food at Denny's, Rob sat back on his bench in the booth. He was wearing his court face. "So what's on your mind, Kate?"

Tired and hungry, she snapped. "Damn it, Rob! Get the stick out of your butt so we can talk about this like the friends we used to be."

His face registered shock and hurt. "Used to be?"

Her chest ached as he said those words back to her. "And will be again, once we clear the air," she said more gently.

Rob lowered his gaze to the table. "I owe you an apology ... Liz pointed out that I shouldn't have run a background check on Canfield–"

"Stop calling him Canfield!"

Kate made herself stop and take a deep breath. *Okay, one step at a time here.*

"Apology accepted. Do you get why you shouldn't have done that?"

"It's none of my business who you're friends with," Rob said, still not making eye contact.

Kate covered his hand on the table with her own. "I don't agree. I'm glad you care enough to worry about me. And good friends should always feel free to point out if the other seems to be doing something potentially harmful. And you did that. Now you have to trust that I know what I'm doing."

Rob wrapped his big hand around her fingers as he raised his eyes to meet hers. "This may piss you off but I've gotta say it anyway. You and Skip are not *just* friends, and if you think you are, then you're the only one who's being fooled."

Kate sighed. "We are currently friends but, yes, there's definitely some strong interest in taking things to another level, on *both* our parts. But I told him it's too soon and he's respecting that."

"What about… what I found out?" He let go of her hand as the waitress arrived with their food.

Kate waited until she was gone to answer him. "I'm not going to violate Skip's confidence. You'll have to take my word for it that there's a good reason why he blew up at his boss and quit the state troopers."

"What about the job instability?"

"That *is* none of your business, Rob. It's Skip's business."

The pain in his face at the sharpness of her tone made her drop her gaze. She stared at the burger on her plate. Her stomach roiled at the sight and smell of the meat. She didn't even remember ordering it.

Rob's voice was low. "Dear God, Kate, I never meant to bring us to this, where we're waltzing around each other."

She covered his hand again and gave it a squeeze. Her stomach grumbled, then heaved a little. "Can I have a quarter of your sandwich? I can't eat this burger. It's too heavy."

He handed her the peace offering.

She took a small bite of the turkey club, chewing slowly. Her stomach settled down some.

Thinking she was changing the subject to a safer topic, she said, "Skip told us about the car. Are you sure you're okay? You were limping earlier."

Annoyance flashed across Rob's face. "Banged my knee up some, but I think it's okay. I'm not convinced it wasn't just a resident whose driving has deteriorated."

"Rob, I was almost run down by a similar car a couple days ago, and Mac and Rose had a close call with him yesterday."

Rob frowned as he processed that information. "So the killer hasn't moved out."

"Or they moved out but are still nearby."

Kate ate another bite of his sandwich while she had a short internal debate. Should she let it go? No, there was too much at stake here, and the whole point of this conversation was to clear the air.

"Why the annoyed look a minute ago?" she asked.

"What do you mean?"

"I assume you're not annoyed with me for asking if you're okay. So you must be annoyed with Skip for telling us."

"I asked him not to say anything because I didn't want to worry Betty."

She narrowed her eyes as she saw the subtle signs on his face. That wasn't necessarily a lie, but she was fairly sure it wasn't the whole truth.

"Which is why he waited until Betty was out of the room, and as it turns out, it's a good thing he told us right away. Now we all know about the other near misses and we know they were intentional. So why are you annoyed with him?" Kate finished off the quarter of his sandwich as she watched him closely.

"I'm not. It's good that he told you." His expression was a little too innocent.

"But you were annoyed, a minute ago. Why?"

"Because..." He stopped.

Kate leaned forward. "Rob, are the words, 'because he had no right to' hovering in the back of your mind, by any chance?"

He pressed his lips together.

"Why wouldn't he have that right?" Her voice was almost conversational, as she picked up another quarter of his sandwich and took a bite.

"Okay, what if I asked you not to tell Liz something? You would respect that request, wouldn't you?"

"Yes, I would. Because she's your wife, so you have the *right* to ask that." In a gentler voice, she added, "What gives you the right to ask Skip to not tell *me* something?"

He dropped his gaze, then reached out and swiped one of her fries. He ate it slowly.

She kept quiet, giving him time to sort it out.

After a moment, he looked up, a chagrined expression on his face. "Damn. I wasn't this bad when the girls started dating."

She smiled. "You were probably more consciously aware of what was going on then. This snuck up on you while you were focused on other things."

"I really owe you an apology, Kate. I've been a bit of a jerk."

She cocked an eyebrow at him.

"Okay, I've been a total ass about it."

She chuckled. "Apology accepted."

They breathed out a big sigh in unison, and then laughed together.

"And I guess I'm applying a double standard here," Rob said. "Since I just got pissed at you for keeping something from me."

She grinned at him. "I was going to let you slide on that one."

"It's human nature, though, isn't it? To want to protect the people you love."

"Natural," Kate agreed. "But not always wise."

Her stomach grumbled. The queasy feeling had subsided and hunger was reasserting itself. "You want half my burger since I ate half of your sandwich?"

Rob nodded.

She cut the burger and transferred half to his plate, then picked up her half.

As she took a bite, he asked, "So, Kate, what's really going on here between you two?"

She looked at him while she chewed, trying to decide if he was ready for the truthful answer to that question. She wasn't even sure if *she* was ready for it.

"Kate, please. We used to be able to just blurt out what we were thinking. I'm only asking what you're feeling toward this guy?"

She put down the burger and wiped her mouth with her napkin before answering him. "Honestly, I think I'm already half in love with him."

Rob froze, another of her fries partway to his mouth. "Oh." He seemed at a loss for a moment. Then he dropped the fry on his plate. "How do you think he feels about you?"

"I'm fairly sure he's about at the same place."

"Really? What makes you think that?"

"Because between all the interviewing and avoiding falling pots, we've been doing a lot of talking. We haven't blatantly said how we feel out loud, but we've agreed the potential is there for us to have a really great relationship. So neither of us wants to blow that by rushing into things."

She paused still feeling a bit awkward talking about Skip with him. But he was right, they needed to get back to the easy place they'd once been.

"We've even talked about how hard it is, for both of us, to resist the physical attraction. It was his idea that we implement a four-foot rule."

"Which is?"

"We have to keep at least four feet between us at all times."

Rob cocked his head to one side. "Uh, is it okay if I play devil's advocate here?"

She hesitated. "I guess."

"So he's not just interested in your body. Could he be interested in your money?"

"Okay, that's a bit insulting on several levels. I think I'm a pretty good judge of character, Rob, and I know Skip doesn't have any ulterior motives. He's interested in *me*. Besides, I haven't even told him about Eddie's insurance yet."

"Sorry, I didn't mean that to sound... Like I said, I'm just playing devil's advocate."

They worked on their food for a few minutes. Rob glanced up at her a couple times. Finally he said, "Uh, is it possible you're attracted to Skip mainly because his personality reminds you of Ed?"

She suppressed the urge to laugh. *Actually, my dear, he reminds me more of you.*

Out loud, she said, "They're both easygoing, but in somewhat different ways. I think the attraction is more because that kind of personality is a good complement to my own."

"As in, one has to be easygoing to put up with you," Rob teased.

She'd known full well he would go there. "Exactly," she said with a grin.

After another minute, he said, "Kate, let me ask a hypothetical question. You both feel like this could be a serious thing between you, right?"

She nodded.

"Suppose you two do get together and get serious, is that going to be fair to Skip? If you, uh, aren't able to be as close to him as you were to Ed?"

Kate looked into his eyes. She felt her own filling with tears. Damn, she hated being so weepy.

"Every time I think about that, I feel guilty, like I'm being disloyal to Eddie." She looked down at her plate. "Because I think I *could* end up loving Skip as much as I loved him. And up until a few days ago, I wouldn't have believed that could happen." A couple tears broke loose and ran down her cheeks.

Rob stared at her for a second, then he reached in his pocket. He pulled his empty hand out and looked at it.

She realized he'd been going after his handkerchief, but she already had it. She gave him a small smile and dug it out of her own pocket. Swiping at her eyes, she said, "I've wondered if you would ever run out of handkerchiefs."

"Sweetheart, I've learned to pack several extras when I'm going to be around you these days, but this trip, even that precaution may not have been enough. I think I've only got one clean one left in my suitcase."

He was smiling at her, but his eyes were troubled. He took her hand in his. "I hope you won't be mad, but I have to be honest. I still have some reservations about Skip. I do trust your judgement, but I don't know him well enough myself to say that I trust him yet."

"That's fair enough."

"But assuming he does turn out to be the totally great guy that you sense he is," Rob's voice was gentle, "then I think it's a good thing that you would be able to love him as much as you loved Ed. Any less than that would be less than either of you deserve."

She smiled at him, blinking back more tears.

The waitress arrived with the check.

"This one's on me," Rob said, letting go of her hand and reaching for his wallet. "I owe you for being such a jerk lately."

Kate decided not to protest.

~~~

Skip was sitting at the table in the suite's living room, pretending to watch television, the volume low. He heard Kate's key in the lock, then the murmur of voices as she and Rob said goodnight to each other.

She slipped through the door and turned to flip the deadbolt. When she turned back around, he started to rise from his chair.

Kate held up her hand. "Don't stand up."

He froze, then sank back down. "Why not?"

"Because if you do, I will walk right into your arms."

He decided 'And that would be a problem, why?' was not the best response. Instead he said, "That bad, huh?"

"No, actually it was good. Started out rough but ended good.

It's just... It's been a long intense day. My emotions are raw." She walked toward the table.

He pretended to measure its diameter with an imaginary measuring tape. "Close enough," he said softly, then tapped the table across from him. "Sit."

Kate sat down.

Skip reached for her hand. She tried to pull away. "Stop," he said. "There's three and a half feet of wood between us. It's okay. Just relax, take a deep breath. The intense day is over."

He'd been back and forth all afternoon, first kicking himself for the damned four-foot rule, then admitting to himself it was a good idea.

Now he gently massaged her hand, ignoring the longing building inside of him.

She closed her eyes and took a deep breath. Then opened them again before he could wipe the desire off his face.

She tried to pull her hand back, but he hung onto it.

"Skip..."

"It's okay. Just relax," he said again. He stroked the backs of her fingers, then couldn't resist lifting her hand to his lips and gently kissing her fingertips.

Her eyes went wide.

"Sorry. Guess that didn't help with the relaxing part," he said, still holding her hand near his lips.

He was an experienced lover. He knew if he turned that hand over and kissed her palm, or better still the soft skin on the inside of her wrist, she would be his for the night. It was an enticing thought.

But he didn't want her in his bed for just one night. With a jolt, he realized he wanted her in his life, for the foreseeable future.

He let go of her hand.

"Would you like to watch some TV for a while, or just go to bed?" He tilted his head toward the door of the room she shared with Betty, so she'd know there was no innuendo intended.

"Bed, I think." Kate got up and walked toward the bedroom.

At the door, she turned with an impish look on her face. She fluttered her eyelashes. In her fake Valley girl accent, she said, "I'm going into the Barbie dream house now. Goodnight, Ken." She blew him a kiss.

Skip's soft chuckle followed her into the bedroom.

CHAPTER TWENTY-SIX

During yet another room service breakfast, Kate brought up something she'd been mulling over since the day before. "I think I need to be the one who talks to Carla Baxter again, by myself."

"I don't think that's such a great idea," Skip said. "You and I can do it together."

"Baxter doesn't like men. She wouldn't even answer her door for Rob yesterday. She'll be much more likely to be open with me if I'm alone. I'm a lot younger and stronger than her and I've had self-defense training. I'll be okay."

"What if she pulls a gun or knife on you?"

"The killer has used whatever weapon has been handy so far. There's no reason to believe he or she is armed. I'll be on my guard." Kate figured this was the one thing she could do for the investigation that the others couldn't readily do. If she could get Baxter to open up and glean something useful, or at least eliminate the woman as a suspect, then she could go home knowing she had done her part.

"Except with Jeff," Skip said. "He was apparently poisoned."

"So I won't eat or drink anything she offers me."

Skip stared at her from across the table. His jaw was tight but the worry in his eyes told her he was concerned, not angry. He opened and closed his fists. The concern morphed into pain. Then he swallowed hard and gave her a slight nod.

He's worried about losing me.

The realization both pleased and disturbed her. She wasn't sure she wanted that much power over the man's feelings, since she had no idea when her heart would be fully available.

"We should probably have another go at Jill Winthrop as well," Rob said. "Maybe Kate and I can talk to her after she sees Baxter and I track down the Murphys."

Kate gave him a grateful look. At least, he wasn't going to buck her on this.

He pursed his lips.

Okay, he wants to buck me, but he knows it won't do any good.
She smiled at him.

Rob smiled back but it didn't reach his eyes. They too were worried.

She stifled a sigh, and glanced in Mac's direction. He didn't look happy either.

Arrghh!

"I want to talk to the director again," Skip was saying, "if she's in today, and sober. But I'm thinking I should tackle Morris first, just in case she orders me off the property when I try to talk to her."

"Do we really think Mrs. Carroll's a strong suspect at this point?" Kate asked, leaving unsaid the fact that she was passed out cold when a car tried to run Rob down.

"She didn't deny that she went to see Doris and she definitely didn't like the woman. Felt she was a troublemaker."

A piece of toast in her hand, Liz gestured at her laptop on the dresser. "Nothing popped in my research on the Murphys or Petersons. They've apparently led mundane lives."

Fishing their summary out of her pocket, Kate said, "Who wants the Petersons?"

"We'll take 'em," Mac said.

Rose nodded. "And we still need to find Joe, which could be tough on a Saturday."

Kate passed the slip of paper across the table to Mac, then pulled out her cell. "Let me see if Lindstrom will tell me more about what's in Jeff's autopsy report." She got his voicemail and left a message.

Rob held out his hand. "While you've got your phone out, let me get his number from you."

She handed him her phone and he scrolled through her contacts list.

"Hey, it's under L, not S for *Saaanndy*," he teased.

Skip shot him a dirty look that Rob didn't see, but Kate did. She rolled her eyes at Liz.

Do convents take widows with small children?

Rob scribbled Lindstrom's number on the back of one of his own cards. Then he looked around the table. "Folks, we've gotten a little too used to knocking on doors and talking to innocent-looking old people. Keep in mind that we're looking for a killer here." He looked directly at Kate. "So *everybody* be careful!"

She nodded, acknowledging that the message had been received.

At The Villages, they had no sooner let themselves into Betty's apartment then the doorbell rang. Rob and Kate were nearest the door. He looked through the peephole, frowned, then opened the door.

Sandy Lindstrom said, "May I come in?"

Rob stepped back and extended his arm in a come-on-in gesture.

Dread lay like a brick in Kate's stomach. She did not like the look on Sandy's face.

The detective had a search warrant in his pocket, but he was hoping he wouldn't have to use it. He didn't want to push Franklin. If the man pushed back, it might force his hand.

He stepped into the apartment and nodded to the group standing around the kitchen area. A whiff of sweat suggested they had just come in from outside.

Walking over to the window at the far end of the living room, he studied the wooden stand sitting in front of it. Green foliage from an array of house plants spilled over the sides of its shelves. "Looks like you have quite a green thumb, Mrs. Franklin," he said conversationally.

He pulled out his handkerchief and used it to pick up a small box from one of the shelves. After examining it for a moment, he turned back toward Franklin, who was still standing near the door. He pulled out an evidence bag and dropped the box into it. "I'm afraid I have to take this."

"What's this about, Detective?" Franklin asked.

Lindstrom waved them toward the seats in the living room. He took the one closest to the door. "It looks like Morgan was poisoned with nitrates, which are the most common ingredients in fertilizers, including plant food for house plants."

Franklin sighed. "I can think of quite a few people around here who not only would have ready access to fertilizers or plant food, but would probably know it was toxic. Aunt Betty has a solid alibi and no motive for killing Morgan."

"Alibis for Morgan's murder will be a bit difficult to pin down, I'm afraid. Traces of nitrates were found in quite a few empty beer bottles in Morgan's recycle bin. *None* of them had any fingerprints on them, except Morgan's."

Lindstrom gave them a moment to digest the significance of that. Those bottles would have been handled by quite a few people, between the brewery and Morgan's apartment. They should have been covered with prints.

"That beer could have been given to Morgan at any time," he finally said.

Kate had a strange expression on her face. It took him a second to recognized it. She was trying to recall some elusive memory or connection. *Or* she had *just* recalled something and was trying to hide it.

Franklin opened his mouth. "I repeat—"

Lindstrom held up a hand to stop him. "As to motive, we're thinking we may have two murderers here. One killed the women, and then someone who had it in for Morgan figured this was a real convenient time to kill him."

Canfield sat up straighter in his chair. "Johnson."

"Who?"

"Paul Johnson," Kate said. "He approached us yesterday with an offer to help. Claimed he was a friend of Morgan's but didn't really seem to know him very well. And he tried to pump us for information about the investigation."

Lindstrom took out his notepad.

"He's in the next building over, Detective," Betty Franklin said. "Apartment 130."

Liz Franklin had been tapping away on her laptop. "An overdose of nitrates causes oxygen deprivation," she said, not looking up from her screen. "It can lead to dizziness or even convulsions, before you go into a coma and die."

She lifted her eyes to meet his. "Detective, did the medical examiner say whether or not Jeff had to be dead before he went over that railing?"

Lindstrom glanced at Mrs. Franklin. He chose his words carefully. There was no reason to upset the old woman anymore than necessary. "There was enough bleeding that the M.E. couldn't be sure. He could've died immediately before the fall, or during it."

Betty Franklin nodded. "So his killer didn't have to be particularly strong. He or she could have given Jeff the beer at any time." Her eyes grew shiny but her voice was steady. "And when the poor man drank it and realized something was wrong, he came out of his apartment, maybe trying to get someone to help him."

"And either had a convulsion or passed out just as he got to the railing," the other Mrs. Franklin added.

Lindstrom was trying to decide if his suspect bringing it up herself that Morgan's killer didn't have to be strong meant she was innocent, or that she was a clever actor.

He nodded. "That's the most likely scenario, although his killer may have been nearby, ready to help him over that railing. If he'd died elsewhere and the killer carried or dragged him there, his heart would've been stopped long enough that his wounds from the fall wouldn't have bled at all."

Liz was tapping away again. "Detective, it's also possible

he committed suicide," she said, without looking up from the computer on her lap.

"Drinkin' fertilizer'd be a weird way to kill yourself," the wiry little guy growled.

Lindstrom couldn't remember his name, which showed how tired he was. He stifled a yawn.

"True, but nitrates are *prescribed* for angina," Liz Franklin was saying. "The body can apparently handle small amounts. Hoarding your heart medicine and taking an overdose would not be so strange."

"Do you know if Jeff had chest pains, Aunt Betty?" her nephew asked.

"Not that I know of, but I just thought of something. Jeff tended to be quite fastidious. He would always carry his own plastic knife and fork to the cafeteria. And he had a little bottle of hand sanitizer with him at all times."

"That sounds pretty obsessive-compulsive to me," Kate said. "It's conceivable he might wipe down a bottle before drinking from it, even when he was trying to kill himself."

To Lindstrom's mind, that sounded like a convenient thing for Mrs. Franklin to suddenly remember. He gave Kate a skeptical look. "It's not like he'd be worried about germs at that point."

She shook her head. "If he had obsessive-compulsive disorder, he wouldn't be able to help himself. He would feel compelled to wipe the bottle down."

"But why would he put the nitrates in beer?" the Hispanic woman said.

Lindstrom's brain searched for her name. *Hernandez, Rose Hernandez.*

Liz shrugged. "Maybe to disguise the taste? It takes a lot to kill you. Maybe dissolving them in something seemed easier than popping a whole bunch of pills."

"I don't know that suicide is likely," Canfield said. "But I think we need to keep it in mind. Ask anyone who claims to know Jeff if he's been depressed lately."

Lindstrom looked at the big man, and couldn't help himself. He grinned at the guy. "I see what you mean about these folks being a formidable team. For a minute there, I thought I was in my squad room brainstorming with my investigators."

Canfield flashed a grin back at him.

Lindstrom sobered as he turned to his prime suspect, in the Blackwell case at least. "What allergy medication do you use, Mrs. Franklin?"

"Benadryl."

"Lab says the substance on your kitchen rug was diphenhydramine. It's the active ingredient in Benadryl and a few other over-the-counter drugs. Works on allergies but it's also sedating. In high enough concentrations, it can kill. Who would know about your allergies and what meds you take for them?"

"Unfortunately, everybody on our suspect list, and then some. I'm afraid old people tend to compare notes on their ailments a good bit."

Lindstrom braced himself. "I need to see your medicine cabinet, Mrs. Franklin. I'll need to take your allergy medication as potential evidence."

"What the hell for?" Franklin snapped at him.

"Robert, watch your language."

The man ignored his aunt as he held Lindstrom's gaze.

He sighed. "It is conceivable that your aunt used her own medication to set up a botched attempt to fake her suicide."

"Oh, come on, Lindstrom. That's pretty far-fetched."

Lindstrom looked at Betty Franklin. "But something a creative person, say a best-selling author, might come up with."

Franklin opened his mouth to protest further. Lindstrom reached into his jacket pocket for the search warrant.

Betty Franklin stood up. "Come on, Detective." She led the way to her bathroom.

Lindstrom pulled his empty hand back out again.

A few minutes later, a second bottle now tucked inside an evidence bag in his pocket, he headed for the door.

Kate got up and followed him. She slipped outside, pulling the door shut behind her. "I guess this means Betty's still a suspect, despite your new theory."

Lindstrom nodded. "Afraid so." His captain had actually been the one to push the theory, as a way to explain away Morgan's death and justify Mrs. Franklin's arrest for the Blackwell murder. Davis wanted somebody arrested for something, to appease the press and get the brass off his back.

"Sandy, we can't go on like this. We're in a total double bind here."

"I know, but the only thing that's keeping Captain Davis from insisting I arrest her is the fact that her nephew's a lawyer, and I've promised not to let her leave the jurisdiction."

Twice, he'd broached the subject with Davis, suggesting they could let Elizabeth Franklin go to her nephew's for the time being, since they did have a reciprocity agreement with Maryland. The captain's response had been that the press would have a field day if it got out that he'd let their prime suspect mosey on down to Maryland.

"It's not hopeless though. I've got a few things cooking," he said, trying to reassure her. "Something will pan out eventually."

"Was anything missing from Jeff Morgan's apartment?" she asked.

"Don't know yet. His kids live out West. They couldn't get a flight yesterday. They'll be here this afternoon."

Kate looked up into his face for a moment. He saw respect in her eyes, and also regret. With a sinking feeling, he realized she wasn't interested in him, at least not romantically.

"Thank you for telling me all this, Sandy," she said. "And thank you for continuing to work so hard to find the real killer. We'll keep trying to help where we can."

"Just be careful, Kate."

"I will."

~~~~

Kate paused before going back inside the apartment. Again,

the feeling nagged at her that she should be remembering something. She strained to capture the elusive memory. But the more she chased it, the more it teasingly danced just outside of consciousness.

Let it be. It'll come to you later.

After she'd filled the others in on her conversation with Lindstrom, they headed out to fulfill their various assignments.

At the corner of the atrium, Kate and Skip split up. "Be careful," he said over his shoulder, and headed toward the fire stairs, to lay siege again at Henry Morris's apartment.

Rob was a little ahead of them, already going out the front door of the building, in search of the Murphys.

Kate watched the receding backs of her favorite men and smiled to herself. It was such a relief to have the air cleared with Rob.

In the next moment, her good feeling evaporated. Her sweet Eddie should be alive today, to be counted among her favorite men. Instead his ashes rested in an urn in her closet.

Another stab of grief and guilt as she realized she hadn't talked to Eddie in at least a couple days. She swallowed the emotions clogging her throat and willed herself not to cry.

Of course, if Eddie was still alive, you wouldn't be feeling what you're feeling toward Skip.

Kate shook her head. Nobody ever said emotions were logical.

It's definitely too soon, Eddie.

There was no response.

Was he unwilling to discuss the possibility of her dating other men?

"Get a grip, Kate," she said out loud. Now she was not only having conversations with a dead man, she was reading meaning into his silence.

I love you, Kate, echoed faintly in her head.

"I love you too," she whispered. Then she squared her shoulders and headed for Carla Baxter's building.

Rose was a trained police officer, and she was armed. She wasn't afraid of some creepy James Dean look-alike.

She and Mac had decided it was much more efficient to split up. So Mac had gone off to knock on the Petersons' door, while Rose tried to figure out how to track down the maintenance man. She was kicking herself for not asking Lindstrom for Fielding's home address.

There had been no Joseph Fielding listed in Betty's phone book. Liz's Google search had produced a multitude of hits, but none of them had seemed to be the Joseph Fielding who lived in Lancaster.

Rose could call the detective, but she decided to check out the management office and the machine rooms in each building first, before bothering Lindstrom. She wanted to search for anything that might implicate Fielding in the murders. And she might just get lucky, if the guy was working on a Saturday.

As she was leaving the recreation building a half hour later, Rose noticed a wooden shed, about thirty feet square, tucked discreetly under some trees. The door was standing open. She walked over and stuck her head inside the small building.

The shed contained a large lawn tractor, two smaller lawn mowers and a wheelbarrow. Hanging from hooks on the wall were rakes and shovels and other sundry gardening tools. Rose noticed there was a smaller area partitioned off in a back corner of the shed, and a set of shelves along one side. She stepped in through the door, scanning the room. After determining that no one was in the shed, she headed toward the shelves.

It did not take long to locate the plastic bottle of concentrated plant food amongst the hodgepodge of small tools and supplies. Using her knuckle, Rose nudged the bottle so she could see the side label better. Sure enough the first two ingredients had the word *nitrate* in them. She nudged the bottle again. It was almost empty.

A grin was spreading across her face when she heard a toilet flushing. The door of the little room opened behind her.

She whirled around. A man stood just outside the room, zipping his fly.

He stopped in mid zip. "Well, hello there. Aren't you a cute little Mexican babe."

Rose had found Joe.

CHAPTER TWENTY-SEVEN

As Kate had suspected, Carla Baxter was willing to open her door when she looked through her peephole and saw a woman alone. But the absence of a male presence did not make the retired professor more forthcoming.

After an exchange of greetings, Kate's warm and friendly and Baxter's a bit stiff and nervous, Kate politely turned down the offer of coffee and they settled in the living room. Two boxes, partly full of books, sat in front of the half-empty bookcase near her chair.

"Are you moving out?" Kate asked.

"No, no," Baxter said quickly. She was perched on the edge of her chair. "I was just cleaning out some things, to give to Goodwill."

Kate leaned over and glanced at some of the titles in the nearest box. Somehow she didn't think Goodwill would have a big demand for outdated chemistry and math textbooks. "Certainly no one would blame you, if you were moving out, what with the murders here. We've seen several moving vans this week."

"No, I have no reason to run away."

Not only was it an odd thing to say but the woman's body language was screaming that she was hiding something.

"Well, I know Mrs. Carroll's concerned," Kate said. "There's been a bit of an exodus apparently."

Baxter relaxed somewhat but didn't say anything.

"Have you lived here for a long time, Dr. Baxter?"

"A little over seven years."

"Do you know Mrs. Carroll fairly well then?"

"Not really." Baxter relaxed a bit more. "Why do you ask that?"

"Oh, no particular reason. We're just trying to get to know as much as we can about the folks here is all." Kate thought it was a fairly innocent thing to say, but the tension was back in the other woman's posture.

"Well, I'm sorry to have to bother you this morning, but I wanted to follow up with you on a few things. Did you know Jeffrey Morgan?"

"No, not really." The professor sat back in her chair. "I mean, we crossed paths occasionally, exchanged greetings, but I never really had a true conversation with him."

"One person we interviewed implied that he might have a secret." Kate used the word *secret* intentionally, and sure enough, the woman's body tensed again, although her facial expression remained neutral.

"The implication was that he might be gay," Kate said.

Baxter cocked her head slightly to one side. The question hadn't seemed to trigger any additional anxiety. After a beat, she said, "Possibly, but I really didn't know him that well."

Kate changed tacks. "We've found out from Detective Lindstrom that nitrates were involved in this latest crime. Can you tell me anything about them?"

Baxter was now sitting quite comfortably in her chair. She wrinkled her brow in concentration, then said, "I seem to recall that they're used in fertilizers."

Kate waited to allow the woman to elaborate. She didn't.

"I'm a little surprised you don't know more about nitrates, when you seemed so knowledgeable about chloroform."

Baxter actually smiled. "While I was still a chemistry student, I was a research assistant to a professor who was using trichloromethane in his research."

Okay, that makes sense. But why the fluctuations between tension and relaxation?

Kate returned the woman's smile. "Well, as I said, we've been doing some background research on folks, not necessarily because we have reason to suspect them, but just to be thorough." As she'd anticipated, Baxter tensed at the word *research*.

"And we found out something interesting about one person." Kate paused, waiting for a reaction.

Baxter leaned forward, her posture stiff.

"This person used to work in a setting where there were some unexplained deaths. Before all these murders started, do you recall anyone dying under circumstances that seemed at all suspicious? Such as someone who was terminally ill, but then died much sooner than expected?"

The professor relaxed back in her chair. She shook her head.

Initially, the woman had made some effort to hide her reactions, but now she didn't seem all that aware of the shifts in her body language. Her anxiety spiked at any implication that they were checking into people's backgrounds, and also whenever there was a change of subject, until she found out what the new subject was.

The therapist in Kate was doing battle with the investigator. The therapist wanted to reassure the poor woman. The topics related to the murders had not made her nervous. Kate thought it was unlikely she'd had anything to do with those crimes.

But the investigator part wanted to know just what was making this woman so tense. Maybe the two goals were not mutually exclusive.

Kate reminded herself that she was alone with the woman; she needed to be careful. Bracing to defend herself if necessary, she kept her voice sympathetic. "Dr. Baxter, correct me if I'm wrong, but I think you have a secret that you're anxious might come out, and I want to reassure–"

"No!" Baxter jumped to her feet. Her hands flew to her face. "How did you find out I killed my sister?"

Rob knocked on the Murphys' door with little hope there

would be any response.

But this time a female voice called out, "Just a minute."

He let out a sigh of relief and glanced down at the slip of paper in his hand. First, find out about any connection to Jeff, then explore their potential access to chloroform and knowledge of nitrates.

A woman opened the door, the safety chain in place. She was about five-seven and seemed to be in decent shape for her years.

Rob introduced himself, offering one of his business cards. He explained that he was talking to people in the community in order to clear his aunt's name.

"Come in then." Mrs. Murphy undid the chain and opened the door. "But I don't know if there's anything more we can tell you. We've already talked to those other folks, who said they were friends of your aunt. We told them everything we could think of that might help."

Rob walked past her. "I'm sorry to bother you again, but there's a couple new things I need to ask you about, if you don't mind?"

A lean man of average height, who looked like he made regular use of the community's gym, had come into the room. Rob assumed he was Mr. Murphy.

"Sure, shoot!" The man pointed his finger at Rob and mimicked shooting a gun.

His wife gave him a repressive look.

Rob politely refused the offer of refreshments. Mrs. Murphy escorted him to a small sitting area, which contained only a loveseat and one overstuffed armchair. The rest of the combination living/dining room was dominated by a huge mahogany table, china cabinet and heavy, carved chairs, which no doubt had once graced a much larger formal dining room.

As Rob sat in the armchair and Mrs. Murphy settled on the loveseat, her husband dragged over one of the dining room chairs. He straddled the seat backward and crossed his arms on top of its back.

Rob cleared his throat. "First of all, I was wondering if you knew the most recent victim, Jeffrey Morgan? Can you tell me anything about who his friends or enemies were?"

The Murphys exchanged a look.

Then Mr. Murphy said, "We *can* tell you that. But then we'll have to kill you." His voice was even, his expression deadly serious.

Rob realized Murphy's chair was between him and the door.

CHAPTER TWENTY-EIGHT

As Kate walked along the sidewalk, she was still processing the sad story she had just heard. Carla Baxter had a dark secret all right, but not the one she'd suspected.

The story Baxter had told her was a variation of the ones she'd heard all too many times in her office–abusive stepfather, mother in denial, children desperate enough to run away. Seventeen-year-old Carla had felt she couldn't leave her younger half-sister behind, at the old man's mercy without her big sister as a buffer.

The second day, they were hitchhiking on the highway when a car stopped. Carla hadn't liked the way the man was looking at her sister and was about to say no, thank you. But her sister was already leaning into the car. The man grabbed Jenny's arm, yanked her the rest of the way in and took off.

A sobbing Carla stumbled along the shoulder until a police officer spotted her. An APB was released and Carla was returned to her home. Two weeks later, her sister's body was found in a shallow grave. Her parents, along with most of the occupants of the small town in which they lived, had blamed Carla.

When Carla had turned eighteen, ten long months later, she had left home and had never returned. But she had carried a tremendous burden with her. In addition to the grief and guilt, she'd lived the next fifty years with the irrational fear that if anyone found out about her past, they too would blame her for what had happened.

Kate had tried to convince the woman that her sister's death was not her fault, but she doubted she'd had much impact. Guilt tended to be the most illogical emotion of them all. She'd encouraged Baxter to seek professional counseling. The woman had tearfully promised to think about it.

Kate had been debating about the wisdom of bringing up Frieda's name when Baxter had started begging her not to tell anyone about her past. Her words had been pleading but she'd had a strange glint in her eye.

Kate hated to make a promise she wasn't planning to keep but she was afraid not to. The woman had become more and more agitated. Kate finally succeeded in convincing her that her secret was safe.

As she entered Betty's building, she was still trying to decide whether to share with Lindstrom her gut sense that Carla Baxter may not be a totally sane person. She definitely intended to tell him the woman had a motive to kill Frieda.

As if her thoughts had conjured him up, Kate saw the detective coming across the atrium. But she never got a chance to tell him anything about Baxter.

Lindstrom hurried in her direction. "Kate, have you seen Joe Fielding around today?" There was urgency in his voice.

"No. What's the matter, Sandy?"

Ignoring her question, he said, "Go back to Mrs. Franklin's apartment and stay there until I call you." Then he turned and walked away from her.

What the hell?

Kate ran to catch up with him. "What's going on?"

"Hair from the last rape scene matches Fielding's. He's my rapist. He wasn't home when we went to his apartment. I gotta track him down before he rapes, or kills again."

Kate's eyes went wide. "Kills?"

Lindstrom's arm shot out to hold her back as he eased open the machine room door.

An officer was rummaging through the cans and jars on the workbench. "No Fielding, sir, but I did find this." He held up an evidence bag with a small bottle in it. "Trichloromethane on the label."

"Good work, Officer Daley."

"Isn't that—"

"Chloroform," Lindstrom answered before she could finish the question. He moved briskly back out to the atrium and headed for the outside doors.

Kate raced after him. "Sandy, wait…"

Outside, Lindstrom stopped, looking around the parking lot. Kate caught up.

But before she could tell him that Mac and Rose might be talking to Joe at that very moment, he said, "There's more. Local FBI office got a partial hit back from ViCAP. It's a national database to match up violent crimes with similar MO's." He took out his cell phone as his eyes continued to scan the nearby grounds.

"Home invasion in Boston, eight years ago. Elderly woman was raped and hit on the head with a lamp, although she wasn't killed. Jewelry box was rifled. Her assailant wore a black ski mask. Guess who the maintenance man for her apartment building was?"

Kate grabbed Lindstrom's arm. "Sandy, Mac and Rose were going to talk to him, to see if he knew Jeff Morgan." She yanked her phone out of her pocket to call Rose.

The detective was talking into his own phone, requesting more uniforms to join the search.

~~~~~~~

A half mile away, Rose was watching Fielding's every move.

At first he'd assumed she was a new member of the housekeeping staff, and had made a couple lewd suggestions about what they could do together after work.

He had grown wary when she'd informed him that she was investigating the murders. Rose had reassured him she was just a friend of Mrs. Franklin's, not a member of the police force that was formally investigating the crimes. Trying to get him warmed up, she'd asked for his impressions of some of their suspects.

But he kept moving nervously from one area of the shed to

another. She had to stay on her toes to keep him from getting around behind her. She wasn't about to let that happen.

"Yeah, that Mrs. Forshite," Joe slurred the woman's name as he flashed Rose a bad-boy smirk. "She's got the hots for me, I can tell. One a shese days, when her ol' man's not 'round...." Fielding gyrated his hips, then stumbled a step. He sniffed and rubbed his red nose.

As Fielding once again paced across in front of her, Rose checked out his pupils.

Aw, shit!

She instinctively put more distance between herself and the man. Fielding wasn't drunk, as she'd first assumed. He was high.

Cocaine or PCP, Rose figured, from the signs he was exhibiting. She prayed it was cocaine. Taking another step backward, she bumped into the shelves.

Her phone vibrated in her pocket, distracting her for a second.

Fielding suddenly stopped pacing and veered toward her. He stepped in so close she couldn't lean down to get her pistol out of her ankle holster.

"Come on now, li'l Mexican mama," he slurred. "'Nough talkin'. Let's party." He took another step to pin Rose against the shelves with his hips, as he reached out to grab one of her breasts.

~~~~~~~

Skip was hiding a smug smile as he sat down on the sagging sofa with the floral print slipcover in Mr. Morris's living room. It had taken him almost an hour but he had finally worn the man down.

He'd tried a modification of Mac's approach–knocking, then calling through the door, "Mr. Morris, I know you're in there. I just have a couple questions. If you don't let me in, it looks like you've got something to hide." Every few minutes, he had repeated the process.

Skip was realizing the springs in the old sofa were shot. His bulk sagged deep into the upholstery, forcing him uncomfortably against the back of sofa. His knees were sticking up in the air and his gun was digging into the small of his back. But he would embarrass this guy if he made a big deal about the uncomfortable seating, which would not make Morris eager to talk to him.

He looked around. No place else to sit anyway. The only other seat was the old-fashioned wing chair the older man was sitting in.

Misinterpreting Skip's appraisal of the room, Morris said, "I know. It's damn crowded in here. Can't turn 'round without knockin' somethin' over. The old bat was the one who wanted to move here. Said she didn't want to clean that big house no more. But then she wouldn't give up most of her damn knickknacks."

Skip decided his late wife was a saint to have put up with him as Morris went on to deride women in general. He was sounding like a true misogynist.

The man paused for breath, and Skip asked him how well he had known the two female victims.

Morris, already on a tear against women, replied, "Damn bitches. Deserved to die if you ask me. One of 'em mean as a snake and the other couldn't keep her nose outta other people's business."

Skip paused. Keeping his voice neutral, he said, "I got the impression from Mr. Reilly and Ms. Hernandez that you'd claimed to not know Frieda McIntosh very well."

The man hesitated for only an instant. "Well, ya didn't have to know her that good to know she was a nosy bitch."

Skip decided to come back to why Morris thought the women deserved to die, after he'd asked about the third victim. "I understand that you and Jeffrey Morgan were friends."

The man stared at the wall above Skip's head for several beats, his eyes growing shiny. "Yeah, he and I were buddies," Morris finally said. "Couple a weeks ago, his doc told him he had cancer. Tumor all twisted 'round his pancreas." His voice was rough with emotion. "Just had a few months to live."

Morris lowered his eyes to meet Skip's. Tears leaked out and ran down his leathery cheeks. "Jeff asked me what'd it been like for Sally. How bad did the pain get? He was hintin' for me, when the time came and he couldn't take it no more, to help him put an end to it all."

The man's head fell forward and he shielded his eyes with a hand, while he shook with silent sobs.

"I'm very sorry for your loss, sir," Skip said quietly, then waited for the man to compose himself.

It looked like Jeff Morgan had a very good reason to kill himself.

~~~~~~~

Police cruisers descended silently on The Villages, disgorging more officers to help in the search of the buildings and grounds.

"Don't worry. We'll find them," Sandy Lindstrom tried to reassure Kate as they stood on the sidewalk by the main road.

Her heart was in her throat. She kept telling herself that Mac and Rose were both seasoned fighters. There's no way Joe would be able to overpower the two of them. She was trying again to reach them on their cells when a faint call came from the other side of the recreation building. "Detective!"

Lindstrom and Kate took off running.

"Detective, over here!" came the voice again as they rounded the corner of the building. They spotted a large shed, with a uniformed officer standing in the open doorway. As they drew near, he stepped aside.

Inside the shed, Rose was kneeling on Joe Fielding's back, a knee pinning one of his arms in an obviously painful position. He was whimpering, his face twisted into a grimace, the other hand underneath him, clutching his crotch.

Rose reached under him and yanked out that hand, slapping one end of her handcuffs onto the wrist. He yelped as she shifted her knee to attach the other end of the cuffs to his other wrist. Ignoring his sound effects, Rose was calmly reciting the Miranda warning in a flat voice.

Relief washed through Kate's body, leaving her weak in the knees. She grabbed the doorjamb to steady herself.

Rose relinquished her prisoner to one of the uniformed officers.

Then she pointed out a plastic bottle on one of the shelves.

Sandy Lindstrom read the label and told another officer to bag it.

Kate backed out of the way as the first officer led Joe out of the shed.

Once they were all outside, Sandy stepped in front of the prisoner, holding up the evidence bag containing the small glass bottle from the machine room workbench. "What's this, Joe? A little chloroform, just in case you need to knock somebody out?"

"Don't know what yer talkin' 'bout," Joe mumbled.

The officer gripping his arm gave it a small shake.

Sandy seemed unimpressed by the denial. He pulled out his cell phone and punched in a number. After listening for a few seconds to whoever picked up on the other end, he said, "Okay, good. Keep me posted."

He turned back to Fielding. "I've got people executing a search warrant at your apartment, Joe. They gonna find anything interesting there?"

Joe blanched.

The detective smirked.

"Hey, Joe," Rose called out, as the uniformed officer led the man away.

The prisoner looked back over his shoulder.

"I'm Guatemalan, asshole!"

CHAPTER TWENTY-NINE

Rob decided to sit for a minute at the little table in the atrium of Aunt Betty's building. His heart was still beating a bit rapidly from his encounter with the supposedly boring Murphys.

After Mr. Murphy's announcement that he was about to kill him, the wife had laughed. "Don't mind Fred. He has a twisted sense of humor."

"Dry, my dear," Murphy had said, a deadpan expression on his face. "Not twisted, just dry."

Silently, Rob had agreed with his wife.

They'd then admitted that Jeff Morgan was their brother-in-law. He'd been married to Mrs. Murphy's older sister, who had died in an automobile accident over thirty years ago. He'd never remarried, and the Murphys had helped him raise his two children. It was on Jeff's recommendation that they'd come to The Villages when they retired.

Rob had probed gently about Jeff's recent mood and the possibility that he had committed suicide. According to Mrs. Murphy, he had seemed down lately, but he was a devout Catholic and would have considered suicide a mortal sin.

"Nitrate poisoning would be a strange way to commit suicide," Fred Murphy said. Apparently Detective Lindstrom had already told them about the doctored beer.

"Now drinking too much *would* be Jeff's reaction if something were depressing him," Mrs. Murphy said. She'd also informed him that Jeff did not have a heart condition.

Both had denied any recent access to chloroform and had

seemed confused by the question. They had also seemed genuinely fond of their brother-in-law, and horrified by his murder.

Rob hadn't sensed anything off about the Murphys, other than Fred's rather sick sense of humor. His gut told him neither of them were killers.

The soothing sounds of the fountain tucked amongst the plants had done a good job of lowering his heart rate. He pushed himself to a stand and headed for his aunt's apartment.

He was fitting his key into the door lock, when Kate and Rose rounded the corner from the atrium. Kate was grinning.

"What's up?" Rob said, as they drew nearer.

"It's all over," Kate said. "The murderer was Joe Fielding, the maintenance man. Lindstrom has him in custody."

It took a second for her words to completely register. The nightmare was over.

He grabbed Kate in a bear hug. "Hallelujah! We can all go home now."

Then he grabbed Rose. Ignoring the look of horror on the young woman's face, he gave her a hug as well.

"Time to round up the troops," Kate said brightly. "I can't wait to get home." She pulled out her cell phone and hit a speed dial number, then held it to her ear.

Rob finished unlocking the apartment door, anxious to tell Liz and Betty the good news.

Kate closed her phone. "Skip's not answering. Come on, Rose. Let's go find him."

Skip had ignored the phone vibrating in his pocket as he watched Morris. The old man was bent over, elbows on his knees, hands on either side of his lowered head. "Jeff was gonna die anyway, but it's a damn shame someone took him out before his time."

A moment ago the man's grief had seemed genuine but now something was off.

Morris looked up before he could completely wipe the

suspicion off his face. They locked eyes for a moment.

Then something in his peripheral vision caught Skip's attention. He glanced across the room. A black windbreaker hung on a hook near the door. Peeking out from under the edge of the jacket was a triangle of black knit fabric. His gut told him it was a ski mask.

He tried to lean forward to get to his pistol, but the enveloping sofa fought him. He quickly looked back at Morris.

The old man was holding a gun. "Don't move, young fella."

Adrenaline zinged through Skip's system, followed by the familiar calm. As Kate had said, unflappable served him well in his profession.

Morris rose to his feet and backed away across the room. "Keep your hands where I can see 'em and stand up real slow."

Skip brought his empty hand back around in front of him. His brain on full alert, he weighed his options.

He lowered his palms to the edge of the sofa as if he were about to push himself to a stand. Hoping to distract the old man so he could get to his .38, he said, "Why'd you do it, Mr. Morris? Why'd you kill those two women, and your own friend?"

"Whadaya think this is? Some plot for some dumb movie." The man's gaze never left Skip's hands. "And this is the part where you stall by tryin' to keep me talkin'. You're gonna die anyhow so least I can do is tell you why I did it, right?"

"Something like that." Skip gradually tucked his feet further back against the sofa, gathering himself to spring up. But his center of gravity was too low. There was no way he could get to his feet in one smooth, fast move.

Morris narrowed his eyes at him. "I told you to get up nice and slow. Do it now, or I'll blow ya away."

He did as he was told. "You're going to find it hard to explain firing that thing at me. People all over the building will come running when they hear it."

"Yeah, but whether I can explain that away or not, you'll still be dead, now won't ya?"

Skip could get to his own pistol now, but he wasn't sure he'd be able to draw and fire before Morris shot him. He changed back to his first tactic, stalling while watching for an opening to lunge for the man's gun.

"So you're not going to tell me why you did it? At least satisfy my curiosity before you blow me away."

"Okay, I'll tell ya, in one sentence." Morris was rummaging blindly with one hand in the top drawer of a chest behind him. He never took his eyes off Skip, but eventually he found what he was looking for by touch.

"The bitch turned me down, twice. I asked her out and she said no, even though she'd been flirtin' with me for months. And that nosy Frieda bitch was goin' 'round tellin' anybody who'd listen that Doris had done that."

Skip actually counted three sentences in there, but he wasn't about to quibble.

Morris suddenly threw something at him. "Catch!"

Stifling the impulse to duck instead, Skip clumsily grabbed at the flying object. It was a roll of duct tape.

"Lean over and wrap some of that 'round your ankles, and I'm watchin' so make sure it's good an' tight."

"What about your friend?" Skip asked, as he leaned over. He pretended he was having trouble teasing the end of the tape loose, while he reassessed. If he dropped to the floor as he drew his gun, would he be able to get off a shot in time, before Morris could? He was a dead man if he let this guy tie him up. Skip glanced up through the hair hanging over his face.

The old man's gaze and hand were both steady. "He was gonna die anyway, so I figured I was doin' him a favor. Watched Sally waste away for months. Ain't no way to end a good life. Instead he went out feelin' no pain, havin' a few beers with a friend… What's takin' you so long? Wrap that 'round your ankles!"

Skip slowly complied, leaving as much slack as he dared. When Morris came closer to tie his hands, he should have an opportunity to overpower the man.

"Thought he was already gone when I left his place." The man's voice was now sad. "But he musta woke up and come lookin' for me. And fell over the railin'."

He cackled. "That threw the cops off real good… Now, slap a piece of that tape over your mouth, 'cause I'm sick an' tired of talkin' to ya."

The doorbell rang, making them both jump. Skip brought his head up too quickly and almost lost his balance.

"Mr. Morris." Kate's voice, muffled by the door. "Sorry to disturb you but we're looking for Mr. Canfield."

Skip froze. He didn't dare make a sound to alert her of his predicament. Morris might shoot her through the door.

"He ain't here. Go away!" the old man yelled, glancing briefly toward the door.

Skip lunged forward with his upper body. He knocked the gun out of the man's hand. It hit the floor and slid under the skirt of the chair.

With his feet hobbled, Skip knew he wouldn't be able to stop his momentum. His plan was to twist around so he could land on his side and roll, while he retrieved his pistol.

He knocked over a small table. China knickknacks went flying. As he hit the floor, his head smacked against the edge of the tabletop.

He fought desperately not to lose consciousness. His vision blurred. He looked up, trying to locate his adversary.

The last image his brain registered was his own gun butt descending toward his face.

CHAPTER THIRTY

Kate stood with Rose outside Mr. Morris's door. She was becoming increasingly concerned about the elderly man as they heard first a crashing noise inside, then a loud thud and several grunts.

"Mr. Morris, are you okay?" she called through the door.

"I said, go away," Morris yelled back, sounding out of breath. "Can't a man have no peace 'round here."

"Are you sure you're okay?" Kate called out again. "Did you fall?"

"Goddamn it! Go away and leave me alone!"

Kate shrugged and started to turn away from the door, but the nagging sense that there was something important she needed to remember was back.

More muffled noises from inside the apartment. Kate put her ear to the door. "Sounds like he's dragging stuff around in there," she whispered.

"I got a bad feeling all of a sudden," Rose whispered back.

Kate tried the knob, but of course the door was locked. Her instincts were agreeing with Rose's.

"Stay here and keep trying to reach Skip. I'm gonna get Mrs. Carroll to let us in."

Rose nodded..

Kate raced for the fire stairs.

～～～

Henry Morris had finished wrapping tape around the man's wrists and had dragged him into the gap between the back of the sofa and the bookshelves that lined one wall of his living room. Ignoring the purring of the vibrating cell phone in the guy's pocket, Morris knelt down and felt for a pulse in the man's muscular neck. He couldn't find one.

Well, now, might just have saved me a bullet.

"Now the question is how the hell to get ya outta here," he muttered. He thought about his old Buick. Only got thirteen miles to the gallon but it had a nice big trunk. "Gotta wait for dark. When everybody's asleep I can probably get ya out to the car," he said to the body behind his sofa.. "Gotta take ya far, far away from here."

But where? If he dumped it somewhere nearby, it wouldn't take long for the cops to link this guy back to The Villages. He needed to buy some time.

Roundtop Mountain!

He and Sally had skied there every winter in their younger years. It was only an hour away and this was off season. Nobody'd be around in the middle of the night. Take him up there. Rip the tape off and dump him off a cliff. Be weeks before he was found. And his head injuries would be blamed on the fall.

And by that time, he'd be packed up and long gone. Hell, nobody would think twice about him moving out.

I'll be just another chicken shit runnin' from the killer. He cackled under his breath at the irony.

But could he drag this guy out of the building without making a bunch of noise? If not, he'd just have to dump him over the railing and then get the hell outta here tonight. He'd sure hate to have to leave Sally's stuff behind, though.

Another knock on his door.

Damn, don't these people never give up.

As he struggled to get up off his knees, his elbow came precariously close to the lamp on the table at the end of the sofa.

"Go away!" he yelled at the door.

~~~

Alice Carroll put a hand to her throbbing temple and turned

to the woman who had literally dragged her out of her office, claiming someone was in dire straits inside their apartment. "It doesn't sound like he's hurt to me."

Something crashed inside the apartment. She winced as pain ripped through her skull. "Mr. Morris?"

There was no answer.

She wrung her hands, staring at the door, hesitant to use her master key. But if the resident was in trouble... She wrung her hands again. The hangover was making it hard to think.

"Look," Mrs. Huntington said. "Something's going on in there that isn't good—"

Alice turned when the woman abruptly stopped.

Mrs. Huntington's eyes were wide. Alice followed her line of vision.

The short, Hispanic woman was holding a gun.

It took a moment to register that the weapon was aimed at the doorknob, not at her.

"Open the damn door," the crazy woman barked at her. "Or I blow off the lock."

~~~

Mac had finally tracked down the Petersons and had asked his questions without learning anything useful. He was entering Betty's building while listening to the message Kate had left on his voicemail earlier.

Alarm shot through him at her frantic words. "Mac, you and Rose are in danger! Joe's the killer..."

The phone message blurred into the background as he heard Rose's raised voice from above him. He couldn't make out the words but she sounded pissed.

Scanning the upper railings, he spotted Kate's curly mop above the plants on the second level. He raced for the fire stairs and up the steps, two at a time.

Bursting through the door on the upper level, he saw Rose and Kate and the old biddy who ran the place standing in front of old man Morris's door. He took off in their direction.

Kate heard feet pounding. She looked up.

Mac came to a halt next to her. "What's going on?"

"We're not sure. But Skip might be in there and we've heard several crashes and other strange noises. Morris won't open up."

Rose glared at Mrs. Carroll. "I *said* open the door!"

Trembling, the woman tried without success to insert her master key in the lock. Kate snatched it from her and unlocked the door.

Rose stepped in front of her, gun still in her hand, and shoved the door open. Mac pushed past her as well.

Kate took two steps into the room. Mrs. Carroll stayed in the doorway, wringing her hands.

Morris was standing in the middle of his living room, arms stretched out at his sides, open palms toward them. "What the hell is this, Nazi Germany? You can't just storm in here! Mrs. Carroll, I'll have your job."

The director started apologizing and backing out the door, tugging at Kate's arm.

But she was staring at the man's hands. Something about those hands. Something she had seen.

Kate dug in her heels and talked over Mrs. Carroll. "We were concerned because we heard crashing noises. We thought you might be hurt."

Morris pointed at a table and a broken lamp on the floor. "I knocked the damn table over."

Mac and Rose had spread out on either side of her. Rose's gun had disappeared. They were both scanning the room, looking for anything that was off.

After a moment, they looked at Kate and shook their heads slightly.

But something was still nagging at her. "Well, we're very sorry to have bothered you, Mr. Morris," she said, stalling for time.

The man waved the back of his hand at her in a get-out-of-here gesture.

And she remembered. In her mind's eye, she saw the back of that hand grabbing a box to drag it through a doorway. On the side of the box was a picture of a tall brown bottle of beer.

She looked down at the tipped over table and shattered lamp, at opposite ends of the sofa. Suddenly the cluttered room transformed into what it was, the scene of a struggle.

Kate glanced first at Mac, then at Rose.

That's all they needed. Mac began to ease around behind Morris. Rose scanned the room again, looked down.

"Hmm," Kate was saying, "that lamp sure rolled a ways before it broke."

Rose sidled sideways toward the sofa and tapped something on the floor with her foot. She looked up at Kate, alarm on her face.

Kate caught movement in the corner of her eye. Her head jerked around.

Morris yanked something from behind the cushion on the chair next to him. "Don't nobody move!" He pointed a gun at her.

Kate gasped, recognizing the pearl handle. It was smeared with red. Her throat closed.

Morris turned slightly toward his left, looking for Mac. "Nobody move!" he said again, in a menacing growl. He glanced behind him.

Mac leapt onto the man's back, bringing the side of his hand down sharply on Morris's forearm. The howl of pain was eclipsed by an explosion of gunfire.

The doorframe shattered beside the director's shaking knees. She screamed.

The gun clattered to the floor. Rose had her foot on it in a nanosecond, her own gun once again in her hand.

Morris and Mac had gone over in a blur of arms and legs. They rolled around on the floor, the old man struggling to free himself. Adrenaline gave him a few seconds of fight, but Mac, younger and stronger, soon subdued him. He rolled Morris onto his stomach, pinning down his arms.

"Check Skip," Rose said to Kate, gesturing with her head toward the sofa without taking her eyes or her aim off of Morris.

He was now howling about invasion of privacy and lawsuits. As if his loud objections could make them forget that he'd been holding a gun on them a few seconds ago.

Kate ran to back of the sofa and tripped over something sticking up from the floor. She looked down and froze. It was a man's sneaker, attached to a leg. She grabbed for the arm of the sofa, staring at Skip. He was trussed up with silver duct tape, his eyes closed, his face deathly still and pale.

She scrambled into the tight space and knelt beside his head. Frantically, she felt his thick neck with her fingertips. She couldn't find a pulse. Tears welled in her eyes, blurring her vision.

She tried to get to his wrists but couldn't get past the tape wrapped around them.

Pushing her fingertips again and again into the muscles of his neck, she prayed, but felt not even a tremor. She couldn't get the words *he's dead* past the lump in her throat. All that came out was a croak.

Her arms futilely tried to gather his broad shoulders onto her lap. Giving up on that, she collapsed across his chest.

Not again! Not again! shrieked in her head. Sobs racked her body.

She froze. Was that a whisper of breath on her neck? She feared she'd imagined it.

~~~

Rob had left the apartment door ajar, assuming the others would be along shortly. He and Liz were trying to determine if they should stay a few more hours to provide Aunt Betty with some additional emotional support.

She'd assured them she was fine. Now that the killer was in custody, all she wanted was to get her life back to normal.

But Rob was thinking they should stay at the motel another night, and check on her again before leaving tomorrow.

A sharp crack. A woman screamed.

Rob bolted out the door, racing in the direction from which the sounds had come, across the atrium and up the fire stairs.

On the second level, Mrs. Carroll was standing outside an open door, wringing her hands and emitting little yelps and squeaks.

Rob ran to the doorway and unceremoniously shoved her out of the way. He quickly scanned the room.

An old man was lying face down on the floor. Mac was wrapping tape around the man's wrists while Rose sat on his back, reciting the Miranda warning for the second time that day.

Despite the din the old man was making, Rob heard sobbing from behind the sofa. In one stride, he was standing at Skip Canfield's feet.

Kate turned her teared-streaked face toward him, and something shifted inside. All that mattered was she cared for this man, and losing him would tear her apart, again.

Rob yanked out his cell phone and punched in 911. Guilt, irrational but powerful, ripped through him. He had hired the man, brought him into this danger.

Kate's hand brushed hair away from an angry, red gash above Skip's temple. Blood streaked his cheek and had saturated the carpet under his head. His eyelids fluttered. His lips had a bluish tinge, but his forehead was beaded with sweat.

That discrepancy triggered a three-decade old memory from Rob's Boy Scout days. "Ambulance. Head injury. I think he's in shock," he barked into his phone. "Villages Retirement Center, G Building, second level."

It vaguely registered that Liz had elbowed her way past Mrs. Carroll in the doorway.

Rob tossed his phone down on the sofa. The 911 operator kept squawking, demanding his name. Why the hell did his name matter? He grabbed the phone back up and yelled, "Rob Franklin. Get an ambulance here. Now! And Detective Lindstrom."

He dropped the phone again. Pulling out his handkerchief,

he tossed it to Kate. "Try to stop the bleeding, but don't press too hard."

She caught the cloth and held it against the wound.

Rob knelt at Skip's feet and tugged at the tape on his ankles. He looked in Rose and Mac's direction. "Knife!"

The old man was still yammering about his rights and how dare they–

"Shut up!" Rob roared.

Mac tossed him a penknife. The old man shut up.

Rob cut the tape on Skip's ankles, then leaned over to free the man's wrists. The backs of his hands were clammy.

Shock. What are you supposed to do for shock?

Reaching back to the lessons that had earned him a First Aid badge, he remembered something about propping the feet up. He reached around the end of the sofa.

Liz anticipated his objective. She yanked one of the seat cushions loose but hung onto it when he tried to take it. "We shouldn't move him if he's been shot."

Kate shook her head. "Don't think... shot," she choked out.

Rose climbed off of the now-subdued prisoner. "Shot went wild." She rushed to Kate's side, then jolted to a stop at the sight of Skip's bloody head. *"¡Dios mio!"* She crossed herself.

Rob lifted Skip's legs and Liz slid the cushion under them.

Rose had sprinted off into another room. She came back with a flowery bedspread and tossed it to Rob. He spread it over the unconscious man.

Kate's eyes were wide, watching their movements.

"Talk to him," Rob urged.

She looked down at the battered face at her knees. "Skip, don't leave me," she whispered. "Please, don't leave me!"

Rob's throat closed. His eyes stung.

Skip's hand jerked. Kate grabbed it and squeezed. His eyelids fluttered again. His breathing seemed more even, and his pale lips had lost some of the blue tinge.

Liz knelt beside Rob at the big man's feet. They leaned against each other.

Two paramedics rushed in the door and headed for Morris lying on the floor.

"Here! Behind the sofa," Rose barked.

Rob scrambled to his feet, one arm around his wife to bring her up with him. "Kate, we need to get out of the way."

Rose hauled Kate to her feet and backed her away, as Mac grabbed one end of the sofa and dragged it several feet across the floor.

The paramedics moved quickly. In a matter of seconds, they had an IV needle in Skip's arm.

Rose maneuvered Kate over to Rob. He took her in his arms. Now that he could do nothing but watch and pray, the adrenaline was draining out of his system. His knees wobbled.

Liz wrapped her arms, as best she could, around both of them. He felt her take a step back with one foot, a petite brace holding up her shaking husband and the woman sobbing against his chest. He let go of Kate with one arm and put it around his wife. The three of them clung to each other.

After several minutes that felt much longer, one of the paramedics said, "He's stabilized. Let's transport."

The others let out pent-up gasps of air.

Kate slumped against Rob. At first, he thought she'd fainted. Then she looked up at him.

She gave him a wan smile. More tears flowed, from relief this time.

CHAPTER THIRTY-ONE

Outside the slightly ajar door, Kate debated whether she should knock or nudge it open a little further to peek in. If the occupant of the room was sleeping she didn't want to disturb him. She wondered again if the smiley face balloon she'd bought on an impulse in the gift shop was too silly.

A rustling noise from within helped her with the first quandary. She gently knocked and a man's voice croaked, "Come in."

Didn't sound like Skip. Did she have the wrong room? She nudged the door open.

The big man's upper body was elevated in the hospital bed. He wore a hospital gown that was too big even for his large frame. A sheet and lightweight blanket covered his legs. His head sported a white bandage on one side, with a sizeable knot on the other providing some degree of symmetry to his bruised face.

His left eye–the one that wasn't half swollen shut–lit up when he saw her. "Hi Kate. Come in." His voice was raspy, a little garbled.

Fear closed her throat. Was his head injury worse than the close-mouthed doctor had implied? She rushed to the side of his bed.

He pointed to a plastic water cup on the tray beside her. She held it up for him while he took a long sip from the straw.

"That's better," he said in a more normal voice. "They're giving me some kind of medicine that dries my mouth out. And this," he gingerly touched his swollen right eye, "isn't focusing very well, which is throwing my coordination off."

His gaze went to the ceiling above the foot of the bed, and his battered face lit up again. Kate followed his line of vision. In her rush to his bedside, she'd let go of the balloon. It now bobbed against the ceiling.

She moved to the foot of the bed and jumped up to snag its ribbon, then tied it to the end of the side railing. "You like balloons, huh?"

"Yeah, but mostly I like the idea that you got it for me." He grinned at her.

Then his face abruptly sobered. "Hey, they didn't call my mother, did they?"

"No, they started to, but Rob stepped in and said he was your attorney and could authorize medical care. They didn't argue, although I'm sure they would've if you'd needed surgery. Rob's got an elderly mother of his own."

"Tell him I appreciate his quick thinking. Mom worries enough about me. She doesn't need to know every time I get a little bump on the head."

"I don't know that I'd call those *little* bumps."

Skip shrugged and the too big hospital gown slid off his shoulder, exposing a darkening bruise. He gave the gown an irritated shove back into place. It slipped right down again. "Nurse said these only come in three sizes, child, adult and jumbo. Damn thing keeps coming untied." He started to reach behind his neck, wincing in pain.

"Here, let me get it." Kate leaned over to tie the strings for him.

"Thanks. I think I landed funny on my shoul–" He sucked in his breath as her fingers brushed against the nape of his neck. She felt his skin quiver under her touch.

Pretending she hadn't noticed his reaction, she gave the bow a final tug, then gently patted his shoulder. "That should hold now."

Before she could take her hand away, Skip had covered it with his own and dragged it around to his chest. "Be still, my heart!" He pretended to swoon.

An electric sensation shot up her arm. She snatched her hand back, then tried to cover the hastiness of her gesture by smacking him lightly on his forearm. "You can't be feeling all that bad then, Mr. Funny Man."

She used her foot to snag the leg of a visitor's chair and dragged it a little closer to the bed. Sitting down, she folded her hands in her lap. "And what happened to the four-foot rule?"

He gave her a lopsided grin. "Don't suppose you'd believe me if I said, 'what rule?' You know, head injuries can cause memory problems."

"You're right. I wouldn't believe you." She gave him a mock stern look. "So how are you doing, *really*? Since none of us are relatives they wouldn't tell us anything except that you were out of danger and quote 'resting comfortably.'"

"I'm fine, really. Doc came in awhile ago. He was forced to agree with me that I have an unusually thick skull, something my mother has known for years. No fractures, no bleeding or swelling in the brain. Just a headache." He tilted his head toward the IV bag hanging from a stand beside his bed. "The joy juice is taking care of that."

Skip grinned again. "Doc raced out the door muttering, 'More tests! Must run more tests.' But if those come back okay, I'm gonna make them let me out of here." He pushed himself up a little further into a sitting position. "So, what happened after my lights went out? Morris didn't get away, did he?"

"Oh, no. Mac and Rose subdued him until the cops got there. She literally sat on him while Mac tied him up."

Skip chuckled a little at that mental image.

"I'm afraid Sandy had to keep your gun for the time being, as evidence. Morris fired it, but he didn't hit anyone."

He scowled at the mention of the detective's name.

Kate reached over and smacked him on his arm, not quite so lightly this time. "Cut that out. You're the only man I'm going to be having non-dates with for the foreseeable future. Anyway, Morris confessed. Said he'd already told you most of it so he might as well. Doris was an impulse. He went to see her to ask her out, apparently for the second time because she'd refused him the first time. She laughed at him and when she turned away, he lost it and grabbed the poker. Then he decided he needed to shut Frieda up."

"Yeah, it's coming back to me some. He said something about Frieda gossiping about Doris flirting with him."

"He was afraid the gossip would draw the police's attention to him," Kate said. "When his attempts to get to Betty and stage a suicide failed, he apparently killed Jeff Morgan to confuse the issue. He also planted a bottle of chloroform in the machine room to implicate Joe."

"He didn't tell the cops the main reason he killed Jeff?"

"I don't think so. Was there another reason?"

"Jeff had been diagnosed with terminal cancer. He'd hinted to Morris to help him commit suicide when the pain got to be too much. Morris figured he'd put his friend out of his misery sooner instead of later, and throw the police off in the process."

"Well, that makes that piece fit into the puzzle better," Kate said.

"Yeah, but there's another piece I'm confused about. Morris came across as a real misogynist. Didn't think much of women at all." Skip started to scratch his head but connected with gauze bandage. He dropped his hand back to his side. "But he did seem to still be grieving for his wife. And if he was such a woman-hater, why would he be pursuing Doris so persistently? You'd think he'd have been content to live out his life as a widower rather than complicate it with another woman."

"Well, some misogynists truly want nothing to do with women, except maybe to satisfy their sexual needs. But others have a love-hate relationship with them, or should I say a need-hate relationship. Underneath the bluster, they're desperate for a woman's love, but they hate themselves, and often the women, because of that neediness. A lot of wife batterers have that dynamic too."

Skip nodded, then winced. "Where'd Morris get the

chloroform? Did Detective Sandy tell you anything about that?"

Kate gave him another mock glare. "Yes, Detective *Lindstrom* told us that Morris admitted to having a little black market endeavor going. He and his wife had been pilfering drugs and supplies from both their workplaces for years."

"That explains how they could afford to retire to The Villages," Skip said. "So where's everybody else?"

"Rose and Mac have headed back to Maryland. I think Rose could have flown home under her own steam, she was feeling so high, after taking down two bad guys in one day. She had a close encounter with Joe. When Sandy and I found them, he was writhing on the floor and clutching himself, while Rose was calmly cuffing him and reading him his rights."

Skip winced, then chuckled. "I don't usually wish that fate on any man but in this case... Must have been quite a blow to his ego, to be taken down by petite Rose."

"Don't call her petite to her face, if you know what's good for you," Kate warned him. "Turns out Joe's wanted for a home invasion in another state. Between that and the rape charges here, he's not getting out of jail any time soon."

"Good. Did Rob and Liz leave too?"

"Not yet. They wanted to make sure you were okay before they did." Kate's eyes stung. "Skip, I... *we* thought we were going to lose you." Without thinking, she reached out and covered his hand with her own. "Rob was the one who realized you were in shock. He... he may have saved your life."

It sounded melodramatic in the re-telling, but at the time they hadn't known that Skip's injuries themselves weren't life-threatening, but the shock, brought on by blood loss and lying immobilized, was.

As they'd sat in the ER waiting room, Liz had piggybacked onto the hospital's wireless network to do a little research–her way of coping. She had opted *not* to share with Kate what she'd learned until after the doctor told them Skip was in stable condition.

If they hadn't forced their way into Morris's apartment when they did, if he'd lain there until nightfall, he might indeed have been a corpse. The shock might very well have accomplished what the bumps on his head had not.

Skip turned his hand palm up and wrapped his fingers around hers. "Tell him thanks for me."

Then he raised her hand to his lips and kissed her fingers, sending a jolt of energy up her arm. It momentarily took her breath away.

"Kate, I...," he began, but she twisted her fingers loose and pressed them against his lips.

"You can tell him yourself," she whispered, pretending to misunderstand. She pulled her hand away and sat back. "The other reason they're sticking around is to drive you home when the doctors release you. You okay with him driving your Explorer? Liz will follow in their car."

Skip's face fell. "Sure. That's generous of him." Staring at the smiling balloon above his bed, he asked in a strained voice, "So is this goodbye then?"

"Heck no. You're not getting rid of me that easily. If they do let you out of here today, I was planning to bring you some soup tonight for your dinner."

His face relaxed into another grin. "You tryin' to kill me?"

"I'm getting it from Mac's restaurant, wise guy. His Aunt Sabrina, who also happens to be his chef, makes a mean chicken orzo soup. Guaranteed to cure all maladies and heal all wounds."

"So does this mean we've progressed beyond non-dates?"

Kate looked at his bruised and battered face for a moment. Ignoring the ache in her chest and the tingling in the rest of her body, she shook her head. "I wish it weren't the case, but no, I'm not ready for that yet. Is it okay with you if we get to know each other better, as friends, for a while?"

"Yeah, that's okay." He shrugged, knocking the too-big hospital gown askew again.

She decided it was too dangerous to lean over and try to fix it for him.

He yanked the fabric back into place. "May I ask why you feel it's still too soon to date?"

"It's a little hard to explain." She looked down at her lap. "I'm afraid I would constantly be comparing you to Eddie. Which would be totally unfair to you..." But the bigger part, that she definitely couldn't explain to him, had to do with her internal conversations with her dead husband. They had been her salvation for months, but now they were a stumbling block. As long as she still had that connection to Eddie, it felt wrong to attempt to establish a new relationship—unfair to Skip, confusing and conflicted for her.

"I just need more time, to finish letting go of Eddie." She was praying he would understand.

"Kate, I can accept that you may not be able to love another man as much as you loved him."

She looked up and met his eyes. *You think you can accept it, but...*

"I didn't say I'd like it, but I can live with it."

She shook her head a little. "How do you do that?"

"Do what?"

"Read my thoughts like that."

"You're not as hard to read as you think. And I'm paying close attention."

She smiled. She liked the sound of that last part. "Skip, I doubt I would ever love any man exactly the same *way* that I loved Eddie, but I... that doesn't mean I can't eventually love just as intensely."

His face lit up. "Any idea how soon *eventually* will be?"

"I hope soon." She realized she needed to get out of there before she promised too much. Maybe she'd better ask Mac or Rose to take his soup over tonight.

She stood up. "Skip, I truly hope that *soon* it will no longer be *too soon* to be more than friends." Leaning over, she kissed his bruised cheek, then quickly stepped back and turned toward the door.

"Kate…"
She slowed her pace and looked back over her shoulder.
"As I said before, I'm a very patient man."
She smiled at him. "I'm counting on that, Skip."

AUTHOR'S NOTES

I have intentionally identified the year when this story takes place as 2006 to point out that Kate and Skip are members of the generation coming right after the Baby Boomers. (Also, there are five more books that happen between this one and 2014.)

Kate's generation is frequently referred to as Generation X, but I've never cared for that name. I've always thought of them as the 'Tweeners.' They are the generation between the post-World War II Baby Boomers (my generation) and the Boomers' babies (my son's generation).

This generation was caught between two strong cultural influences. Their parents were already well into adulthood when my generation threw out the rule books and triggered a cultural revolution. In one generation, we went from pregnant teenagers being forced into marriage or being thrown out on the street to premarital sex and cohabitation before marriage being the norm; from the advice to my mother's generation of housewives that they should freshen their make-up and put on a pretty frock to greet their man at the end of his hard day's work (despite the fact that she had been caring for his children and home all day) to Gloria Steinem burning her bra and demanding the woman's right to choose whether she worked or stayed home with children. And that's not even getting into the issue of separate drinking fountains and restrooms for 'coloreds' to supposed racial equality.

The 'Tweeners' parents were traditional, like those of the Baby Boomers. They tended to follow traditional gender roles and used stricter, authoritarian parenting. But their children were growing up in a social environment that was very different from what they were experiencing at home. At home, 'traditional' values reigned; out in the world, they encountered a freer attitude toward sexuality, the assumption that the genders were equal, and the belief that it was okay to be a working mother.

So Kate and Skip are not the thirty-somethings of today, nor are Rob and Liz like those in their forties today. They are struggling with issues of female independence versus male protectiveness, the acceptability of platonic male-female friendships, whether or not men should cry or curse in front of women, and the angst of leaving one's child to return to work. Come to think of it, I'm not sure that the thirty-somethings of today aren't still struggling with a lot of these issues, but perhaps more subtly.

I bring all this up because my 32-year-old son pointed out that my characters are not like his friends. No they are not. They are members of the smaller-than-normal generation sandwiched between mine and his, and caught between the old school and the new.

Most of my clients, when I was a therapist, were members of this generation. I know them well and feel for them. They had a much tougher struggle to find their own identity than my generation did. We identified ourselves as rebels against the establishment. They weren't real sure what the hell the establishment was (their parents or society?), nor was it clear for them whether the establishment was good or bad.

On another topic, I have taken some liberties regarding technology. The image-based, face-recognition search engine that Liz uses was still under development by Google in 2012 (when this book was originally published), and was not available in 2006. Also, today we find Betty's use of computer disks and unfamiliarity with flash drives amusing, but keep in mind, in 2006, flash drives were a newfangled invention, as were digital fingerprinting devices.

I owe an apology to the current captain of the Lancaster City Bureau of Police's Criminal Investigations Division. I apologize for portraying your fictional counterpart as someone who would railroad an old lady into a murder conviction just to get the press and brass off his back. I have also taken liberties by blending the duties of your Special Investigations Unit and the Violent Crime Unit together (the former would investigate rapes while the latter would handle murders).

Unfortunately, the case Rob describes in Chapter Five (the

woman convicted of murder when she was fending off a rapist) is based on a very real case in Pennsylvania in the late 1980's. In that case, it was actually over a decade before she was pardoned and her daughter was sixteen. This poor woman missed out on her child's entire childhood while she was imprisoned for defending herself.

On a lighter note, I totally enjoyed the time I spent in Lancaster, doing research for this book. Denny's, the Travel Lodge with its Indian restaurant, and Florentino's restaurant where Kate and Skip have their first non-date are strung out along Columbia Avenue on the western side of town. And there is indeed a Home Depot on US 30. However, while Lancaster abounds with retirement communities, The Villages retirement center is a total figment of my imagination.

A huge, huge thank you to all the people who made this book possible, especially my good friend, Angi, who has been an unending source of encouragement. To all my beta readers, my friend and partner at *misterio press*, Shannon Esposito, and all the wonderful authors there, and my editor, Marcy Kennedy, you have my unending gratitude. I probably wouldn't still be writing without the support of these people and also the folks in my online writers' group, the WANAs. And a big thank you to my cover and interior designer, Melinda VanLone, who is not only a great artist and writer herself, but is a very patient person who puts up with my perfectionism.

Last but not least, my special thanks to the Amish family (although I suspect they will never read this) whose buggy pulled out down the block from me on Columbia Avenue, and thus gave me the idea for Skip's envious moment.

And now a preview of Book 3: FAMILY FALLACIES

Kate Huntington is continuing to hold Skip Canfield at arm's length–insisting they go on 'non-dates' as friends only–as she prepares to return to the career she loves. Her enthusiasm for her job is soon tarnished, however, when anonymous notes start appearing at the counseling center where she works.

As these missives become more and more disturbing, Kate encounters a second nightmare. She is being sued for allegedly planting false memories in the mind of one of her clients. Even her closest friend, lawyer Rob Franklin, has several misconceptions about this controversial issue. But despite the friction this causes, he still insists that he will represent her.

Soon, however, his legal counsel is needed for more than a malpractice suit, when Kate becomes a murder suspect! Rob may not understand the nature of traumatic memory but he is certainly going to do his damnedest to keep his friend from going to prison.

Meanwhile the sender of the anonymous notes has upped the ante and is now threatening the children of Kate's family, especially her own baby girl. When she turns to Skip for support, he vows to do everything within his power to protect the woman and child whom he secretly hopes will someday be his family.

As the sexual energy between them heats up, the weight of so many changes and pressures in her life is becoming more than even a strong woman like Kate can handle. Rob has had his misgivings about her too-handsome-to-be-trusted suitor, but now the two men must work together to support the woman they both love, and protect her and her child from a killer.

ABOUT THE AUTHOR

Kassandra Lamb has never been able to decide which she loves more, psychology or writing. In college, she realized that writers need day jobs in order to eat, so she studied psychology. After a rewarding career as a psychotherapist and college professor, she is now retired and can pursue her passion for writing.

She spends most of her time in an alternate universe with her characters. The portal to this universe, aka her computer, is located in Florida, where her husband and dog catch occasional glimpses of her.

For part of each summer, Kass returns to her native Maryland, where the Kate Huntington series is based. She is working on Book 7 in the series, *Fatal Forty-Eight*, plus a third Kate on Vacation novella.

To read and see more about Kate Huntington you can go to **http://kassandralamb.com**. Be sure to sign up for the newsletter there to get a heads up about new releases, plus special offers and bonuses for subscribers.

Her e-mail is **lambkassandra3@gmail.com** and she loves hearing from readers! She's also on Facebook (**https://www.facebook.com/kassandralambauthor**) and Goodreads. She hangs out some on Twitter @KassandraLamb and blogs about psychological topics and other random things at **http://misteriopress.com**.

At *misterio press*, we take pride in producing top quality books for our readers. All manuscripts are proofread several times, but proofreaders are human. If you discover any errors in this book, please e-mail the author at lambkassandra3@gmail.com. Thank you!

Turn the page for more exciting misterio press mysteries...

Karma's A Bitch ~ **The Pet Psychic series**
by Shannon Esposito
Maui Widow Waltz ~ **The Islands of Aloha series**
by JoAnn Bassett
The Metaphysical Detective ~ **The Riga Hayworth series**
by Kirsten Weiss
Dangerous and Unseemly ~ **The Concordia Wells series**
by K.B. Owen
Murder, Honey ~ **The Carol Sabala series**
by Vinnie Hansen

**Plus even more great mysteries/thrillers at
http://misteriopress.com/misterio-press-bookstore/**

CPSIA information can be obtained
at www.ICGtesting.com
Printed in the USA
BVHW081414230922
647636BV00002B/231